FLedGe

I Am Just Junco
BOOK TWO

By J. A. Huss

FLedGe

I Am Just Junco
BOOK TWO
By J. A. Huss
Find me at
Jahuss.com

Edited by RJ Locksley
Cover design by J. A. Huss

ISBN-13: 978-1-944475-79-6

Dedication

To all the nerdy, geeky people who love this SF shit
and birds, as much as I do. Because I love the fuck out of birds.

Prologue

A bead of sweat tickles me as it slides down my ribcage, clings tight as it rounds the curve of my back, and finally drops to settle on the towel underneath my body. I squirm a little to shake the feeling and cool air rushes in where there was once only heat. I flip over on the towel and put my hands under my forehead and try to go back to sleep.

"You're gonna burn, Junco."

"Mmmmhmmmm. Maybe."

I jump a little as the cold squirt of lotion drops onto my back and rough hands begin massaging it into my skin. I pick my head up a little and mumble, "Thank you."

He laughs. "Believe me, it is my pleasure."

He moves his hands to the back of my legs and I laugh and kick him away. "Tickles, Charlie." He increases the pressure to make the tickle stop and I relax back into the small dent my body has made in the sand over the past hour. When he's done he sits back in the beach chair next to me and is silent. I peek up at him with one eye, squinting at the sun. "Quit it. It hasn't changed. Just ignore it."

He looks down at me and nods, but the words tell another story. "What do you think he's saying?"

I let out a huff and turn back around so I can look out towards the lake where the apparition floats, just a few feet off the end of the dock. "Who cares?" I look back up at Charlie, but he's still staring. "We can't hear him, so who cares, Charlie."

"Junco, if he didn't have something to tell you, he wouldn't be here at all."

I lay my head back down and mumble, "Not interested. Not one bit."

Charlie gives up and slides down next to me on the towel, slipping his arm around my body and kissing the back of my neck until I arch my back and giggle. "Let's go inside," he breathes in my ear. "He's giving me the creeps."

I smile and then I laugh. "He's a hologram, Chuck. He can't see anything. Shit, he can't even get the talking part straight. Just ignore him. He'll go away. Eventually."

But he ignores my plea. Instead, he grabs my hand and pulls me to my feet. Then swings me over his shoulder and starts running towards the cabin. My body jerks and bounces with each stride and I laugh so hard it hurts. "Oh, God! Stop! Stop!" I beg, but he just swings me over and plops me on the ground, then grabs my hand again and pulls me inside.

I fall down on the rumpled blankets and laugh as he crawls towards me from the foot of the bed. "No tickling!" I warn.

But he just takes my wrists and holds them over my head and leans down onto me. "No tickling? Since when?"

I laugh and squirm. "I'm serious." But he knows I'm not.

He gathers both of my little wrists into one hand and then slips the other under my back to unclasp my bikini top and covers my mouth with gentle kisses. "I love you, Junco," he breathes as he lets go of my wrists.

My hands go to his back and I draw my fingertips up towards his neck, making him buckle this time. They continue up into his blond hair and I pull his face towards me. I open my eyes and he's staring at me. "It's almost time to go, you know. That's why he's out there."

I shake my head as I search his brown eyes. "No, Charlie. I'm not going back. Ever."

He lets out a puff of air. "Silly, Junco. You can't live in a virtual when you still have a body. You have to go out so you can come back again."

My head is shaking before he is finished. "No."

His lips reach down to my neck and touch me softly. He leans into my ear. "Babe, I'll always be here. They can't ever take this away."

I feel the tears well up in my eyes and he lifts his head to study my face. "Shhh, not now, Junco. Now I just want to love you." His hands remove the loose top and then slide down my thigh and I moan and grab him tight and I thank God for every second we have together, every breath that escapes, and when the release comes I am bathed in the rays of total and complete happiness.

I wake later, when the moon is out and the wind has picked up enough to make the sheer curtains in the window blow in towards the bed. Charlie is gone and I am alone on the cool white sheets. I swing my legs over and dress in a large white shirt and some old denim shorts and make my way out of the bedroom. The moon is so bright that the ripple on the lake reflects the glow indoors through the picture window. I stand near the small kitchen and watch Charlie out on the deck, sitting down in front of the apparition of Tier.

My heart aches for him and for me, because he's right. Tier is here for one reason and one reason only. To announce the end of — whatever this is. My throat tightens up and I swallow hard to fight back the sadness. I walk out onto the deck, making just enough noise to let Charlie know I am out here, but he doesn't turn back to find me and the sinking feeling drops a little further into my stomach.

I walk down the steps slowly and then step into the soft sand that was never present at the lake cabin this virtual was based on. My toes sink in and I walk towards the dock and step on. Still, Charlie remains fixated on the holo hovering out over the water.

I can feel the vibrations on the deck as my feet touch down, and as I move out over the water the planks have a little more give than they do near the shore. Still, Charlie remains fixed.

I am halfway to the end when I hear the voice and I stop. It's Tier's voice. When he first appeared it was like the holo was stuck in a repeating pattern. No sound would play and we sat in front of it, just like Charlie sits tonight, and tried to read his lips. Tried to think of what he might be saying. Added in our own words, laughing at the absurdity of what we came up with. And finally, we just gave up and ignored him.

I cover the rest of the ground and take a seat on the edge of the dock. Charlie takes my hand and I lay my head down on his shoulder.

By then I already know what Tier's message is. He repeats the same two sentences, over and over again.

Trust no one, Junco. Show no weakness.
Trust no one, Junco. Show no weakness.
Trust no one, Junco. Show no weakness.
Trust no one, Junco. Show no weakness.

And I come out of it just like I went down. Swinging for the dumb fuck who just ripped me out of the happiest time of my life.

Chapter One

I burst out of the tank and the desperate gasp for air is like a prairie devil sucking up a farmhouse. My fists latch on to anything that will prevent me from going back under as waves of thick goo slosh around my body. Only the whine of plasma charge snaps me out of it and I allow a multitude of hands to grasp my arms and keep me still as the voice booms next to my head.

"Don't make me regret letting you live, Junco."

I cough and somewhere deep inside my vomit reflex is triggered. Shit comes up, clogging my airway and making me struggle against the firm hands. Since my eyes are still glued shut, I have no idea what comes out.

They pull me up out of the tank – completely out of the tank – so that I'm in mid-air for a few seconds, and then my feet hit the cold tile floor. My legs know what to do, but it's not happening. They drag me and I count six pairs of boots as we travel. Damn. Six fucking avians for me. I'm about to feel special when I'm dumped on the floor. A door snaps shut and I know I am alone.

A hydraulic click makes me twitch as my heart pounds in my chest. I take a deep breath and Tier's words come back to me. Trust no one. Show no weakness. I count to five to calm myself, breathing in and out, up and down, and then scoot on the floor until I bump into a wall. My hands flail out, finding a rail, then I pull myself up and force my legs to stand. My whole body shakes with fear, atrophy and cold, but the legs hold and I straighten my back, let go of the railing, and lift my chin.

And wait as the thick, sticky tank goo crusts in the ventilated room. My body feels lighter than normal and I realize that gravity must be less than one-G.

It helps.

A fine mist sprays out in all directions and I lift my arms up to let it coat me all over. It is only then, when my muscles are asked to respond, that I realize what's happened.

The smile comes out and I laugh, soft at first, then wildly, hysterical, and I turn my face upward to the drizzle as my lids are freed from their prison. Hot water blasts the soap off my body and I finally open my eyes.

I expel the fear.

I've been reborn.

The water drenches me and then I step back to wipe my eyes and look around, holding the handrail for support. It's a shower room, obviously. Small, but I can see through the clear surround that there are close to a hundred of them all lined up. Mine is the only one in use at the moment. I look through the glass to try and see if anyone is around, but the large room outside the stall appears empty.

My attention returns to my shower and I lather my new body with gel provided by a wall dispenser. When my hands touch my chest and upper back I gasp with the changes. My upper body is pure muscle. The smile creeps along my face as I imagine the new power this will bring to my old skills. I turn my head to try and see my wings but all I get is a glimpse of the tips as they roll over to cup my shoulders.

The water cuts off and the hot air blasts me in all directions, making my long hair fly up and whip around my face. Several minutes later the door opens with a click and my hair falls flat as the wind ceases.

I scan the room and count more than two dozen possible surveillance points, then step out and look down the long row of empty showers and start walking. At the end I find a small pile of clothes inside a cubby. One small square filled among hundreds that are empty.

I take the clothes and walk over towards a flat piece of furniture that sits low to the ground. I've worn Tier's shirts back on Earth, so I know it goes over my head. I fuss with the bodice, noticing that the missing fingers on my left hand are still missing (oh well, one can hope) and then the remaining digits automatically track to the SEAR wound that runs the length of my jaw on the left side. I drag a fingertip down the raised line of scar tissue and allow my mind to jerk back to the memory.

And then let it go.

It is what it is.

My attention returns to my girls, which need to be smashed down into the cups of the upper body garment. Tier's shirt never had cups and they feel heavier than I remember, so it's a struggle to get them to cooperate before sealing up the sides.

In the end it fits like it was tailored specifically for me.

The pants are made of the same black material as the top, synthetic, thick as light armor, and soft. They slip on easily up to my hips and it's only then that I notice my SEAR dock under my belly button is completely covered by skin. I touch it and the dock opens, revealing the small blue wand within.

I admit, I have to hold back my revulsion.

"Do not remove the weapon, Junco." The voice on the speaker is emotionless and direct.

I completely ignore it and slip the SEAR knife into my hand. My thumb flicks over the small imperfection near the tapered end and it comes to life with a buzz. Another smile graces my face. I flick it off and dock it, then look up and find what may be the closest surveillance point. "You went through all this just to kill me in the waiting room? I don't think so. It's mine and I'll take it out whenever I want."

I button my pants and move on to the socks and boots.

This time I'm stumped. My feet are no longer feet and I stare at them in awe. Or maybe confusion, I'm not quite sure. Four toes and they are extraordinarily long. All point forward, but the two outer toes seem to have a mind of their own and can point sideways and almost backwards, if I wiggle them enough. I get up and walk around a little, looking down as I try out the new digits. They move and adjust as I change my pace. The talons clack on the hard tile and I imagine what it would feel like to clutch things. I wrangle them back into the forward position and tug on the socks and boots.

When I'm finished a door opens and I walk through.

The space is empty except for a mirror long enough to allow hundreds of avians to gawk at their new bodies at the same time. I stand there, stunned at what I see. I flex my back muscles and the wings respond. One stretches out to its full length and then retracts and folds, cupping back over my shoulder. I squeeze the muscles a little and I feel them collapse completely against my back. It makes me look human for a moment and I grin back at my reflection.

My wings are not black. I get close to the mirror and try to see my back. They are a strange color – not white, not cream, not tan, not brown, not gray – a mottled mixture of all these hues. I squint at my eyes in the mirror, moving my head back and forth to get a clear look at them, expecting to see orange like Moju's or green like Tier's. But they haven't changed at all and a grunt of disgust leaks out of my mouth.

"Well, that fucking sucks. Not only do I still have hazel eyes, but you fuckers gave me hazel wings too." I look up, but get no answer. Then I whisper under my breath, "That is so fucked up."

I'm done looking, satisfied with the novelty of my new body, but the next door does not open. I think of how I should act so that I don't show weakness and decide on boredom. I lean my wings against the wall and then slide my back down until I'm sitting on the floor. I tilt my head back and close my eyes and my mother's voice is in my head. *Patience and inertia are not the same thing.*

She's right after all. So I wait. And think about where Tier is. Hell, where I am for that matter. Are we in the Band? I'm not really even sure where the Band is, but Tier talked about it before we left Earth a few times. And then my thoughts slip back to Earth – to Selia. Did she get the message out? To Slag – what did he do after we left? To Moju. My hearts aches for him and I let a little frown cross my face before I catch it.

This seems to be the magic signal that I am calm and ready to be rational, because the door opens and a man walks in.

He doesn't look avian. For a moment I wonder if I ever left Earth. But I feel the weight of the wings and the lightness of the less-than-G gravity and let that go. It doesn't matter where I am – I am no longer human.

He's not a friendly-looking man with his height and muscular bulk, not to mention the down-turned mouth and intense stare. His suit is black, tailored, and screaming money. His hair is fair and this too is different. So far all the avians I've ever met had black hair. Except me of course. My hair is still the same ugly auburn brown. His complexion is fair as well and his smile as he approaches me is forced.

I look up at him for a moment, then get to my feet and wait.

"I'm Lucan, Junco. Your new commander." His voice is deep and calm. Almost soothing.

"You don't look like a commander," I say, raising my eyebrows at him. For one, he's not that old. Maybe early thirties. And for two, he's wearing a fucking suit. I don't get it.

He gives me an indulgent smile, like I'm a toddler. "You've never seen an avian commander, so how would you know what one looks like?"

I watch his deep blue eyes as he talks, find the power there and make myself behave. "You're right. It's a pleasure to meet you, Commander Lucan. Should I salute? Shake? You'll have to forgive me, I am almost one hundred percent ignorant of your culture."

Another indulgent smile as he extends his hand. "We can do it your way, if you like."

I take his hand and shake it politely. "I would not like, actually. I would prefer to know how I am expected to act."

He retracts his hand. "We'll get to that in time. But for now I'd like to know how you came to be on my habitat when I gave a direct order to kill you two months ago."

I smile. "Oh, that's easy," I say, still grinning up at him, "I was invited, of course."

"Ah, yes, your invitation. Would you like to know where Tier is?"

"Not especially, no."

His brow furrows at my answer and I tuck down a smile. I can play too, buddy. Let's dance.

"Well, Junco, that surprises me. I think he would very much like to know where you are."

My stomach churns, but I shake my head. "No, I don't think so, Commander Lucan."

"And why's that, Junco?"

I shrug and turn my back to him and walk a few paces, testing out my wings and feeling my new talons move and be restrained inside my boot. God, no wonder Moju was barefoot. It's kind of annoying.

"I'm nothing to him. He's nothing to me. Why would we care what the other is doing?" I turn back and wait. Patience is not inertia, Junco. "He brought me back because I can be used and I came because, well – I'm sure you probably realize why staying on Earth wasn't a real option for me."

He smiles again. I don't. My face will crack if I have to keep up this fake shit much longer. He turns sideways towards the door and waves his arm, signaling for me to pass through ahead of him.

I do and I am met by six avian guards with their plasma rifles pointed at my head. I listen to their footsteps and decide they are the same guys who just saw me naked and covered in goo not too long ago and shoot them a smile.

They keep their aim true and ignore me.

Lucan and I walk side by side down a long hallway wide enough to drive a few tanks through back on Earth. My gaze stays straight ahead and I do not gawk up or around, but instead listen to our footfalls echo as we travel. The guards match our pace and they surround me in a semi-circle, walking sideways to target me.

I look at Lucan's face and he feels my gaze and directs his eyes down in expectation. "I think it's possible you've misjudged me, Commander. I'm just one small girl. Do you really think you need six heavily armed men plus yourself to control the situation? If so, you will seriously inflate my ego."

He sighs and I know the charade is over. "Junco, we know exactly who you are, what you do, and what you're capable of — so you will excuse my enthusiasm for protection until we can all come together on the same page. I ordered you to keep that weapon of yours," he hesitates as he points to my stomach and I squint up at him, "sheathed. Yet you insisted on removing it."

"Commander Lucan, that weapon is biologically attached to me. Taking it out and giving it a quick check was like wiggling my new toes. A simple reflex to make sure everything is working." I reach for it and the rifles emit an electric field so strong it pushes me backwards. "Cool it, guys. I'd be happy to hand it over if it makes you feel better."

"Hands off, Junco. You will not use that weapon here, do you understand?" I don't meet his gaze and I don't agree to his terms, so he continues, "I would take it, but it cannot stay away from you for long, we tried while you were under. It was — not ideal."

I shrug. "I lived without it for weeks on Earth."

"This isn't Earth."

Yeah, I think I'm getting that, thanks. "Well, you know, I can't help that the thing is attached to me. It wasn't like anyone asked if I wanted a biological weapon grafted onto my body, ya know."

He stops in the hallway and waves the men off a bit. Without the echo of boots the only sounds are the environmental units pumping out conditioned air. The guards step back but the rifles are still on alert. "Junco, I'm not playing games. This sweet-talking you gave Tier will not work on me. So save your breath."

I laugh out loud this time, I can't help it. He gives it a good shot, but he's unsure what to make of me and it shows. "Commander, I don't know who you've been talking to, but it certainly wasn't Tier if you think the reason I am alive and fucking up your habitat is because of my wily ways with men. Tier and I had no conversations about what he was and was not doing beyond a handful of words the very last time we talked."

Lucan's composure is back and his lip curls up slightly as he speaks. "Is that so? Well, Tier must be mistaken then, because he said something quite different."

I don't even miss a beat. "You're a liar. He never said anything other than what I just stated because that was the truth. And if you know so much about me, then you know that death carries very little meaning at the moment. You can try and kill me if you want – I don't give a shit. I have nothing to lose. You're no different than the assholes I left back on Earth and if you really want to know what I'm doing on your habitat, you better ask yourself. We both know I'm here because you want me for something."

I watch the guard behind Lucan raise his eyebrows at me and smile, then redirect my eyes back to Lucan's face and wait for his reply.

He turns and continues to walk and I catch up and walk by his side. We travel in the echo of our footsteps once again and then he stops at a door, palms his hand over the biometrics and it slides open. He waves me in and I step through, but he stays where he is.

"Goodbye for now, Miss Coot." And then the door closes.

Chapter Two

I turn and find Layla gaping at me from the far side of the room. I look up and around and she smiles and waves the thought away. "No cameras allowed here, Junco. I'm so glad to see you!" She walks over to me and hugs me to her chest.

I return her hug and push her back. "What did they do to Tier?"

She winces at his name and shakes her head. Her mouth drops downward as she speaks. "He's fucked, Junco. On trial for treason."

I stare out at the room for a moment, stunned. Treason. That is the worst. I shake it off and study the room. It's a cross between a lab, a clinic, and a hotel. It screams Junco's new vivarium. I pull a chair from the table and sit across from Layla as she waits patiently for me to settle. The chairs are strange, with only a thin backrest, but as soon as I lean back I understand why. It supports my spine without crimping or impinging on my new wings. I slouch a bit, even though the straight back makes it difficult, and feel very tired and sad. Since Tier's warning instructed me to trust no one, I have to presume that Layla will deliver reports on my moods and behavior and force a neutral expression as I wait for her to give me some sort of explanation.

She smiles and then lets out a long breath. "When we discussed everything that could happen when we brought you back, Junco, treason never even entered the realm of possibilities. But" – she hesitates – "here we are."

"What were the possibilities?" I ask as I avert my eyes and study the furniture. In the living area there is a bed, a desk, a large screen on the wall, and a bedside table. I see a door that might lead to a bathroom. That takes up about a quarter of the space.

About half is devoted to medical and lab equipment — centrifuges of various shapes and sizes, some molecular cloning machines, glassware of course, a bench lined with bottles of chemicals, buffers, pipettes, books, a plate reader, cell sorter, a few medium sized coolers, a hood for tissue culture, four microscopes, a gleaming stainless steel minus-80 freezer for samples, and lots of other stuff that looks like it belongs in a research facility. Let's just call it a well-stocked, scratch that, a well-funded lab.

The other corner has a counter that holds canisters filled with paper goods, 2x2 gauze, cotton-tipped applicators, shit like that. There is also a built-in sink and glass front cupboards that hold enough drug canisters to treat a small town back in the RR.

"Demotion, mostly. We thought maybe if we were really fucked they'd kick us out of the Aves. We spent quite a few hours talking about what we'd do if they did."

My brow furrows and I try and put it together. "Are you and Tier — together?"

Her smile is crooked. "No, Junco. I'm on his team, his scientist. We've been together, hell, since he came out of Fledge really. Not counting that stint I did on Lacerion for post-training in moleculars."

"Sorry, I feel a little lost here, ya know. I have no idea who he is, only that I agreed to let him bring me here. We never discussed anything that might happen afterward, so—"

"We figured you'd be like a bonus — one of the Seven that we thought was lost but wasn't. We were pretty sure it was gonna work fine, Junco. It's not like we were just yanking ya on that end. And it did, right? Look at ya! So pretty."

Her sudden pickup of Tier's speech patterns makes me swallow the sadness once again. "I don't like the color, to be honest."

"Really?"

She looks a little hurt and I wonder if she made me this way on purpose, but it's too late now and I just shrug. "I like the black wings. These," I say, peeking back at their almost yellow paleness, "feel like a target."

"Oh, well. Sorry. I think they're beautiful. And I bet everyone else does too. You'll see. Anyway, the whole purpose of being on Earth was to get the Seven and bring them back. We knew you were the Seventh," her fingers do little air quotes, "and the Seventh Sibling is not well-liked around here in theory. But we discussed this for days before we came to the decision, Junco. I'm pure because someone made me that way. Ditto for everyone else. So, if someone altered you as you grew up, and they did – we know this – then how can you not be pure? Just because your alterations took place after birth, why should that make any difference?"

I look away at her question because I don't want to think about anything right now, least of all my avian biological status. "So, what went wrong?"

"After we put you under we let the others come in, but you were undergoing the morph, so you had special protected status. It's a vulnerable position. Being unconscious for weeks on end, helpless and under the control of your medical staff. They couldn't do anything to you then. They just had to wait it out."

I don't want to ask the question, in case someone is listening or Layla is taking notes on my questions, but I do anyway. "And Tier?"

She shrugs. "He's ranking officer, so they couldn't do anything to him either, unless they wanted to mutiny, which they didn't. But, well, everyone has a boss. And Lucan was beyond pissed when we arrived in the Band. They arrested Tier immediately."

"The charges," I ask, still avoiding her eyes, "are treason?"

She nods and gives me a half-hearted crooked smile when I finally look over at her.

"Because he didn't kill me."

This time she doesn't acknowledge me, just releases a deep breath.

"Anything else? Charges, I mean?"

"Something to do with breaking a treaty. And the old stuff, the unauthorized murder charges. He was on – like a probation – and they revoked it for this last charge."

I nod and get up and walk across the room to the bed. "This for me?"

She nods but doesn't rise.

"And all this?" I say, pointing to the medical equipment.

"Tests. Not today though, it's late and I'm sure you're still tired. And," she hesitates, "maybe it will help to know that these feelings you're having right now, the sadness and lethargy? It's normal, Junco. We all get this way after morph. It's an endocrine reaction, the changes really fuck you up. So whatever you're feeling right now, just give it a few days, OK?"

I sit on the bed and start unlacing my boots.

"We'll have to have guards in here with you at all times, just for a little while, though."

I shake my head without looking up and write her off for good now.

"Ashur is taking the night shifts and Braun is taking

days."

I remove the boots and the socks and finger the blister that has formed on my right foot after the short walk from the showers and I wonder for the first time how I will hold up in this new environment.

Layla stands up and walks towards the door, then turns back. "It'll be better tomorrow. We'll do the tests and then you can leave here. You'll see."

I lie down on the bed and turn my back to her.

"See you tomorrow. Ashur's outside, you remember him? From the battle at your house?"

I ignore her.

"OK, well, I'll send him in on my way out."

"Layla?" I ask without turning to look at her.

"Yes, Junco?"

"Why aren't *you* on trial for treason?"

"I'm his subordinate, Junco. He's my captain. I could no more deny his order to save you than anyone else on the ship."

I close my eyes and never even hear the other avian enter because I simply shut down and go looking for the dock.

But it's gone.

So I settle for nightmares. They come easy. History repeating.

I toss and turn in the bed as my nose wrinkles with a familiar but out-of-place smell. It fades and my dream takes me to my bedroom where I lie on the bed in my shorts and puff on a cigar, happy with who I am.

Wait.

That wasn't a dream, that was real.

Where am I?

"Junco?"

The strange voice triggers my reflexes. The SEAR comes out from under my shirt and I'm standing on the bed in attack mode before I can even process all my actions.

The large avian is bent down in a defensive stance, his plasma weapon pointing up at my head. "Junco! Put it down, now!"

"Fuck!" I let out a long sigh and retract the SEAR and slip it back into the dock. "What the fuck?"

He watches me step off the bed and stand on the other side of the room, but he does not lower his weapon.

"Ashur?"

He nods.

"Put your fucking weapon away or we're gonna tangle."

"You cannot take that knife out, Junco. Ever. If you do, you're going to get hurt."

I shake my head at him. "It's docked. What more do you want? Put your weapon down, Ashur – or we will fight."

He stands upright and slides his weapon in the holster that hangs at his hip. My eyes trace the familiar smell that woke me and I lean to look past the formidable avian. A smoldering cigar is sitting in an ashtray on the table. "You did that on purpose."

He gives me a crooked smile. "I know you like them. And I was bored. Can you think of a better way to be woken up?"

I just stand there, kinda pissed. "Well, yeah, actually. There are about a thousand better ways of being woken up than having some strange guy in my room smoking a cigar that reminds me of home. Thanks."

Ashur walks over to me and takes my arm and leads me

over to the table where he was sitting before I went commando on him. He points to the chair and slides a cigar over. "Here, have one. Relax a little, shit. You're so jumpy."

I don't have it in me to protest and the little gray box that holds the cigar is calling my name. I slide it out, press it to the striker, and puff. "Thanks."

He takes his seat and I do the same, then we both puff in silence as we watch the screen on the far wall. The sound is off, but it's the news so the captions at the bottom of the feed tell all you need to know. I guess some things never change, no matter what world you're on.

"What time is it?"

"2 AM Standard, why? Got plans?" His lips attempt to smile around his stogie.

"What time did I fall asleep?" I say as my attention goes back to the screen.

"Eight or so."

I nod. "Oh."

"Done sleeping then?"

I look back at him. He could be Tier's brother, that's how similar they are. "Probably."

"Want some breakfast?"

"No." Just the thought of food makes me want to heave.

He takes his cigar out of his mouth. "What do you mean, no? You haven't eaten in almost two months."

"Obviously that's not true or I would be dead. I'm definitely not hungry."

He's still holding his cigar in his hand, not puffing. "I've already been warned about your eating habits, Junco. I'm in charge of making you eat breakfast, so we're having some."

I screw up my face at him. "I can't think of a single

person who would even know what my eating habits are, Ashur. So spare me."

"Both Layla and Tier mentioned your lack of enthusiasm for food."

I snort out a laugh. "And how they hell would they know?"

"They said you were severely undernourished when we took you, that's how."

"Which means nothing. You guys got to see the tail end of what a very bad week does to my appetite, so what? I wouldn't base anything off what I did that week, let alone assume I have an eating disorder."

"Good, then we'll have eggs for breakfast."

"Knock yourself out, Ashur." Just stop fucking talking to me, I don't add.

He gives me a look of superiority, like he won the argument or something, then pushes back his chair and exits the room through the door I thought was the bathroom last night.

I stub out the cigar and go back to bed watching the newscreen. It's all in English but it shows a lot of stuff that makes no sense. Winged people fighting each other. Killing each other actually, in what looks to be an advertisement for an upcoming arena fight of some kind. Some more winged people having a party. Some people with no wings in what looks to be a government session. Some personal interviews. I just sit there in disbelief. I didn't watch the screens much at home, only when on the road, but it's all a little too familiar. I traveled hundreds of millions of miles, I'm on a totally different planet, habitat, whatever, and still the news is filled with the same shit. Violence, parties, and politics. The irony isn't lost.

Ashur returns a few minutes later with eggs and toast and beckons me to the table. At least it's real food and not that shit Tier tried to feed me in the cave. It doesn't look horrible, but my head shakes out a no as he slides the plate in front of me. I keep the disgusted look as I meet his eyes. "If you make me eat that I'll throw up."

He shrugs and takes his seat, shoving food in his mouth before he even settles. "It's good, real eggs and everything. Tier said you only eat fresh food, so lucky us, right?" He shoots me a smile.

"Tier would have no idea, Ashur. He saw me eat a total of three meals."

"He's the resident Junco expert, like it or not, what he says goes. Might as well enjoy the food, Fledge food is like military field rations."

I force myself to eat three bites and push the plate away.

"Ya know, you don't have to make everything so difficult, Junco. You can have it made here, if you want."

"And what would I have to do in order to have it made?"

"Follow the program," he meets my gaze, "and just do what you're told for once."

"For once? You're an asshole." I let out a deep sigh, get up, and go flop down on the bed and bury my face in the pillows. "I'm sorry I came here."

I hear him set his fork down and push back from the table and look up to see what he's doing. His head is in his hands. A gesture that reminds me of Tier when he was thinking out at the cabin, right before he told me that he killed my father.

"Ya know something, Junco, we're probably all sorry you came here. Except one person, maybe. And that's Tier. So for fuck's sake, try and do what you're told for his benefit. The guy's sitting in prison for saving you and" — he lifts his head and stares at me with bloodshot eyes — "and if I had it my way, Junco, I would have killed you myself in order to save him from that."

He stands up and walks to the door. "If you need something, I'll be outside until Layla comes."

Good job, Junco. Making friends already.

Chapter Three

Layla is busy getting the equipment ready as I watch from the table. "Ashur's mad at me." It slips out because I can't stop thinking about what he said.

Layla talks to me under her breath between curse words directed at the control panel. "Well, Junco, Ashur is not the sanest guy in the Cluster. He's always been a little touched, don't take it personal."

"He said he should have killed me to save Tier."

She looks up this time. "What?"

I shrug with my hands. "That's what he said." I watch her face as she processes this, expecting her to say something, but she doesn't. She just looks back at the machine, apparently in agreement with the guy who's a little bit touched.

I change the subject because the thought of both of them wanting me dead to save their friend is a little too unsettling. "So what does this test do anyway?"

She curses for a few more seconds before answering. "We gotta map you again. I took some images while you were under, but it was hard to see everything. This way we'll have a good baseline at what we're looking at."

"What are we looking at?" I ask.

She stops this time and gives me her full attention. "Sorry, Junco – I forgot that you haven't seen it yet." My heart thumps as I wait for the reveal. "I've never seen anything like it before, but–"

"But?"

"You've got a lot of technology inside you. Like

everywhere. In fact," she's just warming up, I can tell, "your entire nervous system is controlled by circuits that reside outside of your brain and peripherals. Like in your hands – there's a whole pad of circuits in the palms of your hands. And that SEAR dock?" She stops to shake her head. "I have no idea what that is."

I let out a grunt. "That's awesome."

She ignores me and goes back to the machine. Thirty minutes later I'm naked and standing behind the transparent shield that will allow Layla to see inside me.

She describes the process, how it will feel, and how long it will take but my mind is on Ashur. I feel the need to set this right for some reason. He was the only person Tier allowed in the room with us right before they stuck me in morph and he was the person who shielded me from the battle that happened in my driveway. I don't have to trust him, but I don't have to make him hate me either. And some small part of me secretly wants him to leak out more information about Tier. I wonder if Tier even knows I'm out of morph?

I stand as still as I can as the lights begin to pass over my body. When it's over I get dressed and flop back on the bed to wait for the confirmation that I am a freak. When she resurfaces and calls me over to her I can sense her hesitation.

"See this?" she says, pointing to a large white splotch superimposed at the base of my spine in the full-scale image of my body.

I nod.

"That's your endocrine biog."

"OK, that's not so weird, is it? I mean, Tier said my biog protocols were on that cube."

"Right. No, you're right. The biog isn't weird, hell, I have one too. But…" She stops and looks at me. "Junco, this thing controls your whole body. Your glands don't make the hormones, this thing does."

I shrug, not seeing the big deal. "Anything else?"

"Well, actually yes. See these?" She points to more white blotches on the image, one at each joint of my bones, and more throughout my body.

"Yeah, and?"

"Most of these are in the same place as your lymph nodes, or where the lymph nodes would be."

"Layla, get to the point, OK. I'm not an anatomy expert and I don't feel like digging down to find the memories from school."

"OK, well, you don't process your blood in the same way as most people. It gets shunted through these other things, and then these" – she points to the many white lines running up and down my legs, arms, and trunk area – "take it to the muscles," she points, "the lungs," more pointing, "and then finally back to the heart where it interacts with this" – she screws up her face and raises her eyebrows – "master circuit."

I just stare at her blankly.

"Junco, you're half machine."

I grunt. Of course I am. And why wouldn't I be? My body was altered since I was a toddler, I should have seen this one coming. "You're fucking crazy," I say instead.

She shrugs and snaps the image off the viewer and takes it back into the lab. I follow and watch as she rolls it up and stuffs it into a tube.

"What are you doing?"

She scowls at me. "I have to take this to Lucan right away. Braun will stay with you until I come back."

And before I can protest or demand to know what that will mean to me, she's gone and a guard enters to take her place.

He's tall, like Tier and Ashur, but not as dark and more muscular. Both his wings and his hair are more brown than black and I recognize him as the smiler from yesterday's hallway showdown with Lucan. He looks thrilled to be invited in, so I try not to make an enemy.

"Wanna sit?" I ask pointing to the table.

"I'm Braun," he says as he takes a seat.

"Junco."

"Yeah, I know. Was with you when you were picked up from Earth."

"Oh." I stop, trying to see if I recall him, but I have no memory of anyone but Tier, Layla, and Ashur.

"That was pretty funny the way you talked shit to Lucan yesterday." He laughs. "I bet it's been a long time since anyone's talked to him like that."

"Oh," I say again. "He hates me, doesn't he?"

The avian smiles and his eyes glow a little orange. "Lucan hates everyone. He's an Archer." A shrug. "No sense of humor, those guys. So what have you been doing in here all day?"

I walk over to the screen and pretend to watch the news. "Tests."

"Did you pass?"

I look back at him, trying to decide if he's serious or not. If pushed, I'd peg him as a guy who doesn't get serious unless he's forced, but he looks sincere. "No, I don't think so."

"Wanna tell me about it?"

"No, not especially."

"Wanna play cards then? Pass the time?"

"I don't know your games, so—"

He pulls a deck out of his jacket. "You're a soldier, Junco, all soldiers can play poker."

I laugh. "Oh, well, OK."

Braun is the first normal guy I've met in a long time. We get along and there's no arguing and he doesn't pretend to be better than me or even seem bothered that I have the SEAR tucked under my shirt. We play using 2x2 gauze as chips and it only takes a few minutes and I'm laughing. He's got a nice sense of humor and when he asks me if I'm hungry he doesn't lecture me when I say no. But he does leave to get some food and when he brings it back to the table I am hungry and it's not bad.

We've been playing for hours and I owe Braun six thousand rills, whatever that is, when Ashur enters. Braun smiles and stands up, counting his cotton wipes to double-check his winnings. "I cheated her out of enough paper products to buy a new house, Ash." And then he laughs. "See you tomorrow, Junco, I'll bring beer for the next game."

Ashur just raises his eyebrows. "Braun, don't–"

"Ah, shut up, man. And get off her back, she's stressed. Make her happy, why don't you?" Then he looks at me. "We'll have fun tomorrow, Juncs." And then he walks to the door, his weapon slapping his thigh with each step as he leaves.

I'm still smiling when I look over at Ashur and force myself to dial it back down.

"You'll want to stay away from that one, Junco."

"Why?"

He shakes his head. "He's trouble."

"Oh, I see. He's trouble, yet I'm the prisoner, Tier's on trial for treason, and you wish you could kill me. Well, thanks for clearing all that up." The tension is back and I miss Braun already. I walk over to the bed and flop down. My desire to make things right with Ashur is gone with the return of my sour mood.

He walks into the lab and takes a minute before coming

back in the living area and sitting down at the table. His back slouches and his long legs sprawl out in front of him. "I spoke to Tier today."

My heart skips, but I don't answer him.

"He asked about you."

I turn my back to him and let out a big sigh.

"Do you want me to tell him anything if I see him again?"

"No."

"Do you care to explain that, Junco? I mean, the guy is on trial for you, the least you can do is send a message to say hi."

I turn back. "You know something, I'm beginning to wonder how well you actually know him. The Tier I know does not want to hear from me right now, Ashur. And you're lying if you tell me he's sent a message, because I know for a fact he wouldn't do that. So stop with the bullshit, OK?"

He shakes his head and turns his attention to the screen. We don't speak another word to each other. I don't set anything right. And Ashur makes no attempt to make me happy. I lie there for a long time before falling asleep.

I wake in the middle of the night again. My sleep is way out of whack. Ashur is still slumped in his chair, one arm crossed over his chest, his fingers playing with his shirt on the opposite shoulder while watching the screen. He's got a cigar box in his other hand and he taps it gently on the table until he notices me looking at him.

"Cigar?" He extends his hand out and I lean over and take the little gray box, shake out the stogie, and light it up.

"Thank you."

He hands me an ashtray and I prop myself up in bed and set it on my stomach. He's watching a screen about a girl who is being chased by some psycho murderer on an abandoned habitat. Despite myself, I get into the drama. I can see the draw of mindless entertainment, even though I can count on one hand the number of screens I've seen all the way through in my lifetime.

We sit in silence until the credits roll and then he speaks. "I'm sorry for saying that shit, Junco. I don't want to kill you. And we all like you, we don't wish you never came home."

I stare at him until he looks me in the eyes. "You need to butt out of my life when it comes to Tier, Ashur. It's over. He sent me a message" – I hesitate – "and like I said, he never told you to tell me anything, did he?"

He shakes his head. "No. He didn't. But it doesn't make sense, I watched him put you under in the morph, and you two weren't fighting."

"It doesn't matter, does it? It's over."

We sit in silence and watch the screen as another show comes on. "I've seen this one," Ashur says when it starts. "It's not bad."

We watch it and chat some. After a little bit I fall back asleep and when I wake in the morning he's gone.

Layla and Lucan are standing over me, talking in avian. I squint up at them and try to string the words together. "I'm right here, you know."

Both sets of eyebrows go up.

"Yeah, I understand too, so that shit you just talked about me is not going over well." I push up and extract myself from the bed to go take a shower and when I'm finished, I find a closet full of clothes. It has five identical outfits to the one I was just wearing.

And one that makes me smile.

I tug on the camo fatigues and button them up. They are looser than they were when I put them on last and I make a mental note to try and eat more. Then I wrestle the shirt over my back and stretch and rip at the arm holes of the sniper shirt until I can jam my wings and arms through. I realize I look ridiculous, but I don't care. My old field boots are in there too, but there's no way they will fit on my new hulking feet. Besides, I'm feeling Moju's affinity for going barefoot.

When I walk out of the bathroom Lucan and Braun are at the table talking and Layla is in the lab clanking glassware around.

Braun laughs. "Snipers do it from behind? They saved that for you?"

"I knew you'd appreciate my shirt, Braun." His eyes dance as he laughs again and I catch myself wondering how long I'll have to wait until we can play cards.

Lucan interrupts my daydream. "Layla, Braun. Junco and I need some private time, please."

Braun winks at me as he passes. "Beer's in the fridge, Juncs." I absently wonder if I'm old enough to drink on this habitat or if Lucan will frown on that, but he stays seated and points to the chair Braun just vacated.

"Layla has some interesting developments from the tests yesterday. Do you know what it means?"

I shake my head, but keep silent.

"You're not human."

He waits for my reaction, but I hold it in.

"You're not avian."

Nothing.

"You're not machine."

I laugh now. "OK. So what am I?"

"All three, apparently. It's highly unusual."

I squint, but do not avert my eyes. "Will you kill me now?"

It's his turn to stay silent. We stare, willing the other to speak. I have nothing to say so I am patient until he gives in. "That will be entirely up to you, Junco."

"How's that work, then?"

"We have a strict, structured society here. A lot of people must share space in the hundreds of habitats we have scattered throughout the Band, but habitats are not easily made and resources are precious. Do you understand this?"

"Yeah, of course."

"When we create the clutches of children we do so with the entire population in mind. We try to make them into their genetic ideals but not all of them will be able to reach their full potential. Which is why after they go through the morph they must go through Fledge. Do you know what Fledge is, Junco?"

I shake my head.

"It's a test of sorts. To see which individuals can fulfill the potential bestowed upon them. Everyone you've met so far has succeeded in Fledge. Proved themselves worthy."

Tier's words on the rock on Earth come back to me, *She's worthy. That's what I thought. She's worthy — it's just that no one recognizes it yet.*

"And there is a very simple test to determine if you're worthy or not." He stops and waits for me this time.

"Which is?"

"In this case it is a series of fights. That's what Fledge is. A series of fights to the death."

"So you want me to kill people in order to prove myself."

He nods. "Your clutchmate, Esta, went through Fledge

a few years ago. So she earned her place. And if you want to stay here, you must do the same."

I shrug. "OK."

"You may not use the weapon."

"Lucan," I snarl his name, "seriously, if you think the most dangerous thing about me is that stupid weapon, you are grossly mistaken."

"There is one more thing."

"And that is?" I ask, looking at him sideways.

He hesitates and I notice the slightest crack of a smile beneath his facade. "You must testify against Tier."

"No problem." I catch his shock like a firefly in a jar and tuck down my satisfaction.

He physically moves backward. "And you will tell the truth."

"I always tell the truth, Lucan."

He regains his composure. "Very well. I will set it up."

"You do that," I say to his back as he exits the room. You do that, Lucan. And I'll do the same.

Chapter Four

Braun enters before the door can close behind Lucan and his smile brings me back from the edge. "Junco," he says, "I get that you love the shirt, but you can't wear it like that."

I frown at him as he removes his knife and lifts the fabric up from my back. "What are you doing?"

He leans down into my face. "Making you look presentable, babe. Just give me a minute." His hands get busy cutting the shirt around my wings.

"Don't call me babe." I look over my shoulder at him and he shrugs.

"Sorry, Junco. Forgot." Then he flashes a smile and continues to cut. "I invited the 039 over for poker. And the box is stocked, so should be a good time tonight."

"Why?"

He's finished cutting now and he takes a second to straighten out my shirt before leaning into my face again. "Welcome home party, Junco." His hands take my arm and force it into the shirt. Then he manipulates the cloth so that his cut stretches over the uppermost portion of my wing. When his fingers make contact with the sensitive feathers my back arches involuntarily and I squeal. "Shit, what was that?" I ask, my breath heavy.

"Sorry, Junco. I know, it's weird, right? Don't take it the wrong way, I'm just trying to get them out through the cuts in the fabric."

"What way might I take it?"

He stops and leans around to see my face. "It's kind of erotic, isn't it? The whole wing-touching thing."

I raise my eyebrows at him. "Yeah, kinda."

He wrestles with the other wing, forcing me to stifle the sounds that want to escape my lips. When he's finally done I breathe out a sigh of relief and look up into his eyes. They glow a little more with each passing second and are a warm orange, like a beckoning fire. "This isn't my home, Braun." I pick up the conversation as quickly as possible to avoid the weirdness that wants to creep in.

"Is now. We inducted you as our ninth warrior back on the shuttle while you were out."

"I thought you guys didn't want me to morph? You were all outside the door when Tier and Layla were putting me under."

"Not us. That was the fucking crew and the other two teams that were hitching a ride after the clusterfuck in the MR. We were always on board. Tier would never make a decision like that without us. Just isn't done."

"Oh." I frown.

"What," he says as he studies my reaction, "is the problem?"

But I'm not sure, so I can't say. I shrug instead, thinking about being part of a team. So much has happened in two days it's hard to get my head around it. But this isn't stuff I want to share, so I exhale and push it down for later. "Nothing, just – unexpected, right?"

"It's good?"

I nod. "Yeah. Maybe."

He laughs. "Jasus, Junco, you're so hard to fucking please, ya know that?"

I watch the words come from Braun's mouth but I see Tier's face in my mind. I smile up at Braun, shake off those feelings, and then hug him. "Thanks, though. You have no idea how much I appreciate what you're doing right now."

He lifts his hands high up in the air, pretending to not want to touch me. "What? What did I do? I'm gonna get ya drunk, Junco, and probably take advantage of ya right here in the lab." He winks as I look up at him.

"You wish," I say into his chest.

"Oh, shit, do I ever!" Then he pushes me away and goes to set up the game. "But don't go blabbing it to the rest of the guys, Junco. They all have to feel like they have a shot with ya or they'll mope about all night."

"Where's Layla and Ash?"

He nods his head towards the door. "Talking to Lucan."

"Am I allowed to walk out that door?" I say it before I can stop myself, then get nervous with his silent look and scratch my neck and wince.

He shakes his head. "Not yet, Junco. But it won't last forever. So try not to think of it that way."

I sit down and he deals me in, sliding me a stack of high-value chips since we're only fucking around. "Did you really cheat yesterday?"

He doesn't look up from his hand. "Course I did, Junco." His eyes peer over the cards. "Do I look like an honest guy to you?" Then he winks. "No really, I did cheat. I always cheat, which is why I always win."

I raise my eyebrows at him.

"But I get caught a lot too." He laughs. "Plus everyone knows I cheat so they never pay me anyway. Did you really think I would make you buy me a house with 2x2 gauze?"

I laugh. "All's fair in cards and war?"

"Precisely! Holy fuck, that's poetry, Junco. You should publish that shit."

Ash and Layla walk in just as he's finishing. "What the hell is going on here, Braun? She's got shit to do, it's not poker time."

"Ash, you are such a straight-backed piker. Get the hell out, party's not until later. We're just having some fun, right, Junco?"

Layla interrupts as she walks into the lab. "He can stay if you want him to, Junco. But it's a little personal."

Braun gets up and squeezes my arm. "Just knock on the door when you want me to come back in, be right outside."

When he's gone Ash scowls at me as I walk into the lab with Layla.

"What?"

"I told you, Junco. Braun isn't the kind of guy you want to be hanging around with."

I make a face at Layla and we do the girlfriend laugh. "She's not dating him, Ashur, fuck. Calm down. He's keeping her mind off the serious stuff. You seem incapable of playing that part, so leave them alone."

Ash leaves, presumably to give Braun the same warning. Layla just shakes her head and lets out a deep breath. "Damn, he's so fucking wound up about Tier."

I change the subject. "So what's this then?" I ask, pointing to the screen she's looking at.

"DNA profile. You definitely have the genetics of Gyr. Did Tier explain that to you?"

I nod. "Yeah, some avian who was down in the MR and was taken out to the Camp a long time ago."

"Right. But you also have the genetics of a human and not from your parents or anyone else from the Stag Camp or the RR."

"How do you know? There's no database to check."

She smiles. "Well, actually, Junco, the RR has many databases you probably never knew about. There's no match for anyone in the RR. So we don't know who gave you the other half of your code."

"Is that important?"

She shrugs. "Might be, might not be. Hard to tell at this point. Anyway, the most interesting thing about you isn't the avian or the human genetics, it's the AI code we found."

My heart skips and I suddenly feel dizzy. "What?"

She gives me a look that says, sorry for the message, but someone has to deliver it. "Uh, yeah. You have code in those electronic circuits that was created for an AI."

"Like my HOUSE on Earth?" I know it's true before it comes out but the full meaning of it remains just under the surface.

She pouts her lip ready to say no, but another second of thought changes her mind. I watch her expression change in real time as the idea grows on her. "Maybe. Never thought of that. Good instincts, Juncs."

"So what does that mean? To me?"

"Nothing, it's inert. Not even activated, just no connections whatsoever. So it's a big nothing. We think it might have been a future project that was never started or at the very least never completed."

Yeah, right. I wait for her to say something else but she's moved on to other things. One thing you can definitely say about Layla, she's got a certain detachment for things of a personal nature – it's all science all the time.

Good for her.

Braun tells dirty jokes to me like I'm just one of the guys as we play a few fake hands of poker. It makes me laugh so hard I want to pee my pants, even though Ashur's scowl tells me he thinks it's inappropriate. I'm wiping the tears out of my eyes and fanning my face to make the heat go away when the door chimes.

"Enter at your own risk," Braun calls to the smart security. The door opens and two more guys come in, neither of them familiar to me.

Ashur does the introductions. "Juncs, this is Mish." He points to a tall slender guy with the same black hair and wings as Tier, but with the bluest eyes I've ever seen. "And Goldilocks here is Rikan."

Rikan is the first blue-eyed blond avian I've seen besides Lucan, but since he doesn't have wings he doesn't count. Rikan's wings are a honey cream color and my eyes linger on him a little longer than they should. Braun catches it. "Yes, Junco, we all know he's beautiful, but if ya keep looking at him that way, we'll have to beat the shit out of him to dampen down the ego."

I look away, embarrassed.

Mish takes a seat at the table, but Rikan comes up to me and squeezes my shoulder. "It's nice to see you smile, Junco."

Braun looks up from the deck he's shuffling. "Yeah, I think you've smiled more in the past few hours than you did in six months back on Earth." His eyes go back to his task, but I'm stuck on his words.

"Did all of you watch me?" I glance around the room. Oops. Everyone looks a little uncomfortable. "I mean, I don't care if you did. I just didn't realize my life was such an open book."

The door chimes again and Braun calls out, "Enter at your own risk," then winks at me as three more guys come in. Ashur stands up this time and claps a guy in a formal uniform on the shoulder, leaning in to have a private joke. The four of them chat for a few seconds before turning towards me as he motions to another guy. "Junco, this is Arel." Arel is the shortest of them all, darker than either Tier or Ashur, and he moves toward me to shake my hand like a prairie lion stalking grouse at dawn. I shudder to think of him hunting me. "Isten, who is your new counterpart by the way."

I look hard at Isten who, I notice, has hazel eyes just like mine. His wings aren't as mottled, but they are the closest thing I've seen to white so far. "Cold-bore kill-shot in one?" I ask.

He shoots me with his finger. "You must read minds or something," he says as he pulls a chair next to me.

"And Ryse here," Ashur gestures to a guy who could be Braun's brother and who is wearing the formals, "just passed his qualifiers for officer promotion. Here's hoping you make it, buddy, but if you don't you'll always have a spot flying our asses around."

I smile at him as he takes his coat off and settles into a chair between Ashur and Braun. My eyes travel from one guy to the next, watching them joke and talk with each other in a way only a true military team can. The only two missing are Layla and Tier.

We start the game and Braun is caught cheating on the first hand and is relegated to bartender. He beckons me to join him in the kitchen as he goes to get some beer.

"What's up?" I ask.

He's rooting through the fridge collecting bottles from various brands of alcohol that I don't recognize. "Here, take these. That's for Rikan and those three are for Ashur, Ryse, and Isten."

I take the bottles and turn to leave. "Hey, Juncs?" he asks, still fishing around for a few more beers. "We weren't spying on you, OK?" He looks up then, serious. "I know it might feel that way, but really, only Tier was on the ground most of the time."

I smile. "It doesn't. Feel that way, I mean. It's sort of a relief," I let out a deep breath, "not to have to hide things, actually."

He lets out his own long breath and I wonder if he was really that worried about how I might react. "You don't have to hide anything from us, Junco. We're a team now, you're official, no matter what happens from this point on. You're one of us. It was a done deal back on the transport when we took the vote."

I look down. "But why?" Then I look back up to see what his eyes say. "Why would you guys risk so much for me? You don't even know me."

He shakes his head. "You're wrong, Junco. We know you better than you know yourself. We've watched it all go down in real time."

I turn to leave, but he stops me again. "Wait, here," he says, handing me another bottle that I can barely manage to hold on to, "this one's for you."

I pass out the beers and take my seat again. Isten reaches over and removes the top on mine after I struggle for a few seconds, then hands it back. "That's good brew, you'll like it." Then he smiles and lights a stogie, his attention diverted by a play on the table. I turn the bottle around to see the label and my stomach feels funny. It's called *Little Sister*.

Braun watches me as he's coming out of the kitchen. He drops off his load of beers and then comes over and pulls a chair up next to mine and immediately starts peeking at Isten's cards. Isten punches him in the arm and scoots over next to Arel, leaving Braun to bother me.

"Here's the million-rill question for you, Junco." Braun leans back in the chair and flashes a grin around his stogie, then snags my shirt between his fingertips. "Who the hell did you steal this shirt from?"

My face heats up as I watch the guys start shouting out guesses. I smile at all the names they know, none of whom have ever gotten that close to me. "You're all wrong," I say, looking down at it. The memory floods back in from somewhere and I recall the night with perfect clarity. "Mikah Mesner."

"No!"

"Shit, that loser—"

"Say it ain't so, Junco—"

I look up. "Oh yeah, boys. It is so. Mikah fucking Mesner. He was – a lot of fun." I think I make myself blush.

Isten looks at me with a serious expression. "Hey, Junco, I've got a shirt you might like, too." Every one of them spits beer at that one and I feel the heat overtake my face which makes them laugh even more.

I look around the table and find Ashur, a little more serious than he should be, and challenge him with my eyebrows. "Something on your mind, Ash?"

He accepts my challenge without delay. "You had Tier's shirt for a while there, Junco."

The guys take my side.

"Oh, shit—"

"Ash, why the fuck—"

"You piker, leave it alone—"

My hand goes up as I look calmly around the table. "Since I have been informed that we are all in this together, you might as well know the truth." I pause to straighten up my face and look down. They all lean in, waiting for me to give the details. "I did not sleep with your captain." Braun is so pleased he kisses me. Everyone else seems pleasantly surprised and one by one they lift their bottles in the air and toast me.

Ashur salutes with his beer and I nod and flash him a crooked smile.

We spend the rest of the night talking about each other,

and since they know so much about me already, they tell stories even I had misplaced.

Right before I pass out on the bed between Arel and Isten I make a note to myself. Best day ever.

Chapter Five

I roll over on the bed, bump into another body, and force my eyelids open a fraction. Isten's arms wrap around me and pull me in and I fall back into a dreamless sleep only to be woken up in seconds when the door chimes. I hear Layla shout, "Officer up!"

Bodies scramble all around me and I feel Isten pick me up and throw my feet onto the floor. Before I even have my eyes open I am standing at attention, my right hand forming an Earth salute that may or may not be appropriate. The eight of us are lined up in a column, four to a side, in front of the screen. Layla walks through our pattern and stands at the center on the other end.

I keep my eyes trained upward like everyone else, but steal a peek over towards the commanding officer who stands just to my left.

"At ease, Aves."

Everyone relaxes and I study them quickly to see how I should stand. Feet apart, shoulder width, hands behind my back, eyes to the officer. Some things never change.

He begins with a sigh. "I don't expect you to be happy about this and I don't really care. I have my own team, which you are all aware of. Except the lady here–"

"Junco Coot, sir."

"Junco, then. Tier is out and it looks extremely doubtful that he will be back. So, for the time being I'm your captain, but Ashur remains XO until more permanent arrangements can be made. Are we clear?"

"Yes, sir," we all shout.

"All right then, we'll have a morning meeting every—"

"Why the fuck is Junco on the screen?" Braun's cursing interrupts the captain and we all crane our necks to see the news on the far wall.

"Holy shit, it's Selia! Where is this?" I look around. "How do they have this footage?" I have a lot of eyes looking at me, but only Layla responds.

Layla comes over and takes my arm until I'm sitting on the bed. "A lot has happened on Earth, Junco. It's a huge mess and this" – she points to Selia on the screen, her face burned and dirty, dressed in a military uniform that I don't recognize; every once in a while she cowers from an explosion in the background – "woman has been blasting some video of you all over the fucking sphere. She's got a tape of your mother threatening the governments of no less than four of the Republics, your mother's in—"

"Invaded the MR, yeah, I know that. I gave Selia that shit and sent her out right before I went into the meeting to kill Aren."

Everyone looks at me now, but only the captain speaks. "You started this *war*?"

I sneer at him, instant dislike for his baseless accusation. "Of course not, I needed to get a message out of my compound, so I gave Selia there the video Slag gave me of my mother in exchange for a favor. Looks like she did her job and then some, which is good, otherwise I'd have to go back and kill her on principle."

Mish and Rikan snigger on the other side of the line and Ashur hisses at them to shut up.

The captain directs the guys to take a seat at the table. "Perhaps you should start at the beginning, Junco. This was not in any of the reports."

"Well, it wouldn't be, would it? No one knew but me and I wasn't debriefed." I stare up at him innocently and he draws a large breath in.

"Yeah, OK. Start at the beginning, please."

I run it down in simple terms: the memory dump with Tier, the envelope in the Goat, the trip back to my room, the secret room, the call from HOUSE to see Slag, the discharge – everyone groans at this part, but I move on quickly – then the video message on the cube Slag gave me.

"She set them up?" Ashur's tone says he's doubtful.

I shrug with my hands. "This is all I know, Ash."

"And that part about your childhood, Junco?" Layla asks. "Is it true?"

"You mean the part where I assassinated my first target at six? Or the part where my mother wanted to steal me away and my father had her deported?"

She swallows and nods.

"I found the memories of both," I say, looking from face to face. "We were on vacation, some fancy European ski resort. They went up the on the lift in front of me, I pretended to be adjusting my sock in my boot. The targets got on the lift, then I followed. When we got to the top my parents were already halfway down the mountain. I followed the couple until my parents came out from the trees, then they killed the man and I slit the woman's throat with the SEAR. It was the first time I ever used it – for real, anyway."

All eight of my new teammates stare at me in disbelief and the silence makes me continue. "We changed to cross-country skis in the woods, trekked a few miles down to a road, and were picked up in a long silver car by an older man with white hair." They continue to stare. "That's it. You can close your mouths now."

"And you were six?" It's Isten's question this time.

I look to him and nod. "Six – but if it makes you feel any better, Isten, I hurled my guts out afterward. So anyway, like I said, I knew the reporters were out there beyond the gate at my house, and this girl, Selia," I point to the screen where she is still talking, "got the golden ticket if she would just deliver Charlie's cubes to someone in his family. I'm glad she's telling everyone, that was the purpose of me giving her the evidence."

Ash throws me a little gray cigar box and I breathe a mumbling thank-you as I slide it out and strike it up.

"Now what?" Ash is looking to the captain.

"Well." He stops and looks down, his eyebrows teetering somewhere between surprise and frown. "I don't think we have to worry about her going through the General Fledge."

And the uproar that ensues drowns out any pain I might be feeling from exposing myself.

Ash is irate. "She is Aves! A sanctioned member of the 039. She will not go through the General Fledge!"

The captain sighs. "She's only part Aves, Ashur. It's not good enough for Lucan. I have no say in this and neither do you. Either she goes through it, or Lucan–"

"Or he kills me," I say bluntly. "Tries, anyway. And since I am on his world, breathing his manufactured air, he'll probably be able to accomplish that regardless of how well-trained I am." They all stop talking to look at me, eyes searching my face. "Lucan explained it yesterday, and I agreed to do it. And to testify against Tier in the trial. That was the deal."

Now they look at me like I'm a traitor but I put my hand up. "Don't ask, OK. You all just need to trust me.

Tier asked me to trust him when he brought me here, and I did. Still do." I look straight at Ash. "I still trust him, Ashur."

I look around to the rest of them, even the captain. "And now I am asking you all to trust me. Do you think I want to kill strangers just prove my worth? No. I don't. And I have no information that will incriminate Tier, I promise. He told me nothing. Nothing. There is nothing I can say to hurt him at this point. When he asked me to come with him when we were out on the rock, he said the thing was already in motion, his actions couldn't be taken back, even if he wanted to."

Braun turns away and runs his hands through his hair. They are all so much like Tier it makes my heart ache.

"I never asked him to save me. But he did. I'm sorry if that wasn't what you signed up for when you took your vote. But I can't change it."

I wait to see if any of them will fight with me or maybe walk out, but they don't. I take a deep breath and when I let it out, I feel alone. My team is confused and hurt, my captain is selling me out, and I've told them all to pretty much fuck off. I am just Junco. Again.

The captain clears his throat. "OK. Men? If I were your real captain, I'd stick around and give a shit. But I'm not. Your captain is sitting in Justice on trial for treason because he refused to kill your nine here. Like the girl said, deal with it."

And with that he leaves us alone.

Ashur is furious and stalks up to me, making himself an imposing figure compared to my smallness. Braun intervenes and pushes him back. "Don't do it, Ash, I'm fucking warning you."

"Junco, what were the instructions? I want answers, now!"

I shake my head and Isten takes his turn. "Come on, Ash, back off." Ash pushes him in the chest and Isten bares his teeth. "You better think twice, Ashur, you better think before you touch me again."

"Junco," Layla pleads. "How could Tier have told you anything? You were under morph. There was no message, you dreamed it." Mish, Arel, and Rikan just hang back and say nothing as they watch me struggle.

I turn my head and play with my hair, thinking about it. Then turn back and study each face one at a time. I want to trust them, but Tier ordered me not to. "Layla, if I could tell you I would. But I can't. It was an order. His order."

"Just tell us what the order was," Ryse says, taking my hand. "Really, Junco, he would never fault you for telling us."

"You're wrong, Ryse, it was pretty fucking specific. I'll do what I can, I promise. That's all I can say. I'll do whatever I can to make it right."

Braun steps forward and pulls me away from the group. "All right, show's over. Let's get on with the day."

I break free and head to the shower. The hot water blasts me until my whole body is red and when I step out in my avian clothes once again, the room is empty except for Braun. He's sitting at the table with his back towards me, smoking a cigar and watching some avians fight in a contest on-screen.

"I have to tell you something, Junco," he says without turning around to look at me.

I take a seat on the other side of the table and wait for him to acknowledge me. He just pushes a little gray box in my direction and I light the stogie up, puffing on it to calm my nerves. We sit that way for several minutes and then I push him. "Spit it out, Braun. I don't have a lot of self-control right now."

He lifts his eyes and I can see the wheels turning in his mind. He pokes his cigar in the direction of the screen.

I turn to look at the fight.

"That's Deliverance from last year," he says.

I shake my head. "OK. I'll bite. What's Deliverance?"

"A fight. A big fight that takes guilty prisoners, especially high-value prisoners, right? Famous ones, ones who committed horrific crimes, shit like that?"

I prod him forward with a nod.

"And they have this contest. The winner gets to kill a bunch of bad guys at the end but the real prize is a wish." He stops and drags his gaze around until he meets my eyes, "I have a plan. Not a great plan, but it's something. Only you can never tell anyone I told you this. They'd never forgive me."

"Hey, if there's one thing you can be sure of, it's that I'll keep a secret, right?"

He smiles. "Right, yeah."

"So what is it?"

He takes a puff and blows the smoke into rings as he stares up at the ceiling, then he looks over at me. "Sorry. It's just, I can't believe I'm going to even propose this. But, if I were you, I'd at least want to know of the possibility. Don't feel pressure to accept it, either. Just think about it."

I nod and lean in as he starts talking in a low whisper. We stay that way for several minutes and I look down when he finishes.

"It's a long shot, I get it. But believe it or not, I'm the brains of this operation." I choke on my own spit and he finally cracks a smile. "No, really, Junco. I might just be a big dumb munitions expert to most people outside our team, but I've got a wicked fucking strategy game going on inside." He taps his head with the spittle end of his cigar.

"Yeah? Well, that's one stupid fucking plan if you ask

me."
    "I told ya it was."
    "Has a lot of variables."
    "Yeah, lots of what-ifs, I know."
    "Can't possibly work."
    "Yeah, forget I mentioned it."
    "Oh, it's already forgotten."
    We smile across the table and then we laugh.
    We laugh until we are hysterical.

Chapter Six

Ashur enters the room as I am wiping the tears from my eyes and Braun is hacking on the smoke caught in his throat. He turns and we both look at our XO, small leftover sounds of laughter escaping before we realize he's still very much pissed off.

"I'm glad you're both so fucking pleased with yourselves. Meanwhile, the entire team is coming apart over this shit."

Braun stands up and for the first time I see him as the imposing fighter that he is. Ashur doesn't cower, move, or even flinch. He's one hundred percent secure in his authority, but he doesn't tell Braun to sit down either.

"Ash, you need to back off. This shit is going down Junco's way, no matter what you say about it. She says Tier gave her orders, and that's the end of it."

Ash pushes past him and walks over to me. "Put some shoes on, Junco, you've got a meeting to attend." I look down at my feet and scowl. "Now, dammit!" he growls. "You're not leaving here barefoot, so put them on."

I get up and grab the boots and socks from my closet then sit on the bed and force my feet to obey and conform. When I'm done I stand and look over at Braun. "I'll see ya soon, right?"

He smiles. "Count on it."

Ashur waves his arm towards the exit and my stomach churns at the thought of crossing the threshold into my avian existence. Ash's hand pushes on my shoulder in an attempt to guide me forward, but I brush it off and walk through the door on my own.

The hallway is just as I remember it, wide, tall, and empty. Once again, the only sound is the echo of our boots as we walk. I look up at Ashur. "Where are you taking me?"

He doesn't even glance down at me. "Conference Room Zero."

I nod. "OK, well, who am I meeting?"

"Lucan and some guy from Earth."

"Really? Who?"

He shrugs, but doesn't say anything and we walk for several more minutes. This is the longest hallway of my life. When we come to the end there is a large door. Massive. He presses his palm to the biometrics and it takes a moment for the reinforced gateway to commit to opening. We wait in silence as the mechanisms inside click and adjust to the command.

I feel like a little kid trying to see beyond, but I'm disappointed because it's just another hallway, though smaller this time. We turn right, then left, which brings us to another door.

"Are you ready?"

"For what? This the conference room?"

He smiles, the first one since my outburst. "No, Junco, the real world. It's quite a walk over to CR Zero, it's on another part of the habitat. Out there," he nods to the human-sized door, "are a lot of people. Just stay next to me and don't get lost." He starts to turn away, but then looks back. "And for fuck's sake, Junco, don't do anything stupid like try and run off or I swear–"

"Calm down, I won't."

He lets out a deep breath and I unexpectedly take one in, then his palm flattens against the side of the door and my new world comes into view. I stand there gaping at all the people bustling past. It reminds me of Tokyo or London, there is so much foot traffic. He takes my hand, pulls, and then we're walking in the stream. I try not to look around too much but I can't help it. It's not another hallway at all, it's a city.

I walk along looking up and I hear Ashur laugh. "Junco, watch where you're going. You look like a tourist."

I look over to him and smile. "I am a tourist." It's only then that I notice we're not even on the ground level. I strain my head to see past the throngs of bustling avians, towards a transparent railing a couple dozen yards away. I gravitate towards it, pulling Ashur with me. "Just let me look, OK?"

He shakes his head, but takes the lead and pulls me through the crowd. I stand at the railing and lean over, then swallow and dip back quickly when I realize we've got to be a hundred stories up. Trains whiz past on a suspended track about twenty stories below, and I notice several more as my eyes travel down towards the ground. "Wow, it's pretty incredible."

"This is our capital, do you know what she's called, Junco?"

I meet his eyes and shake my head.

"Amelia. This entire habitat holds eight million people, it's the largest. And busiest, obviously."

I give him a crooked smile. "I love it. How come no one's flying though?"

"Only Aves can fly here, just too crowded. You can fly if you need to. You're in the black Aves uniform, so you'll always be recognized as one of us." He takes my hand and leads me out into the bustle again. "It's about a ten-minute walk to CR Zero, but we can take a train if your feet will hurt."

I look down at them. They already hurt. But I shake

my head. "No, let's walk."

Ashur smiles and pulls me through the crowd. Once we get off the main walkway there are a lot fewer people and he transitions into my guide, pointing out things like stores and offices, bars, restaurants. It's like the Peaks, except nothing like it at all. A dozen or so minutes later we arrive at another biometrically sealed door. He presses his flesh and it opens into a small room.

"We're going up," Ashur explains as he palms the panel. An elevator. My weight sinks with the artificial gravity pull as we ascend and I count the seconds until we stop.

"How high did we just go?"

"About a thousand feet."

"In ten seconds? Damn."

"I have to warn you about the next part, we can go back down and take the train if you prefer, but I think you'll like the view if we walk. You'll probably get really disoriented the first time, just be prepared."

I nod and he presses his palm to make the door open and we step out.

Into nothingness.

The dark star-filled night closes in around me and I hold back. Ash pulls and I think I will fall over, into the black below my feet, but then he's behind me and his hands are planted on my shoulders pushing me forward.

"Just walk normal, Juncs. The walkway is transparent."

"Everything is transparent, Ash. I feel like I'm walking out into space."

"Well, that was the feeling they were going for, so I guess they succeeded."

We climb until the incline evens out and I realize we're standing on the summit of a great arch that dips out from the habitat and into the vacuum. I spin around and almost fall. "Why are we the only ones out here?"

He shrugs. "VIP shit, you know. Not for the masses."

"Feels good to be important, then."

He smiles. "Can you find any stars?"

I search, but I'm lost in the night for the first time ever. "It makes no sense to me, I can't find any."

He points and I follow his finger. "There's his belt, Juncs. Can you see it?"

I don't at first, but then it all slides into focus, like I'm looking at some old 3D art. I find Rigel, then up to Betelgeuse, then Castor and Pollux in the Twins. I turn, carefully, and I can see the entire winter hexagon.

"Wow." Chills run down my body and I shiver.

"Yeah. I know how much you like looking at the stars. I like it too."

I look over to his face and try to figure him out as he stares out into the deep. "I don't really get you, Ashur. I mean, you're a pretty hard guy to read."

He lets out a little laugh. "Says the lion to the wolf."

"Do you hate me? For not telling you? And for getting Tier in this mess?"

His smile drops as he looks down to me. "Junco, as much as I'd like to blame you, none of this is your fault. We fucked up. End of story. And not just with you, with a lot of shit." I stand quietly as he thinks, just taking in the stars and the night. "I'm just having a hard time coming to terms with what we did because Tier is the closest thing to family I have. All the other guys, we're all family too. But Tier and I have been through everything together. We're from the same clutch so we have the same birthday, we grew up together, went to Earth together, came back together. Usually you never have the same morphday as your clutchmates because maturity is an individualized thing. But all of the 039 have the same morphday, so Tier and I are connected through every important life milestone there is. And we've been leading these guys since some of them were eight years old."

I let out a deep breath. "I told you, Ashur, I'll fix it."

He looks up and points to a shooting star. My eyes follow as he talks. "You can't fix it, Junco. The trial is a formality. He's going to be killed."

I shake my head. "No, Ashur. He's not."

He looks into my eyes as we stand there in silence. "I trust you. But don't go and do anything stupid, Junco, because you can be saved. You're a sure thing, darlin'." We both smile at his Tier impersonation. Then he looks down and whispers, "This Fledge has no idea what's coming."

I force down a frown and he takes my hand and leads me down the arch and back into reality.

Lucan is pissed off when we finally make it to the outer door of Conference Room Zero. "Where the hell have you two been?" His eyes blaze at Ashur, then rest on mine. "When I call for you, Junco, you come!"

Ash steps between us. "I brought her straight away, Lucan. Calm down."

"What did you do, walk?"

Ashur laughs. "As a matter of fact, yes. We did walk. This was her first time outside. Shit, man, be reasonable."

Lucan shakes his head. "Watch your step, Ashur. If I've lost patience with Tier, how much do you think I have left for you?"

Ashur shrugs off his threat, then turns to me. "I'll be outside if you need me, Junco."

"That won't be necessary. I'll handle her from here."

"I don't think so, Lucan. She's my nine and I have every right to stick around."

I raise my eyebrows and wait for the fight, but Lucan just grabs me by the arm and pushes me towards the door.

"Don't bruise her, Lucan."

"Don't push me, Ashur, I'm not in the mood."

Ash looks me in the eyes and I shake my head at him. "It's fine, Ashur, I'll see you after."

I'm shoved through the open door into a very normal-looking conference room, if you don't count the night sky view that dominates one entire wall. There is only one man seated at the table that can hold more than three dozen. I almost gasp out loud when I see him.

"Coot, thank God you're OK."

"What the hell are you doing here, Slag?"

"Holy shit, Coot, you have wings."

"Yeah, I'm half avian, remember?" I look over at Lucan. "What's this about?"

Lucan shrugs, trying to look indifferent. "It appears that Earth is unable to continue without you, Junco. Your former commander has something to discuss."

I look at him, then over to Slag. "What the fuck is going on here? Am I being sent back to Earth?"

Slag steps forward. "Calm down, Coot, I'm only here to make an offer."

I look back at Lucan, but he puts a hand up. "I'll give you some privacy."

Slag and I wait for him to exit the room and I get a glimpse of Ash trying to look in before the door closes.

"Explain, now."

He pulls out a com tech from his jacket and hands it over. "I'm to deliver this to you. I have no idea what it says, so I can't speak until you've seen it and made a decision."

I take the com. "You haven't watched it?" I ask with an incredulous frown.

Slag shakes his head. "Biometrics, Junco. It's only for you. Retinal scan. I'll wait outside with them. Just let us know when you're ready to talk."

He leaves the tech in my hand and even though it is impossible for such a small flimsy card to feel heavy, it weighs me down. The chairs are built for humans, with a full back, and when I settle in it feels good to get the pressure off the new blisters on my feet.

The retinal scan flashes my eye and the video begins to play.

It's Moju and my heart thumps wildly in my chest as he screams. A face enters into view, a head I sliced off that night in my driveway. Aren sniggers at whoever is running the camera, and then motions for another person to flame Moju with a torch. "See that, Junco? You think you can get away with what you did?" He shakes his head and barks another order at the torturer. "I've got him, Junco! You might be far away but I've got Moju."

This is a trick, Junco — it's not possible. You killed him! He is dead!

But Aren responds like he's reading my mind. "Do you think you're the only one with clones, you stupid bitch?"

Oh fuck.

"I'm gonna be sending your brother back to you in pieces. Very small pieces that I will personally cut off him each and every day. And just to show my sincerity, we'll make the first cut together." He motions to the man behind him, who proceeds to cut off a finger with a plasma knife. The flesh smokes up in thick tendrils as it burns. My fingers find the SEAR scar on my jaw as Moju's screams turn demonic and I cover my ears.

"I'm sure you remember how that feels, right? Except, Junco, he won't be treated with some special membrane to seal it all up pretty." He laughs and then turns back to Moju, apparently thinking he is off screen, or maybe he just wants me to think that. "She's not coming for you, Moju. She's gonna let you suffer just like everyone else."

And then the screen goes black and a deletion sequence begins counting down. In a matter of seconds the entire video is erased and a smoldering burn begins in the center of the card and spreads outward to the edges. I toss it onto a tray that holds a pitcher of water in the middle of the table and I'm halfway across the room about to kick Slag's ass when I catch myself and spin back around.

Fuck.

Think, Junco. Think.

I take a seat and let my head fall into my hands as my mind races through my options. I know Lucan is in on this. And Slag. I envision six different ways to kill them both using only three moves.

Shit. Think.

I force myself to stop and rationalize it. Why would Lucan want me gone? I ponder all the possibilities, but only one makes sense. To make sure Tier dies. That's the reason.

Trust no one. Show no weakness.

I take a deep breath and count to five before letting it out.

Calm, Junco.

No weakness.

I repeat the breathing until my heart stops racing and then I get up and walk around to make sure I can control it before knocking on the door.

Chapter Seven

They all file in, including Ashur, and each one takes a seat at the table across from me. I smile, and then push the hatred down as Slag begins describing the deal he's been sent to offer.

I interrupt him after only a few words. "Who sent you here, Slag?" My eyes pierce into him, rage at him, but I don't allow a single muscle on my face to move.

He looks at me, confused. "Your mother, Junco. Didn't she explain things on the video?"

I let out a breath and Ashur is on his feet so he can reach into the ashtray and pick up the remains of the tech. Only the extreme edges are left, and they are charred black. He leaves the table and walks around to my side and stands behind me.

"That tech did not contain a video of my mother, Slag. So, I'll ask you one more time, who sent you?"

Slag's mouth sags and it's Lucan who answers my question. "Junco, the launch credentials check out. It came from the Subjective planet pad in Vegas." He tilts his head up like he's thinking. "Recently acquired, since you were picked up."

I laugh. "That is so much bullshit."

He continues without a pause. "A lot has happened on Earth in the time you've been away. Vegas was captured the week after you left."

"It's not a very strategic move on their part. It's a long fucking supply line from Vegas to the Subs, isn't it?" I turn to look him in the face to wait for his answer.

Slag clears his throat and I turn back to him as I quiet down the slip in facial muscle control. "I was sent by your mother, Coot."

"She's not my mother, so quit fucking calling her that. Mothers give birth to their children, or at the very least care for them. She did neither. I'm done here."

I get up to leave but Lucan puts his hand up to halt my progress. "Junco, if you refuse this offer to return to Earth you'll be sent to Fledge. Immediately."

I shrug. "Whatever." I turn back to Ashur. "Take me to Fledge then, Ash."

He smiles and nods but Lucan is on his feet and already in front of me. "Just so I am clear here, Junco – you choose to stay and fight instead of returning to Earth?"

I laugh. "Lucan, you're clear."

Slag interrupts. "Coot, what the fuck are you doing? I was sent by your mother!"

I turn back and growl, "I don't have a mother, Slag. What part of my words aren't getting through to you?"

He crosses the room and grabs me by the arm. My body reacts without the extra squirt of adrenaline that appears during even the most benign of confrontations. My elbow hits him in the face and I turn just enough to knee him in the balls. He stumbles, but stays standing. Ashur steps between us, and Lucan is bending down into my face, his mouth contorting into ugly lines.

My heart never misses a beat and I realize I've wanted to do that for a long time. "I'm not leaving, Lucan."

"Ashur, take him outside and have him escorted back to his ship while I have a private talk with *her*."

They make for the exit and Lucan snarls at me, "Sit down, Junco. We're not done here."

I take a seat and watch him as he formulates his next move. One thing is very clear about Lucan, he has no idea who I am. He's read reports, seen videos maybe. Some first-hand accounts. He knows nothing beyond the few confrontational words between us.

When he speaks, he is calm. "You do realize you've tilted your hand, do you not?"

"I have no idea what you're talking about, Lucan. Please, just get to the point."

"You have no real reason to stay here, Junco. Your morph is over, you're free to leave, you have a long life ahead of you. Your decision to stay is based on your desire to save Tier from his fate, and not this silly rebellion directed towards your mother."

"Are you fucking kidding me?" I burn hot with rage, then see his smile and tone it down. "Are you really going to sit there and tell me you think that tech contained a message from my mother? You fucking piece of shit." I get up and see a slight movement backwards from him. "That wasn't my mother on that tech asking me to come home, Lucan. It was a clone of my first boyfriend snipping off Moju's finger. And I swear to my own fucking God, I will slice your fucking head off with my SEAR if you say another word to me about it."

I realize I'm up in his face – as far as I can manage with the height difference – and I take a step back. Then I turn and walk away.

"I'm staying," I say over my shoulder. "Moju's a big boy, he can certainly handle that little fuck without my help. When I'm done with this Fledge bullshit I'll go back on my own terms."

"When you're done with this Fledge *bullshit*, Junco, you will belong to the Aves Cluster. And you will go where you're told. Is that understood?"

"As long as someone tells me to go back to Earth and kill people, I've got no problem with that."

He lets out a breath and I can feel him roll his eyes at me. I turn to face him. "You're not going to win this game, Lucan."

"Says the one small girl with no power."

"I'm just warning you. Don't be disappointed in the end when I take back every drop of satisfaction you extract from my failures."

He sighs. It hints at exasperation, boredom even, and I sense I may have miscalculated. "One of these days, Junco, we will have an honest conversation. If it's Fledge fights you want, girl. Be my guest. Go and kill. But it won't save Tier. He's been on his way out for a very long time. Long before he refused orders, long before he waged war on the RR for you, and long before he gave away his genetics to a man who helped him kill more than two dozen Earth leaders."

Shit.

I look up at him, too quickly, having misplaced that little secret Tier told me out on the rock. Lucan reads my face and smiles. "Ah, I see some recognition there. Don't worry, Junco – when you testify the drugs will get it all out in the open." He stops and stares into my eyes, burns into them. I look away, feeling a little beaten already.

But he continues, "So, just remember, when we are at the end, when I am standing over you as you break in half, and I am forced to leave you with nothing, Junco – don't say I never tried to help. Don't tell me I made your life a living hell, because you will have done that all on your own.

"And if – this is a gigantic if, Junco – but *if* you *can* take back everything you'll lose by choosing this path, then please know that my satisfaction will come from that, and not from watching you fail."

He walks towards the door, palms it, and then turns. "By the way, has anyone ever mentioned that your language is filthy?" His voice is pleasant, like he's pondering the meaning of something quizzical, but he wrinkles his lip like he has a bad taste in his mouth. "I don't care for it. Cheapens you, Junco."

He leaves me standing there, facing the emptiness of space scowling, and feeling rather cheap and filthy, if I do say so myself.

But not minding one bit.

The door is still open when I walk through a few seconds after Lucan. I watch his figure walk away, down the long hallway, then turn to find Ashur. He's talking to a girl farther down the other end of the hallway and I make my way towards them. The girl is taller than me, but that might be due to her high heels. She has long black hair and wears what I would consider to be housewife gear. I can hear her deep voice murmuring towards Ash, who seems to be on drugs or something. Even though he's looking right into my eyes, it takes half a dozen seconds for him to acknowledge me.

"Junco, there you are."

I raise my eyebrows at him. "You OK?"

The girl turns and a flood of memories waft over me with her scent. I see my toddler self leaving church with my parents, my chubby hands firmly clutched between their palms as we cross the street and head towards the bakery in town. She smells like the bakery.

"Junco." Her voice is deep and entrancing. "I tried to get away as soon as I heard, but was delayed. I am so sorry I was not there when you woke up."

My head spins as I look up at Ashur. "What's going on?"

He smiles but says nothing and my head is swimming.

"Let's go get a stim, that will clear you two up. I was just at the clutch and I'm afraid that the effects won't wear off."

She pulls on us and we follow her.

"– so, like I said, Junco – hey, you still with me? Drink that, will you? It won't get better until you drink it all down."

I look at the drink in front of me and I have no idea how it got there. "Where are we?"

"Oh, for Seven's sake, Junco. I've answered that question seven times. Please, just drink it all right now."

I pick up the glass and bring it to my lips, drinking whatever it contains. I stare out the window, and then get up and press my face against it, amazed. We are at the top of a very tall structure, and the ground is so far away I can't even make out the bottom. I swoon with the realization of how high I am and her hands come out to steady me.

"Sit down, Junco. You're going to fall."

I let her lead me back to the chair and my head clears a fraction. "Where are we?"

She smiles, then breaks into a laugh. "Oh, for fuck's sake. Why don't you just tell me when you're feeling normal and I'll continue talking. I'm tired of telling you everything seven times."

I look at her. "Who are you?"

Her green eyes twinkle. "I'm Esta, Junco. Your sister, from the clutch."

"Why do I feel this way?" I try and look around but my head throbs, like I have a hangover.

"I'm afraid it's an occupational hazard. The wings, Junco. Mine cause people to become sedated and easily controlled."

"What kind of power is that?"

"The kind that makes it possible for me to spend all my days with the Aves Clutch." I squint up at her. "Children, Junco. I raise the children."

I nod my head, understanding. I think. Things are beginning to come in a little clearer and I look around me. The bar is massive. I mean huge. Probably fits like three hundred and fifty people. And every single patron is smashed up against the far wall, sipping drinks and eyeing us with caution. "Shit, Esta. You can really clear a room." My eyes track to the far end of the bar and I spot Ashur. He waves to me and laughs. I wave back.

"Feeling better now?"

"Yeah." I nod. "Wow, you're pretty intoxicating. That could come in handy."

"Yeah, if you spend your life babysitting, it's great."

"No, I mean with anyone. You're like a little drug factory. Controlling people is quite impressive."

"Yes, well, it only works on the Aves, Junco. No one else is affected. Besides, self-healing like you've got is a lot more practical."

"I can't self-heal. I can't do anything." I let out a little sigh and look at the bottom of my drink. "How the hell can I get another one? And a cigar?" I look up at her and wait for an answer.

"Here," she says, taking my finger and moving it towards the pad at the edge of the table. "Press there."

I do and a display pops up. I flip through it and choose a beer and a cigar. It beeps and shuts down. "Did it work?" The words are barely out of my mouth when the servos arrive to deliver my goodies. "Damn, that was quick." I gulp the beer and shake the cigar out and strike it up. I puff slowly and look back at Esta. "Like I was saying, I don't have any powers."

She smiles and I know what the children must feel when

she's about to gently correct them. "All warriors can heal, Junco. And you're dressed as one, so I'm assuming you are one."

"No shit? What else can I do?"

She shrugs. "I'm not sure. Typically you get the powers associated with your Cluster, then whatever special talents you have."

I nod and puff on the cigar.

"Anyway, as I was saying to Ashur back at the conference room…"

My mind drifts again, I'd forgotten all about Lucan.

She snaps her fingers in front of my eyes. "Junco! Over here, dear. I'm talking to you, please pay attention."

I laugh.

"I'm so glad to finally have another Sibling here, it's been awful. I only want to read the history, Junco. And Lucan refuses–" She crinkles her forehead and half a dozen furrows appear.

"Wait, what? You're unhappy?"

She lets out a large breath of air as Ashur walks up. "Feeling better, Juncs?"

I nod. "Yeah. Esta is unhappy."

He pulls back as he looks at her and she covers her face and turns away.

"We gotta get going, Junco." He puts his hand on Esta's shoulder. "She has to fight tomorrow, Esta. She needs to get acclimated. You can walk with us if you want, let me just get a couple stims to go." And then he smiles at me and goes back to the bar.

I can tell she's struggling to hold it together, so I grab her hand and pull her up and lead her back over to Ashur.

She holds my hand all the way to the dorm and when we finally get there, she's even talking again. The stims help keep her chemicals at bay. How fucking horrible to have this effect on people. I mean, it would be cool if she could control it, but just leaching that shit out all over probably breaks a lot of deals in the Aves Cluster.

The dorm is a huge building far out in the middle of nowhere. I'm still not sure how the habitat is laid out because I've never seen a map, but we had to take two trains to get here. And there is literally nothing, I mean nothing, around the building except the train stop and a few benches in front of it.

Ash leaves to check me in and do whatever it is people do when they report for Fledge while I sit with Esta. "So, what was your Fledge like, Esta? Did you do this one?"

She gives me half a smile and shakes her head. "No, the mothers have their own special Fledge. Everyone does, actually. The General Fledge is like a last-ditch attempt to save your life. It's all pretty fucked up."

"So what did you have to do? Take care of kids or something?"

She looks away but the words come out with practiced clarity. "We had to cull them."

"Cull them? You mean kill them?"

She nods. "Yes, the Aves Cluster has specific requirements that must be met by age five. If they don't meet them they must be culled. The Fledging mothers do the culling for a year."

"Holy shit, that's awful. I'd rather kill grown-ups at least." In fact, I find it revolting and my stomach protests with a surge of acid.

"Yeah, me too. I can't do it anymore, Junco." She turns in a sudden jerking movement. "Life like this isn't worth living. I want to do something else, anything."

"I'm not too familiar with the rules here, Esta, do they let you do that?"

She shakes her head. "Not really. Lucan must agree to

it."

I huff. "Well, fucking forget it then, I don't see him giving a shit about anyone but himself."

She looks into my eyes, pleading. "That's not true, Junco. He listens to you guys – you warriors. He'd listen to you, for instance."

I laugh. "Esta, he hates my guts. He literally told me he was going to break me in half back there in the conference room."

She searches my eyes, desperate.

"Plus he hates Tier, and he thinks I love Tier, so–" I look for Ash to avoid her gaze and when I find him he waves me over. "Hey, he's calling me over now so…" I get up and she follows. "OK, you can come too."

He's standing at a long desk, like you might see in a hotel back on Earth. Behind him, in another room farther off, I can see other avians who must be Fledge participants as well. They are looking out at us with interest. "So, Ashur – am I the last one here?"

He smiles down at me. "Yeah, Fledge actually started last week. You don't get to train before the first fight, but you'll be fine, Junco. I'm signing up as your sponsor so I'll come back the day after and we'll train for the second fight, OK?"

I shrug. "Whatever."

"I'm a sponsor too," Esta pipes up to the avian guy manning the desk.

He's about middle-age and a little overweight in the middle. His wings droop low down his back, like they're broken or something and the stubble on his cheeks might look good on any of my teammates, but on him it looks unkempt. "Who the hell are you?" he asks Esta.

"I'm an Aves Mother, and I'd like to sponsor one of these participants. Are there any left?"

Ash takes a deep breath but says nothing. Not our fight, his eyes tell me.

"Lady, I can count on one hand the number who have sponsors, which one do you want?"

She strains to see behind the man, her eyes darting back and forth and then her hand extends and her finger points. "Him. I want to sponsor him." The kid is easily the youngest one in view. He looks to be about ten years old. Half my age. If they're all this young I might have to grow a conscience. I'm no child killer. I look over at Esta as the words form in my brain and I have to hold down a shudder.

The fat guy yells, "Hey, kid, get over here. You want to accept this lady's offer of sponsorship?"

His eyes don't even register Esta. He looks at me and then at Ash. "Sure, why not."

Esta almost claps and I look up at Ash, but he shakes his head at me.

"Day after tomorrow, Ashur?"

He nods to her.

"Great, we'll come together."

Ash leans over and gives me a hug. "Junco, the first fight is a slaughterhouse, just kill anyone who comes near you and don't try and make it to the top. It doesn't count in the first fight. Your scorecard is the only thing that matters."

Esta looks over at her charge. "Just do whatever she does, kid. She's a trained killer, she can't lose."

Ashur grabs her by the shoulder and turns her away as I laugh. I look down at the kid. "Well, shit, you gonna show me where to go or what?"

"I'm not your slave," he says, jutting his chin up at me.

"No, but I'll keep you alive tomorrow if you're nice. So shut the fuck up and take me somewhere."

I'd make an excellent Aves Mother.

Chapter Eight

From my vantage point on the claimed bed I can see the entire dorm. The bunks are stacked seven high and they line both sides of what is a relatively small and narrow room when you consider that the better part of a thousand people are sharing quarters.

Lined up like soldiers in formation, the tables down the middle play host to several dozen smaller groups of participants. Apparently I missed the application deadline for joining one. But I'm not much of a joiner anyway.

The kid sits on the top bunk directly at the head of my own. He said he had a bunk before he went up to the front and was roped into Esta's mid-life crisis plan, but if he did, it's been claimed now. He didn't look broken up about it.

He's eating some ration pack and I feel the need to eat something as well. I kick the metal bunk frame to get his attention. "Hey, where can I get some food?"

He looks down at his ration, frowns, then offers it to me.

"No, where can *I* get some food? I don't want that shit. What else do they have here?"

"They got a machine." He nods his head down towards the front of the room. "If you got money."

"I think I do. Come on, let's go check it out."

"What if we lose our bunks?"

"Who gives a shit? They'll be plenty of them empty tomorrow, right?"

He shows a smile for the first time and I give him one back.

The climb down goes without incident, but he waits until I am on the ground before flying down to join me. As soon as we leave the periphery and enter the throngs of people the trouble begins. A girl snarls and makes a gesture that I can only assume is something obscene. I smile and promise internally to set her straight tomorrow. Farther down a boy, older like me, gets brave and reaches out to touch my hair and hiss at me as we pass. I bat his arm away and he calls me a few choice names.

The kid hangs back for a second, his bravado failing him at the exact moment it needs to rise to the top, and I have to stop and wait for him to make up his mind to proceed. I watch his face play out the conflict and remain patient as he moves past a group of girls that taunt him.

By the time we reach the little galley that houses the machines he's a nervous wreck. "Hey," I call to him as he looks at the long walk back to the bunks. "Forget about them. We'll sleep in here if you want."

He just looks at me like I'm crazy. "There's nowhere to sleep in here!"

I pan my hands out over the floor and then gesture to the tables. "There's plenty of places. Don't sweat it, like I said, the crowd won't be so brave tomorrow. And I guarantee that you and I," I wait for him to find my eyes, "will still be alive."

He smiles again.

I pan my thumb across the panel on a food machine and then let the kid pick something good. I get two and we wait as the autocook prepares it. I have no idea what it is, but when it comes out, my stomach grumbles and we both scarf it down like wild animals.

Afterward I find a cigar machine and grab half a dozen of those, then get a drink for both of us. "Wanna go outside so I can smoke this in peace?"

He screws up his face. "Are we allowed outside?"

I shrug. "Why wouldn't we be? Are we prisoners or something?"

He thinks about that longer than I feel is necessary, but finally decides we are not. The fat guy at the desk tries to stop us when I head for the door, but I shake my head and he backs off.

The day is almost gone when we sit down on the grass and I light my stogie.

"You're not from here, are you?"

I puff for a few seconds. "No, I'm from Earth. Just woke up three days ago. I have no idea what's going on to be completely honest."

He shakes his head at me, but my face convinces him without words. "What are you doing in this Fledge? If you're Aves?"

"That, kid," I pause to exhale, "is very fucking complicated."

I look away, but when I look back he's still waiting for an answer. "Lucan made me, or else I had to go back to Earth with someone I don't care for. I'm only half Aves." I shrug. "So I don't get automatic placement, I guess."

I lie back on the grass and look up. The Fledge building is massive, about half as tall as the height of the habitat, which from this vantage point looks to be a couple miles high. The structure slopes against the side as it climbs and I can only imagine what that does to the gravity in those areas, assuming this is a torus-shaped habitat. That might not be right, but it feels right from the way the horizon curves up on itself.

There are seven distinct segments to the building. "What's the deal with this?" I ask, pointing my cigar at the partitions along the side of the building.

He looks up and sighs. "The fight levels. Fight one is

on the first deck, two on the second. It goes on like that. So, how did you manage to meet Lucan?"

I puff on the cigar and think back three days to when I woke up. It feels like years ago. My mind wanders back to the night I hit the deer and it feels like lifetimes ago. "He was there when they pulled me out of morph. Nasty bastard, isn't he?"

I smile over at him but he's got a weird look on his face. "Is he? I never thought so."

Oops, got a believer here. "Isn't he?" I ask, looking away now. The kid shrugs and shuts up so I take that as a no. "So, you got a name?"

"Isec."

"Nice to meet you, Isec, I'm Junco. So what do you know about the fight then, Isec? Because whatever you know, it's a hell of a lot more than I do."

He tells me, but it isn't much. We stay out for a little longer then make our way back inside. The crowds in the middle of the room have dissipated so we walk back to the bunks with no hassles and Isec is snoring within minutes of hitting the sack. I envy him because I lie awake listening for boot steps on the bunk ladder or the heavy beat of approaching wings the entire night. The adrenaline jacks up a little higher than my previous normal, and I wonder just how safe it really is to close your eyes here.

My mind drifts back to Lucan. The kid obviously doesn't share my opinions of him and it makes me replay one particularly interesting tidbit. *One of these days, Junco, we will have an honest conversation.*

Just once I'd like someone to start the conversation with honesty and not make me wait for it. Just fucking once.

The fat guy is reading off the rules via some amplification device elsewhere in the dorm but to my delight, I can see them as they pan across my field of vision. "Hey." I kick Isec's bed. "Are you seeing this stuff on a vision screen, Isec? Or is it just my Aves shit kicking in?"

"Shut up, Junco, I'm trying to listen."

OK, I guess it's just me. I read along with the announcer, but then skip ahead because he's too damn slow.

General Fledge Fight One
Rule One: One body equals one point.
Rule Two: Only biologically attached weapons allowed.
Rule Three: Fights begin when the shields drop.
Rule Four: Fights end when the buzzer sounds.
Rule Five: No medical attention will be provided.
Rule Six: If you're alive at the buzzer, you advance.
Rule Seven: Those unable to attend the next fight will be culled.

Pretty fucking easy. The announcer demonstrates Rule Four and everyone jumps when the buzzer blares. I look over at Isec and he's panicked. "Hey, Isec?"

I watch him gulp air as he turns to look at me. "What?"

"Stop worrying. Jasus, kid, you're gonna die of a heart attack before we even get in the arena."

He shoots me a weak smile but then gives his full attention back to the announcement.

"Hey, Isec?"

He tries to ignore me.

"Isec?"

"What!"

I smile as he finds my face. "I said you'll live through

this one, kid. Relax, we're a team."

"I don't think you know what you're doing. You're gonna get us both killed."

"How old are you Isec?"

He screws up his face. "What's that—"

"Just tell me how fucking old you are."

"Ten."

"Ten? Isec, when I was ten I had already assassinated two world leaders on Earth. I think I know what the fuck I'm doing. So relax, because if you get killed it will be because you panic and don't do what I fucking tell you. Got it?"

"But you haven't told me how to do anything, we don't have a plan."

"Duh, kid. I haven't seen the arena yet, have I?"

"By the time you see the arena we'll be fighting."

"So?"

He looks like he's gonna scream and I smile at him. "Just trust me."

He doesn't, that much is clear. I try another tactic. "Do you know what the arena looks like?" He nods. "Perfect, describe it to me."

"A large oval arena, small free-G streams on the periphery and gravity wells in the center where the top of the ziggurat is. The terraces hold five hundred on the bottom, then two-fifty, then one twenty-five, then sixty, then—"

"I get it, they graduate upwards."

"We go up facing out, then when the shields go down, we fight until the buzzer sounds."

"How long does the fight last?"

"Five minutes."

"OK, here's the plan, when we get up there, just before they drop the shields, turn and face inward."

He stares at me like I'm a lunatic. "That's your plan? Turn around and face inward?"

"You got a better one?"

He scowls at me.

"Then shut the fuck up and do what I say. Now, Ashur said that body count is what matters, so I'm pretty sure I'm gonna get a boatload, but since I have to make sure your count is high as well, I'll send some of them back for you to finish off. When the shields go down, you get behind me. We'll be back to back. Get it? You call out when someone comes close enough to hurt us. Tell me where they are on the clock face. You know what that means, the clock face?" I use my hand and describe what I'm saying. "Twelve is here, three here, six here." He nods. "Good, you say the clock time from your perspective, and I'll reverse it to my perspective, OK? I've used that technique quite a bit, so it's no biggie for me to switch the numbers around, but if you try and do it, you'll fuck it all up."

My battle plan clearly calms him down and he's got his business suit on now. "Let me see your hands." He thrusts them towards me. "Make your claws go out." He presses on his palms and the razors protrude, not anything as dangerous at Tier's, but good enough for a ten year old. I press on my palms and the razors shoot out like arrows. I look at Isec and smile. "Pretty cool."

"You only have three on your left hand."

"Yeah, nightdog ate my fingers back on Earth, that sucks, but you use what you got, right? Now take your boots off and tuck your socks into them."

"Why?"

"Talons are weapons too."

"Is anyone else going to use talons?"

"Shit, I sure fucking hope so, else they're stupid. Off, now. Tie them to your pants, you got a loop on those?"

He checks and says he does.

"Good, tie them on loose, on the way up to the battle level drop them on the floor, we'll pick them up after the fight."

I look down below and people are beginning to line up near the machines on the far end of the room. Isec scoots over to the ladder, but I put my hand up. "Not yet, let's be last. Oh, and one more thing. I can't fly, so I'll be on foot the whole time."

His mouth drops open. "You're kidding right?"

I smile. "No, I told you I just woke up three days ago. I've never used the wings."

"We can't do this on foot!"

"Like hell we can't. I've been in worse places than this on foot. Alone even. And I've got you watching my back and you've got me watching yours. OK, looks like it's time to go. Shove that fear down now, Isec. When it's over you can think about how fucking scary it was, but for now, this is just another job, another day to get through – got it?"

Isec flies off and I climb down quickly to keep the adrenaline up. We take our place at the end of the line. It's at least an hour before we even make it to the door, that's how slow the line moves. But eventually we do make it and then we are filing around the 3D ziggurat.

We are on the bottom level. Isec steps onto his square-shaped pad and drops his boots. I'm about to step in mine when I realize it's already occupied.

A rough hand directs my gaze upward to an empty space. I look back at Isec and shake my head. "No change, kid!" I call. "Do it like we planned!" I scramble up to the next level and push past the others already lined up and step onto the pad.

I have no time to think, because we are moving upward to the battlefield before I can even take another breath.

Chapter Nine

My neck strains as far as it can. My feet are stuck to the pattern on the ground, so I can't move them to get a better look at Isec, but this is the first fight, which means the arena pops into view in a fraction. I feel my bare feet come unstuck and pull the quick-release loop that holds my boots to my person and they fall to the floor with a clunk that reverberates around in my head, alone, as the silent and slow world of the fight moves in and takes over my body.

I see Isec turn around and look up to find my face. I smile at him, then point and scream "Go!"

The shields evaporate and I'm about to dive down towards Isec when he flies upward and gets pulled into the free-G.

Shit!

And then the stupor of surrealism wears off and everyone is in motion. I have to let him deal so I can take out the girl next to me. My claws extend and I have a second to compare them to hers, which are painted a pretty pink color. A few fractions later the blood from her jugular splats a polka-dot pattern across her face and she slumps to the stone floor, out of the game.

The next guy is the hisser from last night, I jump in the air and swing my newly taloned feet around and take out his eyes, then finish him off with my left hand while my right clasps around the throat of another boy, bigger than Isec, but not by much. He flails at me, trying to scrape his claws across my face, but my reach overtakes him and a few seconds later he's unconscious when I squeeze my fingers together and rip out his esophagus.

I look for the next one but only find a pair of frightened eyes on a girl who towers over me by almost a foot. She flies upward out of my reach and I have a minute to look for Isec. He's fighting, but still caught up in the free-G about two levels up. I clamber along the stone until I get purchase and pull myself up the next level.

A group of girls are waiting for me and one drags her talons across my chest, leaving gaping wounds in my light armor before I can grab her foot and break her leg. The next girl has an illegal knife and I actually take a second to laugh at her. She loses her concentration and I grab the knife and swipe it across her throat, ducking slightly to avoid the hot blood that pulses out of her jugular. The third girl flies off and I find a handhold on the rough stone terrace and climb up the next level, then look to see if Isec is even still alive.

He is, but he's bleeding. I kick a guy with wild eyes off the terrace and he lands on a big mean-looking mother who quickly disables him and throws him down two more levels. The big guy looks up at me and I shrug. "Sorry!"

"Junco!" Isec screams. "Help me, Junco!"

I get a running start and then fling myself off the terrace and soar through the free-G until I bump him out of it. We fall back down to the bottom terrace, rolling to help break the fall. "Get behind me. Now!"

He does and I hear the clock face signals being called out as we twist and turn, back to back, killing anyone who comes near. For a few seconds the fighters around us seek other targets and I have time to notice that the display on my interior vision is rating the attackers, flashing my endocrine biog status and pinpointing any injuries. A team of four swarms in on us and I crank out some epinephrine to compensate. I target the first guy's injured lung and puncture it clean with the tip of my razor and then fling him back to Isec. His buddies grab me by the arms, but I create a standing wave and shake them off, then cross my arms and drag my claws across their faces, pushing them behind me at the same time.

The last guy catches me off guard and knocks me to the ground. He's on top of me as my breath is shocked out of my lungs. I look up and see Isec's panicked face. The guy draws his razors back, and then his body goes flying across the terrace and the big guy I apologized to earlier falls on him and cuts his head off with a razor so long it stops me cold for a few excited heartbeats.

He looks over at me afterward and smiles. "You owe me now."

I shake my head and smile, then take out a spastic girl who looks like she lost her mind several seconds ago and move on to the next one.

I've got a girl by the hair and I'm about to slash her throat when the buzzer rings. I drop her and take several deep breaths and my vision screen says it's releasing cortisone to calm me down. The girl is heaving badly but my data display says she's not seriously injured so I pull her back up to her feet and bend her over and whack her on the back so she can cough. "You OK?"

She nods at me, the fear still plastered on her face.

"Relax, you made it. Fight one is history. Let's get the fuck out of here."

We are instructed to stand on a transport block and then we are moving upward to the level two holding area. Isec and the coughing girl follow me into our new dorm, which is exactly the same size as the last room, but the bunks are only stacked two high. The reality of just how many people were ruthlessly annihilated hits everyone at the same time and we stand there, killers all.

Even with my extensive experience, I've never participated in something so heinous in all my life and it takes whole seconds for me to push it out.

The moderator for this level congratulates us, then instructs us to go shower and pick up clothing and, if anyone gives a shit about us, care packages. The coughing girl sticks to me like glue during showers, as does Isec, much to my dismay, but none of the guys are looking at us girls with anything other than weary apprehension. I wrap myself in a towel and I'm handed a care package, but no clothes. The woman who hands it to me reads my confusion. "Aves only wear standard uniforms, Junco. Your stuff is in the bag." Obviously she never saw me in my *Snipers do it from behind* t-shirt.

I wait for Isec and the coughing girl to get their clothes and then we go back into the dorm and find some bunks. I lie down in my towel and fall asleep thinking about how I forgot my boots on the battlefield.

I thought the care package was from Ashur and the guys, but after I put the uniform on and lace up my new boots I pull a card from the bottom of the bag and my heart stops.

Lucan.

I pick it up and it's written in avian. Isec and the girl lean in trying to look at it. "What does it say?" the girl asks. She shakes her head as I hand it over. "I only read English."

My face screws up and Isec interrupts before I can ask her anything. "She knows that – only Aves read avian."

I squeeze his leg and he jumps. "It's from Lucan and it says, 'Well done, Junco.'"

He eyes me. "I thought you didn't like him?"

The girl looks completely confused but I answer Isec anyway. "Well, he can't be all bad, I guess. He sent me clothes and," I pick up an ionspray, "some drugs apparently."

"What kind of drugs?" the weary girl asks.

I shrug. "How the hell should I know?"

She leans back at my tone. I'm tired and hungry and she's not even on my team but I feel compelled to defuse the silence I've created. It's not her fault I have no clue. "Come on, let's go get some chow."

We skip the ration line and instead go right to the machines. I let them pick whatever they want, then get what Isec orders, plus some beer. We eat in silence. In fact, the entire place is silent, the shock of today's fight still raw and open.

"Got another one of those?" I look up and find the big guy who helped me when I was about to be killed, he's pointing to my beer. Everyone is looking at my beer now. I shrug. "Probably got enough, I have no idea actually. Let's give it a try."

We walk over to the machine. "How would I order for everyone?" I look up to his face and smile. He's good-looking in a Braun and Ryse kind of way.

He takes my thumb and flicks it over the panel, then swipes my index finger along until it gets to the catering section, and he orders beer. "There's no way that's gonna work, but hey–" It beeps an approval and I laugh.

"You must be loaded."

"I don't think it's my money…"

"Kush."

"Junco. Anyway, I'm pretty sure someone will be very pissed off at me tomorrow." I let out a little laugh of satisfaction.

"Maybe you shouldn't do it then?"

"Too late," I say, pointing to the servos. "It's already here." Everyone gets excited and I call out to Isec, "Don't get drunk, you twerp, you'll regret it tomorrow."

The little fucker flips me off and I'm actually taken aback.

I look back up at Kush. "There you are, go grab one."

He does and then comes back and sits down next to me. The coughing girl has moved on and I'm pleased about that. I light up a cigar and lean back into the uncomfortable straight-back chair. I offer him one and he takes it.

We puff in silence for a few minutes, watching everyone celebrate their extra night of life, and then I look up at him. "So, what's your story, Kush? You look a little out of place here."

"Says the lion to the wolf."

"Yeah, you noticed, huh?" I puff, then exhale. Breathe out, Junco. *All the best parts are in the exhale.*

The big guy is still talking. "Well, the whole purpose of the General Fledge is to get into the Aves, Junco. You're obviously already in, so there's no logical reason for you to be here. None at all."

I let out an ironic laugh. "So, your story is?"

He smiles and takes the hint. "Not anything special. I'm in – was in – Political Cluster. I wanted to go for Aves, the draw of it is powerful. So here I am." He shrugs matter-of-factly at this revelation. I have no idea if it's true or not. Don't really care, either.

"Good enough for me, then," I say as I puff out some rings towards the ceiling.

"And you? What's your story?"

I don't even bother meeting his gaze. "Secret mission, that's all."

He nods. "OK, well, thanks for the beer."

I watch him pick up his mug and turn. "Uh-huh. No problem."

As soon as he's gone the coughing girl is back and I let out a sigh. "I'm not your friend, girl. So don't mistake me for one."

She nods. "Yeah, OK. But can I sit here?"

I shrug. "Knock yourself out." Then I get up and walk away to go find Isec and make sure he's not drunk.

He's laughing and talking excitedly with a couple other younger kids who made it through when I find him near the back of the dorm room. They get silent as I walk up. "Enjoying yourselves?"

Isec smiles up at me. "For now, but if you think you're gonna start acting like a clutch mother you better think again. I don't need a mother, Junco."

"No? Well, Esta really is an Aves Mother, ya know. So try and let her down easy, eh?"

I walk away, then stop and turn my head slightly, just enough so he can hear me. "And I could give a fuck about you, Isec."

I take a step and catch his retort. "Back at ya, Junco."

The grin spreads across my face and I go find the bunk where my shit is stashed. The coughing girl is back, lying on the top bunk over Isec's stuff. I'm on the bottom bunk next to Isec. No one has claimed the bunk above me. In fact, all the bunks around us are empty.

I let out a deep breath, stomp my cigar out on the stone floor, and lie back. Exhausted.

"We're not friends," the girl says. "I get it."

"OK."

"But I do want to live and you obviously have no plans to die in here, so I'm gonna stick around anyway."

I turn my back to her. "Sure, whatever. Just stay out of my way in battle or I'll cut your throat next time."

The shiver from her body actually escapes through her mouth and for a second I wonder if I've crossed the line. But then she's silent and soon my world dampens to the twilight of sleep. The thought seeps down into the darkness with me: my guilty conscience never really had a chance.

Chapter Ten

Esta is fussing over Isec on the other side of the training room and I can't help myself when he looks over at me, eyes pleading. I pretend a laugh while pointing and he flips me off. What a little creep.

Meanwhile, Ashur's back is to me and he's pointing up and going on and on and on about free-G flying. He pauses so I interject, "Uh-huh, yeah, that makes sense." He continues as I survey what everyone else is doing.

Kush is on the other end of the training room with some of the older guys. I figure they're all from the Political Cluster since they hang out together, but I could be wrong. I watch him as he tries some hand-to-hand with a partner. He's got some good moves, but I can see ways out of every hold he tries.

I look back and Ashur is staring at me. "Who are you watching over there?"

"That big brown-winged guy. He helped me out yesterday. Got a little sticky at one point and he sort of saved my ass."

Ashur tilts his head. "He sort of saved your ass – or he did save your ass?"

I shrug. "He did."

Ash stares over at the group until they notice him, he beckons with a finger and they point to each other. One at a time Ashur shakes his head until Kush acknowledges him and begins walking towards us.

All I can think about is going outside to have a cigar. "Hi, Junco."

"Hi Kush, uh," I wave my disfigured hand behind me, "this is Ashur, my XO."

I go back to people-watching as Ash and Kush walk off a little ways, talking. If I was a guy, they would never do that. Ashur would never bring him over here to thank him, he'd just shrug it off and tuck it away in case the guy needed a buddy favor in the future. Like I did. But I know damn well that's what he's doing. I've been living with military guys my whole life so I know how it works. It doesn't matter how many people I kill or how many times I save their asses, if just one of them catches me in a weak spot, they go all big brother on me.

I can't take it anymore so I get up and walk out, find the stairs and slip outside without incident. I cop a seat on the stone bench next to the train stop and light up my cigar. This day is so boring. I lie back on the bench and take in the sunshine, then wonder if it's real. Feels real, but there's no sky above me, just the criss-crossing of beamed scaffolding holding up the interior ring of the torus.

My eyes close as my thoughts drift and my body gets heavy.

I wake when I hear someone shouting my name. Several someones actually. I sit up and the long ash drops off the cigar as I move it. Must have dozed off.

I watch Ashur send everyone back inside and then walk over to me. "What the fuck, Junco?"

"What the fuck what, Ashur?"

"You can't just get up and leave the training room like that."

"Well, it wasn't too difficult, so obviously I can."

He lets out a deep breath. "Are you ready to fly or what?"

I smile. "Let's go."

We walk back inside but don't take the stairs. Instead he palms the biometrics on the elevator and we take it all the way up to the Level Seven arena. "Isn't this cheating?"

He huffs. "No. You can't even fly, how is that fair? Everyone else was taught except you. So what if you see the arena." I raise my eyebrows at him, but he continues, "Besides, the only other free-G Fledge facility on Amelia is at Aves, and it's in use right now. So we have no choice."

I scratch my eye and shrug. "Whatever you say."

The Level Seven arena is nothing like Level One. It is a giant sphere with mushroom-looking pedestals shooting up from the ground at uneven intervals. I listen as Ash explains. "Those," he says, pointing to the mushrooms, "are the only gravity wells in the room, OK?"

I nod.

"Everything else past here," he points to a glowing green line on the floor in front of us and then to each of the other regularly-spaced entrances around the perimeter, "is free-G." He pushes me past the line and I go sailing across the middle. "Flap your wings, Junco! Don't get sucked down to the pedestals!"

I can feel the nearest mushroom drawing me in so I stretch my wings and flap a little and shoot towards it at an alarming rate.

"Tilt your wings, Junco! Reverse thrust!"

I do and barely avoid being sucked down completely. I flap my wings, thinking I will go above the mushrooms and avoid them but then I notice that they are growing out of the ceiling as well as the floor. Wait, it's free-G, so there is no floor or ceiling. I twist my body and the ceiling becomes my floor.

Ashur glides up next to me, then tilts his wings to stop his forward momentum. He smiles. "Not so hard, is it?"

I laugh. "Speak for yourself. I'm about to hurl."

"Yeah, takes a little getting used to. Whenever you change direction, in Z-space, I mean," he clarifies, "just pick some random point to be your horizon. As long as you have a horizon, you'll be fine."

"I don't think I'll get the hang of this in one day, Ashur," I say, a little frown creeping out of my lips.

"No, you won't, but you've got time. The second fight is pretty much like the first one, just a different patterned structure. So don't sweat it."

I nod. "OK, well, since we're here I might as well learn how to move and turn."

It gets a lot more fun as I figure out how to move my wings. At first the muscles feel tight and unresponsive, but we stop on the largest mushroom and Ashur shows me how to stretch and move them so that they loosen up. I end the afternoon doing flips, my body careening across the length of the game field and bumping into Ashur as he fails to escape my mad thrashing legs. If I had wings on my feet, free-G would be so much easier.

We swim through the air back to the perimeter gravity field and I start to fall when my feet touch down but Ashur steadies me and smiles.

"You did real well, Juncs. Tomorrow we'll do real training and fly outside, in the regular atmosphere. That way you'll be ready for the second fight."

I nod as we walk back towards the elevator. "So, what did you and Kush talk about?"

He palms the biometric pad and the door slides open. He waves me in and then follows. "I just said thanks, that's all." The door closes and our descent begins with a quick jolt to my stomach. "He's a Political – wants to be Aves. They do this every time, but," he stops to look at me, "don't get attached to him, Junco, they never make it."

"Shit, Ashur, you're a real downer."

"Sorry, just the truth."

The door slides open on two and he squeezes me goodbye. "See ya tomorrow."

I wave and go back to the dorm. Dinner is over and almost everyone is either sleeping or sitting quietly on their bunks. The coughing girl and Isec are playing cards in our corner of the room. I smile at Isec as I walk up. "So, did you learn anything useful today, brat?"

His face is pretty serious, so I pause and listen. "Junco, she said the stuff she taught me today, the Aves kids have to learn by the time they are five, or she has to kill them."

Oh shit, Esta. What the fuck?

"She's crazy, Isec, she's full of shit. Just trying to scare you."

"Why would she want to scare me now, Junco? It's not like I can back out."

My cheeks puff up and then I release the air out in one long exhale as I shake my head at him. "She's having problems, Isec, that's why she's here. She's not happy with her job, so don't take what she says too serious. I'll speak to her tomorrow, and if she says this shit again, we'll get rid of her and you can train with Ashur and me."

This satisfies him and they go back to playing. "I'm gonna go take a shower," I say, but they are busy and don't even respond.

The showers are empty so I strip down and languish in the hot water. My hair is a lot longer than it was before the morph and I secretly wish for a good haircut so it didn't take so long to wash.

When I'm done I walk over towards the counter to see if I can get some clothes, but no one is there and the wall has been replaced with a line of cubbies that have biometric panels on them. They are all empty except the one that says Junco, Aves 039-9.

I pass my thumb over the panel and the transparent door slides up to allow access to another care package. I take it over to the row of benches and sit down, being careful to hike up my towel. This time I fish all the way down to the bottom and find the note first.

Junco,
You have not used the ionspray. Do you think I would put things in the package if I don't want you to use them? Why must you be so difficult?
Lucan

I fish around again and pull up the ionspray. This time it has a label and directions: Quick recovery – To use, squeeze near nose. I consider using it, but I push it aside for now. I'm not hurt, why waste it? Besides, maybe Isec will need one after the next battle.

I pull out my uniform but there is something else in the bag – shorts and a tank. For bed, I guess. I put those on and tuck the uniform back in the bag and carry it with me to my bunk.

The bed is a lot softer than I remember any bed ever being and I drift off to sleep thinking about what Lucan's note will say tomorrow night.

Chapter Eleven

Ashur slams me down on the mat as I focus on Isec's face. Esta is talking to him across the room.

"Shit, Ashur, that hurt!"

"You're not paying attention."

I nod over towards Isec. "Esta was telling him some fucked-up shit yesterday, scared him bad, too. I don't want her telling him that stuff. I need him to learn something useful so I won't be worried about what happens to him if he does manage to make it to the end."

"He's not your responsibility, Junco."

"Like hell, we're partners now. He calls out the people behind me and she's gonna ruin it with her mid-life crisis bullshit."

He laughs and pulls me to my feet. "I'll talk to her later. First try and do some moves that you would normally do on Earth, to see how it's different with the wings and the less than 1G gravity."

I nod and try a spinning kick on the dummy, but fall on my face, laughing. "Hell, I guess it makes a huge difference!"

"Yeah, the last time I saw you do that, you took a guy's head off."

He grins at me, but the image of Aren brings back the video of Moju. *Please, God,* I pray to myself, *let Moju be OK.*

"Junco? What the hell are you daydreaming about now?"

I sigh. "Nothing, let me try that again." I go through the moves and this time at least hit my target, albeit in very sloppy form. After several more adjustments my foot smacks the bag squarely and it feels right. Ashur just sits and watches me, pointing out ways to force my wings to lie flat against my back. It works better that way, less air resistance.

I move on to flips and gymnastics but have the same problem. Ashur holds me as I twist, flip and flop, setting me down like my aerialist coaches would when I was small. Again, the wings are throwing me off balance. He tapes them down and I do it again. And again, and again, and again. I'm sweaty and gross when I notice the crowd watching and feel self-conscious.

"Again, Junco."

I try something new, something I think I can do well regardless of the wings, and I begin a Wan Woo form that I've practiced religiously since I was a pre-teen. It starts out slow, supposed to be done in the riding ring, in the dirt, right? Both on and off the horse. The first twenty-three moves are all balance — standing, weaving, hands, shoulders, and the head. The second part is on horseback, obviously it isn't now, since I have no horse, but I draw a mental box that is ten inches square around my feet to keep me focused. This is how you practice your tricks before going live on the back of an animal that could kill you with a hoof to the head if you fall.

My wings are an added weight that throws off the first of the boxed moves, but I compensate as I spring into a handstand and tilt my legs forward a little. From there I push off one-handed, spin, and catch myself on the other hand. My three remaining digits squeal with the pressure.

The kata pattern speeds along nicely as I rotate between straight flips from the hand and foot position. It's more like a vertical dance than anything, since that's really what mounted acrobatics is. I'm balanced on my head, getting ready to push up with my shoulders when I notice Ashur smiling at me. I smile back and heave, twisting my hips and swinging my knees down in a swoop as my upper body and feet trade places. I land at the very edge of my mental box and throw my arms in the air.

It was pretty sloppy, but I'll take it.

I smile over at Ashur and I'm just about to walk towards him when a big guy, one of Kush's buddies from the other side of the room, steps in front of me. "What the hell was that?"

"Wan Woo long form for aerialists, why?" He's a big brown-winged guy who looks pretty much like Kush — square jaw, intense blue eyes, and stout build, except he's got his head shaved and some marks on his arms. Tattoos or something.

"Never heard of that pattern, or seen anything like that before."

I stare at him sideways, not because he's particularly interesting to look at, but because his words come out like a challenge. A growl of dominance.

"Well, you wouldn't, would you? I mean, unless you've been to Earth, right? I've been told there are no horses in space, so that pretty much rules out mounted acrobatic routines."

Ashur is between us before I can even finish. "That's enough, Junco, let's go fly."

I turn to follow him but the big guy grabs my arm and turns me back. "Hey, I'm still talk—"

I react, I can't help it. My knees are bending on the word "hey," and by the time he gets to "talk," I've smacked him in the jaw so hard with my heel he drops to the ground.

Ashur lets out a deep breath and motions me to follow him, but I kneel down to the guy instead. "I'll let you live because maybe you're just having a bad day, but there will be no next time. Don't ever fucking touch me again."

I stand and glance over at Isec, his smile is so wide I have to shoot him a wink. Then Ashur and I leave the training room and make our way down the stairs to the front of the building.

Outside we stop at the benches so I can puff a cigar. Ashur holds a hand up to his face to shield his eyes from the sunlight. Or whatever it is, since it's obviously not the sun. "Now you'll have to watch your back for that guy, Junco. I hope it was worth it."

I shrug. "He grabbed me, Ash. You can't let guys get away with that shit or they take it to the next level." I blow rings upward and lean back on the bench, my disfigured hand behind my head as a cushion.

"Yeah, I know. But he looked off. Keep an eye out for him."

"Yeah, OK. So we gonna fly or what?"

He smiles down at me, plucks the cigar from my hand, stomps on it, and pulls me up. "This will be a lot harder than in the free-G, you'll be sore tomorrow."

I smile. "I'm ready." And I am.

Flying is not all that fun when you're learning. For one thing, you fall an awful lot. And I'm not talking about some pansy-ass baby fall. Even in the grass that hurts. It takes me hours to get a few feet off the ground and my stomach muscles are burning with the strain of keeping my body parallel. I had no idea it took so many muscles to get into the correct flight position.

Eventually, after Ashur tugs me up into the wind, I find my stride with gliding. The wind is stronger up high so I have to compensate by twisting, using muscles I never knew I had. Well, probably didn't before a few days ago. We take advantage of the air stream and fly out above the train rail, following it into a town a few miles away. People stare at us as Ash lands and I crash and roll near a pub, but we're both wearing the Aves uniform, so they get disinterested quick enough.

We drink and eat, Ash watches some kind of sport on the screen, and I throw darts at a board that has the face of Jax Justice on it.

Internally I find that quite funny.

Some things are universal and hatred for this guy's high-drama action screens back on Earth is one of them, like politics and parties on the news. I hit him in the eye several times, and from the looks of the missing paper pieces in the orbital region, that seems to be a favorite spot for many of the locals as well.

On Earth I don't recall ever having so much freedom. Back home I was in a routine where I did what I was told to do, saw who I was told to see, and went where I was told to go. It wasn't exactly orders, more like habit to the extent that I was unable to even see that I had options. I had boyfriends when we were out on the scrub and on maneuvers, but never at home. As I got older my father got more and more weird about boys, so I kept that shit out of sight. Even the horses were more of a job than a social engagement.

Take Peaks, for instance. I had a vehicle and a Farm Family passport stamped with military privileges, yet I never went to the city alone. Never even went shopping or just to grab a chicken sandwich. It's refreshing, freeing actually, to be in charge of myself. I watch Ash across the room and wish the other guys would come visit too, especially Braun – I really need to talk to that fucker – but the casual routine Ashur and I have slipped into is satisfying in a way I've never experienced before.

Normal.

I walk over and join him and he explains the rules of the sport to me. It's a lot like gridiron, but more violent and takes place in free-G. After a while we leave and grab the train back so I don't have to try and fly against the wind in the dark. Ash gives me a hug at the door and I wave an arm at him as I walk inside.

It's past midnight when I finally get back to the dorm, so I forgo a shower and just slip into bed with my uniform on. I can hear Isec in the next bunk, his breathing even, but the remnants of crying linger in the way he hiccups air. I am thinking about how I will kill Esta tomorrow for scaring him so badly when the arms come up from below my bed and clamp against my mouth. In a blink I am dragged silently down the middle of the room and into the showers. When we get there the door closes and I hear the click of a lock just before the lights flick on.

It's the big guy from earlier.

What a dumb fuck.

His rage is dialed up to maximum and his two buddies stand around him with their arms crossed. "Not so fucking tough without your bodyguard, are you, little girl."

I laugh and he kicks me in the ribs, making me laugh again. "Keep laughing, girl, I can't wait to see you without teeth."

I cough a little to clear my throat, just to make sure I can enunciate everything properly. "Wow. You think he was *my* bodyguard? Shit, I'm *his* bodyguard, you dumbass!" I laugh again, and the boot finds its mark, making me roll a little to the side.

I wait it out because there's only one reason to drag a girl into a locked room and it always ends with the asshole on top. And once he gets that position in his head, he'll have made his last mistake.

"Hold her down, Bann."

"Bann," I say, looking at the guy he was just talking to, "if you hold me down, I'll make sure and kill you first. Don't say I never warned you."

He ignores me and makes to hold my left arm while the other guy tries for the right. I grab Bann's foot first, since I did warn him, and he goes down hard. I wince as his head cracks against the cold tile floor and the blood spills out.

The other guy hesitates, making him already too late for the party. I kick up with my right foot and take out his nose. The blood gushes out in a way that reminds me of nightdogs and caves. I swing my legs back to my head and fling them forward, forcing myself up on my feet. The SEAR exits my shirt silently, but the hiss of power makes the ring leader snap to attention. "What the fu—"

His head is rolling towards the shower drain before he can finish his curse. The broken-nose guy is scrambling to his feet, making for the locked door, when his head goes rolling down towards the blood-red drain as well. The other guy is already dead, so I don't soil the air with any more burning flesh than I have to.

The whole fight is over in less than a minute and I thumb the mechanism on the SEAR and put it away.

I leave the front shower door locked and go looking for the moderators near the cubbies. I spy another care package for me, but decide to take care of clean-up before grabbing it and going back to my bunk.

Chapter Twelve

It takes me several minutes to find someone who gives a shit about the three dead bodies I left in the showers. They want to make me wait in a small room off the office, but I refuse and go back to my bunk with my package. Not my problem anymore.

The entire dorm is awake now and I watch Isec's face as I approach the bunks. "They said they would kill you, Junco. I'm sorry I didn't stay awake to tell you, I thought you'd stay away with your friend."

"Don't worry about it, kid, they're dead now." I rummage down to the bottom of the bag and smile as I pull the note out.

"What's this one say, Junco?"

Poor Isec, he looks like a little baby standing there next to my bed. I read it and laugh. "He says, *Junco, you are a giant pain in the ass. Lucan.*"

Isec screws up his face at me and even the coughing girl is looking down at me with interest. "Are you and Lucan friends?" He says it like it can't be possible, and if he would have asked me two days ago I would've agreed with him. But tonight, I just shrug.

"Maybe, but once he finds out what I just did, he might not be so friendly with me anymore."

It's the coughing girl who speaks next. "What did you do, Junco?"

I look up at her and notice that her eye is swollen shut. It wasn't like that earlier. "Did they hit you?"

She looks down and nods.

"Well, I'll tell you what I did then." I wait for her to look me in the eyes. "I chopped his fucking head off with a SEAR knife. Along with his buddy's. The third guy, Bann – well, he cracked his head open when I pulled his feet out from under him, so I can't really take credit for that one."

She lets out a deep breath and I know relief when I see it.

I spy a moderator walking down the middle of the room towards us. "Shit, here we go."

Isec looks panicked. "What will they do to you, Junco?"

"It was self-defense, Ise, they won't do anything to me. Be back in a little bit."

I get up and meet the mod halfway. He smiles. "Sorry, Junco – Lucan's on a com in the break room. Wants to talk to you."

"Course he does." I follow, a slight bit of panic rising up in my chest.

My knee bobs up and down as I wait for him to appear on the screen. In place of his face is an emblem, a seal actually, like diplomats have. It's hard to read, but I think the little letters around the perimeter say Capitol City of Amelia, or some shit like that. It's bona fide, let's just leave it at that.

My eyes begin to droop when his voice brings me back to attention.

"Explain."

I smile, then lose my bravado and look away. "What do you want me to say? I chopped their heads off. The other guy cracked his noggin open when I pulled his leg out from under him. It was self-defense, Lucan. They were gonna rape me."

He winces as the word leaves my lips, but fuck, it's true.

"Meet me outside immediately."

The screen goes blank and I get up and knock on the door so the moderator can let me out. His dark face peeks through a crack in the door, trying to see past me and over to the screen. "He wants me to go outside. Immediately."

He opens the door all the way and takes me by the arm, apparently I can't be trusted to walk outside without killing people.

We both see Lucan standing over by the train stop bench, so the mod lets go of my arm when we reach the door and I make the final distance alone. Lucan points to the bench when I get there, so I slump down and take out a cigar. His hand stops me and I put it away.

"Junco, you are taking up a lot of my time."

I wait it out because his statement doesn't require an answer.

"Did I or did I not forbid you from using that weapon?"

"You did, but–"

"There were no exceptions, Junco. If people find out what you are there will be a lot of – hostility. Do you understand this?"

"No, Lucan." I look up at him and shake my head a little. "I don't get it. You act like I'm a disease or something. I've had the SEAR my whole life and I never went off and started killing people like a lunatic. So, why? Why do you think I'm so wild?"

His head turns to look down the empty train tracks before he speaks. "How do I explain who and what you are, Junco? You are not human, you are not avian, yet you morph into one of us and have machines in your body. You may in fact be an authentic Seventh Sibling and you have a very dangerous weapon that we cannot remove from you or else–" He stops abruptly and I watch his jaw clench with tension. He straightens a bit and then continues. "We're not sure what you are, Junco." He turns back to me, finished.

"I'm not sure what *you* are, either. And you don't see *me* getting all freaked out about it."

He stays silent.

"Would the SEAR knife kill you?" His expression hardens and I have a feeling I've crossed a line.

"Not much can hurt me, Junco."

"You didn't answer the question."

He blows out a little bit of air in a half laugh. "Do you, or do you not, understand that I have forbidden you from using the weapon while you are here?"

"I do."

"Then why?"

"It was three against one, I needed to stack the deck. They weren't small guys, Lucan. Three against one." The night breeze sweeps my hair aside and I lift my chin up and breathe in.

Lucan is watching me when I look over to him. "Why didn't you use the ionsprays?"

I screw up my face. "I thought you wanted to yell at me for killing people?"

"It happened as you say, so it is excused this time."

"Then why come all the way over here in the middle of the night?"

"I am checking to see if you're OK, Junco. Is that so unusual? I would have called Ashur, but…"

I wait. "But?"

"I was in the neighborhood."

I laugh. "Oh, right."

He takes a seat on the bench next to me, his head eases into his hands and he pushes against his temples. I know the look, it means I'm giving someone a headache. Tier used it frequently.

"I wasn't hurt."

He looks up and then his eyes track down my body. "Yes, I can see that. I'm glad."

"No, I mean, I didn't use the ionsprays because I wasn't hurt."

"Oh." He straightens up again, then flattens out a wrinkle in the sleeve of his black suit. "Right, well, they're just glycogen analogs, Junco, not health sprays. It is forbidden to treat you with health sprays. Besides, you heal yourself anyway. These will help your new muscles acclimate."

"OK, well, I'll use one when I get back in. I learned to fly, ya know. I'll probably be sore tomorrow."

He smiles and I crack one as well, I can't help myself. He goes back to picking at his suit.

"Why are you always so overdressed?"

His laugh blurts out in the night silence. "What?"

"That suit, Lucan. It's so formal."

"How should I dress?"

I shrug. "I dunno, but hell, a suit in the middle of the night? Something a little less rigid would go a long way."

"You really don't know why I wear this suit, Junco?"

"No, I have no idea." I raise my eyebrows at him and he has a genuine look of surprise on his face.

"Well, that might explain some things about your behavior."

"Yeah, want to let me in on it?"

"Who do you think I am?"

I recycle back my memory to my morph day. "You said you were a commander. My commander, actually. In fact you said, *I'm Lucan, Junco. Your new commander.* Is that not true?"

He smiles. "It is technically accurate. I am your commander because I command all the Aves. They are my official military force and the 039 is my personal force."

"What's that mean? You're like the President or something? Commander-in-Chief?"

"Yes."

"Yes? You are the President? Of Amelia? Or of what?"

"Of the avian, Junco."

I grimace. "Oh. I'm sorry, then. I really didn't know. I wouldn't have said all those things to you if you told me that up front."

"It's OK, I find your honesty refreshing."

I snort at this. "Well, I've never been called *that* before."

"Which, honest or refreshing?"

"Ha ha, that's funny." I lean back on the bench and stare up at the fake sky. Windows. Scaffolding, whatever the hell it is. I stare up. "I miss the stars on Earth. I can't see anything here."

"I can take you to see them. If you want."

"How many trains will it take? I'll probably fall asleep."

He reaches out and taps my shoulder and I'm just about to look over at him when the sky changes and the stars shine down on me. I try and sit up before I realize I'm no longer sitting. We're standing in the middle of the night sky, nothing above and nothing below. "Holy shit, what is this? A simulation?"

He takes my hand as I get dizzy. "No, we are outside the habitat. Look behind you."

I do and I smile.

Amelia is beautiful. She's a torus, all right. But she's got four rings to her, not just one. She spins like a top, creating the gravity felt on the outer rim. The spaceports in the center are rather busy even at this time of night and I see several orbitals come and go in the span of just a few seconds.

"Wow." I look over at him and smile, laugh actually. "I'm officially impressed."

He lets out a fake sigh. "Finally, I have impressed Junco the Just One Small Girl."

I look sideways at him, trying to gauge his intentions with that comment, but his face is a blank. He sits down on the air and I follow. Our legs dangle over some invisible edge. "How are we breathing? How is there gravity?"

"We're in a bubble of sorts. I have a few special talents that I won't," he eyes me cautiously, "be sharing the details of with you."

"How did we get here?" He's about to answer when I spy Orion and point up. Everything in the sky for me starts and ends with Orion. He's the first constellation I ever learned. "It's a lot easier to see the stars from here than it was in that tube thing Ashur took me to."

Lucan smiles. "Ashur, I should have figured."

"What's that mean?"

"They are attached to you already, Junco." I am still thinking about this when he switches gears. "I want you to succeed, do you believe me?"

I shrug. "Well, I suppose you'd be a lot meaner if you wanted me to fail, so yeah. I can see that."

"But still, no matter what I do, this will not end well. It will be difficult."

I squint up at him now. "Why?"

"Things have been set in motion. Only going back to Earth would have changed it enough to shift the future."

My voice hardens. "He brought me a video of Moju's finger being cut off, Lucan. He was a plant."

"Yes, that's what you said. So, here we are." He puts his head in his hands and rubs his temples again.

"You know, for a guy who hates Tier so much, you two sure are a lot alike."

His head snaps up. "If you only knew how inappropriate that comment was." The silence between us drags on for a few seconds before he continues. "In which way are we similar?"

He looks over at me and I feel pressure to explain. "Well, he hates when I swear. He actually did mention it a few times back on Earth, and not in a nice way either." Lucan smiles, but does not reply. "And you both rub your head like that when I'm making life difficult."

He nods at this.

"I don't love him, Lucan. I'm not here to save him. Charlie was my love. Moju is part of me, but Tier was just a nice distraction when I really needed one. Someone who held me accountable when it made all the difference. A pretty cool guy, but it didn't get far, and it's going nowhere now. So–"

He tisks his tongue against his teeth. "You're wrong, Junco. All of this is tied up with the dynamics between the two of you."

I wait and the silence is heavy between us.

"Perhaps it is possible that you think you're here for something else, but..." He looks over at me. "I doubt it. We both know you're plotting."

I laugh. "Well, tell me what I can do about it, because to be honest, I'm out of ideas."

"There is nothing, Junco. Truly nothing you can do."

I nod and look down. It's my turn to be silent.

His hand touches my shoulder and we are back on the bench in front of the train stop. "It's late."

"Right, well." We stand up together. "Thanks for the talk."

He bows a little. "The pleasure was all mine, Miss Coot."

And then he is gone.

Chapter Thirteen

The clock in the hallway nearest the stairs reads 3 AM and I know I will regret staying up so late in the morning.

What the fuck are you talking about, Junco? It is morning.

Right.

My feet shuffle up the stairs in slow motion and then try to be quiet as I make my way over to our bunks. When I get there Isec is sleeping in my bed and the coughing girl is in his. He wakes as I'm taking my boots off and shoves over so I can get in.

When I'm settled next to him Isec begins his questions, but doesn't open his eyes. "What did he do, Junco?"

I pat his head and smile. "Nothing, really."

He opens his eyes a little. "That's not true. Tell me, please."

"I just told him it was self-defense." I shrug against him. "And that was pretty much that."

"Then why did you take forever to come back?"

"Has it been long? It didn't feel like we were gone that long."

"Where did you go?"

I think about the trip and smile. "He took me up to see the stars," I say as I let out a cavernous yawn.

Isec is awake now. "Really? I want to hear it all, Junco. Tell me."

"Tomorrow, Isec. I'm tired."

He shakes his head. "No, you'll forget the little details if we wait until tomorrow."

"You're weird, ya know that? You're not supposed to

want to know about the little details of my life, kid."

"I'm from Psyche Cluster, Junco, I'm supposed to know everything about everyone."

"So why are you here trying to get into Aves?" I turn so I can watch him talk.

"I failed our Fledge, so this was my only chance to stay alive."

"Oh, what do the Psyche Cluster do for Fledge? Kill people with their minds?" I smile at my own joke.

"No, I'm not telepathic, you can't pass Psyche Fledge if you're not telepathic."

"Wow, I had no idea that some avians were telepaths."

"It's like a big secret, like how the Aves can read and write avian."

"And now you just spilled it to me! Good going!"

He laughs. "Fuck them. Assholes kicked me out."

"Yeah," I agree. "Fuck them. Telepaths aren't so special."

"That's why I ask so many questions, it's the only way I can understand what people are thinking."

I rub his head and let out a stunted laugh. "Well, ya know what, Isec? On Earth, no one is telepathic. So all the great psychologists have to ask questions in order to figure people out."

He looks up at me. "You're lying to make me feel better."

I laugh again. This time I don't bother to keep it in. "I'm serious! We don't have telepaths on Earth. That's like crazy shit talk."

"Tell me everything."

I hiss out a little breath. "OK, fine. The guy took me to a little room with a monitor..."

When I get to the part about the rape, he stops me.

"Were you really scared of them, Junco? Or were you

trying to make it sound worse than it really was? So Lucan would feel sorry for you?"

"Jeez, kid, cynical much?" I look down at him but he's still waiting for my answer and for some reason his upturned gaze makes it harder for me to justify the lie. "I wasn't scared if that's what you're after."

He nods and I continue. The next probe comes after I tell him about the SEAR. "It's a weapon, Isec. It's very dangerous and on Earth, and probably here too, they are outlawed."

"Then why do you have one?"

"I can't tell you that, but you have to take my word that it's necessary."

He stops me again at the ionspray part. "I'm glad he's not cheating for you, Junco. That's not right. And I'm glad you didn't use them, even though you thought they were health sprays."

He's pretty perceptive for ten. I agree and move on but he stops to question me at every sentence after that.

"How could you not know who he was?"

"What color is Amelia from space?"

"Why does he care what you think of him?"

I think about this one for a while before answering. "I'm not really sure, Isec. Why do you think he cares? You're the Psyche kid."

He smiles, but his eyes are closed. "He likes you, Junco."

"Yeah, I've considered that. It only makes sense."

"Will you like him back?"

"No, I can't afford to, Isec. It's insanely complicated."

"No, not really." His eyes are open and he sits up. "You don't have to act on the like, but you can still admit that you like him, you know."

I smile. "Yeah, that's true. OK, I like him, I guess."

This satisfies him and he lies back down. "So, what do you think he's talking about when he told you things are in motion?"

"I'm not sure, but Tier and Ashur both said the same thing. So there's something to that, right?"

I feel him nod. He is still for a long time after that and my mind wanders over the conversation as well. Lucan is nice-looking, in a blond Western Utopia kind of way. He doesn't add up though, and this puts me off even though he can tick an awful lot of boxes as far as men go.

Isec stirs and I push some hair out of his eyes and then turn over to lie on my back.

"Are you plotting to save Tier, Junco?"

I let out a deep breath before answering. "What kind of friend would I be if I wasn't, Isec? He deserves better than to be killed off for saving my life."

"You do save him, ya know."

I smile. "Yeah? How do you know that, kid?"

He yawns, long and slow, before he speaks. "I might not be telepathic, but I am precognitive."

I lie there in shock, wondering if he's telling the truth. When I finally figure out something to say back it's too late. His little-boy snores have invaded the silence and the moment has passed.

Ash is sitting on my bunk and the entire dorm is empty when I wake up, sore as fuck from yesterday's training and fighting.

"You will join the living today, then?"

"Oh shit, Ashur, do you know what happened last night?"

He nods. "Yeah, Lucan called me right after I got

home. I can't leave you anywhere."

I sit up in bed and yawn. "What time is it?"

"Noon, get the hell up, we've got work to do. Fight Two is tomorrow."

"Yeah, let me take a shower first though. I never got one last night."

"Want me to wait here?"

I'm about to say yes when I have an idea. "No, go teach Isec something useful, will you? He needs some practice." I swing my legs over and start to walk away towards the showers when he calls out.

"Junco." I turn back and find a very serious Ashur. "Do not get attached to that child. He will never make it, you understand?"

"I'm already attached, Ashur. So he better fucking make it, do you understand? Go teach him something. Please."

When I walk into the showers my gaze automatically goes to the drain where the heads were rolling last night. There is no evidence left. I wonder if Kush knows what happened?

The shower feels good and I stand in it a lot longer than I would have if people were around. It's nice to enjoy some privacy when you're naked. I'm not typically shy about such things, I've been showering with the boys forever so I'm just used to it, but that doesn't mean I like it.

After I go looking for my package and find an extra-large one in the cubbie marked Junco, Aves 039-9.

I dry off and put my clothes and boots on before searching through the rest of it. The note says, *Have a very boring day*, and I laugh out loud to myself. Yeah, I could use a boring day. Tomorrow surely won't be boring and if Isec doesn't make it I'm not going to be happy. At all.

There is another ionspray and I dose myself before pulling out the last object.

It's a data reader.

I thumb the biometrics and it's Lucan.

"Looks like you're right, Junco. This came in yesterday. I didn't tell you last night because we weren't finished analyzing it. But it's genuine, maybe the one Slag thought he was delivering to you instead of the one you ended up seeing. Please be careful in the Second Fight."

A new display appears, asking for a fingerprint to continue. I press my thumb and another video pops up.

This one stars Selia and I smile.

"Junco, I hope this reaches you and you are well. I did everything you asked, in fact, I've done more than you've asked and I'm currently embedded with a Subjack Sector. I have met your mother. Delightful woman. No, just kidding. She's scary as fuck and you make a lot more sense now." She stops to smile at the videographer, then continues. "I sent the package on to Charlie's family, but I have to say it did not go well. Perhaps you will return to Earth one day and we can talk about it?" She hesitates here, as if choosing words. "That's not quite true either. The entire purpose of the video is to invite you back to Earth. Subjack would like to hire you. I am making this with the blessing of your mother. She said to extend you an invitation."

That sounded like something she'd say word for word. Very technical and cold. To hire you, Junco.

"I have some rather juicy information about some siblings that might interest you. We could discuss it more in person. I realize you're a long way away, and this is probably out of your control, but…" She shrugs into the camera, her careful words gone. "I have things to tell you, things you should know before you get caught up in it."

She pauses again, then pulls off her hat and shoves it into the side pocket of her fatigues. She's got a long gash across her scalp and half of her ear is missing. "It's been quite an experience, Junco. I think of you every night. Every night," she repeats. "If there is a way, please come. We're moving up North next, to wait."

She smiles, then the video clicks off. A date flashes on screen. January 3, 2153.

I have no idea what the date is today. I was under for two months if Ashur's vague reference to my last meal was any indication of how long morph takes. I went aboard the ship with Tier in November, exact date also unknown. So it is at least late January or early February.

I look around the showers, unable to make a commitment to move or stay, until I hear Ashur calling my name out in the dorm. He pops his head in the shower room. "Hurry up, Junco. Fight's tomorrow!"

I shove everything back down in the bag and lock it up in the cubbie for later. There is one lingering question on my mind and I stop and stare blindly at the transparent biometrics pad. Who the fuck is Subjack? I'm having a hard time believing that Lucan isn't more interested in these new developments, seeing as how she mentioned the Siblings. I look over at the door and find Ashur still waiting.

"You wanna tell me what the fuck that was all about?"

I shake my head and let out a deep breath. "Ashur, if I knew I still might not tell you, but I have no idea, so it doesn't matter."

"Well, what do you expect? It's all mystery all the time with you, Junco. No happy medium at all, is there?"

This time I laugh, because to do anything else will just

make it worse. He grabs my hand and pulls me out and we walk in silence to the training room.

Chapter Fourteen

In the training room Esta has Isec off to one side and he looks very unhappy. Ashur notices the direction of my gaze and pulls me away. "Leave them, Junco. He's her responsibility."

We walk straight through to another hallway and over to the elevators, and then ascend to the top floor. I don't say anything and neither does Ash and by the time I'm floating in the free-G it's awkward.

He swims up next to me, his wings paddling the air with perfect control. "You're mad at me?"

I shake my head and change the subject. "What do you want me to do here?"

He drops it. "I want you to touch down and take off of every mushroom starting here," he points to the near end where we presently are, "and then change Z-space and repeat it on the upper mushrooms, ending there." He points to the mushroom above the starting point.

It's a lot fucking harder than it sounds.

For one, the gravity well isn't just 1G, it's like 2. So you fall hard when you come down.

And for another, that same 2G that drags you down during landing, prevents you from taking off as well.

I complete the pattern three times and I can feel my chest and back straining. I hope Lucan puts a giant dose of G-analog in my package tonight. Ashur, to his credit, does the pattern with me. Much faster and more precise.

On the last round, on the last mushroom, I overcompensate for the drag on my wings and smack into the stone platform knees first. I roll in standard approved fashion, but when I come to a rest I know I have serious bruises.

"Fuck!"

Ashur glides up like this is no big deal. He's not even breathing hard. "You all right?"

I lie on the ground a few more seconds, silent and rubbing my eyes. "I'm tired."

"You wanna be done?" He sits down next to my prone body and waits for my answer.

"I want to go talk to Isec and look at the fight room diagram." I sit up and watch him stare at me. "What?"

He shakes his head and averts his eyes off to some point across the room. "Junco, that kid will get you killed. Do you hear me? We're not doing strategy with him."

"Yes, Ashur, we are. If you don't want him to plan with us in the training room, fine. I'll show him what to do later. But he's getting prepped and either way, we're in this together."

He sighs and looks even farther away before tracking back to my face. "If he gets you killed, Junco, I'll kill him myself. You understand me? We are not here to babysit throwaways." He stands, grabs my hand, and pulls me up. "You are here for one reason only, to leave alive and go back to the 039 with me. Got it?"

I push off and swim over to the exit without replying. The ride back down is silent as well, and when we get to the training room the heat of his anger is dripping off him like sweat. Isec is doing some stupid drills that look like they have zero chance of helping us live tomorrow.

I let out a big sigh, then walk over to Esta, leaving Ashur to fume alone.

"How's it going over here, guys?"

Isec shoots me a dirty look. "You said she wouldn't fucking talk like that to me anymore, Junco. She said by the time the Aves kids are five, they've survived at least six attempts on their lives by their clutch mothers. I think she feels obligated to make me suffer through all six attempts before Fight Two."

Damn, a lot of shit happens to Aves kids by the time they are five. Almost makes my training seem like playschool.

Esta shakes her head. "Can you believe the mouth on him, Junco?"

"Esta, what the fuck are you doing? He's a little kid. He's not Aves, he's Psyche. Either teach him something to keep his ass alive or get the fuck out of here."

Esta huffs at me and my vision screen tells me she's projecting her pheromones at me on purpose. Can't fucking control it my ass. The vision screen suggests a stim analog to counter the effects and I give it permission.

I tap my head. "Doesn't work on me anymore, Esta. So you can keep those drugs to yourself. He's not Aves so it doesn't work on him either. You're just pissed off because you can't control him and I don't like how this is playing out one bit."

Ashur is next to Esta now and I feel the heat rise up in my face at him siding against me. Esta huffs and shrugs as she lifts her chin in the air. "He's my pledge, Junco. I'll train him the way I see fit."

I look over at Isec. "Fire her, Isec. I'll train you myself."

Isec looks over at Ashur and gets a wild look in his eyes. "No, that's OK, Junco. It's fine."

I look over at Ashur as well. "What the fuck are you doing, Ashur? I fucking told you I want him alive, what part of that don't you get?"

He walks over, practically chest bumping me like a fucking alpha male, and snarls, "You don't order me around, Junco. I am the XO here. This kid is going to get you killed and I want you to drop it now."

The last bit makes me start and I step back for a second before I can regain my composure. "Maybe I'll fire you too. Then both of you can get the fuck out of here."

He's on top of me in an instant, but I roll sideways and fall hard on my left side, then scramble backward to get out of his reach before he can grab at me again.

"Don't play with me, Junco. I'm not Tier – I won't put up with it."

"Get the fuck out, Ashur. I'm not your nine yet so I don't answer to you."

"Junco–"

"Esta, shut the fuck up!"

Heads all around turn towards us and I feel Ashur's anger rise again as I get to my feet. I look over at Isec and he looks like he's gonna cry. "You're finally gonna get your wish, huh?"

Ashur's lip goes up revealing teeth. "Meaning what, Junco?"

"You said all along you wanted to kill me yourself, let's go then. You think you can just attack me and get away with it? I don't give a fuck who you are, don't you ever fucking touch me. Ever."

"Or what? You'll take out your little bioweapon and slice my head off next?"

The crowd around us has thickened and I hear them gasp. "I don't need that stupid weapon, Ashur. I can kil–"

He attacks and I flip out above him, my wings spreading to take me high above. He responds and has me by the leg, but I kick. His block is there before I can even register what happened. I fall to the ground with a thud and bounce back up in a crouch. He rushes me and we're grappling, I counter with some mixed martial arts. I put a foot in, but he counters and moves back. I wrap my arm around his neck, grabbing for his shirt, he slips out of it before my hand is even past the first shoulder. I kick my legs back, he's out of reach. I roll, he's gone before I get there. I try and wrap him in a guard, but he's always there, a split second before I am. Like we're in fucking practice back on Earth in a coordinated spar and he's been given the cheat sheet for every attack move I have.

Then he's on top of me, about to slam his fist in my face when I feel him ease up. I flip him off and we struggle for a second and then he grabs my hands as I sit on top of him.

"Stop, now."

I do stop, because I'm in shock and breathing heavy.

"What the fuck was that, Ashur?"

"I said, stop, Junco. This is over." He tosses me aside like a doll and I lie on the mat seething up at him. It's the look in his eyes that gives it away, a cross between panic and guilt.

"I know what this is."

He wipes away a small dribble of blood off his lips. "Get up."

I do, but my anger comes with me. "I know what this is, Ashur."

"Yeah, Junco? What is it, then?"

"You fucking piece of shit! Where the fuck did you learn to counter those moves?"

He growls at the crowd and they dissipate. "Where the fuck do you think, Junco?" It comes out as a whisper and I feel my throat constrict and my face gets prickly. I look over at Isec and now he is crying.

I take his hand. "Come on, Isec. We're out of here."

Poor kid is beyond panicked and can barely eat as we sit in the cafeteria. "Isec, please – I have the battle plan in my head here." I do, too. All of a sudden my Aves vision screen spat it out, right after a minor panic attack at not getting the information before stomping out like a baby. "Look, I'll draw it for you, OK?"

He nods, but doesn't look up. His little feet are swinging off the chair and this makes him look more like six or seven than ten.

Shit, Junco. Ten is young enough, he doesn't need to be six or seven.

I let out a deep sigh and draw the spiral pattern on a napkin. "See, it's exactly like the ziggurat, except a spiral. Same rules, same plan, right?" I smile but he doesn't return it.

The rest of the pledges are back now and the noise level kicks up several notches.

"Come on, let's go take a shower, OK? We'll feel better after that."

He nods and we slip around the corner and into the shower area. It's packed, which sucks, but at least I don't have to shower alone with a little kid. I push him over to the man side and take myself over to where the girls have claimed their own area.

I find him in the dressing area later, sitting with Kush. They are both dressed. Kush looks up at me as I approach. "I tried to get him to leave with me, but he wanted to wait."

I nod and set my care packages down. I forgot that Selia's video was still tucked away in my cubbie. I slip on the bed clothes Lucan left and then grab the bags and we all walk out together.

Kush hangs around our bunks for a few minutes and I have almost no desire to be nice. But I do anyway. I could use another friend and he's the only one interested at the moment.

"So, you wanna tell me what that fight was all about?"

I look back over at him as my hand absently fishes around for Lucan's note in the bottom of today's package. "Not especially, Kush. I mean," I add this to appear nice, "if you don't mind, it was kinda personal."

"Well, I heard some of it, and if you want, I'll help you keep him alive."

Isec's face snaps up to study Kush's motives. I just shrug. "Sure, why not. It would be beyond stupid to turn down help, right?" I pull out the nasal spray and dose myself, and stuff the note in the waist of my shorts.

He smiles. "Yeah, besides, we did OK last time."

I look at him for real this time. "Yeah, you're right. Huh, Isec? We did OK last time." I nudge his leg as he sits motionless on his bunk, but he doesn't speak.

Kush takes the hint and says goodnight.

No matter what I say, the kid won't sleep alone. So he climbs into bed with me. I'm just about to doze off when he finally says something. "Ashur is going to kill me."

I smooth his hair down the side of his head. "Stop it, Isec. He's not going to kill you. That's silly."

"Junco?"

"Yeah?"

"What did Lucan's note say?"

I spy the coughing girl peek over her bunk to listen in and I smile. "It said, Take good care of Isec tomorrow because he's special."

We drift off after that, but I snap awake sometime later when the thought burrows up from my subconscious.

I might not be telepathic, but I am precognitive.

Chapter Fifteen

The four of us enter the second battle together, Kush and I taking up the front and the rear, Isec behind me, and the coughing girl behind Isec. The girl wouldn't take no for an answer and Isec's pleading won out in the end. She had a wild look to her the minute we got in line, and by the time we were all situated on the spiral patterns below our feet, she was half-crazed. Now I am wondering if I will need to kill her myself, just to keep focused.

We are not last this time, so we have to wait a little bit, our bare feet cemented in place. We have a modified plan now that Kush wants to play and the coughing girl said she'd make sure she did her part. Although, looking at her now, I'm having second thoughts.

Anyway, the new formation is a square, each of us taking a point, instead of back to back. We face outward, away from each other at all times. I am listening, but not watching the patterns of movement behind me. We are smack in the middle of the spiral, with several circles above and below. Things in the back slow down and finally the anticipated pause in activity that signals the start of just about anything – be it a horse race, or the release of an arrow into the heart of a pronghorn on the prairie, or a fight to the death to prove you are worthy – stretches out far enough for me to know it is the true beginning.

"Now," I whisper.

I feel them all position and then we are accelerated upward and into Fight Two. It takes a fraction for gravity to catch up to the sudden deceleration and I feel my bare feet lift off the ground and know the hold has already been deactivated even before we settle. I kill the guy next to me and then the girl above me who thought she had it made with her superior positioning before anyone else notices we've been released.

The rest of the bodies come alive and I smile as I watch Isec pull his claws out of his lower target and shoot up in the air to sweep his talons across the face of a kid not much older than him on the level above.

What Kush and the coughing girl are doing, I can't see, I just take up my part in the formation and we walk up the spiral, somewhat discombobulated, yet a hell of a lot more organized than anyone else in my view.

I kill the next person up the ramp and then turn as Isec screams.

A small boy has jumped up from above and knocked Isec down the next level.

A girl swoops in to kill him and I rake my foot across her eyes, then kick her in the face and she pops off the spiral like a starling diving through an open barn door.

I pull Isec to his feet and Kush comes in and knocks a big guy down who was about to take my head off. I don't have time to thank him because there's another girl right behind Kush who has a knife aimed at his back. She's in mid-air, knife in full forward motion, when the coughing girl grabs her by the foot and swings her off the platform. I turn to choke out another kid next to me, but I can hear the sound of a skull crashing on the floor below and smile at CG's save.

We form up again and this time we're running up the spiral, almost everyone is off the platform and fighting in the air, so we make it up a good full turn before we stop and start killing again.

The precipice is directly above us now and I wait for

Kush and Isec to finish off their targets before whistling the command. We lift up, wings beating and crushing against each other in the confined space until we ascend to the top platform where there is a ferocious battle between the other politicos.

Kush charges in and has a guy down in a fraction, while Isec and CG fight off a very tall girl with dark skin. I crouch down, in position, waiting until someone notices me. My eyes scan the group and I pick the leader. He's too busy to notice a little lump on the floor and I crawl on palms and feet, knees bent and my belly almost scraping the ground – slowly, like I've done a hundred times before in a ghillie suit out on the prairie – until I'm so close I could reach out and trip him.

In those few seconds he's killed off a good number of pledges and I am patient as he looks around for his next target.

My head is bowed, but my eyes are up to keep him in view.

He sweeps around, desperate for another target.

Finds the swirl of glowing colors in my eyes.

And I spring up like a lion going for the wolf.

My hands are around his throat and my knee slams into his chest, knocking all the air out of him as he falls backwards. I choke him until he goes limp and crumbles, then rip my talons across his throat to seal the deal.

Sound returns to my world like the rush of the wind across the tallgrass and I pick out Isec's scream of panic. I whirl around and see him fighting off a girl with razors so long they could belong to Kush.

She swipes at his face twice before I can cover the ground and she's about to draw them across his throat when CG plunges down and lands on her back.

Isec goes reeling down with razor girl and I am just

about to clean up when CG snaps the girl's neck, pushing her away with disgust.

Things are getting less chaotic and I know the buzzer is about to blow, but I scan the area once more to make sure. The four of us have acquired the top level of the spiral. I look back at CG and I'm about to congratulate her when one last politico pulls himself up over the ledge behind Isec and grabs him by the throat.

"No!" I scream and everything is silent and in slow motion again as I book it on foot towards Isec. I see Kush on the other side of the platform in my peripheral vision. He turns and begins to react, too late.

Isec reaches up for his throat and wiggles free.

CG hurls herself at the politico as the buzzer wails in my ears.

And I watch as the asshole cheats and slits her throat midair.

Real time catches up and CG is thrown down the spiral and lands in a heap at the bottom, next to a pile of bodies, broken just like hers.

Isec is screaming.

Kush is walking slowly towards me.

And I just stand there and feel a little rush of relief that it's her and not Isec.

The moderator is on the speakers telling us to line up on the spirals to be shunted up to Level Three and life comes back to me.

Until I hear my name.

"Junco, Aves 039, you will remain behind for pickup. Junco, Aves 039, you will remain behind for pickup."

I step off the spiral and have just enough time to see Isec run forward in a panic before they stun me from behind with a bolt of plasma and I fall to the ground, shaking uncontrollably.

I come to in an operating theater, bright lights shining on me from above, my hands and feet strapped down, and the blood from the battle crusting over my ears so I can't hear right. My back flames from the plasma burn as I struggle and my coughing gets out of control. My lungs try to do complicated tasks like inhale and don't seem to be making much progress.

There is chaos and I hear the 039 yelling – at least most of them. Braun is not present. My head bobs around, trying to take things in and get a grip on the situation as quickly as possible, when I spy Tier.

He's strapped to a gurney just like me. Mere inches separate our eyes.

"Tier," I croak.

"Don't trust them, Junco."

I manage a smile between coughs. "Thank you."

"For wha?" he says, slurring his words in a drugged-out stupor.

I whisper between my smile. "For making that real."

Ashur is down in my face then, yelling at me to shut up.

My head bobs around again and I see Isten and Lucan screaming at each other, pushing each other, until razors come out and other Aves step in to break it up.

It all becomes too much.

My eyes close and I am gone.

When I wake Tier has vanished and the room is quiet. Life is clear and the nightmare I witnessed before is over.

"Witness is awake and conscious."

"Witness, can you tell us your name?"

Who the fuck is the witness? The words type out on my vision screen automatically.

Then a reply: *You are the witness, Junco.*

"I'm the witness?"

"Correct," says the voice in the room.

Do not answer out loud unless I instruct you to, the vision screen types.

"OK."

That was out loud.

I had no idea vision data displays could be testy.

"Witness will say her full name for the court."

Say: Junco Abigail Coot.

I say it.

"Physician will confirm that the drugs have been administered and are working correctly."

A voice next to my head. "Confirmed. The cortical feedback loop has been enhanced, witness has normal vital signs, and witness is in full complacency and submissive mode as described by Psyche Cluster Protocol 41."

"Witness will recall the evening of November 9, 2152. Does witness recall?"

Say: Yes. "Yes."

"Witness will describe events which occurred from 1830 hours to 1915 hours."

Say: Aren attacked Tier after I agreed to go with him.

Say: Tier attacked Aren.

Say: I burned Tier with a plasma rifle.

Say: Aren and I escaped.

Say: Aren poisoned me so he could take me back and hand me over to the Mountain Republic.

Say: Tier grabbed me and administered first aid to combat paralysis from the wound.

Say: Tier took me back to a cave which he was using as base camp and completed treatment from the poison.

Say no more until instructed.

It's a lie. My thoughts type it out on the display.

Of course it's a lie, Junco. You want to save Tier, correct?

Yes.

Well, one charge at a time. This one we can knock off tonight.

Who is we?

Silence from the data display, but the room is murmuring like cicadas on a summer night.

The murmuring stops and the voice is active again. "Did witness see a treaty exchanged between parties during this time?"

Say: Yes.

"Did witness see Captain Raubtier read the treaty and submit to it?"

Say: Yes.

"Did witness see Captain Raubtier break the treaty?"

Say: No.

The murmuring gets excited and loud until the voice commands silence.

"Did witness hear Captain Raubtier mention that he killed numerous humans without orders?"

Say: No.

"Did witness hear Captain Raubtier mention that he killed children without orders?"

Say: No.

"This witness' question list is completed."

The bright light above me grows dimmer and dimmer until I am left in total darkness.

Chapter Sixteen

I come to again. This time I'm in a pale yellow room and there are machines beeping around me. I rip out the IV and sit all the way up before Ryse pushes me back down on the bed and Arel slaps a towel over the blood spurting out from my arm.

"Relax, Junco. You're with us now," Ashur says, his voice even and disinterested.

I'm filled with rage. "You asshole, I told you he'd live. And so fucking much for not spying on me back on Earth, right? You piece of shit! Did you have fun watching me all that time?"

Arel steps back, a little annoyed. "What the fuck is she talking about now, Ashur?"

Isten comes up to the bed and then Mish and Rikan follow. They are all here, except Braun. "Junco," Isten starts. "It wasn't like that."

I swallow hard and cough. "He did, Isten!" The tears well up in my eyes and I am about to cry from all the stress and drugs. "He knows all my counter-attacks and I only ever practiced them in one place!" I scream it, I am so angry my head wants to explode. I dial it down and the words come out as a whisper instead. "One secret place, Ashur. Down on the holomat in my bedroom. And you know every single move. Every single counter-move."

His face is a mixture of anger and guilt as he looks up at his team. "How the fuck do you think we could bring her back if we couldn't control her, huh?"

They stare at him in silence.

"He watched me in my room. And not," I stress, "the princess room. He watched me in my real bedroom." I turn away and push Ryse off the bed. The towel Arel placed slips and the blood starts to flow again. It gives up and coagulates half way down my wrist, then becomes sticky until I absently wipe it on the sheets.

The silence is broken by Lucan's voice across the room. "You will all leave now."

They don't even say goodbye, either. They just file out and leave me there.

"Would you like to stay here tonight, Junco?"

I shake my head and more tears spill out. "No. It's not fair that everyone else has to sit there tonight knowing that we killed all those people and I get a choice."

I turn around and his face is so sad I almost take it back.

But I don't, I just let the tears slide down my cheeks.

"I should have to see what I did, witness the number of bunks shrinking as the space between them grows wider, so that I know what a fucked-up piece of shit you've turned me into and how much worse you avians are than–" I let out a sob and take a moment to wipe my wrist across my nose and pull myself together.

When I speak again my voice is low, but even. "I hope you got everything you needed, by the way. That was a classy fucking move, pulling me out after the fight and filling me up with drugs – you fucking *shot* me!"

He just stands there, looking at me. I watch as he swallows hard but even if he is sorry, it won't make it better. Not this time. "I trusted you." I turn back over so he can't see my face.

Tier was right all along. Trust no one.

Not Ashur.

Not Lucan.

And certainly not Braun who hasn't even come back to see me once since the day I left.

"You wanted to break me, right? That's what you said?"

"Junco—"

"Well, congratulations. You should feel very proud of yourself."

Lucan's private flyer drives me back to Fledge. I'm pushed up against the door on one side, my face pressed against the cool glass as I watch the high atmosphere mist part around us. Lucan is sitting, straight-backed, on the other side of the rear seat. I've got the blanket from the bed wrapped around me because the drugs have tricked my body into thinking I'm freezing-ass cold even as sweat pours down my back and puddles inside the waist of my pants.

The ride takes a lot longer than I thought it would and when we finally stop I'm almost asleep, still half intoxicated and the other half exhausted. Lucan gets out and walks with me into the Fledge building. He palms the elevator and the moderators watch with long frowns on their faces as I try to walk straight, but can't.

We ride up to level three and he takes my arm and leads me into the dorm. The lights are all on, but everyone is in bed, sitting up looking confused.

Kush gets up and runs over, then Isec joins him.

"What the fuck did you do to her?" Isec demands. He takes my hand. "Junco?" His little voice is full of fear and he begins to cry.

Kush drags me away from Lucan and takes me over to a bed.

My dried-up sobs are just small hiccups as I lie down shaking.

I hear Isec's little bare feet pad a few paces out into the center of the room. Then he screams at the receding click of expensive shoes on the tile, "She doesn't *like you* anymore, Lucan. She doesn't like you *anymore!*"

A fading laugh wakes me up and the first thing I think is that I'm dead. Eventually, as the seconds pass, I realize I'm not dead, I just wish I was. My entire body hurts. I shuffle and kick the heavy blanket until I unwind my legs, then push myself up and look around the room.

There are only single beds now and we've got a large portion of the room dedicated to a casual sitting area filled with couches, chairs, and tables. The news is on a screen that takes up one entire wall, almost floor to ceiling, but the sound is turned down.

Ashur is sitting on the next bed over.

I don't look at him, but I know he's there. I swing my aching legs out the side that faces an empty bunk and rest my feet on the cold tile floor, massaging my head to make the throbbing recede. It doesn't work.

I stand up and give the dizziness a second as well. Then slowly shuffle over towards the showers.

"We need to talk, Junco."

I ignore him.

I've got the hot water spraying down and I'm just about to try and remove my shirt when I see him standing in the doorway. "You will talk to me."

I stare at him, then release the seams on my shirt and whip it over my head, biting back the pain as my arms and shoulders protest.

When I look back at the door he's gone.

I stand under the barrage of water until my muscles are relaxed, then search out what the vision screen personality can do for my condition.

You there?

Yes.

Got anything to make me feel better?

A series of diagnostics run and the data presents as a graph showing which hormones and macromolecules are in what ratio. The ones that need improvement are blinking red.

Shall I initiate a recovery cocktail?

Is this legal for Fledge?

There are no rules for self-healing in the General Fledge.

OK, yes. Make me feel better.

I am not obtuse, I realize she wrote General Fledge. Which means the Aves probably have some restrictions. But hey, I'm not in the Aves Fledge, now am I.

I lean against the wall as the cocktail floods my bloodstream. The relief is almost instantaneous, and much appreciated.

So, you gonna tell me who you are?

Silence from the vision screen.

Figures. I don't really give a shit, what can I do about it? If there's an AI living inside my body, well, it's not like I can make her go away, can I? Live with it, Junco.

I adjust my towel as I walk over to the Aves 039 cubbie and there are a lot of packages there. I choose one that looks like the rest of Lucan's packages, pull out the clothes and boots, then stuff it back in and let the biometrics lock it back up with the rest.

I have no intention of opening any of them.

After dressing I walk back out into the dorm and head for the cafeteria. I thumb through the selections but

I can't remember the things Isec ordered for us in the past, so I choose something that looks like a biscuit or cookie and force myself to eat it. I grab a drink and a six-pack of cigars and head out.

Ashur is waiting in the hallway.

I walk right past and don't even glance his direction. I'm feeling a lot better with the cocktail and I hop down the stairs and walk towards the outside door.

The thick-around-the-middle moderator glances up from his reading at the front desk. "Hey, Junco?"

I turn. "Hey–" I don't know his name.

"Hey, uh, Lucan's outside waiting for you, honey." He shrugs and makes a face at me. "Just thought you might like a heads-up."

I nod at him. "Thanks."

"And that other one is around here too. Your–"

Ashur comes down the stairs and the mod shuts up. I shake my head and walk towards the door. Outside the fake sunshine is bright, so bright it blocks my view of the bench for a second. I put a hand up to shade my eyes and I see Lucan. I can hear the door behind me whoosh open to let Ashur catch up.

Nowhere to go.

So I light a cigar and make for the grass before either of them can get close enough to order me around. I lie down and stretch back, one hand behind my head, one bringing the cigar to my mouth, and let out a deep breath as I cross my legs and close my eyes.

I feel fucking spectacular. That was one hell of a cocktail.

Ashur reaches me first since he was closer, but he remains silent until Lucan joins our little party.

"You will come with us, Junco. We will have that conversation now."

I don't even open my eyes. "No, I don't think so, Lucan." I take another puff and blow rings, eyes still closed.

"Junco," Ashur growls at me. "You will do as you're told."

"Fuck off. You can try and make me come with you, if you think it's worth it. But I'm not going unless you plan on shooting and drugging me again. I'm not going anywhere with either of you as long as I have a choice." I open my eyes, shade them with my hand, and then sit up. "You both fucked up. I'm not your friend." I point my cigar at Ashur. "And I'm not your…" I stop and look at Lucan because I'm not at all sure what I am to him. "… whatever it is you thought I was."

Ashur's fingers grab me and yank me to my feet, my cigar goes flying, and I overcompensate and stumble backwards a few paces. I want to get angry, but I force it down and then bend over to pick up my cigar to wait it out.

Lucan breaks our standoff. "Ashur, please leave us now."

Ash shakes his head at Lucan. "No way. I'm not leaving."

Lucan smiles like Ash is a toddler. "You are, Ashur. Immediately. Or I will have you forcibly removed. You are evoking far more anger in her than I am, so let me handle this."

I look back and forth between the two of them and my head throbs a little as I clench my teeth in frustration.

Ashur walks back into the building and I watch until he's no longer visible through the transparent doors. I look back at Lucan, but he just stands there, staring at me. I realize after a few seconds that he's scrolling in his own data display, reading something. It's the same look he got when he was telling me about the Vegas planet pad takeover. Distant and searching.

Is that how I looked in the testimony room? I sure fucking hope not, otherwise he knows.

"I know you lied in testimony, Junco."

Shit.

"I just can't figure out how exactly. The drugs were fully accepted into your profile, your vitals screamed the textbook readout of someone under the influence, and you never acted out of character. Nonetheless, I know you lied."

I smile. "Well, good fucking luck with that one, Lucan. Maybe you avians are allowed to make shit up like that and get away with it. I wouldn't know, not my world after all. But I have no idea what you're talking about."

"I know you lied, Junco," he continues, "because not twenty minutes before your testimony Tier admitted to breaking the treaty."

"Maybe his memory isn't so good, Lucan. I, on the other hand, have perfect recall."

"What did he say to you in the testimony room, Junco?"

"He said, *Don't trust them.*"

I watch his face as he realizes I'm telling the truth.

"Pretty good advice, if you ask me. I'm gonna take it now."

I turn to walk towards the doors but he reaches out, not unkindly, and touches my shoulder. And then we are in the darkness of space and I fall forward as my mind adjusts to the nothingness below me. His hand reaches out again and steadies me. I'm steady, but he doesn't let go.

"Junco," he starts, then stops to sigh. "You've asked a few questions since we first met, but I am more surprised at the ones you don't ask."

I wait it out, not to try and gain momentum or anything, I'm just too tired to give a shit.

"Still nothing?"

I look up at him then. "No, Lucan. Nothing. I just don't care."

"What do you care about, then?"

"Well, I could tell you – but then you'd just take it away from me like I'm a child that needs to be punished."

"Do you not want honesty, Junco? Isn't that what you've always been after?"

"It's really not all that important right now, so no thanks. My interest in you, like I said, is gone."

"You'll turn down the answers? Take ignorance instead? Just to be stubborn."

"No, that's not it at all, Lucan. Sure, I'd like the truth, but getting it from you is like burning wood infested with wheat beetles. It heats your house for a while, but the poisonous fumes kill you before you're warm anyway, so what's the point."

"Who will you accept it from, then? If not me? Ashur? Isten? Braun?"

"Tier."

He laughs, a genuine hearty laugh, and it makes me flash with heat. "Ah, yes. You mean the one who instructed Ashur to plant spying devices in your bedroom? He's perfect."

I smile up at him. "You don't get it, do you?" I wait for his complete attention. "It doesn't matter what Tier did before. I granted him absolution back on Earth for all of it. It doesn't matter if he spied on me himself, or if he killed Charlie, or even if he was the one who turned me into this monster. None of it matters, because he was forgiven. It's a done deal."

He stares down at me, his features hardening as the seconds tick off.

Patience and inertia are not the same thing.

He taps my shoulder and we are back in the grass at Fledge. The sky is dark around us. "Well, I guess your secret is out then, right?"

I shake out another cigar and touch it to the striker, inhaling and exhaling before answering. "It's never been a secret, Lucan. You had me pegged right at the start. From the 039 with their plasmas at my head after morph, to the little speech about how sweet talk doesn't work on you. You got it in one. But you know what I don't understand?"

He turns away, so I don't wait.

"Why you let yourself be drawn into my little act. The stars, Lucan? Please, that is so predictable."

He turns back and I expect anger at the very least, but he hands me indifference. "If you interfere with what I am doing, Junco, I will be forced to punish you."

"Like I said that first day in the hallway, Lucan — death means nothing to me. I can kill myself tonight and be one hundred percent satisfied with how things end. Or you can kill me right now and be done with all of it. Because that's the only way you'll know for sure that Tier will die at the end."

I'm slammed onto the ground before I can blink, a sharp pain throbbing up the side of my face. I spread out my arms, crucifix style, and close my eyes to block him out. "Do it," I whisper.

But the fractions pass and I know he's gone.

Chapter Seventeen

Kush finds me like that sometime later. I didn't doze off exactly, just didn't see the point of picking myself up. He sits down next to me and when I don't speak, he lies back and waits. I've noticed some things about Kush over the past week or so. He's patient. And he keeps his distance. It's refreshing.

My grin grows as I turn my head to face him.

"What are you doing, Junco?" He smiles back.

"Lucan hit me and I fell down."

He laughs at me and shakes his head.

"And I don't know, it really wasn't worth the effort to get back up." I turn my head back and look towards the ceiling miles away. It doesn't matter if I spend all the rest of my days under this roof, I will never get used to looking up and seeing ceiling.

"Should I bother asking why he hit you?"

I shrug. "I sort of threatened him. In a roundabout way."

He nods. "Ah. OK. Well, that probably doesn't go over well in the best of times, and you seem to bring out the worst in lots of people."

"Yeah, probably."

"So, you gonna stay out here all night?"

"I dunno."

"Wanna see the cool rooms we have access to now?"

"What rooms? I didn't see any rooms."

"Did you go out past that lounge area? There's a giant mast with all sorts of stuff on the way up. And at the top there's an observatory."

I turn, interested. "Huh, what are the chances?"

He gets up and offers me his hand.

I hesitate, but he pulls me up without waiting for my answer.

I manage to pry Isec's fingers off my arm long enough to get into the bottom of the mast and look up. It looks fucking far. Like miles away to that observatory. In fact, I squint and I'm not even sure if I can see the opening. I might just be imagining it.

"Let's go up," Kush says.

I shoot him a dirty look. "Kush, I've flown a total of like three times. There is no way I can fly up there. Zero chance."

He points to his back. "Hop on, then."

I shake my head. "Nah, I've done that before and it was a struggle to get a fraction of that distance."

He screws up his face. "You've done what before? What are you talking about?"

"On Earth, when Tier and I–" I catch myself and turn away. *Fuck*. "Fine, then. If you think you can carry me…"

He smiles. "I can, Junco."

I hop on and he does. It takes a few minutes, but this is nothing like the escape flight Tier and I took up through that cave opening back in the RR. And even though I keep looking down, Moju's head never pops up from the floor.

When we get to the top he stands on the landing and then I hop down and look into a stairwell that goes up through the ceiling.

"Have you ever been in a gravity curve, Junco?"

I shake my head. "Don't even know what a gravity curve is, Kush."

"You know how the building is curved up against the outside wall?"

I nod, still looking up into the dark hole.

"Well, the gravity fluctuates as you go up. That's why the flight wasn't so hard. The G was decreasing as we went up. So anyway, when we get up in there, it's gonna feel weird – your perspective, that is. Just let me take you to a booth and try not to puke."

I laugh. "OK."

He grabs my hand and starts climbing the stairs. As we go up it gets darker and my breathing picks up the pace a little.

"Close your eyes now, Junco."

I do, and he takes my elbow and leads me. My body is swaying wildly and I can see what he meant by the gravity curve. It's not the same from step to step, very erratic.

"OK, open your eyes, but don't move."

Holy shit! I'm standing on the side of the wall looking sideways at the giant viewing transparency. He pushes me back a little and I fall into a long lounger and then I am lying down instead of walking sideways. My head spins a little and Kush blocks my eyes with his hand. "Close your eyes if you get dizzy." I do, and then he leans back with me. "It's weird, isn't it?"

I laugh and open my eyes. The darkness above me is filled with tiny pricks of light and I smile. "Very fucking weird, Kush."

He looks over and smiles.

We sit there for a long time like that. Silent. Looking. Thinking.

"I already know you're from Earth, Junco."

I don't bother turning away from the stars to face him. "Did Isec tell you?"

I feel him shake his head. "No, you've been on the newscreens for the past two days. Ever since the morning Lucan brought you back."

"What? It's been three days since the last fight?"

He lets out a heavy breath. "Yeah, Fight Three is tomorrow."

"I slept for two days straight?" Wow.

"Yeah, we all figured out what happened afterward. They had you on the screens, your testimony. There was a big inquiry and some people accused you of lying."

"Yeah, like Lucan."

"No, he didn't. The Archer of Justice did though."

"Huh, well, Lucan accused me of lying to my face, so same difference."

"Did you lie?" He looks over at me.

I return a snarl. "Please, Kush. If I did, I wouldn't tell you. Besides, it's not even possible to lie under the drugs. That's what they told me anyway."

He shrugs. "I didn't bring you up here to talk about that stuff."

"Then why did you bring me up here?"

"Junco, it is very hard to get your attention. I figure I'd have a captive audience. And," he says with a smile, "you can't exactly escape, can you?"

I laugh. "I'm sure I'd have better luck getting down than I would have had getting up."

Despite his confession he remains patient and aloof.

And we just lie there, observing.

At some point he puts his arm around me, pulls me close into his golden brown wings, and I doze off. I wake only once, when his hand slips down my belly and I feel a tingle on the skin near my SEAR. I grab his hand and gently move it up higher and then go back to sleep.

I'm pulled out of the best sleep I've had in a long time as Kush is carrying me to the exit of the observatory.

"Gotta go down, Junco. Fight will start in a few hours and Isec's been up here half a dozen times wondering when you're gonna come talk to him."

I nod as I look up at him. "OK."

He sets me down at the stairs and holds me by the shoulders as I make my way to the platform. I wait on the landing, not really wanting to take the leap. Kush bends down and I hop on, grateful. When he jumps off the ledge I feel like I did that night when Moju, Tier, and I were heading out towards the Ramah tunnels. Exhilarated. Kush was right, there's lots of stuff all up and down the mast. I look around and make a mental note to come back after I'm done killing people.

At the bottom Isec is pacing around like a mad wreck and when I'm on the ground he releases his breath in a rush.

"Relax, kid. We're fine."

He shakes his head. "No, this fight is different, Junco. Way different."

I sigh. "Well, let's go sit down and make a plan then, OK?"

We settle on my bed, the soft blanket from Lucan's house heaped around Isec as we talk. Kush sits in and listens, but doesn't interrupt to make suggestions. On the sidelines I guess. Isec has few details of the actual fight arena, but he does fill me in on the new rules. I ask for them on the vision screen and they pop into view. The only real difference is that the fight will not end until our numbers have been cut to seventy-five individuals and weapons will be hidden throughout the field. I glance around the room and try and estimate how many of us are left from the original one thousand.

Two-fifty, I guess. Damn.

Collectively we've killed seven hundred fifty people in the span of about a week.

On Earth we call this internecine. Mass murder. Mutual slaughter and destruction.

Here, apparently it's called growing up.

When it comes time to line up we still have no idea what the floor plan will look like but neither does anyone else. I make us line up near the front this time. Kush is like tenth in line, then Isec, then me. We stand there, shifting our weight from foot to foot, agitation growing around us, nerves fraying, and the buzz of what's to come percolating up from the depths like a salamander lifting up out of a muddy river bank after the spring thaw.

I've never seen the initial process of fight day since we've never been at the front. Our attention is focused on a large metal door as it creaks to life and draws up into the ceiling. We file in and step onto the cube patterns where our feet should go.

I study the lines that criss-cross the holding room, trying to get a sense of what shape it might be. I glance over at Kush and he shrugs. Isec is red-faced and panicked. "Isec, dammit, don't fucking crumble on me now, you understand? Stop it!"

He nods out a yes at me and takes a deep breath.

I look up at Kush as the rest of the people file in and take their spots on the pattern and he raises his eyebrows but says nothing.

Studying the lines again, I see the pattern. I've seen it before at least, but I cannot recall where. I search my memories but only come back with a vague reference to an early childhood education workbook.

It doesn't fit.

More and more people are shuffling around and Isec is doing some kind of meditation. "Isec!" He opens his eyes. "I'm only like six feet away, buddy. We'll do it together, OK?"

He smiles and the quiet of almost time pokes its head into the room.

What is this pattern?

Are you asking me?

I smile. *Absolutely. What's the pattern?*

The floor vibrates and my feet are stuck – I watch Isec lose it in real time.

It's a maze.

And then we are being rushed upward into battle.

Chapter Eighteen

One second I'm locking eyes with Isec's little flushed face.

And then the darkness envelopes us.

He's gone.

My eyes adjust and my night vision kicks in even as I lurch forward, and then slam into the mirrored wall that now separates the two of us. I stop, and the screams start. There is no one around me because I'm positioned in a small nook. I hear footsteps approach and I ready myself to attack.

They move slow and deliberate and I hear the hands dragging across the wall, trying to understand where they are.

No one else has night vision.

The hand stops when it gets to the edge of my nook and the green face on my vision screen is filled with panic. It's a girl, not that much older than Isec, and she's breathing so hard I swear she's gonna pass out. She waits, listening in my direction. Trying to decide if someone is there or not.

Screams around us jolt her into action and she runs forward, then slams into the wall and falls to the ground.

I step out and walk towards her. "Don't move. I'll pick you up, OK?"

She starts crying.

"Look, kid, if you cry I'll just kill you. I'm not in a great mood. I'll pick you up and you follow me, but stay out of the way, got it?"

She nods as I pull her to her feet. I place her hands on a belt loop at my waist. "Hold on, but if I start fighting you let go and drop to the floor, all right?"

She nods.

"Good, now no talking unless you're gonna save my life. Let's go."

Substituting for Isec already?

Shut the fuck up.

I know there are people fighting ahead of me and when I turn the corner I can see them flailing around in the dark. I reach for the SEAR because I'm in a hurry and Lucan can go fuck himself.

I walk up to them, within a foot or so, then push the little girl off me. She slumps to the ground as I flick my thumb over the tiny little imperfection on my weapon. The SEAR comes to life and faces all around look in my direction, stunned.

I cut them down with one elegant swoop of the blade and turn it off.

"Let's go."

"What was that?"

"Shut up and stay close."

We move forward and we repeat the action half a dozen more times. My score card is up to twenty-five when we turn the corner and find the honey hole. A large group of cowards is in control of a cache of weapons, swords mostly, but some small plasma knives too. I scan them and see they have night-vision goggles on as well.

I backtrack and pull the girl with me. "Lie down on the ground and do not move. You understand?"

She looks up at my face in the darkness, scared shitless.

"If they come near you, you don't move. Play dead."

"Where are you going?"

"To kill everyone I can to make the fucking fight stop. If those assholes are just going to stand there hoarding the weapons we'll be here all fucking day before we get down to seventy-five people."

I get down and crawl, sniper style, over bodies and through thick sticky puddles of blood until I reach the corner. I let my body drop to the ground and then, a fraction at a time, I push myself up so my eyes can look around the corner.

There are a lot fewer screams in the arena now. Which means people are hiding and not fighting.

I watch each of the guys, all pretty big, as they strut around in their eye gear. I've used night vision before, it's standard for night patrols. And there's one thing I know about them, they really fuck up your peripheral vision. I whistle and they all turn in my direction. I let them get a good look and then duck behind the wall and wait.

They argue and are just about ready to dismiss me when I hear my name mentioned.

I peek out and smile at them. "I'm gonna kill you," I whisper.

The dumb ones come at me and I step out when they are within reach and the SEAR blinks into existence, slices through all three necks before they can come to grips with what they're seeing, and everything goes dark again.

The others back away instinctively and I am thinking about how much trouble I will be in when this is over when I hear Isec scream somewhere beyond the group. They fling him out into the middle, then kick him in the head and I feel the heat rise up in my face.

I run at full speed and the first guy braces himself for contact when I flip up in the air, do a twist, and thrust my foot into the neck of his buddy behind him. He goes down choking as the SEAR comes out and slices off the hands of the first guy. He slumps down, writhing in pain from the metabolic effects of the weapon. For a few fractions I'm transfixed by the melting of his skin and connective tissues, but then I jolt myself up out of it and the SEAR finds a neck, then a leg, and then there is just me and Isec.

I pull him up and start stuffing weapons in his hands. "Isec, fucking snap out of it, take these, goddammit!" He does, stuffing them into his pants and shirt. "Keep one ready, Isec! Jasus, think, kid, or you're gonna die!"

He arms himself and pulls it together. I grab a pair of night goggles off one of the heads and slap them over his eyes so he can see. "Better?"

He nods.

"OK, look – everyone is hiding, trying to wait it out. But we'll be here all fucking day unless we go do some damage."

He nods at first, but then understands what I'm saying, and shakes his head instead.

"Yes, Isec. If you want to get out of here we have to go kill."

I pull him with me and start to follow the guys who ran. "You call out the clock from behind, OK?"

Silence.

I turn around and grab him by the neck. "Fuck, Isec, answer me when I'm giving you orders!"

"OK, Junco. I got it."

I let go of him and we move forward.

Vision screen, give me all the data you have on the arena.

It floods with so much data I can barely see. *Scale back to everything I need to know within twenty feet.*

The screen clears out enough for me to see, but it's still packed with shit. For one, the group of guys are huddled just around the second corner. "Keep up, Isec," I whisper, "we're going kamikaze. And if I catch you hiding or not using that knife to kill everyone you can, I'll kill you myself, Isec. You get that?"

"Yes, Junco."

"They're around the second corner, all of them. When I say go, we run full out and I'll make the first cut and you finish them off."

"OK."

"And stay the fuck out of the way of my SEAR knife, Isec. Unless you want to die a very hasty death. You stay back!"

He lets out a breath and I whisper, "Go!"

I run, making a lot of noise, and the first head pops out to take a look. I charge at him and he steps back behind the wall and I follow. Another guy grabs me from behind, holding my arms. I lean forward with all my weight and then double back-kick him in the shins as he holds me. He falls backward but his fingers are not ready to let go and make a mad grab, flailing out to grasp whatever is in reach. The pain in my wing almost overtakes me and then the blood is everywhere. I spin around and cut his torso in half, then turn back to find my first target. He's got a little plasma knife raised, thinking he's some kind of ancient warrior out on the steppe, but I slice open his gut from sternum to groin and he falls.

The rest run and I follow. At some point I look back and see Isec is gone, but I keep going, the data screen feeding me intel as I pass over hallways that have no bodies and stop to kill anyone who happens to be hiding in the others. Fucking cowards, if everyone went out and did their killing we'd be done by now. The screaming is back in full force and I'm just about to take off the heads of two tall girls when the buzzer sounds and the lights come on.

The walls drop into the floor and the fight is over.

I search, find Isec, search, find the little girl, search.

"Kush?" I yell it. "Kush!"

"Junco, over here."

I whirl around to find him. He's breathing hard and covered in blood, a sword in his hand dripping with blood.

He's alive.

And he did his killing.

"Exit to the right. Exit to the right. Exit to the right."

The voice keeps insisting, but I wait as Kush rushes towards me. My vision starts to waver and it's only then that I notice the blood is still pouring out of my damaged feathers, flooding the floor around my feet. I start to fall but Kush picks me up and leaps into the mast. I feel my body bounce as he rushes me across the dorm and when I finally force myself to take a look around he's tapping my finger on the cafeteria food machine. He places me on a table and my whole body is sticky and wet from the blood. He rolls me over on my stomach and lifts my wing and stretches it out. I lie still as he massages something into the broken feather shaft and then after a few minutes I hear a long sigh.

Kush leans down into my face. "Junco?"

I grunt, but don't speak. Just don't have the energy.

I taste his blood-covered fingers as he smears a paste across my lips and gums. "Swallow it, Junco."

I do.

I hear him pull up a chair and listen as Isec's small voice asks if I'm OK.

I want to wait and hear the answer, but the blackness takes over.

Chapter Nineteen

I come to with a sharp sting to my face. "Junco!"

"Shit, don't hit me, dammit."

I hear a laugh and when I open my eyes Kush is smiling down at me. "You're so lucky you're already Aves. You lost a lot of blood."

I try to sit up but fall back down. "Help me up, Kush."

He pulls me up so I'm sitting on the table and steadies me as I wobble back and forth for a few seconds. "What the hell happened?"

"Someone snapped two of your primary wing feathers."

I just stare at him and when he doesn't elaborate I shrug. "So?"

"Oh, OK. You don't know. You can pull them straight out and be fine, but break them down near the shaft and you bleed to death, Junco. It was a pretty dirty trick, but this is Fledge after all."

I turn to look behind me, then grab my left wing and pull it out to see the damage. My normally golden flecks are stained dark brown from dried and coagulating blood. Sure enough I have a gap where the two longest feathers near the tip used to be.

"I pulled them out, Junco. Then," he lifts up a food ration that has a small packet attached to the outside, "I used the extra starch from the mapolina packet to stop the bleeding. You just dunk the ends in there and it soaks up the blood and makes it clot."

"Mapolina?"

He holds up the packet. "You know, mapolina. That gross shit they feed us constantly because it's cheap."

I smile weakly. "OK, mapolina." I let my wing drop back down. "How did you know what to do?"

He grins. "Politicos, Junco. We come to the General Fledge on purpose. Train for it for years. They teach us shit, like how to use what's available for healing."

"Thank you, Kush. You saved my life I think."

"Nah, you were already healing yourself. And the color is already back in your cheeks, so you're making blood as we speak. I just sped it up a little, that's all."

"Well, thanks anyway. You're a good friend."

"Come on, let's go take a shower."

I walk out of the cafeteria with him but head over to the lounge area instead. "I'm gonna sit down for a while. I'll take a shower later."

He nods and walks off.

I sit in the lounge area to wait for the crowds to leave the showers because showering with Kush and Isec is not going to happen anymore. The news is on the screen and I fiddle with the controller until the sound comes up.

My giant face is plastered up next to Tier's.

"… due to testimony given several days ago, the former captain of the Aves 039, Raubtier, was cleared of one count of insubordination in the field. The second insubordination, failure to kill a target – referring to Junco Coot, the Sibling currently fighting her way through the General Fledge on Amelia – is still pending. Sources within Justice say they have no current plans to call her back for additional testimony and some have even accused her of manipulating the drugs and beating the detectors.

"In related news, another video feed has been filtered from Earth from the now infamous ex-Mountain Minute reporter Selia Manchen. Manchen went missing back in January after the Aves teams were evacuating when the war broke out. She later went on to join up with the Subjective armies. She's been an outspoken mouthpiece for Subjack ever since. This latest feed comes out of the Tetons where the armies are lying low, waiting for some undisclosed signal."

The images on the screen cut away and there's Selia wearing the same battered uniform as the one I saw her in earlier. She's interviewing soldiers and hunches down to a guy sitting on the ground, knees bent as he laces up his boots. "The system is watching, tell them what you're fighting against."

"The shadow government they have going here," is all he says.

"Explain. Most people who will see this don't understand what that is."

He stops what he's doing and looks up in the camera, straight into my eyes. "You've been lied to your entire life. It's not real," he says, swiping his hand around in the air. "The governments, the people in charge – they make the rules that you," his finger stabs at the camera, "have to follow. But they don't. I'm tired of it. I came all the way from the Western Utopia to fight here and I don't care what happens to us, they're going down."

Then his attention is back on his boots and Selia moves on.

She repeats this several times, and while each soldier says something a little different, they all have the same underlying theme. Lies. Manipulation. Fed up.

The screen cuts back to Tier's trial and I watch them question him under the drugs. When they ask him why he didn't kill me, he's silent for a long time. I hold my breath, afraid of what he'll say.

"She's one of us."

I let the air out and notice there are a lot of people around me now. I catch the eyes of a tall girl sitting in a chair near the couch and recognize her as one of the ones I almost killed at the end.

She shrugs at me. "No hard feelings, right?"

I nod. "Sure."

"Are you really from Earth?"

Everyone crowds in now and I look around to try and get a sense of the mood. Interested, maybe a little too interested. But no hostility. "Yeah. I was born and raised there."

"Are you really one of the Seven?"

I laugh. "Well, I guess it depends. I am one of seven individuals created in the Rural Republic with Aves genetics. But if you're asking me if I'm part of that myth you all have, the answer is no."

Another kid pipes up, not one I recognize, but he's tall as well. Darker like Arel. His shoulder-length black hair is wet and hints at curls. He reminds me of Tier. "So, they gonna kill him for disobeying, you think?"

I search his face to look for hidden meaning, but can't find any deception. "No. They are not."

He raises his eyebrows at me. "Well, I hate to break it to you, Junco, but they seem convinced otherwise."

I let out a breath. "Yeah, but…" I trail off for a second. "I'm not done fighting for him yet. You'll see."

"What is it like on Earth?" It's the little girl from the maze.

I smile at her and she sits down next to me, her hair a mess of wet ringlets and the smell of soap covering up the smell of SEAR death that still lingers in my nose. "When there's no war, it's pretty nice. Where I lived there was grasslands filled with wild animals and blue skies during the day and black skies at night. You don't have to go to an observatory to see the stars, either. You just walk outside and look up."

She grins up at me. The fearful face from the maze is gone.

Another boy appears, about the same age as the dark kid. "Were you a soldier or something? On Earth, Junco?"

I nod. "Or something. Yeah, my father was a commander in the RR. I was an as–" I hesitate as I watch their eyes wait for me to finish. These kids are not soldiers, I remind myself. They are only here to try and save themselves. "I was a specialist in the field. A sniper."

All their mouths make an O shape as I get up. "Well, time for my shower now. See ya."

I pass Isec on my way and he smiles and I have trouble reconciling him as the kid I was strapping bloody night-vision goggles on an hour ago. In the showers I look around for Kush, but he's gone. I stand under the hot water and let it beat the death off me, then scrub my body down until I rub it raw and wrap myself in my towel to face the cubbies.

Junco, Aves 039, is overflowing with shit. I start pulling it all out and open one bag after another. Clothes, shoes, soap, shampoo, a brush, a reader, a com, food, and other little bits of crap that try and convince me they all care.

I want to put the bed clothes on and go to sleep, but I have a feeling I'll be called away for using the SEAR in the fight. So I dress in uniform and even lace up the boots nice and tight. I pocket the com and brush my long hair out until it is smooth. I'm not sure how, but I feel normal. I keep the food and then stuff the rest back in the cubbie before leaving the showers.

When I go back out almost everyone is over in the lounge area or in bed sleeping. I see Kush's head sticking up over the couch where I was earlier and walk that way. He's piled high with kids and I laugh and toss the food on the table nearby. He pushes Isec out of the way to make room and I slip in and rest against him.

Sigh.

And close my eyes.

Isten's voice draws me up from the depths of sleep. "What the fuck are you doing here, Junco? Playing house? Get the fuck up, we've got a meeting. Lucan wants to see the entire 039 immediately."

I sit up and rub my eyes. Isec and the little girl are sprawled out all over me and the rest of the dorm is quiet and still with weary fighters.

"What are you doing with these kids, Junco?" He paces back and forth, his heavy boots clunking on the tiles with each step. He looks a lot bigger and more intimidating than I remember from our poker game. His eyes shine yellow and target Kush. His wings go up slightly behind his shoulders in an offensive position. "And who the fuck is this guy?"

I push the kids off, get up and then walk away before he says something that will make me react. I'm just too tired. He trots to catch up with me and then keeps the pace so I have to trot to keep up with him. We walk outside and there's a flyer waiting.

"What's the meeting about?" I ask as we approach.

He huffs. "What the fuck do you think the meeting is about, Junco? You. They're always about you."

Chapter Twenty

It's bright outside and dark in the flyer, so it takes me a minute to see that everyone is crammed inside. I scoot in next to Rikan and Isten sits next to me. Braun is on the other side of Rikan slumped up against the window, not looking at anyone. Ashur is across from him, and then Mish, Arel, and Ryse.

No one says hi.

Fuck them.

I close my eyes and the rocking motion of the flyer lulls me to sleep. Several times Isten pushes me off his shoulder and Ryse kicks me when I start to snore, but I am too tired to care. I wake up when we stop and I'm sprawled out on the floor, their boots resting on me in various places.

Isten pulls me up and holds down a smile as I wipe the drool from my mouth.

I recognize Lucan's parking garage from the other night and everyone files through the doors into the building.

"What is this place?"

Arel is next to me so he answers. "Lucan's apartments."

"This is an apartment?"

"It's Aves headquarters too, so…"

Yeah, well, that explains everything, then. Thanks.

They take the stairs up several levels and I'm shuffling my feet and out of breath when I finally catch up with them. They start walking again, leaving me behind.

Assholes.

I turn the corner and bump into Ashur. "Sorry," I mumble. And keep walking. He stays behind me for the rest of the way. We meet up with the guys in the outer chambers of Lucan's offices. Some lady with no wings shows us into a conference room and says to wait.

The guys all take seats at the crescent-shaped table but I wait until Ashur points to the one next to him. "You're the nine, Junco, this is your chair."

Ryse is at the far left, Ashur is at the far right, and Braun is in the middle. Isten, myself, and an empty chair are situated between Ashur and Braun, while Arel, Rikan, and Mish are between Ryse and Braun.

I sense there is a method to this seating arrangement, but I don't see it.

Lucan enters in a rush. "Good afternoon, 039."

"Good afternoon," they say together.

I look up at Lucan. "Uh, good afternoon."

He smiles. "Junco, it's nice to have you at a meeting for once."

I scowl. "I've been busy, you know."

"Very busy," he agrees. "Which is why I'm wondering why you insist on breaking the rules and forcing me to take you off task."

I stare at him as the understanding creeps in. This is not a friendly chat, this is a military meeting and he is my commander. "Sir, I am fighting for my life in there and the SEAR is really not against the rules, in fact the rules state that only biological weapons can be used and my weapon certainly qualifies."

"Uh-huh. 039, do you agree that Junco should be allowed to use the weapon in her Fledge?"

They say various things but in general they agree. I get a smug look on my face.

"Well, if this were a democracy, Junco, you'd win, wouldn't you?"

I scowl at him.

"But this is not a democracy, this is the military and the 039 is my personal Aves team. Which means you are my personal soldier. And as such, you will do what I tell you. Is that clear?"

My eyes look straight ahead. "Yes, sir."

He smiles, happy with my obedience. "You make a much better soldier than you do a woman, Junco. Sorry, but it's true."

The guys let out little laughs as my face heats up, but Ashur cuts it off with a curt, "Enough."

"We will discuss your weapon after we conclude the team's business." He turns and takes a seat at the front of the room. "Oh, and by the way, good job staying alive today."

I mumble a "thank you, sir" and then the meeting begins.

Basically, they've cut Tier out. Ashur has been promoted to captain, Ryse to XO, and Braun to the up position. Which, from what I can gather through conversation, means he is training to be a pilot and then he will eventually go through officer school like Ryse just did.

Braun doesn't strike me as officer material, not because he's not competent, but because he's got a little too much rebel in him. He doesn't look particularly happy either. He stands and gives a report on the status of his training and then slumps down in the straight-backed chair. Ryse and Ashur give reports on what the rest of the team are doing. Isten will be guarding some local big-shot in town for the night and the others are just on patrols in places I've never heard of.

Lucan's attention comes back to me. "Junco, report on your status."

I stand. "Well, I killed, uh–" I stop to count them up in my head. "Fifty-two people today." Then I blow out some air and try to explain my injury. "Someone broke my feathers and Kush had to help me again." And then I sit back down.

"Nothing else to report?"

I groan and stand up again. My chair scrapes against the tile and the noise makes me wince. "Sir, I took a shower and a nap."

"Two naps," Isten corrects me. "She slept on the floor of the flyer on the way over."

The guys all think this is funny, but I ignore them.

"Did you eat?"

Oh, fuck. If they start up with me about eating again–

"Junco? Did you eat?"

"Not yet, but–"

"Ashur, the team will make sure she eats before escorting her back to Fledge."

"Yes, sir."

Now it's my turn to slump down in my chair. They make me feel like a child. It doesn't help that I look like a child next to them. Even Arel is giant next to me. They talk about stuff I don't understand for another twenty minutes and then everyone but Ashur and me is dismissed.

Lucan begins talking before Rikan can close the door behind him. "Junco, what does it mean to be a captain in your Earth military?"

"It's a middle-rank officer."

"Here," he continues, "it is not a middle rank. It is the highest rank – under the Archers, do you understand?"

"I get the point, if that's what you mean."

"That is not what I mean, do you understand how we rank our military?"

"No."

"I'll send you a file that you can study."

"Send it to me where?"

"You have your com, correct? My vision display says it is on your person."

I scrunch my eyebrows together and he sighs. "Yes, we track you with it. But at least we don't implant it in your body."

I reach into my thigh pocket and pull out the flexible card and put it on the table.

"Good. Ashur will program it for you before you are dropped off and I will send you information that way."

"Yes, sir."

"Were you allowed to disobey your commanders on Earth, Junco?"

"No, sir."

"Will you disobey Ashur?"

I look at Ashur. "No, sir."

"Wonderful. Ashur, you may wait outside."

I let out a giant groan and both heads snap back and show annoyance at my grumbling.

When Ashur is gone Lucan walks over to a terrace on the far end of the room. "Come here, Junco. The meeting is over and you are free to speak."

The doors slide open as we approach and the noise of the city bombards my ears. There are flyers going by at eye level and the city lights are all on now that the afternoon is winding down.

He leans against the balcony railing and so do I, suddenly feeling weary. "Everyone knows who you are now, thanks to that woman on Earth, so you may continue to use the SEAR if the situation requires it."

"Thanks."

"I'm afraid you've misunderstood what the General Fledge is about, though, Junco. You see, you're making a few mistakes and Ashur is worried about how they will affect your chances for success."

I groan again and wait it out.

"You're collecting children? To protect during the battles?"

I shake my head. "That's not exactly true, Lucan. I'm not collecting them, it's just I've grown fond of Isec, and the little girl today – it was just too much. She's just a kid."

"You're not doing them any favors, Junco. Even if those kids make it because of you, they'll be killed in the Aves for not being strong enough. It's futile what you are doing."

I shrug. "I'm not going to stop."

"You'll disobey?"

I look him straight in the eye. "Yeah, I will."

He pauses to see if I'll add anything to that statement, but I don't. "Here's where I think you're getting confused, Junco. You're already an extremely well-trained soldier so you've been taught from an early age, a very early age I've heard, that you're a member of a team. This is what makes a good soldier, you have that cohesive property in you. I get it. If you were in the Aves Fledge, you'd be part of a team, that is a major difference between the General Fledge and the Aves Fledge."

He stops and looks at me until I nod. "OK."

"The General Fledge has no teams, Junco. And you keep insisting on trying to build one out of these throwaways."

"That's not what this is about, Lucan." I lean over and rest my hands on the top rail, then sink my head down on them and close my eyes. "I just can't kill the little ones."

I look up again and study his face, but he's stoic. "And I'm not killing Isec. I'm not."

"Well, this is interesting. Because, you know, we all feel that way about you, Junco. Very protective."

I have to admit, this catches me off guard.

He smiles. "Of course, you're highly qualified, and there's the difference. Tier was correct when he refused to kill you. Because you're the perfect Aves warrior."

I put my head down again.

"These kids will not make it, Junco. They will not."

I stay silent and wait for it.

"However, if it will make you happy, I will have Ashur and the men train them for you."

I look up and smile. "You will?"

"But they will still die, Junco."

I nod.

"And the end will not shift. You will still end up in the same place. Recall that I told you before that the time to change the outcome was past?"

I nod.

"You will still hate me in the end, Junco. But it wasn't me who put you here. It was Tier. And it was you."

"I get the feeling that you know a lot more about what's going on than I do."

"That is the understatement of the millennium. You know nothing. And now," he turns back to the apartment, "this conversation is over. I will send Kush a personal thank you. Goodbye."

The guys are all waiting for me outside and none of them look happy about it. "Finally," Ryse says. I try to catch Braun's eye but he ignores me. They all shuffle out the doors and again, I'm last. I walk out and find Ashur waiting for me around the corner. He lets me pass and then takes up the rear.

We get food to go from the cafeteria and pile in the flyer. I eat whatever it is they hand me and it's not bad. When we finally reach the Fledge building I get out and they close the door and issue half-hearted goodbyes.

And then I am alone.

And for the first time in a very long time, I feel lonely.

I lie down in the grass and look up at the ceiling and puff on a cigar. A little while later I hear wings and turn to see Ashur landing on the sidewalk.

"I forgot to program your com, Junco." He sits down next to me and I hand it over. He hands it back a few minutes later. "Are we good?"

"I guess. I mean, you're the captain, right?"

"That's not how the 039 works, Junco. We're tight. Perfect."

"What do you want me to say? I forgive you? I do. I doubt I've ever had a real moment of privacy in my life. Why should I care about one more person watching me? It's absurd."

He pulls me next to him and wraps me in his wings. "I'm sorry, OK?"

I squirm in his arms but he doesn't let me go. "I was never really mad about you watching me, Ashur. It doesn't matter."

"Then what's your deal, Junco?"

I look up at him. "I'm not in control of *anything*. I mean, yeah, soldiering is something I can do. But no one asked me if I wanted to be a soldier here. Or on Earth for that matter. I get that I have to do the Fledge thing, that's not an option if I want to stay. But don't I ever get a say?"

"I never got a say. Tier never got a say. None of us did."

"Yeah, but maybe I'd rather be a woman than a soldier. Did you guys ever think of that?"

His eyes search mine. "Would you really? Is that why you're sleeping with that Kush guy?"

I laugh. "I'm not sleeping with Kush. Don't be ridiculous."

"There's been reports that you spent last night with him up in the observatory."

"Well, yeah. But I was sleeping. Not fucking him."

He chokes on his laugh. "Junco, soldiers talk like that, not women."

I shrug and chew on a fingernail.

He's silent for a few minutes and I wait patiently. "It's just a job, Junco. And compared to some jobs on this stupid habitat, it's a damn good one. Like I said when you first came out of morph, you can have it made here. You just have to give it a chance and try to follow *some* directions."

This, I think, might be the crux of the problem. "I want to go back to Earth, Ashur. The thought of staying here forever makes me—" I stop and shake my head without finishing.

He hugs me tighter. "I get it. We'll go back, I promise."

"How can you promise that?"

"Because we never finished our job. We still have four Siblings to find. Believe it or not, we spent a lot of time on you. Years, Junco – you and Moju both, actually. You two really sidetracked us big time." He stops and pushes me away, then pulls me up on my feet with him. "When Fledge is over we'll do something else, OK?"

I nod. "OK. Thanks. I'll see you later." There's just nothing good going to come of any of this and there's no room for regrets because I chose this path. It's move forward or die.

Chapter Twenty-One

I don't get more than a few paces inside Fledge before my com beeps. I pull it out of my pocket and stare at the screen. I don't get it. It doesn't say anything, just has some symbol flashing at me. I shove it back in my pocket and start walking towards the stairs when Lucan appears and scares the shit out of me.

"Jasus, Lucan."

"You will ignore my file?"

I stare at him. "What? File?"

He points to my pocket. "The file I just sent you."

I fish the com back out of my pocket and stare at it again. "I don't know how to use this thing. I never had my own com on Earth."

He reaches out and I hand him the com. "Come here and sit, I'll show you."

"I'm tired, Lucan. Can't we do this–"

"Sit."

I take a seat on the bench he's motioning to and he sits next to me, then his fingers move across the com screen and things move and flash and generally do all sorts of stuff. Then a hologram bursts into the air in front of us. Lucan's holographic head is rotating in the air. He's smiling.

I laugh and look over to him.

"What's funny?"

I laugh again. "That fake smile on your fake head."

He ignores me and his fingers begin interacting with the hologram like they were with the com. His head flashes and then eight more heads appear.

"These are my sitting Archers. The most important of which are Rache, the Archer of Justice. And Gib, the Archer of Clutch. Together the three of us run all the worlds in the Band."

"I thought you were the one in charge?"

"I am, but I am not a dictator. I can override them if they disagree with the actions I want sanctioned, but if they gather enough support they can override me." He looks over to me. "That has never happened. We work well as a team."

His finger sweeps around the circle of Archers and then a bazillion more appear, taking up space far out into the room. "There are many Archers and each runs something that keeps our worlds together and each reports to me." He removes the other less important Archers and only he remains. His fingers make Tier appear. "I have not updated this yet. Ashur is here now. The 039 is my personal team to use as I see fit. Each of the eight higher-ranking Archers has a team for this purpose." He taps Tier's head and then the entire 039 appears, including me. We all rotate in a small circle around Tier with a rank above our heads. Ashur, then Ryse, then Braun, Isten, Rikan, Mish, Arel, and me. There's a nine floating above my head.

"Huh."

"You have a question?"

"I just think it's," I stop and choose the correct word, "interesting that you updated my status on that little chain of command, yet you left Tier in place."

He smiles but doesn't address my remark. "You report to Ashur now. And if Ashur is not around you report to me. Or Ryse or your other team members. If you need something you come to one of us. No one else is above you. You cannot command the personal teams of other Archers, but if you command any of the regular military warriors, they will accommodate you, within reason. If they do not, they will have to answer for it. You speak for me."

"That's a lot of power for someone you barely know." I look up at him and study his face.

"Tier gave you a rank of 039-9. I could undo it, but why? I don't see any reason to prohibit your rank. From what I've been told and what I've seen, duty is something you take seriously."

Every time I see Lucan his opinion of me seems to change. Which is funny, because I seem to be revising my opinion of him on a regular basis as well. Do I take my duty seriously? I have no idea to be honest.

His fingers move around once more and then the entire room is filled with avian warriors, they take up space in every direction, piled up to the ceiling, one on top of another. I look through the window and see them stretching far out past the train tracks. "This is my military."

I cannot even begin to think of the number represented by these floating faces. "How many?"

"Fifteen million active warriors. A third of which are based on the other tori below Amelia proper. But they are also spread out in the Band where they are needed. There are millions more. Inactive warriors who have moved on to something else, but are still available if necessary."

"Why?"

"Why what?"

"Do you have such a large military?"

"It is not necessary for you to have that answer right now, Junco, but they represent a very small percentage of our overall population. It is not that unusual. Do you have any more questions?"

"How many avians are there? In all?"

"Billions, Junco."

"Where do you keep them all?"

He smiles. "That is the central issue of these times. Where do we keep them all? The simple answer is we cannot keep them all. This is why we have Fledges. Any more questions?"

I look away. I'm not sure I like where this conversation is headed. "No, I guess not."

The military collapses back into my com and we sit there in silence for a few moments. "I'm sorry this has been hard on you." He stands up and I follow. "I am trying to make it as easy as I can."

I look up at him. "Why? You didn't even want me to stay."

"That's not true at all, Junco." He puts a hand on my shoulder. "Expect Ashur tomorrow. Goodnight."

And then he's gone.

I shake my head to clear things up, but I'm more confused than ever. I walk up the stairs slowly and then change into my bed clothes and fall asleep without speaking to anyone.

Something wakes me. A small sound of feet on tile. I sit up and look around. Isec's bed is empty. Maybe he just went to the bathroom? Another noise out past the lounge area has my feet on the cold tile, covering the distance to the mast in my bed clothes.

I look up and see a flash, high up on the sixth level.

I hesitate because my skills are so raw, but curiosity takes over and my powerful new limbs carry me upward. It's not a snappy ascent, like Kush's was, and it's definitely not pretty or graceful. By the time I get to the fifth level I have to stop and climb up the ragged walls covered in relief art. Ultimately, I find myself swinging out under the sixth-level platform for several seconds before I force myself to let go and flap like mad just to make the landing. I lean against a large wooden door to catch my breath, and then look up. There's a symbol over it that leaves no mistake as to what is contained within.

It's a church.

I lean my weight into the door and it opens in front of me. There's a vestibule with a statue of some presumably important winged person. The door behind me closes with a shush of air and I push through the second one.

And stand there stunned. "Holy fucking shit," actually escapes my mouth as I take in the altar.

"Junco, what are you doing here?"

I whirl around and find Isec plastered up against the far wall. "I saw you."

"You scared me."

I smile at him. "Sorry."

"You're not supposed to swear at the syrinx."

I nod in the direction of the upside-down avian woman hanging on the crucifix at the far end of the church. "That her?"

He nods. "Yeah, you're not—"

"I get it, Isec, sorry. It's just – the whole image, from an Earth religious point of view is just – wrong."

He frowns at me. "Oh, how so?"

"The symbols, they're backwards. It's nothing, just cultural differences, but seeing someone hanging upside down from the crucifix just goes against the grain."

"What's that mean?"

I shake my head. "Wrong, is all."

He walks forward out of the little space filled with avian iconery and chooses a bench about halfway between front and back and takes a seat.

I slip in next to him. "So, what are you doing here?"

"Praying, Junco."

"What do you have to do to make her listen?"

He looks at me funny. "Pray, Junco."

"Oh. Well, does she have special prayers?"

"Yeah, but I'm not wasting my time teaching them to you, so don't ask me. They're printed on the cards in the back. Now leave me alone, I'm busy."

I get up and go back to the little nook he was hiding in and grab some cards, then slump down on the floor and pour through them.

Calm Ion Storms? I chuck the stiff little card at the wall next to me and move on to the next one.

Fledge Protection? Chuck it.

Fearlessness? Chuck it.

Clear Thinking? Chuck.

Acceptance of Fate? I look at the picture for a long time because it's the syrinx on the altar, then flip it over to read the prayer.

Out of the night that covers me,
Black as the pit from pole to pole,
I thank whatever gods may be
For my unconquerable soul.

In the fell clutch of circumstance
I have not winced nor cried aloud.
Under the bludgeonings of chance
My head is bloody, but unbowed.

Beyond this place of wrath and tears
Looms but the Horror of the shade,
And yet the menace of the years
Finds and shall find me unafraid.

It matters not how strait the gate,
How charged with punishments the scroll,
I am the master of my fate:
I am the captain of my soul.

It's a straight ripoff of Henley's Invictus. And yet so unquestionably appropriate it could have been written for me, for this very moment. I look up when Isec approaches.

"Did you find one?"

I breathe out my words. "Yeah. It's a poem from Earth, too. Isn't that weird?"

He smiles. "She sends you what you need, Junco. I'm going back to bed, you coming?"

"Nah, I'll be along in a little bit, OK?"

He nods and leaves me alone.

I get up and go sit down on a bench up front and stare at the sacrificial woman. Her left foot is bound to a vertical wooden post. The horizontal post is situated across the top of the vertical post, so it's more of a T shape than a cross. Her right leg is bent, splayed out behind her. Her arms reach back, touching her outspread wings, and her head is tipped so her eyes look down and not forward, exposing her throat. Her long red hair trails on the ground.

Syrinx.

I search my memory for a meaning and come up with two possibilities:

The voice organ of a bird.

A water nymph in ancient Greece.

I close my eyes and say the prayer out loud from recall. When I'm finished I add my own silent personal touch. *Please let me accept my fate with courage. Let me be brave in the end.*

My vision screen comes to life. *Do you wish to accept the sacrifice?*

I don't understand.

Do you wish, Junco Coot, Aves 039, to accept the sacrifice required to fulfill your prayer?

Who are you?

Is that a no?

Wait. I accept.

The screen blanks out and I have a bad feeling about what I just did. I stuff the card in the waistband of my bed shorts and leave the church, more unsettled than when I came in. I get to the ledge and realize I have to jump if I want to get down. Either that or wait until everyone wakes up and ask someone to come rescue me. I pull out the card and stare at the last part again.

It matters not how strait the gate,

How charged with punishments the scroll,

I am the master of my fate:

I am the captain of my soul.

And I jump, Cygnus-style, into the pit.

Chapter Twenty-Two

"Get up now!"

Ashur's voice booms in my ears and I jump up with a start.

But he's not talking to me, he's talking to them.

Isten sits on my bed and pushes me back down. "Not you, Junco, you're with me today."

I watch as Isec is dragged up and pushed over next to the little girl. The tall girl I almost killed in the last fight is in line, as is the guy who reminds me of Tier and his friend who asked if I was a soldier.

Ashur is screaming at them from the front while Ryse, Arel, Mish, and Rikan lean in from behind to add choice words. The little kids stand there looking like they will piss themselves at any second. Ashur comes to Kush, who yawns with his eyes closed, and then pivots without saying anything and goes back to screaming at Isec and the little girl who has given up her name between sobs.

Kete.

"You are nothing! Nothing, do you understand?" He bends down to Isec and Kete and they step back with a start, but Rikan pushes them forward.

I make to get up, but Isten pushes down on my chest. "You wanted this, Junco. Now butt the fuck out."

"Isec," Ashur growls, "when you understand that your only reason for living right now is to make my nine happy, we'll get along and be just fine. Do you understand that?"

Isec, to his credit, looks up and meets his gaze. "Yes, sir."

"If you live through this Fledge and she doesn't – I'll kill you in your sleep. Do you understand?"

Isec swallows and nods.

"Your only purpose in life right now is to hope you have a chance to give up your worthless life for her promising one. Do you understand?"

"Yes, sir."

He moves on to Kete, who breaks down and cries. "You'll be the next one to die if you don't stop that fucking crying. You think I'm your clutch mother, Kete?"

She can't answer and Ashur moves on to the tall girl.

"What's your name and excuse for being here, girl?"

She takes a large gulp of air. "Tessen, sir. I quit my Cluster."

Ashur scowls at her. "You quit? You're a quitter? I hate quitters. Junco's not a quitter, she talked the fucking President into making the 039 train you, you sorry excuse for a soul. If you quit on me…" He extracts his razors and they are as long as short swords. "I'll take you out to a docking bay and throw you into oblivion. Am I clear?"

Tessen nods. "Yes, sir."

He moves on to the boy who asked me if I was a soldier yesterday. He's older, not as old as Kush, but Ashur passes him by after getting his name, Joll.

The last boy is Wyrd and Ashur leans down into his face. "I don't think I like you, Wyrd. You look like you think you can take me. Can you take me, Wyrd?"

Wyrd squints his eyes. "No, sir. I don't think that *at all.*"

Ashur paces back the other way and Kete starts to cry again. He stops in front of her, and then looks over to me and his voice is back to normal. "Junco, sorry – I'm gonna go out on a limb here and predict this one will not make it."

He moves on to Isec. "I'd pick you to die as well, Isec. But since Junco always puts you first, she'll save your ass yet again."

He moves on to Kush. "You're the only one I'd take home."

He tracks back to Tessen. "You'd do if no one else was available." She looks at him and smiles, but he cuts her down. "That's not a compliment, Tessen."

He walks all the way back to Wyrd. "You come from Science?" Wyrd looks at him and nods. "We'd keep you for that and that only, then. But it's not a bad job, if you can get it."

He tracks back to Joll. "I don't see it in you, to be honest. Have you killed anyone in these fights, Joll?" Joll's eyes go wide and he shakes his head. "Well, at least you didn't lie."

Ashur walks over to my bed and rolls his eyes when the others can't see. "Is this it, then, Junco? Your team?"

I shrug. "Thank you."

He pulls me up from the bed and gives me a hug and leans down to whisper in my ear, "We're good now, right? You'll love us again if we do this?"

I push back and look up at him. "We're perfect."

Ashur looks to Ryse. "Take them up to training while I talk to Isten and Junco."

The screaming begins anew and then they are gone.

Ash sits down on the bed and he pulls me between him and Isten. "OK, Junco – you're gonna fly up and down the mast today with Isten. Things get vertical from here and you'll need new skills for the rest of the fights." He leans past me to see Isten. "Make her walk around in the observatory, Is. That will probably help with Fight Four, don't you think?"

Isten nods. "Yeah, I'll make it relevant."

Ashur looks back to me. "And don't fuck about, Junco. The levels are nothing like you've had or think they will be, so don't get complacent. Besides, if you die I'll have to kill all those pledges, and we wouldn't want that, would we?"

I smile. "I owe you. I know this is purely for my benefit."

Ash's face softens. "I get it, Junco. You have a big heart for someone who has probably killed more people than Is and me together. Just don't expect them to actually live, OK?"

I nod.

"Except for Kush. He might make it."

My eyebrows go up. "Really?"

He shrugs. "I think so, yeah."

And then he kisses me on the head and walks out.

I look over at Isten and my face gets hot. "He likes you, Junco. Whatever you said to him last night after we dropped you off," he hesitates and shakes his head, "made him *very* fucking happy."

I track back to find what it might be as I dress in my uniform. But only one thing stands out.

I didn't sleep with Kush.

Isten and I spend the entire day in the mast. At first I can barely manage it. Oh, it's not bad going from level three to level four. Or even level four to level five. But the span of space between five and six is just as enormous today as it was last night. I end up clinging to an aging architectural detail on the side of the wall before Isten comes to my rescue. This happens several times, actually. Then the flight from six to seven feels insurmountable and he has to tow me up in the light G to even make it to the observatory the first time. I can only imagine the horror inside these massive levels to require such vertical expansion.

And then he makes me fly down in a dive that reminds me of ancient dogfights. The first time Isten has to grab my uniform shirt and yank me back up to him so I don't splat on the hard stone floor. He makes me glide down slowly after that.

From the bottom we start the process all over again and I struggle back up, gradually with each assent I manage to go a little further. But in no way would I ever be considered an expert flier.

We're resting on the platform underneath the observatory when Isten catches me eyeing the church. "You want to go in there or what, Junco? You've been staring at the place the whole day."

I soar down to the sixth-level platform and land clumsily in front of the large door. I wait there until Isten reluctantly follows. "I went in last night." I wait to see his reaction, but he holds it in. "I prayed to her."

Isten laughs. "She's not real, Junco."

I shrug. "I found these prayer cards in the back, right? And the one I chose was called *Acceptance of Fate*." I look up at him. "It was an old Earth poem. Don't you think that's weird?"

He shakes his head. "So they stole some poetry from Earth? That sounds typical to me."

"I was raised in church, did you know that?"

He smiles. "Yeah, I know. But this isn't your religion anyway, so don't waste your time. This is some really old-ass shit, Junco. Before Crage and Inanna, before all the Seven Siblings. She's ancient – something else entirely."

"So why does she have a church here?"

He steps off the ledge and flies upward to the observatory before calling back to me, "Who cares? Let's go practice walking in the gravity curve."

I flap frantically to make up to the top one more time, but no matter how hard I try Isten has to push me the remaining hundred yards. I step onto the landing and we climb the steps together.

Chapter Twenty-Three

I don't close my eyes when we enter and I'm immediately sorry because this shit is just wrong. I can't tell what is up and what is down and my head begins to spin.

"Close your eyes, Junco." I do and things calm down. My feet float up off the ground and I feel my stomach lurch. "Keep them closed, then when you're ready open them and decide where is up and where is down, OK?"

I nod.

"There are couches all around us."

"I know."

"Oh, I forgot you spent the night with Kush up here."

I huff out some air. "I did not sleep with Kush, Isten. Fuck, you guys think I sleep with everyone."

He laughs. "Not true. Anyway, just pick a couch and then I'll follow you."

I open my eyes and choose up, then use my wings to adjust my body a little and pick a new up. I head for a couch and stand next to it.

Isten comes up next to me and pushes me back and then gravity takes hold and I'm lying down, not standing.

It's still weird.

He climbs in next to me. "You know what this place is for, Junco?"

I shake my head. "Well, I'd guess it's to look at the stars, but something tells me that's not right."

He lets out a little laugh. "Technically, of course it is to look at the stars, but Fledge is filled with superstitions and the observatory is one of them. People come up here to be reminded about how little they matter in the universe."

"That's dumb."

"Just listen. You're supposed to come up here with someone you love, which is why we jumped to conclusions with Kush. Anyway, you're supposed to cling to each other and tell each other stories about your life. Did he tell you stories, Junco?"

I shake my head. "No, we fell asleep."

"Oh, well, he blew it. But I'm not gonna." He pulls me close. "I fully intend on telling you stories."

I laugh. "Yeah, like what? Not a myth, I hope." I look up at him questioningly.

"No, my first kill."

"Oh."

"I can't get the image of you out of my mind, Junco. Six years old and being sent on missions like that."

"So how old were you?"

He smiles down at me. "Eight."

"That's pretty young too."

"Yeah, but I wasn't told to do it, I just lost my temper."

"At eight? You lost your temper and killed someone?"

"I was on Earth with my foster family. They send us at five, you know that right?"

I nod. "Tier told me about his."

Isten sits up a little at this. "Really?"

I nod. "It was the quick version, he said."

He's silent for a few moments, like I caught him off guard. "Well, I wasn't supposed to be killing anyone, I was just supposed to live with this family until I got called back. Usually it takes about ten years before they want you back to Fledge. But I saw something and when I tried to tell someone about it, you know, to make it stop, they didn't believe me."

"What did you see?"

"My foster brother molesting my little sister."

"Oh, shit."

"Yeah, so I followed him one day and took a rifle with me. My family had guns all over the house, ya know. This was Texas. Anyway, I followed him out to this pasture where he was fucking around with another girl, his own age this time at least, and I shot him in the head while they were getting it on. I got away with it too, on Earth anyway. Hid in the bushes, the girl never saw me, got home before anyone noticed, cleaned the gun, put it back. It was pretty fucking simple. But I confessed in my next report and they pulled me. Called me home to Fledge out early."

"Well, I'd be proud of that kill, Isten. At least you helped someone."

He looks over me and grins. "Do you know who you killed that day on the slopes, Junco?"

I shake my head. "No, I never did ask."

"Well, we looked it up after you told us that. And it was the President and First Lady of Sovienna. They were some fucked-up people, so if that memory ever gives you nightmares, well, I can show you what they did to children for decades before you showed up and put a stop to it."

"Hmm. I don't have nightmares anymore, Isten. They're all gone."

"That's great, Juncs. But if they ever come back, you gotta ask yourself if it's worth it, right? Because from what I can tell, you killed a lot of very bad people over your career."

I lean into him a little.

"Anyway, when I got back to Amelia they put me in a holding status, because you can't go out in the regular population until you Fledge, you have to stay in the clutch. But it just so happens that there were like sixty other guys in the hold with me. All guys who had fucked up their fosters for whatever reason for another. It was like an epidemic that year, they checked the food supply and all kinds of things even, that's how weird it was.

"So, they had to have a special Fledge to make room – we call it the Fuck-up Fledge. I was in the Fuck-up Fledge and so was everyone else in the 039. Tier, for killing his father. Ashur for killing a teacher at school. They were the oldest and most experienced." He laughs. "They were both twelve."

"So you all Fledged out together? And you all survived it?"

"Well, we didn't know each other at first. When we got to 313–"

"What's 313?"

"Oh, it's the asteroid that hosts the Aves Warrior Fledge. It's got like half an atmosphere, after a thousand years of terraforming if you can believe it, but very thin. You have to wear suits or you'll die within hours."

"Did you have to kill each other?"

He looks down on me. "Nah, Juncs. We have to work as a team, to survive the shit on 313. Poisons, weather patterns, orbital fire – shit like that."

"And you all, the 039, were all on the same team?"

"No, see, this is how it works. They airdrop us all off – like I said, there were sixty of us or so. Then you have to get from one end of the asteroid to the other before your air and supplies wear out. So, when you get there you're not a team, right? Just a bunch of guys. But if you make it to the end, the guys you make it with – that's your team. The conditions create the winners, get it? Create the team."

I nod.

"And we were the ones who lived. Me, Arel, Ryse, Rikan, Braun, Mish, Ashur, and Tier. That was it. Out of sixty guys. We were the only ones left."

"And how did Tier become captain?"

Isten smiles. "He's the strongest, the most ruthless, the smartest. And the most reasonable, caring, and hopeful. He's the perfect fucking Aves warrior, Junco – they were talking about making him Archer. So they gave him the command. He saved every one of us during Fledge. We owe him every second of life we've lived since we were kids."

"And you'll just let him be killed, Isten?"

He frowns. "We're doing what we can."

"It's not enough."

"Maybe not, but that's what we've got." He stays silent for a few minutes, perhaps he's mad at me for questioning him. Or maybe he's just thinking. Eventually he gets back around to our conversation. "You know why Lucan didn't send you to the Aves Warrior Fledge even though it started at the same time?"

I shake my head.

Isten pushes me back a little so he can see my face. "Because, Junco, if you went through all that shit with another group of guys, you wouldn't belong to us anymore. You'd belong to them. You'd make your own team and not be part of our team. And Lucan couldn't stand to let you go. He said that, Junco. To each of us. That's why we're worried about these kids you're helping. It's not supposed to be this way. There are no teams in the General Fledge. You're not supposed to bond with them. You're *our* nine. You understand what it means to be the nine?"

I shake my head. "No."

"The team hardly ever gets to nine. I mean, it does happen, but it's so rare, no one even thinks about having nine – not including your science contact, right? Layla is our science contact, but she's not a part of the team because that only includes us warriors. To have a real ninth member is special. It's powerful. It carries a lot of meaning around here. And you're the nine. We voted you in and even Lucan agreed."

"Only as long as we include Tier, and he's gonna be found guilty, I'm told. For not killing me. And Lucan will let him die."

"He's doing what he can, Juncs. He really is."

"Tier hates what he is, you know that right?"

Isten is quiet now.

"He told me, quote, *I feel like I've lived a hundred lifetimes of misery. And when I wake up each morning I don't want to keep doing it, Junco. When I wake I ask myself, how much longer before they will just let me die?* Unquote."

"But, Junco, he saved you because he wanted you. He wanted you to be with us. We talked about it for years. You can't even comprehend how much planning went into making the decision to disobey and get you here."

"Except Tier will not be here so I won't be the nine for long, will I? That's pure bullshit, Isten. Just let me do it my way."

He sucks in his breath. "Junco, do you have any idea of the cost?" He looks at me, the fun gone, the pain in full force. "It's higher than you might think. It's higher than anything you can imagine. And don't fucking pray to that stupid Fallen Archer again, either. For fuck's sake, that's all we need, her sacrificial spirit fucking things up at the very last fucking second."

When we fly back down the pledges are already back in the dorm and Ashur is watching the screens, waiting patiently. Isten says goodbye and leaves, while I go sit down next to Ash. "How'd it go?"

He smiles. "You first."

"Pretty good, I guess. My flying will not win trophies, but it'll have to do." I smile back, but my heart's not in it.

"They did OK, Junco. Kush is pretty good and Wyrd is all right. The girl, Tessen, could be helpful. But that little Kete, she won't be back tomorrow night." He looks at me hard. "And I do not want you to save her, you understand?"

I nod. "What about Joll?"

"Oh, shit. That kid is beyond useless. I have no idea how he survived so far."

We sit in silence for a while, watching some movie on the screen. Ashur must like horror shit, because it's another screaming half-naked girl running from some crazy demonic thing.

"You wanna go get some food, Junco?" He looks over at me, his face kind.

"Sure." I smile. "We can do that."

We grab a train back to that pub we were at before and it's like our fight never happened. We eat and talk about stuff that has nothing to do with Tier, or the Fledge, or death.

And it's nice.

Normal.

Chapter Twenty-Four

There are no patterns on the floor this time. Instead the Fourth Fight begins with all seventy-five of us being stuffed, one at a time, inside capsules. When someone gets in the lid slides shut and the capsule is shuttled somewhere out of sight. I look at Isec to see how he's taking it, but he's calm. Calmer than I've ever seen him in fact. I squeeze his shoulder as we wait our turn. "You doing OK?"

He smiles back at me. "Yeah, sure. Why?"

I shrug. "Well, usually you're freaking out. And this is completely different from all the other starts."

"I feel good, Junco. No matter what happens, I'm OK with it."

I nod. "All right." He turns away from me and I let out a sigh. They grow up so fast. I have a feeling Ashur has something to do with this, but whatever it is, I'm grateful. He's come to terms with the fights, and that's a good thing.

I think.

Kete is first to be stuffed in the capsule. She's screaming like the spring wind on the prairie. I don't move to calm her. I believe Ashur, she's done and there's no sense in making it worse.

Tessen is next and she gets in without incident.

Isec is next and he turns. "See you when we're done, Junco."

I smile. "Fight hard, friend."

He climbs in and lies back and before I know it he's shuttled up and out of view.

My capsule comes and I climb in, settle on the hard pad, and watch the capsule close above me. It moves fast and jerks from side to side. The capsule stops and is loaded into some mechanism below. Then I hear a loud click and everything goes still, the only sound my own breathing.

We were near the front, so the wait takes forever.

And then I'm accelerating hard. I feel the bullet catch on something below my back and my feet slam into the floor of the capsule and I'm shunted out of the tube and into free-G. I twist in the air and create back thrust with my wings to slow myself down. I hear screams as people smash into the wall and then the smell of burning flesh.

They've been electrocuted.

For a moment I'm stunned still, and then I see her. Dead, her mouth open, her eyes wide, and she's wet herself. Kete is finished before the fight even starts.

I snap out of it and begin killing as I pass through the air. I leave the SEAR tucked away. No sense in complicating things unless I have to. Enough people are dead from the launch.

I swim though the air and take stock of what's happening here.

There is a single transparent partition that divides the arena into left and right halves. Except it is better described as top and bottom. Except that doesn't work either, because the gravity well is on the surface of the partition. Towards the floor, except the floor is relative.

It's a mirror image.

I swim down to my floor and get my feet planted on the ground. Only one other fighter has made it so far so I charge towards him as he shouts encouragement to a friend. I swipe my razors over his throat and he falls dead just as his buddy is floating down towards me. I grab him by the leg and swing. He goes careening off and hits the wall, the electricity surges though him and his body sends off sparks in all directions.

I hear screaming and look down to the other side of the partition. I see Isec fighting for his life, his small razors slashing and to my delight, hitting their mark. He looks good and I smile.

A girl comes at me hard from above and knocks me down. I scramble up before she can get the gravity under control and kick her in the face, my talons clawing her skin off as they pass through her flesh. I walk towards her as she flails half in and half out of the full force of the well. She screams at me to leave her alone.

"Honey, you picked the wrong girl to attack if you're looking for mercy." I pull her by the foot and she tries to kick me. I bring her down to the ground and twist her neck and then fling her up and let her float away.

I run over to the edge of the partition and do a handspring and fling myself over the other side, grabbing at the floor so I don't drift off, then bring myself upright. This side fared much better in the initial launch and they have a lot fewer casualties. A big guy rushes at me immediately, but Tessen is there and she grabs him by the throat and digs in her claws. He's choking when we kick him off and point him at the wall.

I see Isec, still fighting off kids twice his size, and Tessen and I launch upward, swim across, then flap like demons and launch ourselves at his attackers. They go down. I grab the nearest boy and stomp on his mouth and watch the blood spurt out, then swipe my razors over his throat to end it quickly.

Isec comes and stands next to me and Tessen and we just watch. We are alone on the floor. Even when we look below our feet, there is no one there.

They never even understood what it was.

So we stand there like spectators.

Whole minutes go by before the buzzer goes off and we are floating, then swimming, over to the exits. This time I don't hesitate, I jump off the fourth floor and sail down to the dorms. Tessen, Isec, and I wait in the lounge to see who makes it.

We laugh hysterically when we count up the living and find only Kete is missing.

Ashur really did his job with these guys because it only takes seconds and we barely remember who she was.

Ashur shows up sometime that afternoon when I am sleeping on my bunk. He nudges me awake and then slips in next to me. I smile at his good mood.

"Just Kete, then?"

I nod and he's happy. "You did a great job, Ashur. It was amazing."

He sighs. "Let's go somewhere, Junco."

"Where?"

"The city. Wanna go to the city with me?"

"Am I allowed?"

"I'm your captain, remember? I make your rules. Only Lucan can tell you no above me."

"Will Lucan care if we go to the city?" I study his face to see what he's up to, but he just flashes me a smile.

"He told me to take you out, Junco."

"Really?"

He picks up a bag from the floor and hands it to me. "No uniform for you. Tonight you're not a soldier."

I hold my breath at his comment and feel something.

"You OK?"

I nod as I exhale. "Yeah. It's just – thank you for that, Ashur."

He shrugs. "It was completely inappropriate for Lucan to say that about you being a better soldier, Junco. And when I told him you said maybe you'd rather just be a woman, well, you really know how to pull his strings because he fell all over himself to try and clarify. I said he should take you out and treat you nice, but he said it would make things weird. So, apparently, me taking you out isn't weird."

I look at him sideways. "Well, it sort of is."

"Yeah, it is, but I don't care. Go get dressed." He pushes me until I fall off the bed and then he kicks me away with his boot.

I practically rip the bag open in the dressing room. Inside is a card from Layla. The clothes are tailored to my uniform specs, so they should fit perfectly. I am relieved to see that they are not fancy. If I had to wear a dress in front of Ashur all night I'd be too embarrassed to have fun. But Layla has made me a pair of jeans, a fitted black jacket with a thick belt that cinches my waist, and a pair of knee-high black boots.

It's pretty perfect for being picked out for me on a foreign world. She's right too, once I figure out how to get the jacket to seam up they are the best-fitting clothes I've ever worn. Besides the uniform, of course. There's some make-up in the bag so I paint a little bit on. I'm not usually a make-up girl, but fuck it. I might as well make the most of it.

Tessen comes in when I'm brushing my hair. "What's going on, Junco?"

I smile. "Ashur's taking me out to the city tonight."

"Ohhh, what I'd give to have a date tonight. You have no idea."

I laugh. "It's not really a date, Tess. It's Ashur."

She raises her eyebrows at me. "Uh-huh. Ashur is a man, Junco. Men who show up with bags of custom-tailored clothes to take you out just to make you happy consider it a date."

I shrug. "I don't care. I'm excited even if he does think that."

She smiles as I brush my hair. "Have twice as much fun as normal, Junco. And bring some back for me."

I walk back out to the dorm and Ashur is waiting by the door. "Shit, Junco — took you long enough." But he smiles and takes my hand to twirl me around. "You're very pretty."

"You're supposed to keep that shit inside, Ash."

He shakes his head. "Not tonight."

We walk outside and Lucan's flyer is waiting. Ashur opens the door and I slide in. He takes the seat across from me and smiles. "How about dinner first?"

I nod. "Yeah, sounds great."

He opens the partition between us and the driver and gives him a location and then turns back to me. "So, I know you were with Charlie, Junco. But when's the last time you went out? Like a normal nineteen-year-old girl?"

I shake my head. "I've been on some dates and I've had boyfriends. But that was all field stuff, really. Just messing around on scrubs maneuvers or after patrols. If you want to know the last time I went out like other girls, then that would be never."

He screws up his face. "Last time at a bar?"

I shake my head again. "Besides the pub here with you? Never."

"You never went to a bar on Earth?"

"No, I wasn't old enough."

He laughs so hard he almost chokes. "Wait, so you're old enough to assassinate world leaders at six, but you can't go to a bar when you're nineteen?"

I sigh. "Yup, that's pretty much it. Besides, the RR doesn't have bars. I'd have to go to Peak City and I only went there when my father took me."

He looks serious. "I guess I never realized that, Junco. How much you've missed out on. Shit, no wonder you're wondering if there's something better out there."

"I thought you watched everything I did?"

"We never watched your personal life, not really. I mean, when all that shit went down with Charlie it was pretty hard not to take a closer look, but other than that I never paid attention to what you were doing in your free time."

"That's because I never had free time, Ashur."

He looks away. "Yeah. I guess not. Except for the horses. And neither Tier nor I liked to watch that shit."

I smile and think of Tier in the barn with me back on Earth. "You should have seen his face when I practiced in front of him."

Ashur watches me smile and it's contagious. "We all watched you do that last contest on the newscreens, where was that – Asia?"

"Japan, yeah."

"I thought Arel was gonna have a heart attack." He laughs out loud now. "He couldn't sit down and every time you flipped in the air he jumped, like a fucking little old lady worrying about her kittens or something."

I laugh. "I took first place."

He nods. "I know, Junco. You were fabulous as usual."

I feel my face go red and my heart starts to race. *Shit.*

"Don't get nervous, Junco." He watches me struggle. "It's just me."

"I know, but that's why I'm getting nervous." I take a deep breath and let it out. "It would be very easy to mess this all up, ya know?"

"Relax, we're just gonna have a night out, OK? Sometimes I have to remind myself that a couple weeks ago I was a complete stranger to you. But for me, Junco, you've been a constant in my life for a very long time. I know it's not fair, and I know that probably bugs you, but that's just how it is. So, if I make you uncomfortable, just say so. I'll back off."

I nod and scoot over to the window to look out. "OK."

He scoots over to the window too and starts pointing things out below. It eases some of my nerves.

"It's kind of funny though, if you think about it."

"What's that?" I ask, looking over to him.

"That complimenting you makes you all flustered, but if I were to try and kill you right now, your heartbeat would barely register."

"Yeah, well, I've had many years of practice, Ashur. So many that I'll probably never be normal."

"Is that what you want? To be normal?"

I shrug. "It was hard not to think about it back on Earth. I was in the RR, after all, where women pretty much just get married and have babies." I look up at him. "Having a life like that was normal – but having a life like mine never was. Here, I have no idea what's normal. But I can tell that you don't have a lot of girls in the warriors, do you?"

He shakes his head. "You're the only one."

My eyes absorb the little details of Lucan's flyer as I think about this for a few seconds. "I was wondering about that."

"Does it bother you? Being the first and only?"

"It really does."

"How come?"

"Because it turns me into a symbol that I don't want to be. I just want to fit in and be like everyone else. And if I'm the only girl in the warriors then I'll never fit in. I might rather be a wife than that, to be honest."

He sits back in surprise. "What?"

"I know what you're thinking. But, like I said the other night, Ashur, I never picked this soldiering stuff. And I realize that I'm not even a regular person – whatever the definition of that is, I'm not it. But inside I feel like I should have the chances that other girls have. Not to be forced to kill people all the time just because I can. And I don't even know if it's possible to change at this point anyway, but all that shit with Charlie made me think about what I might be giving up. I wanted that baby, Ashur. I was gonna keep it."

"What baby?"

I stare up at him and realize my mistake.

"What baby, Junco?"

I shake my head. "Shit, I thought Tier told you everything?"

"What *baby*, Junco?"

"I was pregnant, Ashur. My father dosed me with an ionspray to get rid of it." I watch him stare at me open-mouthed and then I look out the window at the lights as my face gets hot and my eyes begin to water. I count my heartbeats to get myself under control. "That's why things got a little weird with me those last few months on Earth. I was–" I stop and search for the words, my eyes squinting.

"Not thinking clearly. I was maybe even a little bit insane."
I look back and him and wait.

"Do you want to quit?" His eyes search me. "The truth, Junco."

"The truth is no, Ashur. I don't want to quit. I just want to feel like I'm the one who made the choice. I'm good at what I do. And I want more than anything to be near you guys, it feels so – necessary. Besides, quitting is even scarier than losing out on being normal."

He shakes his head and squints down at me. "Why?"

"Because I don't know how to do this stuff." I spread my arms wide at the flyer and my clothes. "I don't know how to go out and have dinner. Or relax. Ashur, I couldn't define a normal nineteen-year-old girl if my life depended on it. And maybe back on Earth there was the possibility of a life as a mother or a wife, or something besides a soldier. But I'm pretty sure that possibility is gone now." I watch him struggle with my words and he's silent for a few minutes as he looks out the window. "I just want the opportunity to make the decision, Ashur. That's all."

He takes a deep breath. "Are you hungry?" he asks, finally turning back to me.

"No, not really."

"Would you rather go for a walk?"

"Yeah, I would."

He gives new instructions to the driver and we stop on the ground level of Amelia proper and lie down in the grass. I spend the next hour looking up at the city tucked inside Ashur's wing and for the first time since I've been on this stupid habitat, I don't miss the stars.

Chapter Twenty-Five

I wake with a start to Ashur screaming at my team again, but Ryse shushes me back down into the blankets when I try and sit up. "Not you, Junco. You're with me today. You can go back to sleep if you're tired."

I let out a small laugh. "I'm not breakable, Ryse. So whatever Ashur told you guys about last night, don't fucking treat me like that."

He leans over me and I open my eyes. "Everyone is breakable, Junco. So shut the fuck up and go back to sleep. I only got two hours of it myself, so I'm fucking tired, got it?"

"Mmmmhhhhmmm. Got it."

"And when we're done sleeping, we're gonna go have some fucking breakfast. And then, we might even go watch a fucking screen just because I'm your XO and I can make you come with me."

I smile as I drift back off. *It would be so easy to love them.*

A few hours later I'm done sleeping and Ryse is watching the screen in the lounge. I pad over to him and plop down on the couch. There's a reporter on screen covering a ceremony. On stage are about two dozen girls dressed in Aves uniforms and they are being congratulated on their new promotions to warrior status.

I laugh. "Who did this?"

Ryse looks over to me. "Lucan, who else?"

"Why?"

He stares at me for a few seconds, his normally brown eyes glowing a little orange. I don't know Ryse all that well. He's not fun and boisterous like Braun, or serious and caring like Isten. Or even possessive and overbearing like Ashur. He's more aloof. More detached from me, like he hasn't made up his mind yet.

"Because, Junco, if you don't want to be the first, then fuck it. It's an easy fix, right? Just promote some girls and poof, that problem is solved. You'll never have to think about it again."

I nod and pull my legs up to my chest. "That was pretty nice."

He smiles at me, maybe for the first time ever. "We thought we knew everything there was to know about you, Juncs, but it turns out you've kept a lot of secrets."

I get up to go take a shower but Ryse calls back after me, "There's a bag of clothes next to your bed. No uniform today. Wouldn't want to steal the limelight from the new kids."

After breakfast we spend the day generally fucking around. He takes me to the zoo, which is populated with Earth animals, so I've seen them all, and then we go to the screens and see a movie. Not horror, thank God, but some action-drama thing that also runs on Earth.

Afterward we're walking along a path in a park looking at a small pond filled with familiar fish. "Do you guys have anything here that is pure avian? Like not something we have on Earth?"

Ryse stops and rubs his unshaven chin for a moment. "You do realize we're from Earth, right, Junco? We're not real aliens."

"Well, the Seven Siblings myth said–"

He cuts me off. "It's not really a myth, Juncs. It's mostly true."

"Which parts?"

"Well, the genetic engineering stuff, the fucked-up bloodlines, the part where they were cast out–"

"You're full of shit, Tier said it was a myth. Both versions."

He shrugs. "Tier's got his opinions. I've got mine."

I just stare at him. "So where do I fit in?"

"You want to see where you fit it?"

I nod as he pulls out his com. "Give me a minute." He walks away talking and I turn around and look back at the fish in the pond.

... Down below the water you can see the scales of brightly colored fish reflecting the sunlight...

"Nice, aren't they?"

I look up at the new voice. He's tall and fair with a mess of hair that looks like he's been in a wind tunnel. He smiles down at the water. "The fish?"

I look back at the fish. "Yeah, they're nice."

"I'm Kadian." He puts out his hand to shake and I stare at it, confused.

"Sorry, I thought you were–"

"Juncs!" I look over at Ryse who's trying to talk to me and the com at the same time. "Get the fuck away from that guy, he's a reporter."

I look back at Kadian and shake his hand. "Junco. Since you must already know, there's no point in being rude." I turn to walk back over to Ryse, who is occupied with his other conversation, but Kadian puts his hand on my shoulder and I pause and then turn back.

"Wait, you're her, then? Really?"

I look into his eye at a small red blotch and realize he's recording this. "If you're asking if I'm Junco, then yes. I said I was."

He smiles. "How's Fledge going?"

"Still alive, Kadian."

Ryse is in his face and Kadian goes flying backwards and lands hard on the ground. "Back off, Kadian." Lucan appears and he and Ryse shuffle me away from the stunned reporter. I look back and mouth the word "sorry" as Lucan touches my shoulder and we disappear.

And reappear in a corridor that looks a lot like the one where my lab was just after morph. "Junco," Ryse explains, "reporters are reporters, no matter where you are. He's not a nice guy, and he spies on us all the fucking time. Don't talk to him."

I look up at Lucan. "Is this an order?"

Lucan just shakes his head. "I don't care who you talk to, Junco. But if Ryse says no, then it's no."

"Whatever."

"Are you interested in your part in the myth or aren't you? I'm busy, so if you're just going to pout about Ryse's heavy hand, we'll do it another time."

"No, I'm interested, really."

He smiles and steps over to a door. It opens and he waves me in.

It's a very busy lab, with screens from floor to ceiling filled with genetic profiles, data, charts, and a lot of molecular biology. Models of protein structures and crystals. Stuff I've seen from school, but never actually worked with myself.

There are at least two dozen white coats milling around at various stations, some working on screens, some talking in groups, and some I can see through a window that looks into another lab.

Lucan waits for me to take it all in and in the meantime work seems to come to a halt as everyone turns to look at me. I look up at Ryse. "What's going on?"

Lucan places a hand on my shoulder and guides me down a half-flight of stairs and over to a conference room. We enter, but the wall facing the lab is a window, so I continue to watch the activity after the door closes behind us.

"Have a seat, Junco, I have a story to tell you."

I make a face. "I don't like the stories, Lucan."

"Yes, well, this one is true."

I position myself so I can watch the lab as we talk and Ryse sits on the table next to me, while Lucan has his back to the window. "Layla has told you, correctly, that you are a product of the genetics obtained from the missing Aves plant, Gyr?"

I nod.

"That is not true for the other avian siblings. They do not come from Gyr, only you do."

"Oh, does it matter?"

"Not to you it doesn't, because it takes you out of what we do here. We aren't interested in Gyr's genetics, we're interested in the genetics of the six remaining pure avians. Esta, for example. And Moju. The four we have yet to find."

"Oh."

"And the reason is because those genetics are ancient. In fact, they pre-date the time of flight."

I nod. "Uh-huh. OK, well, I don't get it."

"They represent our true genome. Unaltered by generations of engineering and pure as it was before we left Earth."

I shake my head. "Pretend I'm obtuse, Lucan, and just spell it out, OK?"

"We need that code. In fact, we must have it to make changes or we will not survive as a species."

"Well, you have Esta, isn't she enough?"

Lucan's face is serious. "She is not enough, Junco. We need all six or the code makes no sense. It's hidden, you see, wrapped up and inaccessible."

"So why do I care? I mean, not to be a bitch or anything, but what does this have to do with me if my code doesn't matter?"

"You could help us, Junco. Get these siblings to come home."

"Right."

"This is important, Junco. Which is why I took time out of my day to bring you here and show you just how many people are working on this problem. The Six have one job, to keep the genetic code. But the Seventh also has a job, and that's to keep the Six…" He stops for a second. "You could call it safe, or just in line, or maybe act as a shepherd. The translations are – muddied. But the Seventh does have a job."

"If I'm so important, then why did you want to kill me on Earth?"

He looks away and for a few heartbeats I figure he's not gonna answer. I look over at Ryse and he shrugs.

Lucan clears his throat. "Junco, I was wrong about you. You were a very difficult mission for Tier and the team. It was too long, they had too much freedom, they quite frankly spent far too much time on you. It changed them. You changed them."

I raise my eyebrows. "And?"

"And we thought that even if you were the Seventh, we could do without you. You were a lot of trouble for the part you were to play."

"So, you don't need me."

He smiles. "We do need you."

I stand up and walk over to the window to take another look. "How much time before you have to have the code?" I glance back at them. "I mean, it's not critical or anything, you guys all look normal to me."

Lucan gets up and walks over to me as I turn to watch the white-coats. "It is extremely critical, Junco. Our children are not surviving."

I spin around, furious. "Well, for fuck's sake, Lucan! Why the fuck do you kill them all off then? You could just let them live!"

"They are *damaged*, Junco. It's been happening for many generations now, and we are not able to obtain the same quality of individual as is necessary to ensure our survival. We cannot afford to allow the code to be further diluted. We stopped the clutches seven years ago. There are no children younger than seven at this very moment."

"Oh." I turn away again. "Well, that's pretty fucked up." I watch a bustle of activity in the lab for a few minutes as someone calls up a 3D protein model up on the large central holotable and a small group of scientists stand around pointing to it. Finally I shrug and turn back. "Of course I'll help. Why wouldn't I? Is there a reason they wouldn't want to come here? I mean, you're not going to mutilate or dissect them or anything, are you?"

He laughs a little and I realize that he doesn't do that often. "No, we would not mutilate or dissect them. But we've not had a lot of success convincing Moju."

"Well, shit, you better try to get him quick, there's no telling what Aren's done to him by now."

Lucan shakes his head. "You were correct in your prediction about that, Junco. Moju escaped shortly after and has been on a rather extensive killing spree ever since."

I smile. "Oh, well. Good for him. I knew he'd be fine if I stayed."

"But he might come back if you convinced him."

I shake my head. "I'm not so sure. Tier says he's wild. Besides, I never had any control over him, that was all Tier. Moju acted like he hated him but when the time came he followed his orders." An image of Moju saluting Tier in the hallway of the tunnels pops into my mind as I look over at Ryse and then back to Lucan.

"Yes, I've heard. But we don't need to discuss this now. We'll visit again after Fledge."

I huff. "How do you know I won't be killed in Fledge, Lucan? I mean, isn't it kind of risky to put me in there if you need me so bad?"

He laughs again, twice in one meeting. "Don't be silly, Junco. You've never been in any danger from these fights. You practically sat around filing your nails for the entire fourth battle. The other Archers think we're helping you cheat, that's how well you're doing."

Ryse is close now and Lucan taps us on the shoulders and delivers us to Fledge. "It was very nice to see you, Junco. Take care tomorrow."

And then he is gone.

I look up at Ryse and shrug. "OK, so this reporter thing?"

"Junco, he spies on us. Makes shit up about Tier and Ashur. He's on the screens like every night talking shit."

"That's not the point, Ryse. I'm not a little kid. You shouldn't be allowed to make up social rules for me."

He rolls his eyes at me. "Fine. Talk to whoever you want, OK?"

I smile. "Thanks." He turns to leave me there at the door but I hesitate. "Hey, Ryse?"

He turns back. "Yeah?"

"Tell Lucan thanks, too."

"What for?"

"For asking me to help, instead of telling me. I know it's just a token choice, but it sorta feels real. So, thanks for that."

He salutes me and I turn and go inside.

Chapter Twenty-Six

I'm on a mountain. By myself. Apparently Fight Five is a personal challenge and begins with being at the bottom of a mountain and ends with being at the top of a mountain. This whole stupid fight is climbing a mountain. Something I can do in my sleep. However, I'm currently on a ledge that was previously occupied by a rather angry bunch of eagles who now want it back.

The big one lurches at me for the tenth time and I kick out at it again. It snags my last toe and I scream as the blood squirts out.

Something in my thigh pocket begins to vibrate and I stop to pull out my com. I'm getting a call. During a fight. The screen says push to answer.

So I push.

"This better be a fucking emergency, Lucan."

"Uh, Junco?"

It's not Lucan. "Yeah?"

"It's Kadian."

Silence.

"The reporter from yesterday?"

"Oh. Yeah, OK. What do you want?"

The eagles are back and I miss his words as another one tries to attack my already bleeding toe – he lunges in and snags a bit of skin. "Fuck, that hurts! You stupid motherfucker, get the fuck out of here. I'll be gone in a minute, just let me get my fucking breath!"

I hear talking coming from my com and pick it back up. "Kadian, I'm a little bit busy right now."

"Are you in Fledge right now?"

"Yeah, I'm busy."

"Well, why are you answering the phone?"

"Hold on, there's an eagle who wants to eat my toe." My fingers pull up a small stone and I peg it good. It screams as it dives off the ledge and I cover my ears. "Ha, I got it in the eye!"

"Junco, put the com on your Aves shirt, near the upper left shoulder, so you don't have to hold it and I can see what's happening."

I slap it up there and his voice is amplified.

"So why did you pick up the phone?"

"Huh?" I answer, scrambling out of the way of another, smaller eagle. "Shit! Why? Oh, well, this is the first com call I've ever gotten, ya know. I was never allowed to talk on coms at home and I thought you were Lucan or Ashur or someone I shouldn't ignore."

"What are you doing in this fight?"

"It's not a fight, Kadian, it's a personal challenge. And they dumped us out at the bottom of a mountain and we're supposed to climb to the top. At least I think that's the point, they never really tell you, but what else could it be, right?"

"Describe what you're doing now."

"What the hell does it look like, I'm fighting eagles. But you know what, I'm done here. They can have this fucking ledge back, I'm done resting." I walk out towards the ledge and two big raptors are waiting to try and get my toes, but I fall to the ground and sweep them off with my legs and then I run to the edge and jump, grab a hold and begin to pull myself up past the outcrop that acts as a roof over the mountainside cave. My bare feet find their holds and I climb, one hand and foot at a time until I can see another ledge above me. I stop, breathing hard for a few seconds, then listen and hear the tell-tale whine of something I never wanted to hear again. "Holy shit, they've got nightdogs up here!"

"Nightdogs?"

Oops. "Oh, I didn't know you were still there."

"Yes, the whole habitat is with you right now, Junco, in real time. You have to fight a nightdog?"

I snort. "I don't have to fucking do anything and I tell you what, I'm not fighting any nightdogs, they already ate two of my fingers. I'm climbing straight around these fuckers."

"Why don't you just fly to the top?"

"Can't – there was a sign at the drop-off that said no flying. Some kid tried, they shot him."

I lurch out over a slight overhang and the snapping to my left makes my heart jolt for a second. I grab with my left hand and then swing again, my legs scrambling to find purchase, and then my right hand finds a hold and I pull up a few more feet.

I repeat the process until I find a rest spot.

"How far from the top are you, Junco?"

I turn and look down. "Pretty close, I think."

An eagle soars by and makes to grab at me with its talons but I kick out at it, and when it turns away I resume climbing, one hand, one foot, one hand, one foot.

And then then I am almost there and I smile. "Kadian, look!" I pick the com off my shirt and pan it around. "I'm almost there!"

I stick it back on and climb again, and again and then I'm on a flat ledge and I stand and turn. "Holy shit! I'm at the top!"

I scramble over a few more outcroppings and stand on the peak to see if anyone else is around. "No one else is at the top. There's no one!"

"You're the first, Junco?"

I cup my hands to my mouth and shout, "Oi! Oi! Pledges! Where are you?"

"Junco!" A faint call to my left, and I twirl around. "Kush!" I wave frantically. "Kush is alive, Kadian! He made it! Tessen! Where are you?" I watch as a few more people clamber to the top, but no Tessen. "Tessen!"

"Junco!" Wyrd calls from just over to my right, and I wave. "Wyrd's alive too!"

"Shit, where are you, Isec?" I don't expect him to make it, but I hope he does.

"Who's missing, Junco?"

"Tessen, Joll, and Isec."

"Junco!" I whirl to my left and there's Tessen waving. I wave back. "Tessen's alive!"

Fuck, Isec, where are you? I wait. The silence from the com and the few people who pop up at the top who are not Isec make things worse. I scan, and scan and scan. "Isec!" I look around. "Isec! If you can hear me don't stop climbing, Isec! Keep going!"

I hear Tessen, Wyrd, and Kush calling for him too, encouraging him, and I smile. "He's gonna make it, I know he will." I let out a long breath and then I hear his tiny little voice. "Junco! I did it!"

I scream. "I knew you'd make it, I knew it!" I jump up and down and I can hear Kadian telling me not to fall, but all the pledges at the top are whooping now – we scream and dance at the top of our mountains and then the announcer comes on and tells us to prepare for removal.

We are whooshed down a tube and spit out onto a large web and I bounce into the others, happy at making it, happy my friends made it, and then I swing down to the ground and run towards the ledge. I hold back until last and then I hear Kadian asking me questions, and I dive like a swan down to the dorm a thousand feet below.

I land in a heap with everyone else and I take the com off my shirt as I walk into the lounge and see my feed live on the screens. Everyone is pointing at me and I look into the com and smile.

"Junco, what was the best part of Fight Five?"

"I made it, Kadian, and I didn't have to kill a single soul to do it. Goodbye!"

I push the off button and the feed disappears from the screen.

It's only then that I realize Joll is still missing. But am I surprised that I've already forgotten about him? Or that the rest of the team have also?

No. We all knew. Joll was already dead to us.

There is only one day between the Fifth and Sixth Fights, so we spend the next entire day in training. Ashur has gathered everyone in the gym, including me. Out of the original one thousand pledges, there are exactly thirty of us remaining.

The entire 039 is present, except Braun of course, fucking asshole. Plus four more teams that I've never met before. I've got Kadian on my com on my chest, as does Ashur. He says it's good PR. My wings are taped securely to my back, as are Ashur's. This can only mean one thing.

He paces up front screaming about how worthless we will be if the Aves are forced to take us into their Cluster. I stifle down a yawn and then kick Isec to pay attention when it's contagious. If Ashur sees him do that he'll make an example out of him.

"Junco!"

I turn back to the front. "Yes, sir."

"Up here with me."

I get up and go to the front. He pulls me over and stands behind me with his hands on my shoulders. "For the rest of the day you will fight, and watch your fellow pledges fight, an Aves warrior. You will watch with a critical eye. You will look for weakness and strength. And you will ask yourself for each and every opponent, will this person save my life if I have to be on their team? You will rank them in your mind. Yes or no. Yes, this person is as good as or better than me. Or no, this person will get us all killed."

They stare at him like he has three eyes.

"Do you understand?"

"Yes, sir!" they shout.

He growls, "As Lucan's personal warrior, I am the ranking captain and I choose to fight Junco." He turns me around. "Junco, we will finish that fight now."

"Yes, sir." I'd like to tell him to go fuck himself, but he wouldn't tolerate that shit in front of the other teams. So I suck it up and prepare to get my ass kicked.

I walk towards him and grab him with both hands, one behind the neck, the other on his bicep, and swing into a flying arm bar, taking him down and slapping him on the mat. I hear him laugh. "Jasus, fuck, Junco!" He gets out of it easily and I end up on the bottom, but I have momentum on my side and I use my shoulder to flip him again. He catches my foot and gets me off balance, but I get my other foot hooked around his neck and get him in a leg bar, pulling just enough to make him know I won this move. He's not done with me yet, and flips over, but I hold tight to his leg. He struggles for a second, scooting back and forth to break my hold, but I hold on.

He hooks his leg around my hip, grabs my other leg, and pushes my ankle back until I cry out. I bite down the pain and let go of his leg to make him change position. He doesn't let go and the pain is searing back through my joint. I feel the tendon stretch and I think for a moment he might actually snap it if I don't tap out.

His foot appears by my head like a gift and I snatch it up and hold on, pushing his ankle back now. He rolls over on my hips and I use the motion to swing him all the way over as I twist on the mat. My foot slips free and I smack him in the face with it and he laughs. I still have a hold of his ankle though, and I twist and his laugh is cut off. Asshole.

He uses his considerable weight advantage to swing free and now he's lying across my chest as I take a few seconds to catch my breath, then swing my right arm over his neck and fishhook him to at least pop myself onto my stomach. Unfortunately, he's got me in a good shoulder lock and he's practically sitting on my neck. I take another second to rest, then let him flip me over and squirm away, my smaller size giving me room and advantage that no other person in the room might have, except for maybe Isec.

And then I've got him face down on all fours and I absently log people cheering for me in the background. I mount his back and hold his head in a choke, but since I weigh almost nothing compared to him he simply stands up. I unhook my legs and push off him into a back flip, miss the landing and slide across the mat. I scramble up as he's turning and hook him in the jaw with my foot as I spin. I watch his head snap to the side and a small trickle of blood seep out of his lip.

I stop, bending over and breathing hard trying to catch my breath. The whole room has been stunned into silence as they wait to see if he will take me down.

"Junco," Ashur says over his own heavy breathing. "You're fucking amazing."

I laugh. "Yes, sir." We meet in the middle and bow.

He points to the water bottles stacked up on a table at the other end of the room and I go to grab us some when I hear him talk to the pledges in a low voice. "That, you worthless throwaways, is a warrior who could beat every ass in here. But before you go getting jealous, she's also the one who will save you when you need it. You all fucking remember that."

We disconnect Kadian and sit down on one end of the gym to untape each other's wings and cool down. The remaining pledges repeat what we just did. The other Aves are really more into punching, flying and kicking than the grappling stuff Ashur and I did and most of the pledges suck so bad the entire encounter lasts for mere seconds. But some, like the biggest guy called Annun and a few of his buddies, and Kush, do OK, if not well.

It doesn't take long to see what Ashur's point was in facilitating this exercise. Some of the remaining pledges are very weak candidates to be warriors. And Isec's shortcomings are so painfully obvious I can't bear to watch and instead I head to the stairs and go outside to smoke. Ashur doesn't follow me.

I lie on the grass in what seems to be the late afternoon sun and after a few minutes Kush finds me. I look up at him as he approaches and pat the ground next to me. "You looked good today, Kush."

He smiles as he sits down. "Where did you and Ashur learn that stuff, Junco?"

"What stuff?"

"Those fighting moves?"

"Oh, it's a specialized art on Earth. You don't have jujitsu here?"

He shakes his head. "Never heard of it."

"Well, shit. You guys should get some teachers. It's pretty fucking useful for close combat like that."

"Where did Ashur learn it?"

I shrug. "I dunno." I puff on the cigar and then blow out some rings. "Watching me, I guess."

He's silent for a while so I fill in the gaps. "The 039 were my watchers on Earth." I look over at Kush to gauge his reaction but he's a blank. "He had years to see what I was up to, so I guess it just interested him and he decided to teach himself."

"Hmmm."

"What?"

"He's pretty infatuated with you, Junco."

"Kush, he's my captain. I'm his nine. He certainly loves me, but he's not in love with me if that's what you're getting around to."

"He definitely could be, that's all I'm saying. One word from you would be all it takes."

I shrug and blow smoke rings. I'm not even remotely interested in having this conversation with Kush and I let the silence hang until I hear Isten calling me to come back upstairs from the door.

I leave Kush out there on the grass.

Chapter Twenty-Seven

Later, Ash and I are sitting in the lounge as we watch a horror screen. "Go take a shower, Junco. What are you waiting for?"

I look back at the showers and shake my head. "I don't like to shower with people here. It feels weird. Especially with Isec and Kush, ya know?"

"You're suddenly shy?" He grins at me and laughs. "That's a first."

He's right, too. I've never been shy about my body before. "I know. I just don't feel comfortable with these guys. It's too personal."

"I was gonna take you out to dinner."

"I'll eat later, I want to go look at the church again. Wanna come with me?"

"No, I'm hungry and I'd rather go out to dinner."

"No one's stopping you, go."

He looks sideways at me. "Why do you want to go up there?"

"Because it's strange, why is it here? I asked Isten but he ignored my question." I pull out the prayer card that I've been keeping in my pocket and hand it to him. "I went in there that night that you programmed my com. I followed Isec up there and I found that prayer card."

He reads the poem. "Huh. Never heard of this one before."

"No? It's an old Earth poem, Ashur. Don't you think that's weird?"

He flips it over to look at the syrinx on the front. "Is it a famous poem?"

I shrug. "Not really. Maybe it was once, but it's a few hundred years old or something."

"How did you know it, then?"

"See, that's the thing. I had to memorize this poem in school, Ashur. Was assigned it in sixth year, right before I went off to cadets."

He hands it back to me and I pocket it. "Well, you don't ever want to ask Isten about the syrinx, Junco. He's worthless about religion. Refuses to even talk about it. But the syrinx was an ancient…" He looks up and struggles to find the correct word. "I guess the only proper way to describe her is the Fallen Archer."

I stand up and grab his hand. "Come up there with me."

He scowls. "Will you take a shower and go eat with me afterward?"

I smile and nod and he gives in.

Ashur stands behind me as I bend down to pan my fingertips across the ancient markings around the wooden door frame.

"Well, are you gonna go in?"

I look up and shake my head. "No, it scares me."

"Junco—"

"I just want to see if I can read this." I point to the markings.

"It looks like chips in the wood to me."

"It's not, it's ancient Sumerian cuneiform."

"Oh, well that explains it." He shakes his head and laughs.

My finger traces the various images, ticks, and lines one graphic at a time and I reach back in my memory to find the key. It's far back, from grade school, year three or four maybe, but it's there.

"Junco, can you really read that shit?"

I open my eyes and Ashur is bent down next to me, his face right up to mine. "I could, if I had enough time. I have the key in here." I say, tapping my head. "My father took me to the British Museum once, for birthday week. His friend was some big-shot curator guy in the Ancient Near-East section and he gave me this book that had worksheets and stuff."

Ashur looks at me strangely.

I shrug. "I can't help it, I just remember weird shit like that. Plus, we had like a whole semester on it in regular weekday school. Learning gods and goddesses and stuff. Like we do the Greeks. But this door is odd, because these markings are a mixture of several different forms. It encompasses the entire span of ancient Sumerian writing stretching over a period of almost four thousand years."

"What's it say?"

I smile because he's interested now, he can't help it. "I don't really know, I'd have to decipher each one, then try and apply it in context. I'd have to go back and read the books about the mythology to make sure it was correct. It would take months, years maybe."

His fingers pass over the carvings. "Oh, well, it is kinda cool."

"Don't you have anyone who can read this, Ashur? I mean, surely you must have some book or something that tells what it says."

He shrugs. "Yeah, maybe. I could look into it if you want."

"I do," I say as I look into his eyes. They are green like Tier's and they glow a little as we stare at each other. I break away first. "The thing is, Ash, when I went in there to pray, I prayed to be brave when the time comes. I said, *Please let me accept my fate with courage. Let me be brave in the end.* And I got an answer."

I watch his eyes again as it sinks in. "From who?"

I scratch my head and think of a good way to put it.

"Junco, from who?"

"My vision screen."

"What vision screen?"

"Huh?"

"What vision screen?"

"That shit that scrolls across my vision, the data."

"What the fuck are you talking about?"

"You can't see stuff on your field of vision? Stuff like documents and your personal biogs, or the injury status of an opponent?"

He stares at me, his eyes glowing like fuck, and I feel my heart stop. "You're not supposed to have a vision screen, Junco. That has to be gifted to you by the– ."

He stops mid-sentence and stays quiet. Like he's said too much.

I let out a breath. "Well, I have one."

"What did it say to you, Juncs?"

"She said–"

"She?"

"Yeah, she said, do you wish to accept the sacrifice? And I stalled, and she asked if that was a no, and I said wait, yes, I do. I'll accept the sacrifice. And then she was gone."

"Is this the only time she's talked to you?"

"No, when I was giving testimony, she was the one telling me what to say."

"What?"

"I woke up after talking to Tier and she was on my vision screen, she typed out word for word what I should say. And I did. She said they would knock off that charge if I said what she told me to."

"You *did* lie."

I nod. "Tier did break the treaty. I lied. Are you gonna tell Lucan?"

He looks at me. "No, of course not, Junco." His hand wraps around my head and he pulls me into his chest as he slumps back against the door. "What the fuck is going on, though?"

"Did Lucan or Layla tell you what they found inside my body?"

He huffs out some air. "There's more?"

"I'm part machine, Ashur. I'm littered with circuits all through my body. And when Layla explained what she saw she said that there was AI code inside me, but that it was inactive and inert."

He snorts. "Some fucking scientist she is."

"I know, right? When she told me that I immediately thought of my HOUSE back home. You know we had an AI running our house?"

He nods. "Arel corrupted her once, so we could get inside. But I don't know anything about it, really."

"So there's something inside me. Are you sure we shouldn't tell Lucan?" I pull back and look at his eyes.

"Has it done anything bad to you?"

"No, she shows up in stressful situations and helps me."

"Let's just wait."

"Sure, I'm fine with that." But not really. I'm worried, I want to say. I'm a little scared even.

"Back to the Fallen Archer and your original question. The church is here because she's like the equivalent of your Jesus on Earth. The sacrifice, to let everyone else live, right?"

I nod. "Yeah, that was his purpose, his death saved the rest of us."

"The syrinx isn't that magnanimous, she's here to remind you of *your* sacrifice."

I look up at him, my eyes wide.

He nods. "Yeah, funny timing. The purpose of the church is to make you ask if you're good enough to live. Can you contribute, can you help, can you save others. Like the stuff I was saying to the pledges today."

I let out a little laugh. Synchronicity.

"Anyway, by the time you get to Fight Six, you're supposed to reflect on this and then make a decision. Either say you're worthy and prove it, or give yourself up for the good of the others. That's her purpose."

I'm silent as I consider what my acceptance of the sacrifice means, but it's not particularly attractive. "So why is she called the Fallen Archer?"

"She gave herself up so we could live too, way back, like when we were still on Earth. Self-sacrifice is her thing."

"But *why* did she have to?"

He smiles down at me as his fingers absently play with my hair. "I thought you hated the myths?"

I shrug. "It's hard to ignore this one."

"Yeah, well, it's complicated because we have so many different mythologies that it's hard to keep straight. But the Fallen Archer, even though the Seven Siblings has Old Crage in it in some versions, is one of the twelve original myths. Which means it's way older than Crage.

"So anyway, the story goes, the avians were getting ready to leave Earth to go find the Seven Siblings but they"

– he stops and bends his head over to look at me – "I'm improvising here, Junco, I haven't read this myth in like twenty years so don't quote me or anything – but they needed stuff they didn't have. From what I can remember they needed to reach escape velocity and plot a course, and build the habitats out here in the Band, and all the technology we'd need to leave Earth and survive. And the story says she gave herself up so that we could get that from the High Order."

"What's the High Order?"

He shakes his head at me. "For this you do have to go to Lucan. I'm not allowed to tell you this part, sorry. He's the Archer."

"Oh. Well, since I have to go to him anyway, should I tell him everything then?"

"If you trust him."

"Do you trust him?"

"Unconditionally."

I nod. "OK."

We stay that way for a few more minutes and then he pulls me to my feet. "Time to shower, I'm fucking starved." He pushes me off the ledge and we soar down to the dorm.

Chapter Twenty-Eight

The tubes we are placed in for the Sixth Battle are upright and in the shape of a streamlined bullet. There are so few of us now, only thirty, that we all approach the circle of cases together. The transparent doors slide open simultaneously, and we all take a step forward and turn around.

The case slides shut and the only sound I hear is my own breathing. It has not been possible to predict the moment the fight starts for some time now, and I shuffle my feet with impatience. Somewhere deep below in some hidden layer of the habitat a mechanical ratcheting vibrates and then I am accelerating upward.

The top end of the bullet slides back in anticipation and then the case abruptly stops.

But I don't.

Momentum propels me up and out onto the field of battle. I am sailing through the air and then my upward acceleration reaches zero and I hang there for a fraction.

And fall.

My feet slam into the metal grate that pops out from the side of a deep well about the width of my arms. My ankle twists a little as it gets stuck between the metal crosses and I fall backwards.

"Shit!"

"You OK, Junco?" Kadian is on my coms but I ignore him and look around at where I am. It's obviously another personal challenge because there is no one else in the pit except me. I try my twings to see if I can fly, but the space is too tight. A sudden memory of Tier fighting nightdogs in the cave comes back and I push it down.

"Junco?"

"Kadian, one more fucking word from you and I'll cut the transmission. I'm motherfucking serious, seal your fucking mouth shut."

I stand and wince as my ankle cries out in pain. Just fucking great, I have to climb out of a pit with no rope and my ankle is fucked.

A timer beeps on the side of the ragged sandstone walls and begins to count down from three hundred seconds. A rush of water fills the chamber below my feet as I hear the snapping of jaws and almost pee myself.

I look down.

Crocodiles.

I scan up the side of the wall and spy another timer, about twenty feet vertical, then see the mechanism that will close another grate over my head and trap me down here if I don't start climbing now. I reach up for a handhold and pull up, find a foothold with my good foot, and repeat. The timer races down but I put it out of my mind and find another handhold and pull.

I am almost to the first gate and still have a full sixty seconds to get past the mechanism when the first grate below me slaps open. The crocodiles claw at the sides of the pit and jump at me. I lose purchase and slip a few feet backwards, my feet kicking out as the crocs jump into the air to grab a foot.

I try again, the timers down to forty-five seconds now, and pull. My ankle screams at the strain of my weight, but I force it down and climb. I reach the grate with fifteen seconds and use it to haul myself up quickly. I push my back and legs against the opposite sides of the pit wall and rest as the gate below me slams shut.

I put my feet down and take a real rest as the water is funneled out through some unseen drain and the crocodiles disappear. The bottom grate slides back in and becomes solid just as the side of the pit opens up and nightdogs are released below me.

Shit, they probably took that fear straight out of my mind. Dammit, Junco, push that shit down!

A litter of pups appears in the side of the pit wall next to me and they begin screaming for their mothers. I study the wild dogs below me and see that they are all bitches, their teats swollen from recent birth and nursing. They jump up and almost snap my fingers off that are clutching the grate. I pull back and get to my feet in a panic as the pups continue their call for help.

The timer for this phase beeps and starts counting down from two hundred forty seconds. I put a hand up and climb, trying my best to block out the vicious growl of dogs. I get a few feet up and the grate below me slides back into the wall, exposing my legs to the wild animals below. I let out a whimper and scramble up the wall as they jump and gain a hold of the boot of my drooping leg. I shake hard and pull the foot away, find another handhold and pull. They jump again and take a chunk of my pants with them as they fall, and I cling hard to the wall, then watch the timer begin counting down my final minute.

"Fuck!" I reach again and pull, the cries distract me and I slip as my foot falsely assumes the porous rock will hold my weight. The dogs jump again as the pups in the small nook on the side of the wall scream for attention. I watch the milk drip off the bitches, their need to nurse and fight driving them upwards towards my body.

The timer is at forty seconds and I reach up again, pull, find a spot for my foot, test, reach up, pull, find a foothold, test, and make it to the third gate and scramble my ass off as the timer says I have five seconds before I will be chopped in half. The thought of the nightdogs getting to eat my legs as a reward pushes me up just as the grate slams out below and I drop and rest.

I don't watch as the pups and bitches are removed from the pit, but I listen for the silence. It is a short reprieve, because the nasal growl of a pack of prairie lions echoes in my ears. They fight and claw at each other for a second and then the timer beeps and begins to count down what may be the final one hundred and eighty seconds of my life. I scramble up the pit wall, one hand over the next, one foot in, test, next foot, test, and repeat. The timer is at one hundred twenty when I hear the mechanism for the grate begin to slide.

I calculate the distance between myself and the prairie lions and know with surety that they can leap far higher than that short distance.

My ankle is not only burning, it swells against the side of my boot and the heat threatens to make it burst. The gate slides open and the hissing begins as the pride realizes they can get me. They leap and I scream and pull myself up, trying not to look down. I feel the claws scrape the flesh off the back side of my calf as I pull my ankle from their reach. *Pull, Junco! Pull!*

I do, but they figure out that the soft sandstone is perfect for long sharp claws to gain purchase as they try and catch a good meal.

I scream, "Fuck!"

One gets close and I have to stop and kick out to knock it back as I hold on desperately by one hand. The rocks begins to slide and loose bits of wall crumble beneath my fingers.

I reach up with my other hand and grab, then shake my head and think.

"Stop fucking thinking, Junco, and climb!"

For a minute I think it's me talking, but it's not. It's Kadian on the coms. "Climb, you stupid girl, climb!"

I do.

I climb and I ignore my ankle and after what seems like too many kicks at the leaping prairie lions my hands reach the lip of the pit and I haul myself up and over, struggling mightily in the sudden increase in G. It is so thick I immediately feel exhausted.

The lions make one last attempt and gain a hold of my boot with claws and teeth and I slide back. But I'm done by then, I kick those fuckers in the teeth and they scream as they fall back into the darkness.

I scramble out of their reach and take a minute to calm down before looking around. It's only then that I realize I could have just pulled out the SEAR and killed them all. And I didn't. Lucan will be so proud.

"Junco!" I hear a voice from behind and get to my feet, limping on my bad ankle and huffing in the heavy gravity. It's Annun. I smile and wave. "You beat me!"

He waves back but he's not smiling. "That fucking sucked."

My smile falters and I swallow hard. "Yeah," I say more to myself than anyone. "It really did."

I take a good long look around. I'm standing on the top of a spire-like rock formation, as is Annun, and I assume, as would everyone else if there was anyone at the top with us. But there isn't. There are thin rope bridges connecting each spire and I make to cross over to Annun when I hear him shout, "Stop now!"

I recognize a command when I hear one, so I do stop. And look up at him.

He points over to a spire across the center circle and then I see the body lying at the bottom, limbs all splayed out at angles not seen on living things. A broken rope bridge hangs down either side of the two spires. The heavy G is too much for that little bridge.

I look back at Annun. "Shit. Thanks."

We only wait a few seconds before the others begin pulling their way out of the pits. Annun's buddies Merkar and Pike are out first. I watch with apprehension as one by one those who made it claw across the small flat area surrounding each pit opening. Kush comes up, and another kid I don't really know. His friend is next, and then Wyrd. I smile with relief. At least he will make it.

Another guy is there, then so is Tessen.

A few more materialize, and then we are at fourteen and I'm just about to give up on Isec when I see his head appear and then the rest of his little body follows him as he drops to his side in exhaustion.

I smile, but I don't call out, I just breathe hard, still not fully recovered from the challenge.

We all made it.

It's too good to be true and I catch myself wishing they hadn't, that it was over, and that the final deaths were all behind us.

But as I look around at each spire I don't see anyone who shares my sense of dread. They jump and call out and scream their happiness from the top of the world.

But I know better.

The top of the world is the worst place to be.

It just makes the fall back down to Earth all that much farther.

Chapter Twenty-Nine

Ashur is taping my ankle up on my bunk while everyone else races around to get ready for the party. Lucan has sent a fleet of flyers and we are going to the 039 to celebrate.

I pleaded with the vision screen to mix me a cocktail for the pain, or start the self-healing stuff or something, but she is gone. And I don't really know how to run the equipment yet. So I suffer.

Two days and it will all be over.

"What are you thinking about, Junco?" Ashur is still taping but his eyes are on me.

I shake my head and exhale. "Just glad it's almost over. You know, Lucan said that these fights were not challenging for me, that he was never worried about me making it. But I have to disagree. Kush saved me the first fight and stopped the bleeding from my wings after the third fight. And believe it or not, it was Kadian's voice that snapped me out of the panic I was in in the pit. And I don't know if you saw on the screen, but Annun saved my life when he stopped me from crossing that rope bridge. There's no guarantee, Ashur. That's stupid of him to think that."

He smiles, a gentle smile, as he puts my foot down on the ground. "Stand up and try it out."

I do and it feels better, but I won't be wearing boots tonight. He takes my arm and guides me as I limp out of the dorm and out to the flyer. He loses his patience before we even reach the door and scoops me up to carry me the rest of the way.

We get to ride alone and I'm glad I don't have to share transport with all those excited people. He leans me back against the far door and puts my foot up on the seat, then settles on the opposite bench.

"What's wrong, Junco? You should be happy, your whole team came out of Fight Six. That's pretty amazing."

"I know, I am. But…"

He raises his eyebrows. "But what?"

I shake my head. "Nothing. I'm just really tired, that's all."

To my surprise he drops it and lets me doze on and off for the duration of the ride. The flyer lands on the roof of a very tall building overlooking Amelia proper. Ashur lifts me up and carries me down the landing pad stairs to a large terrace filled with green plants and flower beds and then through a large open door.

The guys are all there, even Braun, and they laugh and joke with me about my almost fatal ankle injury. Ashur sets me down on the couch as they all crowd me.

I look around at the apartment. It's what I might call ultra-minimalist on Earth, with sleek white floors and a sunken living room filled with white couches and loungers. The accents are chrome and it almost reminds me of my bedroom at home. From my vantage point on the couch I can see the terrace outside, as well as the lights of the buildings across the expansive boulevard.

Mish hands me a beer and Rikan throws a cigar in my lap. I strike it up and puff, then take a swig of the beer.

It feels awesome to be here with them.

Braun comes over and lifts me up into a bear hug and I choke and complain, but it feels so good I give in and throw my arms around his neck and plant a kiss on his cheek. He sets me back down on the couch and slides my legs over his lap and I fall back into the pillows and relax.

"Sorry I've been missing all the fun, Juncs. Lucan had me running all over the fucking worlds doing bullshit stuff. I think he was trying to keep us apart, you being my one true love and all."

Ryse interjects, "Braun, the only way Junco would love you is if the rest of us were all dead."

I smile up at Braun. "Not true, Braun."

"Shit," Rikan says, "She'd love Lucan before you!"

I laugh. "So not true, Braun."

He shrugs. "She says she loves me guys, I'm going with it!" He pulls me to his face and kisses me on the head. "I'll always be your favorite, right, Junco?"

"Always, Braun."

"Now, about that house you owe me, honey..."

I slap him and Ashur pulls him off of me and takes his place.

Isten yells from across the room, "Flyers upstairs."

The apartment bustles with activity as the other pledges pour into the party. Someone gets some kind of loud music going and the drinks begin to flow. Tessen makes her way over to Ash and me. "Junco, you can't mope on the couch all night. Get off her, Ashur." She physically pushes him aside and pulls me to my feet. "Let's mingle."

I laugh and look back at Ashur's stunned face as I limp away with Tessen. "Bye!"

We poke around all the rooms one at a time and discuss the quality of food from the autocook in the kitchen, the potential for large parties at the dining room table, the type of stone used for the tiles on the floor, and the wall art. Lucan appears from nowhere and scares the shit out of us as we peek into the various bedrooms.

"Junco, are you looking for your room?"

I stare up at him. "I have a room?"

"Of course you do, this is the 039. You live here."

Tessen nods and gives me the girlfriend look of approval.

"Come."

He takes my arm and helps me walk down a few stairs into the sunken living room, then across the other side and up a few more to a separate part of the apartment. I spot Ashur talking to Annun but he excuses himself and follows us as we walk into a small hallway that leads to another room.

When I walk in I'm a little bit taken back. It looks almost identical to my room at home, only much larger, and with an incredible bay window that almost bumps out into the traffic of flyers.

I look back and all the guys are peeking around the door to see what I think of it.

"Damn, Junco! Can I move in too, Lucan?" Tessen is clearly impressed.

I walk over to the piano and sit on the bench. "Where—"

"We looted your house, Junco. I hope you don't mind." Isten sits next to me and squeezes my arm. "Rikan and I took a bunch of shit while that fight was going down in your driveway."

My fingers touch the keys and I play the little lullaby I learned when I was just a toddler to try it out. It's even in tune. Isec wanders up and pulls on my arm. "Can you play it?"

"I actually play very well. Wanna hear?"

He nods and I push Isten off the bench so I can have room. "It might sound funny, I haven't played since my fingers were bitten off."

Nobody cares.

I play the first few lines of Asgarth's Genius from memory to test the left hand, but to my surprise, it sounds perfect. My fingers fly, picking out the sweet melody that made me fall in love with the piece in the first place, and then transition into the deeper notes that take it down to the dark place of Asgarth's nightmares. In the opera, Asgarth is an insane prince who thinks everyone is trying to kill him. It doesn't end well for the people around him.

I stop after I finish the first song and turn around. Everyone is silent and somber and then they clap gently and I smile and get up and bow.

Lucan is gone, but Ashur comes over and takes me to the book shelf to show me the photo albums they managed to get out of my room. "We got what we could." He looks away. "It probably makes you miss it even more, but–"

I smile and exhale. *All the good parts are in the exhale.* "It's very touching, Ash. Really."

People file past us after looking at the view and then we are alone and he sits me down on the window seat. I hear Tessen's loud laugh down the hallway and smile as I lean over and look down. The street is so far away and the boulevard so crowded with trains every twenty floors or so that there is no possible chance of getting a glimpse of it. I pull my legs up and hug them to my chest as I stare out the window. Ash goes over and turns the lights out. "It's beautiful at night."

I agree and lean back against the edge of the window frame. The lights outside really are stunning.

"Why are you so unhappy today?"

I shrug. "Because there's still one more fight and I'm getting hopeful that things will turn out OK." I look up at him and shake my head. "And things never turn out OK, so why bother enjoying it? It'll all be gone soon enough."

He sits next to me and takes my hand. "Not all of it, Junco."

I smile up at him. "I don't deserve you."

He leans in and kisses me, then stops to search my face for a reaction. His eyes glow green and I wonder what color mine are at the moment. I reach up to his cheek and stroke him with the tips of my fingers, then slide my hand around his neck and draw him in close to kiss him back. It lasts for so long I lose time.

I pull away and turn my head so he can take his kisses to my neck and then down my chest. His hands go to my waist and then he pulls back. "Fuck, Junco." His breath is heavy as he bows his head.

I nod and exhale as I play with his hair. "I know."

He pulls all the way back and sits up as I smile. I get up but he stays seated. "I'm gonna go find Lucan."

He nods. "I'll be out in a minute."

Chapter Thirty

Lucan is out on the terrace sitting on a porch swing that looks like they might have stolen it right out of the RR. I walk up next to him and he pats the seat so I sit down and pull my legs up into my chest. He makes the swing move back and forth and it reminds me of the lullaby I played on the piano.

"You look like I feel, Lucan."

He smiles and pats my arm like I'm four. "Yes, you and I feel it more so than the others, Junco. The end is getting closer now."

"Will I really hate you?"

He raises his eyebrows. "Perhaps not. I can't say without knowing what you feel for me now."

"I think you've been pretty wonderful to me, to be honest."

"I'm not sure wonderful will cover it."

"Are you going to kill me?"

He laughs. "Oh, Junco, I hope that was a joke."

I feel my face go red. "OK. It was."

He looks over at me and shakes his head. "Never, Junco. I would never do that."

"Will you let Tier die?"

I watch his face drop as I feel his heart skip a beat. "Believe it or not, that is not even in my control. I have no say at all. I used up all my gifts on Tier, there are none left for him."

I avoid his gaze as he looks over to me. "What's that mean?"

"It means that I've given him every advantage, illegal and otherwise, since the day he was born. There are limits as to how I distribute gifts and well, I have run out in his case. I've used them up. So, I am rather helpless to help the closest thing I will ever have to a son."

I stare at his mouth, trying to understand the words. "Tier is your son?"

"In an avian sort of way. I didn't make him, but I was there – for some reason I cannot even remember at this time – when he was pulled out of the womb. And I chose him. I poured it all into Tier."

"Why?"

"I cannot even say for certain, only that I felt compelled. I even named him. It doesn't really fit him though, that name. He's so much more than a predator."

I put my head down on my knees and we are quiet for a while. "I lied, Lucan. In the testimony. That AI is not inert, Layla was wrong. She told me what to do when I was under the drugs."

He looks over to me, sad. "I know, Junco."

"And I was praying to the Fallen Archer up in that Fledge Church, and she asked me if I wanted to make the sacrifice, and I said yes."

He nods again. "Yes, I saw some of that as well."

"Saw it how?"

He taps his head. "In my brain, one of my special talents."

"Oh, you know, Isec says he's a precog."

"Is he? Isn't life cruel? He needs to be a telepath to live, yet his genetics give him precognition, which does him absolutely no good because he must be a true-blood Aves to control it."

"Yeah, life is a total bitch." We swing in silence for a few seconds. "What's the High Order?"

I look up and watch his face crinkle. "Who told you about them?"

"No one, but Ash mentioned it when he was telling me about the Fallen Archer myth. He said he wasn't allowed to talk to me about them. I had to ask you."

His eyes sweep over to mine. "Everyone has a boss, Junco. Even me."

"That's it?"

He laughs. "That's it for now. Do you want me to tell you what to do with the AI?"

"Can I do anything? Or am I just stuck with it?"

He takes a moment to think. "Yes, you can make choices, but only you can decide which one is best. I can tell you to ignore her, take her advice, or refuse to do so. But in the end it doesn't matter. I do not think she can make fate shift."

"Well, shit. It sucks to be us, right? But oh fucking well. That's who we are. So, I guess the only thing left to do is finish it off, Lucan. When we get to the end, we'll revisit all this and see where we stand."

He smiles. "You can stay here tonight if you want. Sleep in your new room."

I take in a sharp breath. "I better not. No offense, but I should probably go home with everyone else until I can think a few things through."

"Would you like a bit of advice?"

"Absolutely," I say, looking up at him.

"Take your time, Junco. Think about what you really want. Last week you could not picture yourself living here and being happy, yet today I think you'll agree that has changed."

"Yeah, you're right."

"Ashur is a very good man."

I look up into his eyes to see if they are judging me. But they're not, they are kind and sad. "I know, Lucan."

He changes the subject so fast I almost feel dizzy. "Your piano playing was impeccable, even with missing fingers. Do you find that odd?"

I look down at my left hand. "Yes. It's funny, ya know, when it happened Tier took me back to the cavern and I woke up later all freaked out about it. But right before I passed out again he said, *You'll never miss them, Junco. I promise you, you'll never even know they're gone.*"

I smile and look up at Lucan. "And he was right. I never think about them. Ever. And I never miss them when I'm doing anything, not even when I'm climbing a wall or fighting or playing piano. It has no effect on me."

Lucan stands up and takes my hand. "Take the day off tomorrow, no training for anyone. Just do something fun."

I nod and he lets go of my hand and disappears.

I avoid Ashur for the rest of the night, but I watch him from across the room as he talks to Annun or one of the other pledges that he must think of as worthy. I sit at the table and play poker with the guys and let Braun distract me with his jokes filled with sexual innuendo.

At the end of the night I slouch against Tessen in the flyer on the way home and begin the process of making choices.

I can't sleep. Everything is somehow off balance and my mind refuses to let any of it go. I want to be with Ashur and forget everything else. Forget Tier and the last battle, and the Seven Siblings, and the myths.

I swing my feet out and walk over to the mast and before I can even think about what I'm doing, my wings are carrying me up to her. I land hard outside the huge wooden door after a dozen or more minutes of frantic flying and then go inside. The vestibule smells sweet with some kind of incense, which means other pledges have been in here recently. It makes me feel better that I'm not the only one drawn to her and her questions.

I pull open the second door, half expecting someone else to be inside, but it's empty. I walk up to the altar and stand in front of the offering. My eyes begin at the feet and trace down every inch of her writhing and twisting body until I get to her throat. I kneel down and sit back on my butt as I look at her half-outstretched wings. One falls to the side, bent at the elbow, the tip stretching outward. The other looks as if it is desperately trying to stay tucked up next to her back, but if the moment were released, it too would drop out.

I peer under her head to see her face. Her mouth, hidden unless you're underneath her, is open in a scream, her eyes wide.

"What do you want from me?"

"What do you have to give?"

I stand up and turn around. "Annun, what the fuck – you scared the shit out of me!"

"Sorry, I saw you come up here and I needed to make my visit anyway, so–"

"What will you do in here, Annun? I'm not quite sure what the purpose is besides convincing yourself that you're worthy."

"It's not to convince myself I'm worthy, Junco. It's to convince her. She chooses, not us."

"But she's not real. Is she?"

He smiles. "It's faith, right? If you believe, she's real. If you don't, she isn't."

"OK."

"Do you believe, Junco?"

"In her?" I pause and look back at the icon. "I already have a God, Annun. I'm just a bit infatuated with her persona at the moment."

"Has the Fledge changed you? I barely know you, so it's hard to tell if you've changed from the first fight."

I shrug. "Of course, yeah."

"I only ask because I don't even recognize myself anymore."

"Is that a good thing or a bad thing?"

He shakes his head. "Bad, I think. Killing all those people–"

"Yeah, that has changed me. My scroll is so long now, I'll never fit through the strait gate."

He looks at me funny. "Huh?"

"Nothing. I just mean, I've done a lot of bad things, way before I ever came to the avian world, and the only way to get past it is to push it down. Put it away. Only bring it out when you need it, Annun. That's the only way to get up in the morning."

"Sounds risky."

I huff out a laugh. "It definitely is, but it gets you through, right? To the next step. We're at the end now. We're done. Lucan says we have to take advantage of our last day, no training or nothing. And I agree, push this shit down and enjoy each other for one more day. Then whatever happens at the last fight, we'll at least have something good to counter the bad."

"You're for sure getting through, Junco."

"Yeah, I know that, Annun – but do you see my friends? Your friends are for sure getting through with you.

So you're light-years ahead of me in that department. And the really ironic part is that all along Ashur warned me not to get attached to the weak ones. He warned me, but I thought I could save them."

I let out a huge sigh and shake my head. "It would be a lot easier if they were already dead." I look up at him, meet his eyes. "Because I'd have that shit locked down already, and be on the other side of death. That's the best place to be, ya know? On the other side of death."

"So, that's it? You can just turn it on and off like that? Forget about stuff and move on?"

I shrug.

"That's pretty impressive, Junco, really, I envy you. But it also makes you a little bit insane."

I laugh. "You should have seen me on Earth, Annun. I was beyond insane."

"So if Tier dies? If Ashur were to die? You'd turn that off too."

I look over at the syrinx and breathe, letting a few seconds pass before answering. "You bet, Annun." I look back up to his face, meet his eyes. "You fucking bet I would."

He shrugs. "You're the perfect fucking warrior then, right? Do what they tell you and then say more, please."

He's judging me now, but I don't even feel it. It's already turned off. "Annun, I was born the perfect fucking warrior, I never asked for it. They made me this way. If I were to let it go, what would I be then?"

His voice stays soft. "Just Junco, maybe?"

"And who the fuck is Junco except one small girl from Earth whose only worth is tied up with how accurately she can hit a target in the head from four thousand yards away?"

He watches my face for a moment. "I've heard she does a pretty mean flip on horseback. And she plays the piano so well it makes you want to cry."

I feel my chest heave and turn away, the tears filling up my eyes.

He walks over to me and puts his hand on my shoulder. "Sorry, Junco. I'm sorry. I'm no different. In fact, I'm much worse. You didn't choose to be here, but I did. I did. I left my safe life with the politicos to come here knowing full well if I made it I'd have this blood on my hands. At least you can say they made you what you are. I made myself this way. I wanted this."

I shake my head and look down at the syrinx and whisper, "I'll let you in on a secret, Annun. Since we're sharing. I like who I am and what I can do." I look up at him. "I do. I'd like to think that given the chance, I'd choose to be someone else. Someone kind and loving. Maybe a mother. But I think the odds of me actually doing that in an honest-to-God real situation are almost zero."

"I like it too, Junco. That's why we're both here in the church telling the syrinx we're OK with what it took to get here. And she should mark us worthy because we want to be here. We're not sorry we made it. We're proud. And when the last battle comes, we'll do what we have to because it's these shitty fucking moments that will show what we're made of. What kind of warriors we really are and what we have to offer. How much of ourselves we're really willing to sacrifice to hold it all together."

I stay silent for a few moments as I let his words sink into my memory. "They're gonna give you the command, I bet. Make you a captain."

"If they do, it'll only be because you're already taken."

"I'd follow you, Annun." I look up at him. "I would."

He smiles. "I'd definitely follow you, Junco. Just say the word and I'm there."

This is what Isten meant when he said the Fledge makes the team. I can feel it, how bonded I am to this guy I barely know. This stranger who will stick it out with me in my darkest moments and give me the words I need to hear so badly it makes my chest ache. I want to tell him, but I just smile instead. He grabs me by the shoulder and turns me around so we can walk out of the church together. Then we jump off the ledge and go back to the dorm to sleep away our midnight confessions.

Chapter Thirty-One

I wake to the whine of plasma rifles charging against my head and I lie still.

"Junco, please open your eyes and make no other movement until instructed to do so."

I open them. There are seven Aves warriors, not my team, and another man who looks a lot like Lucan, but who is definitely not, standing around my bed. The fair man smiles at me.

I wait.

"I am Rache, the Archer of Justice. We require your testimony today and when I instruct you to do so, you will get up, shower, dress, and come back out for transport over to the Justice habitat for the proceedings."

"Yes, sir."

"You may get up."

All seven warriors follow me to the showers and train their rifles on my head as I clean up and dress. I exit and am offered some type of food, which I refuse. Rache is waiting by the door and we take the stairs down the three flights to the ground floor. I watch the mods frantically talking on coms as I pass by the windows and I know they are speaking to the 039 or Lucan.

There is a large transport flyer waiting in the space where I usually puff on my cigars. As we approach, the doors open and I am ushered inside and take a seat in the middle, surrounded on all sides by plasma rifles on target.

Rache takes a seat opposite me and smiles.

I raise my eyebrow at him.

"This went better than expected."

"Really?" I say calmly. "You thought I'd, what? Kill you with my SEAR because you want to ask me questions?"

He sniffs and straightens his back. "Junco, you have an unprecedented wild side. We cannot be too careful."

"Huh." I stare at his blue eyes. "Well, good luck if Moju comes back. If you think I'm wild, I can't wait to see how you treat my brother."

"There's no need to be spiteful, Junco."

I shrug. "You're the one with the weapons trained on my head, Rache. If you're so afraid of me, why not just let the 039 bring me over to Justice? Or Lucan?"

"Because I wanted to meet you."

I squint at him. "Well, you're not making a great first impression."

He flicks his fingers and the guys back off. I nod to them and they nod back. It's not their fault he's excitable. I hold on to the arms of the chair as the flyer banks hard to the left and we glide into a parking structure.

"Have you been off Amelia before?"

I shake my head. "No, except to look at the stars with Lucan."

He stares at me for a split second and I catch his surprise before he locks it down. "Well, you are about to leave. We need to transfer to the ship that will take us to Justice. The men will remain on alert but will not target you. If you attempt to–"

I cut him off. "Rache, we're on the same fucking side. I'm not gonna make any attempts to do anything."

He smiles. "You'll excuse me if I'm suspicious. You are the only person that I know of who has successfully lied while under the truth drugs."

I keep my mouth shut for that one.

"Lucan confessed your actions, Junco."

I shrug. "It's always a bitch trying to predict how a drug will react with certain metabolisms. That's pretty basic toxicology and you should really have a handle on the possible side effects if you're gonna give that shit to humans."

"Half human," he corrects me.

"One third actually," I say as I turn my head away.

The door opens and we all exit and transfer to a waiting ship only a few dozen meters across the terminal. The G is light and feels artificial so I figure we're near the center edge of the torus. I enter the ship and buckle myself into the harness. A warrior sits next to me this time, his weapon stowed. He leans over and extends his hand. "Monk."

I smile and shake it. "Junco."

"Don't mind Rache, he's really not bad."

"Yeah, OK. So, is this gonna take long? This is my last day before Fight Seven and I wanted to spend it doing something fun."

"You'll be gone all day, sorry."

I nod and look away. "Not your fault."

I watch out the window as we are propelled out into the blackness of space and jump a little bit when the thrusters rumble alive to push us to wherever we're going. Being out in space in a little transport ship like this isn't as exciting as it sounds. In fact, there is absolutely nothing to look at and you're constantly adjusting yourself in the harness chair because free-G and sitting in one place don't really go together. I sleep the entire way and only wake up when Monk's hand forcibly shakes me back into reality.

I unbuckle my harness and stumble a little in the light G as I make my way to the door. From there the gravity evens out and I get heavier as we move through a series of polished tile hallways until we reach an unobtrusive beige door.

The guards talk on implant coms and we wait until some unknown signal tells us to proceed through the door. Rache goes first and turns left, I am directed to go right, led down another long hallway and through another door that leads out into what I could only describe as a courtroom.

Lucan is already there, but the other 039 aren't. He must have used his little teleportation thing to get there ahead of us. He comes over and dismisses the warriors around me with contempt.

"I apologize, Junco. They did not inform me of this until this morning."

"I figured, obviously."

He leads me over to a chair in the center of the room and motions me to sit. "Any advice?"

He smiles. "Just tell the truth, Junco. And if the AI gets involved, refuse to listen this time. It is important that we build trust with Justice."

I nod and he leaves and takes a seat in the circle of chairs which surround my own. Nothing like being in the hot seat.

"State your name for the record."

I look up at an officiator who stands in a corner of the room with a panel of other people, monitors maybe. "Junco Abigail Coot."

The officiator comes over with a red book and places it in front of me. "Put your left hand on the Bible and hold up your right hand."

I do.

"Do you solemnly swear to tell the truth, whole truth, and nothing but the truth so help you or may God strike you down dead?"

I almost laugh, but I hold it in. "I do." He takes the Bible back. "But my God doesn't strike people down dead. Just to be clear, that's not how the oath goes."

"Junco."

I look over at Lucan and shrug. "Sorry."

"State your age and place of residence."

"Nineteen. The Fledge place on Amelia. I don't know what it's called."

"Did you lie in the last testimony?"

"Yes."

"How were you able to lie?"

"I have a program inside me that can counteract the drugs."

"Did you ask the program to counteract the drugs when you were giving testimony?"

"No."

"Why did the program run?"

"I don't know." I hear a lot of murmuring from the back panel and look over, squinting my eyes.

"Are you running any programs now?"

"No."

He looks at me dubiously. "None?"

"Nope."

"Why not?"

"Because I don't know how to run them."

Lucan stands and speaks like he's bored out of his mind. "Objection. The topic has been exhausted."

"Sustained." The ruling comes from a voice in the ceiling and I figure out the process. The officiator is a prosecutor. Lucan is my defender. The voice is Rache, the judge.

The officiator tries a new tactic. "We've thrown out the treaty charge for Captain Raubtier at any rate, so we will not rehash that issue today. Today I want to know why he didn't kill you as he was instructed."

I frown. "Shouldn't you ask him that?"

"I have asked him that, now I am asking you."

I sigh. Loudly. "He told me that he made the decision to disobey orders when he saw how I reacted after I crashed my Goat into a tree on my way to The Stag."

"Continue."

"He said I was fearless, that I wasn't a quitter, and that he felt I'd have a lot to offer you, the avians, if I was just told the truth once in a while."

"Continue."

"That's it."

"That is all the reason he gave?"

I nod. "Yes. That's it."

"Did he mention the reward for bringing you back?"

My heart skips. "No."

"Did he mention what he might receive if he brought you back?"

"I actually did ask him that, believe it or not. I'm a rather suspicious person by nature. And he said he was looking for redemption."

A lot of murmuring from the back panel now, and I can't help myself, I turn and look over at them.

"From what, specifically, was he seeking redemption for?"

"Killing a lot of people I think."

"Did he tell you who these people were?"

"No, but I was told by someone else who they might be."

"So you knew that he was responsible for killing children?"

"Objection, this is embellishment."

I look over at Lucan but stay silent.

"Overruled, continue, Miss Coot."

"I know he killed mutant children out at The Stag Camp, he said they were monsters."

"Who else did you think he killed?"

"Corporate humans. I don't really know."

"It wasn't worth asking about? To know this for sure before you decided to leave your planet and come to a strange world, uninvited?"

"Well, I've killed a lot of people myself, so you know – typically we just do the old wink and a nod at that stuff, right? Like the code among thieves."

"Junco." I look over at Lucan and he shakes his head at me.

"I absolved him," I say, shrugging.

The officiator looks at me strangely now. "You what?"

"I absolved him. From whatever it was he did."

"Miss Coot, please explain how that works for those of us unfamiliar with the process."

I exhale loudly. "I forgave him, in advance. Before knowing what he did."

He stares at me now, like I'm a wart on his hand. "Why?"

"Because I needed to trust *someone* and I really wanted it to be him. And I didn't want to hear what he did. I tried to prevent him from telling me, in fact."

"Did anyone send you here, Miss Coot?"

"No."

"What do you hope to receive from the avians, if we should allow you to stay?"

I stare at the officiator, then look over at Lucan as my heart begins to race. "You're kicking me out?"

"I didn't say that, Miss Coot. What would you want from the avian people if they should allow you to stay?"

I take a breath and calm myself as the vision screen comes alive. *Tell them: to be accepted and allowed to prove myself.*

"To be accepted and allowed to prove myself."

"And how could you prove yourself to the avian people?"

Say: I will bring back the Siblings on Earth and deliver the code you need to survive.

I say it and the room erupts in a gasp. I look over at Lucan and he gives me an ever-so-slight nod.

"I have no further questions."

The voice above erupts. "Miss Coot, you are free to leave with your Archer."

Lucan comes over and takes my hand, leading me towards the door, then touches my shoulder and we are outside Fledge.

"Well done, Junco."

"She told me to say that."

"Well, thank the gods above that she did because it probably just saved your life."

Chapter Thirty-Two

I walk into Fledge and it is so quiet I think that the entire place is empty. But when I look around I see that all fifteen of us are there, just spread out among the many, many extra beds.

"What's going on?"

At first no one answers, then Kush comes up. "There was a pretty big fight earlier, everyone's upset."

"What was it about?"

He shrugs. "Who will live and who will die tomorrow, Junco. Fuck."

He walks away and I go sit down next to Tessen. "Bad day, huh?"

She nods. "Where have you been, Junco?"

I sigh. "I was on trial, I think."

"What?"

"Yeah, at first I thought I was there to testify against Tier, but I think I was on trial myself. To see if they will let me stay or kill me, or whatever."

She looks at me, stunned. "So what happened?"

"I promised to bring the Siblings back from Earth if they let me stay. Who'd have fucking thought that I'd be bummed about being sent back to Earth." I look up at her. "But I am."

"Then why did you volunteer?"

"I had to. I think they were gonna kill me, Tessen."

I leave and go over to my bunk. Isec's bunk hasn't changed from when I woke up, but he's either sleeping or pretending to be asleep and has his back to me. That's OK with me. I can't face him right now anyway. I change into my bed clothes and lie down, thinking about tomorrow until I drift off.

The next morning there is no alarm, but we all wake early. I sit on the side of my bunk moving my almost healed ankle around in circles and looking around at everyone, then get up and take my shower and dress in my uniform. I grab all my junk in my cubbie and take it over to my bed. I don't know what will happen after the battle, but I want to sort through things before we have to leave.

I find a bunch of notes from Lucan and the guys that I never saw. From after the first testimony when I was mad. It seems so long ago, that fight with Ashur. I sort the stuff out into three bags and leave them at the foot of my bed.

And then I sit there. Just like everyone else. And we do absolutely nothing until the call comes to line up for the fight.

The prep room is small and the markings on the floor are back. This time they have a moon shape and they line us up in a crescent, all facing the same direction. I am in the middle somewhere, between Annun and Tessen. Neither Kush nor Isec are talking to me this morning and I don't even note where they are in line.

I feel the silence before start, and swallow as we are shunted upward. We erupt into a large arena that I recognize as the free-G room where Ashur taught me to fly, but the perimeter is filled with people. The mushrooms that I practiced flying and jumping on have been turned on their sides and they flank us, five on one side and five on the other. My feet are stuck to the floor and I jump a little as the observers begin to clap politely.

Annun looks down at me and I shake my head and shrug. I see Ashur and the guys in the center, behind Lucan, and then as I look around I see other Archers, with their personal Aves teams sitting behind them. I even see Rache and his guys. Monk catches my gaze and waves. Behind the Archers are more warriors.

Lucan puts up a hand and the room goes silent. "Welcome to Fight Seven of the 2153 General Fledge. We are here today to declare a winner and choose a new team of Aves warriors."

The Aves clap until Lucan begins to speak. "We will begin with the winner." He backs away and Ashur comes forward. "The 039 is proud to declare that Junco, Aves 039, is the winner of the 2153 General Fledge with a total of eighty-seven kills."

My vision falters at the number. Eighty-seven people dead because of me playing this game.

"Junco, please come forward."

I feel my feet come unstuck and I walk up the stairs to Ashur. He shakes my hand, a very human congratulations, then kisses me on both cheeks and places a medal around my neck.

"Choose the warrior you would have first on your team."

I take deep breath. Here we go. I look at each of my fellow pledges as my eyes move down the line. Isec refuses to look at me, Kush is angry, and Tessen smiles. I smile back at her. "I choose Annun."

Ashur squeezes my shoulder and bends into my ear. "Well done, Junco. Come with me now."

He flies over to the first mushroom across the room and I follow. When we get there I hover for a second and then he pushes me back and I am locked against the stone. Unable to move.

Annun is beckoned to the stage and the process is repeated.

"I choose Merkar."

"I choose Pike."

"I choose Kush."

Kush stands on the stage and we wait as he looks down the line. I stare at him, glad he's on the hot seat for once. Not so fucking easy when it's you who has to make the choice.

He chooses someone I don't even know and I huff out some air. Ashur looks back at me but I shake my head.

The next kid chooses his friend.

And the next kid chooses his friend. All pledges I can't even identify by name. That guy chooses Wyrd.

Wyrd walks to the stage and takes a hard swallow to shut down his panic and relief. There is only one spot left and six hopeful faces look up to him, begging for a chance. "I choose Tessen." She screams and I feel the relief wash over me. Since she is the last she is escorted to the final mushroom, directly across from where I stand. I catch her eye and smile. Then look over to Isec and my face falls. He's crying.

My back comes unstuck from the stone and then Lucan is talking to me. "Junco, Aves 039, please come forward."

I fly over and land next to him. Ashur shadows me and stands behind us. "Junco, as the Fledge captain, it is your responsibility to cull the unsuitable members."

My heart pounds as I look up at him.

"Do you understand, Junco?" he asks me kindly and in a low voice.

I nod and whisper, "Yes, sir."

I look up into the crowd, to judge them, but I come away unsatisfied. There is nothing but sympathy for me. There are no hoots or hollers now, no clapping, no laughing or smiling. Only pity. I look over to Annun and he nods and I read his lips as they say, "Show them, Junco."

To his credit, Lucan stands patiently and watches me sort through the reality of what I have to do. I look down for a minute and bring back Annun's words in the church... *And when the last battle comes, we'll do what we have to because it's these shitty fucking moments that will show what we're made of.*

My breath comes faster as I walk down the stairs, then walk behind the pledges and remove my SEAR from my stomach. I hear the crowd gasp and whisper as I activate it and dial it down to dagger size.

I cut their heads off from behind. The crackle of the plasma through tissue sends tendrils of burning flesh up into the air and I watch as the entire arena wrinkles their collective nose at me.

When I get to Isec he's crying hysterically and I know that if his feet were not stuck to the floor, he'd be running from me like those girls Ashur is forever watching in his horror screens.

I step out in front of him, to at least look him in the eyes, but he squeezes them shut, tightly sealed from reality. His tears drop down his cheeks as I remove his head. And then I shut down the SEAR and stick it under my shirt and stand there, looking down at the rumpled heap of bodies and the wide-eyed expressions on the floor. The audience remains quiet and somber until Ashur appears and leads me away and out of sight and then the whispers begin.

They sound like a flock of starlings in the trees over winter.
That seals the deal.
I know exactly what I'm made of.
Cold fucking stone.

Chapter Thirty-Three

I don't even know how I got here, but I am kneeling at the syrinx's head in the church, the silent tears streaming down my cheeks. I hear the door open behind me, but I don't turn until Lucan kneels down next to me on the red carpeted floor. He puts his arm around me. "Junco, let's go home."

I shake my head and push his arm off. "No, I'm not done."

"You've been in here for an hour, Junco. Everyone is gone now, let's go home and you can think about it there."

"I fucking said no, Lucan. I'm not fucking done."

"What do you need to do to be finished?"

"An answer."

"An answer to what question, Junco?"

I let out a deep sigh. "Why am I so evil? How much longer do I have to keep killing?"

"You could quit, if you want."

I snort. "Yeah, I could die, too."

He stays silent after that.

"She's here, I know it. She just doesn't want to answer me because she wants something, just like everyone else. She wants something from me and it's gonna be you next. Or Ashur. Or Isten. It's gonna be you guys next, just to make me pay for all the shitty fucking things I just added to my scroll. I can feel it. Someone will come up to me, maybe that Rache guy, and he'll say, *It's your job, Junco. Kill your best friend now, kill your favorite. Kill your Archer.*" I look up at him and it's painful to see the look in his eyes. "And I'll do it, Lucan. I know I will."

"You won't, Junco. You're with us now."

I shake my head. "How could you ever trust me again? I'm a total sell-out. I'm nothing but a programmed robot waiting for new orders. It's great if you're the one in charge of me, yeah. Sure. That's great. But God fucking forbid you be on the receiving end, right? Because I'm just a good little soldier. Follow orders and then say, more please."

"Junco, this is what every General Fledge winner goes through. It is predictable, this grief. These doubts. You did follow orders, but those pledges would not be suitable for this Cluster. And they were not suitable for their own Clusters. They were defective."

"I don't mean to make comparisons like this, Lucan, and normally I never would because you're entitled to your own culture, but on Earth we love the defective just as much as the average. More, sometimes."

"This is not Earth, Junco, and we are not human."

I sniff up some snot. "Yeah, I know."

"We are at a critical stage, we have no genetic stock to speak of, Junco. None that we can afford to use. Do you know that the General Fledge used to yield more than two hundred new Aves warriors? It wasn't always ten."

I look up and take a deep breath. He smiles at my new attention to his words.

"We produced so many quality warriors. We were overfilled with candidates, those qualified for command, and those fighters who had everything it took to make our ranks successful. But this is what the bad code has done to us. Reduced us to the one-percent rule. And if we can be perfectly honest here, you and I both know that only four or five, at the most, of those ten today were really qualified."

I swallow because I knew it instinctively as I watched them line up. Even Kush is questionable.

"Why didn't you choose Isec, Junco? It was completely up to you."

I drop my head and close my eyes. "Because he would have chosen Tessen or Wyrd or Kush."

"But they were all chosen anyway."

"I know, but it would have been a lie." I look up at him. "I'm not supposed to lie unless it's war. Isec was not my pick. Isec never saved my life. Annun did. And I didn't know." I turn my head away and let the tears spill out. "I didn't know, Lucan. If I had known— " I let the words drop unsaid. I'd like to think I would've lied and picked Isec, but I'm not sure. I'm not sure and I cannot even bring myself to lie about it now.

"Do you know we purposely reworded the question this year, to make it less strict as to who can be chosen? And that all the sitting Archers signed on, just to give you the chance to save your little friend – in case you needed to retain that human element to stay with us."

"What?" I look up in his face and feel my heart shrivel up with sadness.

"We usually ask which of the remaining warriors you would follow into battle. And this Fledge we decided to ask you to choose the warrior you would have first on your team. We gave you an out if you needed it."

I stare at him, sniffing and unsure what to think.

"Of course, we would all have been disappointed if you took the out. And when you didn't, when you chose the best of the remaining warriors to follow, you earned the respect of the entire Aves population. You were objective under enormous emotional stress, and you came through for us."

"I don't feel well."

"You are exceptional, Junco. Exceptional. You have natural gifts that we cannot even comprehend yet. And you have given Amelia and the rest of the worlds hope with your promise to deliver the Siblings."

"How the fuck can I deliver them, Lucan? She made me say that, I was scared and she made me say it! I have no power to deliver them."

"You do have power, Junco, you'll see. Moju is waiting for you. He's waiting for you to just come and ask him to come home. He's not waiting for Tier, no matter what you think, he's holding on for you. I saw it." I look up at him and he nods. "I would not lie."

He takes my hand and pulls me up.

I consider fighting him but I don't. He leads me down the stairs of the altar and back between the always-empty benches of the syrinx church. And then we are out the door and Ashur and Isten are waiting. I look up at them and force the tears back, then paint an angry frown on my face as they grab my arms and fly me down to the dorm.

We hear the uproar long before we land and walk the short distance to the lounge area. All the guys are there, as are a few I don't recognize, and they are shouting and pointing to the screen on the wall.

Lucan is arguing with several others who look like him, so I assume they are Archers, and Isten and Ashur join the fray as they push for dominance.

It takes me a few seconds to turn and log what's scrolling across the screen.

It's Tier.

He's dressed in some nondescript uniform, not the Aves uniform, and his eyes look distant with drugs. He's on the gurney, under testimony. A reporter flashes across the screen and summarizes the event that has everyone here riled up.

He's pleaded guilty to treason and Justice has accepted the plea.

The trial is over.

I stare at the words that splash across the screen. Then watch as a camera shows a large crowd rioting outside the Fledge building. I walk over towards the door and make it down two flights of stairs before I hear the 039 calling my name. I hop down the stairs faster, pushing down the residual pain from my ankle injury as a banging noise from below draws me down. I race out towards the front door and skid to a stop, sliding on the floor and landing on my hip sideways as a window shatters from the blunt force of some large object.

The rioters are wild, screaming and pointing at me like I am the one who is guilty of treason. I scramble up as they break down the barrier keeping them at bay and then they are spilling into Fledge. The SEAR comes to life in full sword length just as I hear the heavy boots behind me.

The plasma loop illuminates their faces in the dim evening light that leaks in from outside and it's their turn to skid to a stop on the gleaming white floor and fall on their asses. I crouch with the SEAR in high ready position and shake my head. The little red lights in the eyes of some tells me they are reporters, or at least recording the scene. "Don't even fucking think about it."

Lucan appears between the mob and me. Then the 039 and I are standing shoulder to shoulder. Ashur puts his hand on my weapon arm. "Put it away, Junco. You're just making it easier for them to hate you."

I wait a few seconds as Lucan barks orders and the other Aves teams push them back outside with force. I breathe, and the SEAR slips back into place. "What the fuck was that?"

Ashur shakes his head. "They blame you. For Tier's fate."

My eyes squint as my mouth draws down in a long frown. They blame me. Because he should have killed me like he was instructed. Just like I had to kill Isec when I was instructed. I watch Lucan argue with several individuals who appear to be reporters and then he grabs one and escorts him over to me.

It's Kadian.

"Junco," Lucan snaps, "come upstairs." He has a pretty good grip on Kadian's arm and then he touches me on the shoulder and we appear up in the dorm. I am immediately drawn towards the unbearable noise coming from the far wall and I absently walk over to the lounge. The screen is alive with action and my eyes track to a familiar landmark. I feel dizzy as I realize the footage is from Earth.

Peak City is bursting in explosions. I look over at Lucan and I can see his shock as well. The reporter's voice isn't registering in my brain, because when I look back all I see are the words *Tactical EM Pulse and Nuke Explodes over Peak City* scroll across the lower edge of the screen.

I hear boots running up the stairs and then Ashur is next to me. I look up at him and watch the flashes of destruction flicker across his face for a few seconds before he looks down and meets my gaze. Lucan's hand is on me then and he is pulling, yelling at Ashur to turn the fucking screen off, and yanking on Kadian's arm so hard he's begging desperately for him to let go.

"Stop!" I scream as my hands come up to my ears. "Just shut the fuck up for a minute, all of you!" I breathe in and out repeatedly as Ashur moves to turn the screen off. "Stop, Ashur. Leave it alone. It's my fucking home that was just blown up, so if anyone has a right to watch as it falls apart, it's me."

The room is hushed of human sound and all eyes are on me. Only the explosions make it into my ears. I look over at the stairs and most of the guys from downstairs, and all of the Archers, are there, quiet and still. I walk over to the couches and take a seat, then lean back into the cushions and turn up the volume and log every detail, every scream, every dead body, and every demolished building that used to be the rock of my existence as it falls into ruin.

A little while later an additional nuke is reported. This time it takes out Council Three in the RR. A hovercopter flies as close as it can get in the northwestern sector to show the world the burned land that used to be my tallgrass. The tears finally begin to fall. My whole life, everything I had before I came here, is wiped away in a single day.

They stay there with me and watch the screen, every one of them, my team or otherwise. Warrior or Archer. They all stay. And they say nothing. We just watch as the entire middle section of the United Republics erupts into total war.

Eventually Ashur takes my hand and pulls me up. "We're going home now." On the ride home I stare out the window and think. My home is gone, Tier is guilty, I have promised to deliver something that might not even be possible, and I killed someone who trusted me.

And millions of people are dead, Junco. Maybe Moju too, so this might signal the end of the entire avian race. And all you think about is how it affects you? Nice.

When we land on the upper terrace of the apartment I push Ashur off and go directly to my room. My biometrics release the lock and I close it behind me before anyone can follow.

I leave the lights off and sit down in the window seat, looking out at traffic and the bright lights of Amelia proper. My vision screen comes to life but stays silent.

Is there a way to salvage anything from this event?

There is always a way, Junco. The question is, as always, what are you willing to sacrifice to make it happen?

"What do you want?" I say out loud.

Your compliance.

"Tell me what I have to do."

You know what you have to do. You've known it all along. It's the reason you stayed behind when Slag came for you. It's the reason you fought with Lucan. It's the reason you lied under testimony. And it's the reason you will push Ashur away.

I shake my head. "There is only one way to make it right."

Yes. So shut the fuck up and get on with it, why don't you? Quit looking at the things you've lost and see the things you have.

Chapter Thirty-Four

I wake up in the new bed, luxurious blankets and pillows strewn about from my thrashing. My door is open and I can hear voices coming from the living room. Ryse's for sure, and a few more that I don't recognize. They joke a little and get loud and Ryse tells them to keep it down. I hear the familiar sound of poker chips and listen for Braun, but his voice is not among the cacophony of maleness that floats into my room.

I get up and go into the bathroom and start a bath, adding bubbles as I watch it fill up, then strip my Fight Seven uniform off and sink into the hot water with a heavy sigh. I slip under a few times to get my hair wet, then use the provided bottles to wash and condition it.

When I'm done I wrap up in a white robe that hangs on the bathroom door and stuff my hair up in a towel. Back out in my room the voices are louder now and I tap the door shut and go find something to wear. A few minutes later I hear a knock.

"Enter."

"Sorry, Junco. I hope we didn't wake you up." Ryse smiles at me and I try to smile back, but I'm just not into it. I just go into the closet and pull on some bed shorts and a tank top. Then find some white fuzzy socks that slip over my feet and go back in the bathroom to brush my hair.

When I come back out he's sitting on my bed, waiting for me.

"What?"

"You want me to call Ashur and tell him to come home?"

"Why? Where is he?"

"Working on something for Lucan."

I shake my head. "No point, really. It is what it is, Ryse. And there's nothing any of you can say or do to change it."

He nods. "Yeah. OK. Well, when you're hungry you just let me know. I'll help you pick something you'll like from the autocook."

He walks over to the door and I walk over with him and close it as he leaves, then go over to the window seat and plop down. It's a fabulous space and looks out over the boulevards. Several stories down I can see the train, then several more there is another one. I can't see the bottom during the day either, but there are tall buildings across from me that are interesting to look at. Plus, there is a lot of eye-level traffic that captures my attention.

I pull my legs up to my chest as I watch the people who pass by inside the flyers. A noise over on the pile of clothes in the bathroom pulls me out of my reflection and I jump up and go grab my com from my pants pocket.

"This is Junco."

"Hi, Junco. It's Kadian."

I sigh. "What do you want, Kadian?"

"Oh, I just wanted to check up on you, make sure you're OK. I'm very sorry, Junco. Everyone is very sorry."

"Yeah, except those crazy people who wanted to kill me last night for Tier's stupid decision."

"They have calmed down due to the – circumstances. Have you watched the screens today? There was a public apology."

"No," I sigh. "I just woke up."

"Well, I have an ulterior motive for calling you."

"Yeah, what's that then?"

"I want to take you somewhere tonight. Will you come out with me?"

I'm shaking my head even though he can't see me. "Kadian, I don't really—"

"Junco, I promise you, this is something beautiful you won't want to miss."

"How would you know?"

"I heard you that day we met, when you asked that barbaric XO of yours if there was anything he could show you that was purely avian, not human. I have something I can show you. Something that fulfills that request."

I'm interested despite myself. "What is it?"

I listen to him tisk his tongue. "Surprises, Junco, mean you have to trust me that it will be worthwhile."

"I'm not really into surprises, Kadian, people tend to get killed when they try to surprise me."

He laughs. "Nonsense, Junco. You're a woman and that means you like surprises just as much as any of them. You've just been around all those killing machines for so long you've forgotten how it feels."

He's got a point there. "I'm not really good at" – I search for the word – "socializing, Kadian. In fact, I'm pretty terrible at all that stuff."

"No, Junco, you've just never been taken out properly before."

"Look, I'm not interested—"

"Me either, Junco. I am happily attached to a very beautiful woman who I would like for you to meet tonight. I just want to show you something, OK?"

I look down at my clothes. "What should I wear?"

"Not those bed clothes you have on."

"How do you—"

"I live across the boulevard, Junco. Exactly opposite your window. And before you go thinking I'm some stalker, we've lived here for years. It's just a happy coincidence."

I walk over to the window seat and peer out, training my eyes to the building across the way, and see a small figure waving at me through the breaks in traffic. "So Ryse was correct? You're a spy and you write terrible things about us? You peep into our apartment?"

He gives me an exasperated huff, "This is a family home, Junco. Someone in my family has owned it for centuries."

"So you make stuff up about us?"

"I absolutely do not. Everything I've ever reported on the 039 has been one hundred percent true."

"But maybe it was secret? And you reported it anyway?"

I hear a small laugh over the com. "Perhaps. But that's what reporters do."

"So you want to take me out so you can report on me tomorrow?"

"Well, of course I will report on you. You're news, Junco. But the venue is worthwhile, and does deliver what you're looking for. Something that cannot be seen on Earth."

I hesitate.

"It is beautiful, Junco. And you could use a little beauty in your life today."

He's right. I could just sit here and listen to Ryse and his buddies play poker. As if my whole world wasn't in the process of coming down on me. Or I could go out and forget for a while. And isn't that what always gets me through the disasters? Forgetting? Shit, if there's one thing I can do it's push it all away. "OK, I'll go."

"Perfect, I'll pick you up in five minutes, wear anything you want."

And then the com goes dead.

I throw on some pants that look like human jeans, but aren't. And a shirt that isn't too complicated to pull over my head and seam together. I slip on my uniform boots because they are comfortable, and then head out.

Ryse and his friends look up as I enter and walk over to the terrace to go up to the roof. "Hey? Junco? Where are you going?" Ryse's cigar bobs up and down in his mouth as he talks.

"Out," I say. I'm halfway up the terrace stairs when I hear the flyer on the roof. Ryse is running to catch up with me, but I don't stop. The door opens on the flyer and Kadian is smiling at me.

"Oh, fuck no!" Ryse steps in between the flyer and me, blocking my advance, but I shoot him a dirty look.

"Ryse, I'm not a prisoner anymore. I'm Fledged out now and if I want to go out, then I will."

"But Junco," he pleads a little, "this is Kadian, he's a total scumbag."

I stick my chin up. "I have my com so Lucan can track me all night. I'm going, and there's nothing you can say about it."

"Ashur is not going to—"

"Ashur isn't my keeper, Ryse. I'm not on duty so I don't have to take orders from you or him."

Kadian has exited the flyer and steps up to Ryse. "I promise to deliver her home safe and happy."

Ryse actually growls at him and I push him back and jump in the flyer. Kadian gets in with me and then the door closes and we take off.

The flyer banks hard into a parking structure and I have a fleeting moment of déja vu at the suborbital station with Rache. I push it down and get out. Kadian stays seated and I poke my head back into the cab. "You coming or what?"

He smiles and shakes his head. "Girl stuff, Junco. I'll pick you up in two hours."

Before I can protest there are female hands leading me away and into a steamy shop filled with tantalizing flowery scents and the bustle of girls. I am subsequently plopped down onto some large cushions as a team goes to work on my fingernails, talons, hair, and to my horror, a full face of make-up including eyelashes that make my lids feel heavy.

When they bring about a mirror a while later I don't even recognize the girl on the other side. My hair is piled high on my head with soft tendrils slipping out every so often to soften and frame my face. My hazel eyes appear large and the color is brought out with make-up. My lips are a pretty pink just like my cheeks, and when I tilt my head to see the SEAR scar along my jaw it has all but vanished.

The ladies all nod and smile, then tug me up and guide me into a dressing room where a severe woman with a tight silver bun and wings to match sits with her lips pursed.

"It is a genuine improvement, Junco. Do you approve?"

I look in the full-length mirror. "Yeah, I like it."

She smiles. "I'm Anni and now we will dress you for the night. The dress is a gift, of course. So you may keep it."

"OK, thanks."

She brings out a stunning floor-length gown that is the prettiest shade of spring yellow I've ever seen. As she goes about instructing her helpers in fastening it around my wings I catch a glimpse in the mirror.

"Wow."

They top it off with a slight jacket made of some kind of fur that is a shade or two lighter than my hair. I scowl at the shoes as they place my feet in them, but Anni clicks her tongue at my balking and after I give in and cooperate, I'm suddenly three inches taller.

Anni takes my hand and lifts it in the air as she turns me slowly in a circle. "You are ready."

She claps and her attendants escort me into another chamber, then through a closed door to the parking garage where the flyer is waiting. The door opens and Kadian appears, dressed in a very nice dark brown suit that complements the tones in my hair and jacket. I take his hand as he offers me help into the cab.

"Junco," he breathes, "you're stunning."

I pick up the high-society manners I was forced to practice all growing up. "Thank you. You look exceptionally handsome as well."

He is tight-lipped about our destination. I watch as the flyer takes us a few wide avenues over to the boulevard, then banks to the right and slides into a slot in the side of a building. I read a marquee above a large expanse of wide brass colored doors: *Enki and the World Order*, last night on Amelia.

When my eyes come back to Kadian, he is grinning. "I think you'll enjoy it, Junco. It's a beautiful retelling of the myth in nargala."

I nod, but I have no idea what he's talking about.

I've been to the opera on Earth, Handel's Messiah in Berlin and London, as well as The Marriage of Figaro in Vienna and of course, Asgarth's Genius in just about every city it opened in during my lifetime. My father indulged me in the arts for reasons known only to him.

This feels like the opera.

The women are dressed in expensive finery while the men wear complementary suits to match something on their lady's person. Kadian is a nice-looking man to begin with, and his suit is cut to perfection, so we fit in with the crowd. We stand in the lobby as people take pictures of us. Normally I'm self-conscious about stuff like that, but tonight I feel like I have a costume on and don't have to be the gawky Junco. I don't smile, I can't smile, but I do paint on a neutral expression that passes for acceptable.

An usher directs us to a chamber that contains several seats. We take two near the edge of a balcony, and Kadian leans over to talk in my ear. "The nargala is sung in avian, but I have been told that you understand it. Yes?"

"I do."

He smiles. "Good, good. It's an old story, but the fourth act is especially poignant. I think, anyway."

He gives me a conspiratorial look and I nod a little. "OK."

A little while later the lights dim and the show begins.

Kadian calls the woman rotating in mid-air in the center of the theater the Ilat Nargalist, and he genuinely beams with pride when he suddenly announces that she is his girlfriend.

She is beautiful, dressed in a bright blue gown that hangs to the floor several stories below. She floats like an angel, her outstretched wings the color of a robin's egg. They don't flap, so I can only assume she is controlling herself via a free-G zone that doesn't touch the rest of us.

When she begins her song my chest heaves with the beauty of it. It is not a song any human can replicate, the notes are so high they barely exist in my hearing range. I see my vision screen come to life and adjust my capacity for sound detection, and her true talents flood into my body. She is singing several notes at the same time, like an orchestral arrangement coming from the mouth.

I am so taken by the sound, I forget to listen to the words. Eventually I catch on to the story. Enki is the all-powerful creator and he's going about to various family members allocating supervision duties. Each god and goddess is bestowed a realm with special powers. He has quite a big family, so this lasts the first three acts.

The fourth act begins with a twist.

A very young goddess Inanna complains that she has been overlooked. I think back to what I know of Inanna. Not much except for her journey to the world down below as told to me by Tier. In this story she begs to know why Enki, her uncle, has forsaken her.

Why do you treat me so badly?
My sisters have all been given domains to rule over.
My sisters have all been given powerful husbands.
My sisters have all been given special skills.
My sisters have all been given the ability to please you.
But I, the woman Inanna, have been given nothing of this new world.

Her uncle replies,

Tell me what you require, Inanna.
Tell me how I have wronged you.
Tell me what more could I give you?

You shine brilliantly in the evening,
You brighten the day at dawn
You stand in the heavens like the sun and the moon,

Your wonders are known both above and below,
I made you strong.
I made you the destroyer of all that cannot be destroyed.
I made you cunning.
I made you the speaker of words known to no man.
I made you the twister.
I made you the manipulator of the threads that bind the world.
I gave you sight.
You see further than any other, you see what no other can.
I made you beautiful.
You have endless suitors ready to lay down their lives.
You cut off the heads of those that cannot be cut.
You make the final decisions,
You make the sacrifice.
You stand apart.
You make us whole.
You complete us.
What more do you want?

Chapter Thirty-Five

I feel a tear slip down my cheek as I listen to her song and I wait for Inanna to accept her gifts with grace. But she does not, she demands the Carrier of Light and she is denied. The nargala ends with her behaving badly and being cast aside. Someone grabs my hand as another tear slips out. I look over and Lucan is sitting next to me. He squeezes as the theater goes dark.

We are standing in the lobby a short time later when the Ilat Nargalist comes to greet us. She bows low from the waist at Lucan and he takes her arm at the elbow and squeezes with both hands. She slips her free hand to his elbow and bows again. A very avian greeting that I have yet to master the nuances of.

I am introduced but my world is spinning. Lucan excuses us and taps me on the shoulder and we are out in the dark of space.

I sigh. "Thank you, I was beginning to feel dizzy."

He smiles and wraps my hand into the crook of his arm. "Yes, I could tell it was becoming too much."

"Why did you come?" I look up at him and he does something that surprises me, he shrugs.

"I would not have taken you there, Junco. It is—" He stops and searches for a word. "Too close."

I think back to the story. "Yeah. Why do I feel like it is talking about me?"

He laughs a little, but it's not a happy laugh. "You are so much like Inanna it is becoming painful."

I let out a large breath. "What's going on, Lucan?"

He shakes his head. "You are the Seventh Sibling, Junco. We know this now, and we can state this openly, correct?"

I shrug. "Hell, Lucan, if you say so. What am I gonna say? I don't know any better. But I'm not here to kill anyone."

He pats my hand, the one still holding onto his arm. "I think we are past that, but there is still a long way to go before we can sort it out."

I stay quiet for a few minutes and look up at the stars, enjoy the view for once. How many people can say they've been out in the middle of space with no suit? Not many, I bet. I count myself lucky. "Thank you," I say, looking down again.

"For what, Junco?"

"Everything. I feel so ungrateful. Always looking at how much I've lost instead of how much I still have. I don't want to be Inanna. I don't want to be hungry for power. That's not me. I want to be satisfied." I look up to him. "And even though there is still a lot to be sad about, there is also a lot to be grateful for. I'm thankful that you're here helping me through this. Even if I don't show it all the time."

He squeezes my hand and we are on the terrace at the 039. "You lost a lot in the last few months, Junco, and even though grief is a negative emotion, it is still necessary. There is nothing wrong with grief."

I look over and see Ashur lingering in the doorway. Then Lucan takes my arm like he did the Ilat Nargalist and says goodbye in a way that touches my heart.

I watch the air after he's gone for a few seconds, then walk over to the open terrace door to look up at Ashur.

He smiles. "Did you have a nice evening?"

"Yes, but…"

He raises his eyebrow at me. "What?"

"It would have been better if you were there with me." I shrug, then lift my long gown slightly as my fancy shoes click past him, past the guys sitting in front of the screen, and down the small hallway to my room where I take the costume off and soak in the tub until I am red with heat.

I'm in bed, not sleeping since my days and nights are mixed up yet again, when Ashur, dressed in some thermals and a t-shirt that makes him look more like one of my scrub buddies back on Earth than my avian captain, knocks on my open door. He walks over to the bed and sits down. "I have something for you." In his hand is a book and I sit up a little, interested.

"What is it?"

"The translation of the syrinx church door inscriptions."

I scoot over and open the covers. "Get in and read it to me."

He smiles and does what I ask. I lean up against him as he opens the book and we flip through the pages, looking at what the inscriptions mean. It's an obscure creation myth that even Ashur is unfamiliar with.

He loses interest and hands the book over as I pore through the translations, then go hunting for a few in my own memory to compare them. They are not exact word-for-word matches, but close.

Ashur is almost asleep when I close the book and sink down into the covers with him. "You were so beautiful tonight, Junco. I could barely look at you."

I smile. "I did look pretty good."

He turns his head and opens his eyes. "You know, you make a much better woman than you do a soldier."

"Thank you."

"You should stay a woman, Junco. Retire and be soft for the rest of your life. You don't have to do this if you don't want to."

I shake my head and let out a sigh. "I am what I am, Ash. It can't be helped. This hardness is what keeps me alive and soft is not really something I do. I'm OK with that, for a while anyway. And I promised to go back to Earth and bring home the stupid Siblings. I can't quit now."

"I could do that for you."

I turn and look at him. His green eyes study me back. "I made the promise, it had conditions attached. Besides, Tier might have given up on himself, but I haven't. It's not over until it's over."

He props himself up on his elbow. "What? Are you fucking kidding me?" His eyes dart back and forth, trying to see the meaning behind my words. "He's done, Junco. I don't like it either, but he's done."

"Maybe he is, but I'm not. I owe him."

"You don't owe him, you owe us, the 039! We're the ones who saved you, and we're still here with you!"

I rub my forehead and close my eyes.

"There is nothing you can do. What more is there?"

I shrug. "There is always another way, Ashur. If he can be saved, wouldn't you want to save him?" I sit up and search his eyes now. They are glowing green, bright enough to create shadows in the dark room. "I think it can still be done."

"Junco, you're not rooted in reality. He pled guilty to treason, it carries an automatic death sentence."

"We'll see, Ashur."

He gets up out of my bed and stands over me, shaking his head. "No, I'm not doing this with you, Junco. I'm not going to watch you do something stupid just because you can't sort through your feelings for him."

I sit up, angry. "That's not what this is about, Ashur. Not even close."

"No?"

I stand up too. "It's not about you, Ashur." I stand on my tiptoes and reach up to wrap my fingers around his neck and he puts his arms around me and tries to pull me in as I step back to see his face. "I'm not going to let them kill him."

He shakes his head and pushes me away. "No, I'm not participating in this. Did you talk to Braun?"

I squint up at him. "What?"

"Braun, did he tell you this shit? Fill your head up with this bullshit? He's crazy, Junco. I told you that from the fucking beginning, don't fucking get involved with him!"

"I haven't see Braun since that party here after the Sixth Fight."

He looks down at me suspiciously. "If he's put ideas into your head, Junco, do yourself a favor and forget you ever met him. He thinks he's this super tactician, but he's fucking impetuous and reckless in everything he does."

I slump back in the bed. "Are you going to come to sleep, or what?"

He shakes his head and walks towards the door. "While you plot out some harebrained idea about saving Tier? Forget it."

I watch him leave and then turn over in my covers as I hear a door slam somewhere else in the house.

The guys are all gone in the morning and I'm alone. No babysitter for the first time since I came to Amelia. I sit around in my bed shorts and tank top, sample a half dozen dishes from the autocook, puff on cigars on the terrace, and generally make a mess as I watch with as much detachment as I can muster as the newscreens flash images of Earth and the recent destruction.

They have the numbers.

Eight million dead.

Three million displaced throughout the Mountain Republic, the parts of the Rural Republic that were not affected as much by the fallout, and Texas. Texas is pissed off and has claimed the entire Rural Republic as reparations. They already have the scrubbers in place on the ground. Debris clean-up for the Peaks has been contracted out to some obscure company that goes by Yukichi from the Gulf Coast. The whole Peaks area is going to be covered with a layer of concrete twenty feet thick by the end of the summer and full habitation is predicted in less than five years.

Lovely.

Let's all pretend that millions of people never existed.

I'm seething in rage when the door chimes.

"Enter."

Kush makes his way down to the couches in the sunken living room. "How you doing, Junco?"

"Just fucking great, and yourself?" I'm mad at him, but my reasons aren't clear. Maybe because I saw the blame on his face during Fight Seven, or maybe because he too decided that Isec was expendable. But mostly I think it is because he reminds me of the little brat and I can't push it down if he keeps popping back up.

"I've volunteered for the Deliverance fight."

I look at him with my mouth open. "The wish fight for killing prisoners? Why would you do that?"

"I want the wish. I figure I've been through six of them already, right? And this one isn't even a fight to the death. What do I have to lose?"

"But you could die." They've been advertising Deliverance on the screens for weeks and I guess if you're hard up, a wish is a pretty big draw. "I mean, haven't you had enough killing yet? Maybe you should have been the one to kill the defective pledges at Seven? That might have cured you."

"Look," he says impatiently, "I get that you've been through a lot, but you're not the only one. I haven't been granted the gifts of the Gods like you apparently have. I need this wish."

"What could you possibly need? You're in the Aves, wasn't that what you wanted?"

"Yes, but I am not satisfied with the captain we have directing us on the new team. Annun is good, but he's not that good."

I shake my head in disbelief. "Who gives a fuck who's captain? Seriously, I'm the lowest one on my team, do you think I give a shit? You think you can do better than Annun? You have to earn the rank, anyway. And you didn't earn it. No one will follow a captain who was given the rank as a gift. You're supposed to want to support your captain because he supported you when you needed it."

"Annun helped you, Junco. Not me. He never did anything for me."

I let out a deep sigh. "Well, good luck then. I wish you success. You're a good fighter, so you'll be fine, I'm sure. And you've got just as much chance as anyone at winning."

He huffs. "Yeah, thanks for the vote of confidence. You know, you're pretty fucking condescending to anyone not on your level."

I laugh. "Oh, I'm sorry, did I hurt your feelings? You want me to pretend you're the big strong guy and I'm the weak and stupid girl? Get over yourself, Kush. You're slightly above average for an Aves warrior, but if they get someone in there with real Aves blood, you're toast."

"Someone like you?"

I laugh. "Now why the fuck would I want to fight for something as stupid as a wish. Get real."

He smiles as he gets up and walks over to the door. "Because, Junco, they just announced that Tier will be killed in the Deliverance fight. And ya know, I thought since you're all hung up on the guy, you might like to use your wish to save his fucking life." He salutes me. "See ya around."

My mind races back to Braun's plan before I left for Fledge. How the fuck did he know? Shit, maybe he's a precog, too? I take a deep breath and try and put the pieces together.

I'm still sitting there thinking when Rikan and Mish show up a half hour later. I found the announcement about Tier on the screen and it's playing when they come down into the living area to see what I'm doing.

I look up at them as the realization sinks in and then get up and go to my room to play the piano. My hands pluck out simple tunes at first, building the idea in my head, and then they begin tapping out more complicated melodies as the plan takes root. By the time I've got it all figured out I'm playing Asgarth's dungeon murders in E flat major.

Chapter Thirty-Six

The Fledge building has been repaired since the altercation after Tier's guilty plea. It's locked up tight when I approach the door, but I swipe my palm in front of the biometrics and they open for me anyway.

I walk across the clean tile floor of the lobby, feeling a bit strange when no mods are there to notice, and go directly to the stairs and fly up to the third floor dorm. I walk through, barely managing to push down the memories made here, and walk into the mast.

My flight up is smooth and quick.

Inside the church the syrinx is still upside down in her silent sacrificial scream. I lie down on my back and scoot underneath her so I can see her face again.

"What the fuck do you want from me?"

I stare into her eyes, which glow a faded green, perhaps hinting that at one time she was avian. None of the other Archers have wings, yet she does. None of the other Archers have glowing eyes, yet again, she does. She doesn't have the look of an Archer.

She's not fair, she's a redhead.

She's obviously not male, and all the Archers I've met so far are.

It just doesn't add up.

"Who are you really?"

"It's very perceptive of you to notice these things, Junco. For someone not familiar with the local customs."

I slide sideways to avoid hitting my head on the statue as I jump to my feet and then stare open-mouthed at the woman sitting on the first bench. She's got the red hair, but she's also wearing a long red gown. The syrinx on the cross is wearing some ancient garb I don't recognize. I'm silent as I look at her.

"For someone so demanding, you suddenly have very little to say."

"Do you want something from me?"

She smiles. "Of course I do."

I let out a breath of air. "So, you gonna tell me what the fuck it is you want?"

She clicks her tongue at me. "I don't suffer insolence, Junco. You will refrain from speaking to me in such a common manner."

I rub my forehead to stave off the growing tension, then take a seat on the top step in front of her. "Sorry, then. I'm just very tired."

She smiles. "But you have a destiny and you prayed for courage and bravery when you meet your end."

"So this is the end?"

She nods. "An end, yes."

"An end to what, exactly?"

"To you, of course."

I nod and swallow. "What do you want me to do?"

"You have a well-thought out plan. That you composed today?"

I shrug. "I guess. That's the best you can do? My stupid little plan?"

"Set it in motion."

I am about to object when she disappears and Lucan is standing in front of me at the bottom of the steps.

He sighs. "Junco, what are you doing?"

"Looking for answers, Lucan, why else would I be here in this crappy little church?"

"Your trip on the trains has drawn attention. There is a crowd outside waiting for you."

I shrug. "So? I don't need saving, ya know. Tier needs saving, not me."

He shakes his head. "This business with Tier is over now, Junco." His voice is calm and rational, but I detect that I'm pushing buttons under the surface that might set him off. "Ashur told me that you've still got it in your head that he can be saved."

"He can," I say simply.

"He cannot."

I shrug. "That's just your opin—"

He's got me by the shoulders and is shaking me. "No! It is not my opinion, Junco. It is the future as it is told. I have seen it. Tier dies, Junco."

I don't pull away but I do look him in the eyes. "Isec said he saw it too. And he said I can do it. Did do it, actually."

"Isec? He wasn't a precog, Junco! He was a failed telepath! You're comparing millennia of skill in the foretelling of what will come to the erratic second sight of that throwaway child?"

"The syrinx is on my side," I say simply. "Maybe you should take it up with her? Because I'm not really sure she's as understanding as you might be if I disobey. I'm pretty sure she expects obedience."

He looks into me, searching, willing it to be a lie, but when it rings true, he lets go of my shoulders. "What did you do?"

"I fucking told you, Lucan, that night I said the prayer, I asked her for bravery and courage in the end and she asked me for a sacrifice." I look down. "I said yes, remember? Obviously you dismissed that part of my story, because if you took me seriously you wouldn't look so shocked right now." The last part comes out soft and I wait for his anger. He's still got the look of confusion when I look up at him. "I already agreed, get it?"

"You agreed to nothing, Junco. Do I make myself clear?"

I shake my head. "No, she's one scary bitch. I'm not even allowed to swear at her. She said she doesn't suffer insolence. And I'm pretty sure if I called her to tell her no thank you on that deal we struck, she'd kill me dead."

"This was never in the plan, Junco."

My stomach churns and I hold down the urge to vomit. "This was always in the plan, Lucan. Some fucking precog you are. You know what your problem is? You're just not cynical enough. Don't you know that things will always get worse? When you've lived through the shit I have, you come to expect it. Hell, rely on it like an old friend, even."

He looks at me, his eyes sad and his mouth drawn down in a frown.

"It's not going to end well, you said it yourself. That's just the way it is. But hey, you can take comfort in the fact that it wasn't you who put me here, right? It was Tier. And me. In the end, we're the ones to blame, and I recognize that. I don't hate you."

"You will come with me now and I will take you home."

I shake my head. "No. I don't like the time slip that comes with your teleportation trick. It's got me all fucked up. I don't want to lose time just to get a free ride home. I'm taking the train like a normal person."

"You will stay inside and I will send a flyer to pick you up, is that satisfactory?"

I smile and agree. "Yeah, alright."

He's gone in an instant. I consider calling out to the syrinx again, but don't. She gave her order. Set it in motion.

I get up and fly down the mast, then take the stairs to the lobby and inhale deeply a few times. I walk over to the doors and step through to follow her command.

The reporters have made themselves comfortable, probably not expecting me to turn up, and are lounging around when I exit the building. They look at me for a second, disbelief written on their faces, then spring to action like a prairie lion jumping on a newborn antelope.

They crowd me and I let them.

I am pushed and pulled as questions are hurled at me one after another.

Yet I stay silent and let it drag on for maximum effect.

Finally they calm down and stand as still as you can expect from a mob of vultures.

I clear my throat. "I have an announcement to make." They lean in. Some clamber up a few nearby trees trying to get a good shot. "I've been informed that my former Fledge teammate Kush will be participating in the Deliverance fight." I pause and they wait, so quiet that I can hear the wind blow softly through the leaves. "I will be participating in the Deliverance fight with Kush."

Now they erupt with questions but I ignore them and shake out a cigar, strike it up, and puff with satisfaction when the flyer arrives and I can climb in, giving the scene a more dramatic end that I could have hoped.

When I arrive home Ashur is waiting for me on the rooftop parking pad. He shakes his head as I exit. "I forbid it, Junco. As your captain, I will not permit it."

I don't even slow down as I pass him. "Then I quit, Ashur."

He grabs me by the arm and swings me down on the ground, hard enough to knock the breath out of me, and then holds my hands and straddles my chest with his full weight, making me choke. "I don't think so, Junco," he snarls as he leans down into my face. "You think I'm fucking playing around here? You will not fight in Deliverance!"

I am not stupid enough, or so full of myself, to think I can take on a warrior like Ashur, all things being equal, and this is decidedly unequal from my vantage point. So I stay still and silent until the guys are there to pull him off and fight my battle for me.

Ryse grabs me by the shoulders to tug me upright, then pushes me back behind him. "What the fuck are you doing, Ashur?" he asks calmly, shaking his head at him. "Don't do that. If you've got a problem you don't manhandle her, for fuck's sake."

Ashur is pacing, breathing hard, and his eyes never leave mine. "You want to be a warrior, Junco? Fight like a man? Then fuck it, I'll treat you like one. You're not fighting in Deliverance. That is a fucking order and you are not quitting."

I remain calm. "You were just fine with me quitting last night when all you could think about was sleeping with me, though, right? I can quit as long as I do it on your terms?" I shake my head. "This isn't about you, Ashur, how many fucking ways do I have to say it?" He's about to say something predictable but I cut him off. "It's not about Tier either. Or you guys." I point to each of my team members. "It's about me."

"Junco." Isten walks up to me. "I get it, I really do. But there's a very good fucking chance you'll win. Do you really want to be the one who kills Tier?"

I look down, then force my head back up to meet his gaze. "I'm definitely not going to kill Tier. This fight is happening. It's done."

Lucan arrives in front of me then. "No, Junco, this is not happening. And you said the same thing about not killing Isec if I recall correctly."

My rage boils over and I spit at him, "How dare you. After you talked me up with all that shit about Isec not being good enough, all those sob stories about your goddamn gene pool, how fucking dare you."

He stares at me but no apology comes forth.

I look at each one of them and let my eyes stop with Ashur. "You fucking people think you know me because you spied on me for a while? You don't know me, you showed up when I was seventeen, after all the fucking psychological torture and conditioning was over. When the fucking die had already been cast and I was already complete. What about all those years you missed? You've got no idea the shit I live with every day. You think those teeny tiny little secrets you learned about recently are it? That's all there is to my fucked-up existence? Do you really tell yourselves that my childhood was nothing but a protected life of piano lessons and horseback riding?"

I shake my head and start again in a calmer, more controlled tone. "You don't want to know what I've done because it would take about two seconds for you to realize I'm not fucking worth any of this shit. There is no cure for what I am."

I stare at them in silence.

No one says a word so I look Lucan in the eye. "I fucking told you she gave me orders. This is what she said to do. And you can take it up with her if you don't fucking like it, but as of today I've got a new boss. That bitch has the look of eternal vengeance to her, so I'm proceeding as instructed. At this point I don't give a fuck how it ends – just fucking make it end!"

Ryse interjects, shaking his head and squinting his eyes at Lucan. "What the fuck are we talking about here?"

I look up at Ryse. "Ask Lucan, he's Mr. I-see-the-fucking-future, not me."

Chapter Thirty-Seven

I walk away, jump down the stairs to the terrace three at a time, and find shelter in the window seat of my room.

My com vibrates in my pants and I answer. "What?"

"Kadian here, Junco. I see you in the window and you don't look so sure of your decision."

I huff. "Kadian, I'm very fucking sure of my decision."

"I saw the little fight up on the roof. That Ashur has a violent side. It's quite disturbing."

"If you show that to anyone, Kadian, I will–"

"Relax, snowbird. I'm not interested in your little lover spats. I called to ask if I can have the pre-fight interview."

I scan across the traffic outside my window to see if he's over there, then see him wave. "I guess. Why not?" My Farm Family breeding and manners kick in, I can't help myself. "I never did thank you for the lovely evening. It really was spectacular. And your girlfriend, she's amazing."

"Yes, she is. But she's gone on tour now, so I only have you to distract me."

I smile. "I don't care for Inanna though, I have to be honest."

"Yes, good instincts, Junco. She's wild. But she lives in a man's world, so how can we blame her? When you're blessed with the skill set she was given, it's got to be hard to remember that you're just a girl sometimes."

I snort. "Gee, thanks for the dig, Kadian. As if I don't have enough to think about, now I can brood over how wild I should or should not be in order to accomplish the heinous things they make me do."

He's silent on the other end, but I hear him exhale. Frustration with me?

"If you only knew what they've told me to do over the years, Kadian, you wouldn't say that shit to me, even if you think it's a thinly veiled joke."

More silence.

"And when you add in the fact that I've been forced to kill like a rabid nightdog since I was six, well, then you could maybe cut me some fucking slack when I get a little wild."

I end the call and flip him off in the window.

Lucan appears a few seconds later, like he was waiting for me to end the call or something. He is calm when he speaks. "Junco, Ashur will take you to Layla. I want a complete medical workup."

And then he is gone.

I huff out some air as the door chimes, then pull myself together and open the door to meet Ashur.

His eyes turn away as he mumbles, "Sorry, Junco."

"You know what, Ashur? That's not the first time you've lost your temper with me, but I'm going to tell you something right now. It is the last. You do it again, and I'll fucking kill you just like I did that motherfucker in the dorm showers." I wait for his eye contact to see if he'll challenge me, but he doesn't. He just nods and walks out towards the terrace and I follow.

The ride over is painfully silent. We don't even argue. We just sit. Apparently my first home on Amelia was Layla's lab to begin with because that's where we end up.

The table and screen are both still there, but the bed is gone. Ashur takes a seat at the table and starts changing channels while I let Layla pull me into the lab.

"How have you been, Junco?"

My lips pout a little. "I've been better, to be honest. How about you? Haven't seen you in a while."

She smiles at me. "Yeah, I've been busy. Lucan says he wants another body scan so we can compare it to the ones we did when you came out of morph."

I nod at her.

"To see if there have been any changes."

Right. Changes.

I strip and stand behind the transparent screen. Last time it took a while to get the machine set up, but Lucan must have had this planned before my little outburst, because she's right on top of things. As soon as I get in position, the laser is reading my body.

I can see Ashur out of the corner of my eye and then the door chimes and I watch him get up to go answer it. I hear some muffled talking and then Monk appears around the corner.

"Hey, Junco," he says.

I shake my head.

Layla clicks her tongue. "Stand still, Junco, now I'll have to do that again."

"Do we have to have an audience? I'm naked, you assholes, get the fuck out!"

They both step back at my tone and then retreat around the wall, but I don't hear the door chime, so I know they didn't leave.

"I said, get out! Not fucking hide behind the wall!"

Layla loses her patience and goes around the corner. "You heard her, get out! You know better!"

This time the door does chime.

"Thank you," I say, letting out a breath of exasperation.

"Fucking children, I have no idea how you put up with them, Junco. If I had to spend all my time with those assholes, I'd go crazy."

I smile. "Really?"

She nods. "Oh, yeah. Tier was one thing, he's different. But the rest of them are just giant babies. I can't stand it. I feel sorry for those girls they promoted to warriors. They have no idea what they are in for. Now hold still and we'll run it again and be done."

When she's finished I put my clothes back on and take a seat at the table where I played my first poker game on Amelia.

"Hey, Layla?"

"Uh-huh?" she answers from the lab.

"Have you seen Braun?"

She pokes her head around the corner of the wall that separates us. "Why?"

"He's been avoiding me since…" I think back. "Since I left here to go to Fledge, really. I miss him."

She comes over and sits at the table. "Lucan is keeping the two of you apart."

"Why?"

She shakes her head and shrugs. Then she puts her hands up in a helpless gesture. "He thinks you're plotting something."

"Holy fucking Christos, you're right. I can't spend another fucking minute with these overbearing fucking little boys. I can't take it anymore. I'm going to lose my mind."

She smiles and then laughs. "I see him all the time, I'll tell him you're asking. He'll like that. He's my second favorite, after Tier." She looks at me for a few seconds.

"So, you don't have to tell me, but if you do I won't say anything. I can call it doctor-patient confidentiality."

"What?"

Her face falls and gets serious, then sad. "Do you really have a plan? For Tier?"

I nod. "Yes."

"Will it work?"

Her eyes plead with me, but I can only throw up my hands. "I don't know, Layla."

"Well, you may not have been talking to Braun these past few weeks, but I have. And he got me to agree to something I might not be one hundred percent on board with."

"Which is what?" I ask.

"The plan you two have. He won't tell me what it is, just asked that I be ready and to come when he calls. You know anything about this?"

"I can't say either way, Layla."

She nods and pulls herself together, then gets up to go check on the tests. A few minutes later she calls out, "You should come take a look, Junco."

I get up and walk around the corner to the viewing screen. My body image is almost white with circuits now. I shake my head and feel my throat start to ache as the tears well up. "What is it?"

"It's you." She looks at it for a long moment, then turns to me and gives me a sympathetic smile. "You're wired from top to bottom."

"Will it kill me?"

She shakes her head. "I doubt it. The first rule of symbiosis is do no harm. Otherwise you lose the host."

I'm a host. "What does it mean?"

She lets out a prolonged exhale. "Well, I'd guess it makes you capable of doing a lot of fucking stuff no one else can."

"Like?"

She laughs. "I dunno, eavesdropping in on people's coms? Hacking into databases? Stealing money from accounts? You have a very bright future, and I mean that literally," she says, pointing to the bright white lines on the image, "in stealth circuit ops."

I grunt and laugh with her despite myself. "Gee, just the career I've always wanted."

The door chimes and we both go silent. She snaps the image from the viewer and begins rolling it up as Ashur and Monk appear. "Well, you're all done here, Juncs. I'll get this over to Lucan." She shrugs. "But what he'll do with it I have no idea. Don't let these assholes get you down, they are just boys in the end." She slips the rolled-up image in a tube and heads out towards the door.

Monk, Ashur, and I stand there looking at each other. Then we all start talking at once.

Ashur and Monk are yelling face to face, complete with finger-points to the chest, meanwhile I can't even get them to look down and notice me at all. I stick my fingers on my tongue and whistle so loud they both hold their ears. "Shut the fuck up for a minute." I let out a breath. "OK, what is going on?"

Monk speaks first. "Rache wants me to bring you back to Justice, Junco. I'm under orders."

Ashur shakes his head. "Rache isn't Junco's Archer, Monk. Lucan is."

"She volunteered for the Deliverance fight, so he is her Archer until that's over. She comes with me."

Ashur looks down at me. "You're still going through with this fight, Junco?"

I lift my eyebrows and nod. "Yup. Still going through with it."

Monk smiles. "Well, good. Let's go. The fight is day after tomorrow so you'll want to get settled." He takes me by the arm and leads me towards the door.

"Junco?" I turn at Ashur's call and wait. "Good luck."

I sigh. "Thank you." And then we walk through the door and down the hallway.

Chapter Thirty-Eight

The ride over to Justice is just as silent as the ride over to the lab was. Monk tries, I'll give him that, but I'm not interested so I just ignore him completely. I don't need any more confusing relationships.

When we get off the inter-world transport he leads me through a series of hallways, only this time we end up in Rache's outer offices, and not the courtroom. Monk points to a straight-backed chair and I take a seat as he disappears through a large door.

I wait around for what seems like a very long time before a woman directs me to enter where Monk went through earlier. Inside is another hallway but I see Monk sticking out of a door near the end and walk towards him.

He's talking to someone inside when I reach him. He looks back at me and opens the door and directs me in, then backs out into the hallway and closes the door behind me.

Inside there are nine Archers sitting behind a crescent-moon table that looks similar to the one the 039 used at our meeting. My face goes tight and I feel the anger rise inside me. "Now what did I do?"

Lucan sits in the middle with four Archers on each side of him. He points to a chair in front of him and I walk over and take the hot seat once again.

I want to cry. But I don't. I sit and look at the ground.

"Junco," Lucan begins. "Layla said she showed you the scanner image?"

I nod, but say nothing.

"There have been a great many changes, do you agree?"

I nod again.

"Is the syrinx who talks to you inside of you? Or is she real?"

I shrug, then finally look up and meet their eyes, one set at a time, coming to rest back on Lucan as I answer. "How should I know? I saw her outside of me, if that's what you're asking."

The guy immediately to Lucan's left takes a stab next. "Junco, I am Gib, the Archer of Clutch. Can you describe her?"

I take a deep breath, then exhale. "She's pretty tall, long red hair, long red gown – kind of silky. Know what I mean? Like she's dressed up for something. She's not dark, but not fair like you guys." I shrug.

They look at each other and nod. Then Rache speaks. "Does she have wings, Junco?"

I shake my head. "No."

"What does she want?" another man asks without introduction.

"She wants me to save Tier."

"And how did she tell you to do that?"

I look at them all individually one more time. "I'm not going to tell you."

Lucan huffs. "Junco, you will tell us or we will punish you."

"I will not, Lucan. You can kill me for all I care. I don't plan on being around much longer anyway." His head pulls back at my statement.

Another one speaks without introducing himself. "Then we won't let you fight in Deliverance."

I stand up and knock the chair back. "I DON'T GIVE A FUCK!" I walk back towards the door.

Lucan is there in front of me before I can reach it. He puts a hand on my shoulder. "Junco, please. We're just trying to understand what you are and what you're doing."

"I told you, dammit. She wants me to save him. You can make this very simple and just let him go." I look around. "But you won't. Why? He was already halfway forgiven for those killings, you're just pissed because he brought me here. Well, there's an easy fix, just let him live and we'll both go back to Earth and then you won't have to see us ever again."

Lucan's hand is still on my shoulder and I shrug it off as he starts talking. "We can't let you go until we know what we're up against."

"Fine, put me in jail, or whatever it is you're going to do with me because I'm tired and hungry. I just want to get some fucking sleep and eat something right now."

Lucan opens the door and Monk is waiting outside. He looks at me with raised eyebrows and it reminds me of Braun that first time I met Lucan and told him off in the hallway. "Take her to her room on the Deliverance floor." Monk nods and takes my arm, pulling me away before I can look back.

We walk for a long time through so many convoluted hallways I have a little panic attack about getting lost and my feet actually hurt by the time we make it to the room that will be mine. Monk opens the door and begins showing me around. "Kush is next door, you can open the connecting door if you want."

I look up. "He is?" My chest heaves and I drop my head and begin to cry unexpectedly.

Monk just stares at me. "Junco, I'm sorry. I'm not used to dealing with girls in situations like this. Should I call for Ashur and have him come talk to you?"

I shake my head and wipe my fingers across my face to get rid of the tears. "No, I'm OK. I'm just tired, Monk. I'm tired."

"And hungry, right?"

I nod and smile. "And hungry."

"OK, well, I can get Kush, if you want?"

"No, I'll talk to him later."

"You want me to go?"

I nod.

He smiles. "Oh, here. Rache wanted me to give you this." He fishes into his thigh pocket and pulls out a com. "It's coded to our team, the 399, you're number eight. So, if you want to give someone your number, like Ryse or Ashur, you tell them Junco, Aves 399-8."

He hands it over and I slip it in next to my other com.

"That old one won't work here." He shrugs. "We're off Amelia now, right? You gotta use a Justice com."

"All right."

"OK, I'm number one. So if you want to call me, just push one and it'll go to me. Or if you want to call Rache, just push zero."

"What's Kush?"

He looks at me funny. "We didn't give him one."

"Why not?"

He smiles. "While you're here, Junco, you're on my team. You're my eight. Kush is just another fucking fighter."

"Oh." I let out a breath. "Thanks, and sorry for crying. I'm just—"

"Tired, yeah, I get it." He squeezes my shoulder and then leaves without another word.

I walk over to the floor to ceiling windows and stand on a little ledge that butts up against the glass to look out. It's a view of the fight arena. It's a pretty big place, a lot bigger than any arena I've ever fought in for Fledge. At one end is a stage-type riser. Scattered throughout the open central area are mushroom gravity wells, similar to the ones from Fight Seven. My room is almost dead center opposite the stage.

Surrounding the upper portion of the arena are seats for the spectators. It will be weird to fight in front of people, but not much weirder than anything else I've done since I became an avian.

My com buzzes and I immediately wonder how Kadian got my new number so fast. "Hello?"

"Junco?"

It's Ashur. "Yeah."

"You all right?"

I nod, then remember he can't see me. "Yeah."

He lets out a little laugh. "Monk is freaked out. He's never had a girl on his team."

"I don't get it, how come I'm on his team?"

Ashur is quiet for a few seconds. "Rache wants to keep you, Junco. So…" He stops, maybe not wanting to finish the thought, or maybe he's listening to me breathe erratically on the other side as I begin to realize what's happening. "Don't be surprised if they treat you real nice."

I've done it now, my team is about to be ripped away before I even get the chance to enjoy them. I'm silent as I choke back my tears and try to swallow down the ache that prevents me from talking.

"Junco?"

I push it down one more time before I speak. "Yeah."

"You want me to come see you?"

I shake my head, then catch myself again. "No." I breathe the word out with a half-hidden sob. "No, I'm OK. Really. I'm just going to go to sleep. I'm tired."

"Tomorrow then?"

My nose is running and I sniff a couple times. "Yeah, OK. Tomorrow."

"OK, if you need anything, just call Monk. He's not a bad guy."

"All right, I will. Bye."

I end the call and sit down on the ledge to rest my back on the window and let the sobs out, a little bit at first, then I give up and the tears run down my cheeks like rivers.

How ironic.

After barely wriggling out of my father selling me to the highest bidder, then traveling a hundred million miles across open space to another world, it turns out I can't escape that fate after all.

Chapter Thirty-Nine

Ashur is sleeping next to me when I wake up. When I stir he reaches over and puts his arm around me. "Junco?"

I open my eyes and stare at him. He smiles. "You're not OK, Junco."

I look at him, first the one green eye, then the other. "I know. What time is it?"

I watch him check his vision screen and I realize I could have just checked my own. "5:42 AM."

"Too early to get up."

He pulls me to his chest. "Way too fucking early to get up."

"What time did you get here?"

"About an hour ago."

"Thank you."

"You're welcome, Juncs."

My eyes close and I fall back asleep clinging to him tightly and counting the slow up-and-down motion of his breathing.

The next time I wake Ashur is gone and Monk is giving me a vigorous shake.

"What the fuck?"

"Ah, sorry. But Rache said you have to eat something."

I flip open my eyes and stare up at him. "You're fucking with me, right?"

He screws up his face. "No, why?"

"What is it with you people and my eating habits?"

"I dunno, Junco. Get up and get dressed and I'll take you down to the cafeteria."

"Where did Ashur go?"

"Oh, he said to tell you he'll be back later."

I watch him leave and I force myself up and into the shower. There is a clean uniform waiting for me on the bed when I'm done and I slip it on. Monk appears just as I'm lacing up my boots and stands in the open doorway, talking to someone else outside for a few seconds before directing his attention to me. "Ready?"

I nod.

The hallway is bustling with activity and all sorts of people say hi to me as I pass them. "Who are all these people?" I ask as we start hopping down the stairs.

"Just other fighters."

"Oh, how many are there? Looks like a lot."

He hesitates at the bottom of the stairs as he waits for me to catch up with him. "Thirty-two? Thirty-five? Not sure this year."

"So, what type of person typically wins this fight?"

He starts walking down the hall, then looks over to me and smiles. "Warriors, Junco. Like you."

"And what do people usually ask for, in the wish department?"

"Oh, shit – healing mostly, if the winner isn't Aves that is. I mean after they're done, they're typically pretty fucked up."

"Oh, I thought that was included? This is not a fight to the death, right?"

"Right, but there's a limit." He shrugs. "Or they ask for status positions."

I think of Kush. "And how does that work? They just get promotions, based on the fight?"

"Yeah, pretty much. Nothing spectacular, I mean, it's a gift, it's not earned."

I grunt. "Yeah, who wants to follow a guy who never earned his appointment?"

He looks down at me as we walk. "Exactly. They never seem to figure that out, though."

"What else do they wish for?"

He stops at the cafeteria counter and starts grabbing food. "What do you want?"

I shrug and make a face. "Some of that," I say, pointing to the biscuits.

He shakes his head. "I'll choose for you. Ashur says he always orders for you, else you only eat cookies."

I smile. "He does. What else do they wish for, Monk?"

"Money. A better place to live, shit like that. What are you going to wish for, Junco?"

"I haven't decided yet."

He looks back at me and shakes his head. "Right."

He takes the tray over to a table full of guys and gestures for me to sit. "This is my team, Junco." He points and names them one by one and I say hello. He introduces me as the eight and I feel weird.

I watch and listen to them interact and realize they are pretty much just like the 039, only different faces. I breathe out and wonder if I will ever get to go home. Then I have to stop and ask myself where home is. It seems to be relative these days.

Ashur finds us before we are finished eating and slips onto the bench next to me, saying hi to everyone on Monk's team like he knows them well. He looks over my half-empty tray of food and smiles. "Looks like Monk's on feeding duty?"

I nod. "Yeah, I don't get why you guys are so interested in what I eat, but whatever. So what have you been doing all day?"

He turns and doesn't meet my gaze. "I went to see Tier." Then he looks down to me to see my reaction.

I look across the cafeteria and spot Kush watching me. "Oh."

"He wants to see you, Junco. Tonight."

"Well, I'm not so sure–"

"You're going," he says sternly.

I look up at him, to read how serious he is. "Why? I just don't think it's a good idea, I won't know what to say, it's gonna be awkward and–"

"It's his last night, Junco."

I shake my head at him and smile. "No, it isn't, Ashur."

"Oh, for fuck's sake." He takes my hand and pulls me up. "Let's go for a walk, OK?"

Monk takes an interest at this development. "Hey, Ashur, she's mine now, you don't get to just take her–"

"Fuck you, Monk. She's yours until tomorrow night and then she's going home, so don't fucking get used to her."

I smile back at them and let Ashur pull me out to the hallway. "So, is there an outside to this place? Or is it just an endless maze of interior corridors?"

"No, there's an outside, wanna go take a look?"

I nod. "Absolutely, I better get my sightseeing in before tomorrow, right?"

He puts his hand on my back, right between my wings, and it gives me a little chill. He feels it and looks over at me, then moves it up to my shoulder. "Is this bugging you?"

I shake my head as we pass through a doorway and the outside suddenly springs to life. "Oh, this is nice! It looks like Earth's sky!" The blueness of the upper atmosphere takes my breath away and I halt on the walkway to take it in for a moment.

Ashur agrees with a grunt, then leads me over to a patch of grass under a tree and we take a seat. "Yeah, I knew you'd like this part. And at night," he says, smiling at me as I lie back on the grass to look up, "you can see the stars."

I look over at him. "Ya know, ever since we sat and looked up at the city I haven't missed them much."

This makes him happy and he doesn't even try to hide it. Instead he leans back with me and we are quiet for a while. I think about Tier and wonder what it would be like to talk to him again after so long. Will it be like old friends? Or will it be weird? Does he know Ashur has feelings for me? All these questions are running through my mind when I notice Ash is looking at me.

"What are you thinking about?" he asks.

"Tier. And what it would be like to talk to him again."

"Are you going to go then?"

I swallow and nod. "Yeah, I can't exactly say no if he asked to see me. He did ask, right? I'm not going to show up and have him look surprised."

Ashur laughs. "He gave me an order. Apparently Tier still thinks he's captain." He smiles at this thought, like it's typical of Tier to be bossy like that, even when he's in prison and about to be killed for treason.

"You think I'm full of shit, don't you? You don't think he'll be alive tomorrow night."

He shakes his head. "No, I don't."

"Do you think I'll kill him?"

He shrugs. "If you're in the fight, and you win, Junco, you better fucking kill him. That's what you've signed up for."

"Right." I exhale. "I'll make sure not to win then."

He looks over and frowns. "That makes no sense."

"Yeah, well – you'll have to take it up with the syrinx. Let's go do it now. I want to get it over with."

He stands and pulls me up. "You sure?"

I nod. "Yeah, let's go."

Chapter Forty

Ashur and I walk through a series of biometrically secure doors and at each one we must announce ourselves, then wait, sometimes for a very long time, for someone to come and let us in. Each time I pass over the threshold of a secure station my heart beats a little quicker and soon my whole body feels flushed.

Finally we arrive at the prison and then we are asked to wait yet again. Ashur points me to a straight-backed chair and I go take a seat while he arranges things with the people behind the desk. They seem to know him pretty well and I begin to wonder just how many times he's been here to see Tier and never told me.

After several minutes he comes and takes a seat next to me and smiles. "Be just a little bit longer, OK?"

I nod and play with a loose string on my thigh pocket. There is no one else in the waiting room with us, which should not be surprising considering how difficult it was to get back to this point. I begin to question how common it is to even have visitors here.

A buzzer sounds and Ashur gets up and looks down at me. "That's us."

I get up and my heart goes wild. My vision screen pops to life and I watch as my biogs begin to excrete cortisol to calm me down. Ashur looks at me funny. "You OK?"

I swallow and smooth out my uniform shirt, even though it never wrinkles, it's light armor for fuck's sake.

"Yeah, I'm OK. No, I'm not. I'm nervous. So fucking nervous."

He takes my hand. "It's Tier, Junco. You spent quite a bit of personal time with him back on Earth, just be yourself."

I nod. "Yeah, OK. I'm good." I breathe.

He leads me to the doors where guards are waiting and then we pass through and they clank shut behind us. Ashur seems to know exactly where he's going, so I just follow, my stomach churning with each step. And then we turn a corner and I can see Tier through the glass at the end of the hall. He sees me at the same time and even from dozens of yards away, I can see his smile. My heart calms down and I smile back.

Ashur waits at the door and Tier goes over to the far wall and sits down on the bench. Then a buzzer goes off and the locks click to signal the door can be opened. Ashur grabs the handle and pulls.

And then Tier and I are in the same room. Ashur enters as well and then the door closes and locks behind us.

"Junco, yer so pretty." Tier gets up and walks over to me. I drop Ashur's hand and meet him halfway and he takes me in his arms and hugs me tightly, pushing my face into his chest and dropping his chin down into my hair. I wrap my arms under his and bring them up to grab his shoulders, letting out a deep sigh of relief. We stay this way for a long time. I tilt my face to the side and close my eyes as his hands stroke my hair.

"Ashur, hey, fuck off for a while, eh? It's my last night, let me have her to myself."

I don't hear a response but the door buzzes and mechanisms clank, a few seconds later we're alone. He pulls back and takes me over to the bench, then sits down and tugs me down into his lap. I straddle his legs and put my hands around his neck and look at him, noticing the dark circles and the strain on his face. "Why didn't I come sooner?"

"Yer here now, so who cares?"

I flash him a crooked smile. "Are you OK?"

He looks into my eyes and the glow I've missed so badly is there again. "Nah, not really."

I frown. "I'm so sorry, Tier. This whole thing is my fault."

"It's not, Junco. It's not. I did this. But I did give ya all those instructions in the virtual and ya didn't even follow one!"

"What? I did follow them, and there were only two, anyway."

"No, Junco. I had a whole list to help ya get by without me, but ya did it all backwards."

I shake my head. "I only got two sentences, Tier, it said trust no one and show no weakness."

He laughs. "Fucking Sera, I knew she'd screw it all up, probably did it on purpose."

"Who's Sera?"

"The redhead, ya seen her?"

"The syrinx?"

"Is that who she said she was? What a fucking liar. She's Sera." He shakes his head. "But anyway, I don't want to waste our time talking about her. If ya thought the only thing I wanted was for ya to trust no one, then why did ya go around handing it out like a fucking Utopian welfare payment? You've made more best friends in the last month than I made in my whole life."

I laugh. "Well, everyone has actually been pretty nice to me. It was hard to stay suspicious and aloof. And I didn't do too well with the show no weakness shit either. I've been an emotional wreck on several occasions."

His hand goes up to my scalp, lifts the hair away from my head, and then traces the scar down the side of my face. "That one healed pretty well." He lifts my chin up and looks for the SEAR scar. "That one too." Then his hand goes behind my neck and pulls me in. I stare into his eyes as he takes my left hand and holds it up to look at my missing fingers. "This been giving ya any trouble?"

I shake my head. "No, none at all. I played the piano last week and it sounded exactly the same, like there were no fingers missing."

He smiles. "And I saw ya in the fifth and sixth fights, so I know you can climb—"

"You did?"

"Oh yeah, Juncs. You're like a celebrity with all the screen time you get. I know all about yer life during Fledge. And I saw ya in that dress at the nargala." He shakes his head and exhales. "If I could have one wish it would be to take ya out like that instead of that stupid reporter." He lets out a small laugh, just a breath of air really. "I hope Ashur didn't get a look at ya in that dress, else I know what the two of ya did that night."

I blush and turn away and shake my head. "I haven't, Tier."

He smiles and then leans in to kiss me, but stops just short of my lips and looks into my eyes. "Yer sparklin', Junco."

I reach up to touch my face. "What color are they?"

"Gold, the color of the goddess. Like yer wings."

I breathe out and his lips cross the distance and I open my mouth just a tiny bit to let his tongue slip in and caress me. His hands go behind my head and then he pulls away. "No sense in making Ashur any more jealous than necessary."

I pull back. "It's not like that, Tier."

"You don't have to make excuses for him, he told me."

"Told you what?"

"That he kissed ya, Junco. It's OK, I'll be gone tomorrow."

"No you won't."

He hisses some breath through his lips. "Don't get yer hopes up, Junco, I don't see any way out of it."

"I do."

He smiles. "Well, if so, best to keep it ta yerself for now, eh?"

I nod. "Yeah."

The door lock buzzes and I jump a little. "Yer escort is back." He looks in my eyes and kisses me again. I lean my head into his shoulder and begin to cry.

"Junco, it's OK." He reaches his arms around me and tugs me in tight but my back heaves up and down with my silent sobs. It's not OK. I cannot live without this man. Ever. It might have been possible before this visit, maybe. But now that he's fresh in my memory, and not a distant shadow in another lifetime, I can't let go. His hands stroke my hair over and over again to comfort me, but mine is a sadness that feels like forever.

I start counting to bring myself back from the sobs and when I get to number five I have it locked down, just like I told Annun I would. I pull back and stand up but he stays seated, the pain in his eyes almost too much for me to look at. I force myself to see him, so that tomorrow I will not forget.

"I'll see you tomorrow after the fight."

"I love ya, Juncs."

I let out one more choked sob. "I love you too, Tier. More than I can ever say."

He nods and frowns at the same time.

"But," I sniff and wipe the tears from my face, "I can show you. And I'll do that tomorrow."

I turn and walk away, past Ashur, out the door and down the hallway until I get to the end of the corridor. And then I wait, with my chin up, for Ashur to make them let me out.

We walk back to the Deliverance sector in silence, and then when we get there Ashur takes my hand and leads me outside. I lie down and bury my face in the grass as I cry. He doesn't pull me close, just lets me get it out and for that, at least, I am thankful.

Chapter Forty-One

Ashur leaves to go back to Amelia and I climb the stairs back to my room alone. There is a huge party going on in the arena for the fighters, but I have no interest in going. I palm my hand over the biometrics at my door and go in.

"Don't turn the light on, Junco." Kush is standing over at the window and the door that connects our rooms is open. "Fucking reporters out there, just waiting to get a look at you when you turn the lights on."

I sniff down a leftover sob. "What are you doing in here?"

He turns around. "Waiting for you to come back."

"I went to see Tier." I watch his face as I say the words, but he turns away.

"Yeah, everyone knows already, Junco. Your life is like a screen around here. That's why they want a look at you. To see how upset you are, get ratings for tomorrow's fight and all that good shit. They have you the odds-on favorite to win but the real money is on whether or not you'll kill him in the end. Pretty sick, right?"

I cross the room to the window and stand next to him to watch the party below. The free-G is on and people are floating around like drunken angels. I climb the little lip against the window and when I look over at Kush I'm not that much shorter than him. I smile despite my current situation and he smiles back.

"What?"

I let out a sigh and shake my head. "God, I'm glad you're here. When Monk told me you were next door I cried, I was so relieved."

He lets out a small laugh. "That's a fucking first. Where's Ashur? I thought for sure he'd be here to comfort you the night before."

"I think it got weird, him seeing Tier and me together. I like Ashur, a lot. I mean, I really do. But I love Tier. Love him, Kush. There's no comparison."

Kush looks over at me. "What happened on Earth, Junco? What did you do together that made you so connected to him?" He turns back to the party. "No one can figure that out. Not even your team. So, whatever you guys did down there, he never told them."

"Yeah." I huff out some air with my words. "I found that out along the way. They've been lacking in some seriously critical information. Stuff Tier knew, and they should've known, but didn't."

"So, what happened? Why is he so special?"

"Well, I–" I stop and look at him for the first time, I mean really look at him. He's a very good-looking guy. Tall and muscular. Not fair, but not dark either. Golden, really. Why is Tier so special? I want to say, *Do you understand what a fucking horrible piece of shit I am? And do you understand that Tier was the first person who ever thought to be careful with me?*

But I don't. I go right for the kill-shot instead. "Did you know that I tortured my father with my SEAR knife?"

His eyes squint at me. "You did what?"

I breathe out and nod. "Yeah, see, he found out I was dating this guy from the Mountain Republic and had him killed. And then I found out I was pregnant and he killed my baby. So, I went a little crazy." I look over at him to see what he's thinking, but his face is neutral, not yet ready to judge. "I tortured him with my SEAR and left him to die. And Tier…" I breathe out again to slow myself down. "He was there watching me that night, and went down and killed my father after, so he wouldn't suffer."

His blue eyes just stare at me for a few seconds. "Shit, Junco. I had no idea."

"No, I've never told anyone that story. But that's not what made me love him. That was just how it all started. He just—"

Kush is waiting now, with expectations in his eyes.

"Gets me. He gets me. And he saved my life, shit, a couple times at least. We fought some nightdogs together, and that's how I lost my fingers. Then he healed them for me. And we escaped from the MR soldiers through this fucked-up cave system, and killed this seriously evil genetic engineer, and battled with mutants and machines down in these tunnels."

I stop and watch the smile creep across his face as he pictures our adventures on Earth. The truth is though, these aren't the things that made me love him either. It was him washing my hair, healing me, telling me stories, eating the dinner I cooked, sitting behind me on my favorite horse, and revealing his secrets that made me love him. But I'm not going to tell anyone that.

So, I just nod my head and keep going. "He introduced me to Moju, who is wilder than I am. And he was always on my side." I shrug. "We just fit together, like a puzzle. He was so patient when I couldn't remember what happened. And he was genuinely hurt and apologetic when he had to be the one to tell me the truth. He refused to leave me behind. You should've seen the warriors descend down on my house to fight the Mountain Republic's military, Kush — it was fantastic! They swooped in and fuck—"

"I did see it, Junco, it was all over the newscreens before you came out of morph, before anyone knew who you were and what was going on. There were reporters everywhere and that shit was beamed from Earth within days. Everyone's seen it. They call you the snowbird."

"I had no idea." I laugh and pause to think about it for a second. "But the most important reason why Tier is so special, and why I can't let him die tomorrow, is because he risked his life to bring me here and put me through morph." I look up again and this time I see myself through Kush's eyes. I smile and he returns it. "He gave me a choice, a chance really. A whole new life."

"You're so lucky, Junco."

"That's funny, Kush." I play with my uniform again, adjusting the wrinkles that aren't there. "The bad shit about me far outweighs the good, take my word on that one."

"I doubt that, Junco. You have a giant heart, and" – he smiles – "they all love you now. It's like all the good shit is about to come your way, you're right on the edge of something wonderful."

I look away for a second and my voice lowers and loses the excitement it just had. "If he does die tomorrow, Kush. I'm going with him." When I look back he's frowning at me and I feel bad for admitting my secret. Burdening him with it.

He moves closer and puts his arm around me. "Don't talk like that, Junco." He pulls me in front of him and we lean on the window together to watch the party beyond. There are a few reporters that are floating close to the glass, trying to see in. "Can they see us?"

I feel Kush shake his head behind me. "No, when it's dark in here it's a mirror from out there." His hand parts the hair from the back of my neck and I feel a tingle go up my body, then his mouth on my neck as he kisses me. At first I instinctively pull away a little bit, but he doesn't back off and the longer I let him continue, the better it feels.

I turn my head and his mouth finds mine and then I let him kiss me there too. It's not tender and filled with love like Tier's kisses, but it is passionate.

His hands slip under each arm to release the seams on my shirt, then they gently tug it over my head and return to my back. I buckle as his fingers slide across the sensitive skin between my wings.

He pushes his chest into me and the pressure on my wings makes my throat stretch up and to the side, exposing my neck even more. His mouth slips up to my ear and my eyes flutter as a small groan rumbles out. His breath glides in and tickles pleasure receptors I never knew I had. Fingertips are tracing along the top side of my wing, making it extend out automatically, inviting him to touch the many rows of feathers. His right hand slides down the length of a secondary covert feather and he massages it slightly between his fingers before flitting across the tips and drawing back into my waist where he slides his hand up to cup my breast. His other hand eases down the length of my stomach, pausing lightly at the SEAR to investigate, then unbuttons my pants and slips inside.

My eyes close and I let my whole body sink back against him. I've never experienced such a slow pleasure with a man in my life.

I turn to face him, thrusting my lower body into his. He grabs my wrists and pushes them up above my head, clasping them together and holding me against the cool glass with one hand as the other tickles the small of my back.

He doesn't stop when I look up at him, but instead presses his lips near my cheek once more, allowing his breath to trickle into my ear. The combination of all these new sensations is almost too much. "Oh shit, Kush." I release my passion out in a hoarse whisper.

"What?" He breathes it back into me, then pulls away slightly and lowers his chin.

"I'm going to regret this in the morning."

"No, Junco." He exhales. "You won't. I'm going to make sure of it."

I look up into his eyes and they glow a lovely pale blue, so gentle, and so soft. He meets my gaze and then his mouth finds mine, his tongue inside twirling and probing me, until I give in completely.

Later, I'm puffing one of Kush's cigars and watching what's left of the partiers out in the arena as I recycle back my conversation with Tier.

Kush approaches and leans into my back. He stretches his arms past either side of my shoulders, pressing on the glass, pushing us towards the window. He kisses me and whispers down across my cheek, "You gonna tell me the plan, Junco? Or you just gonna go in there and do it all on your own?"

I grunt as I try to ignore how the air traveling into my ear makes me feel. My words come out just as gentle as his. "What plan is that, Kush?"

He pulls back and then turns to lean his back against the window so he can see my face. "The one that involves winning the fight and saving your boyfriend."

I let out a little laugh with my smoke ring and shake my head with a sigh. "Believe me, I'm not really planning on winning. Killing the person I love is not my kind of prize." He just looks at me and I try to ignore his blue eyes as they start to light up a little, but I can't. "What?"

"Then what the fuck are you doing, Junco? What's your plan?"

I puff again, then blow more rings as I ponder this line of thinking myself. In the end I shrug. "I don't know, Kush. We'll have to wait and see what happens."

We stand there for a little longer, looking out at the arena, probably both of us wondering what tomorrow night will bring. And then he pulls me back to bed and we fall asleep.

Chapter Forty-Two

When I wake up I am alone in bed, but my room is filled with people. Ashur, Isten, Arel, Rikan, Mish, Ryse, Lucan, Rache, and Monk. They are not paying much attention to me, instead they are all talking at once in several smaller groups. I screw up my face as I try to figure out what's going on, then remember Kush. My eyes dart over to the connecting door and I feel a little relief when I see it's closed.

When I look back, Ashur is watching me. It's only then that I realize I'm naked under the covers and yesterday's uniform is strewn about the floor near the window.

Fuck it.

I throw back the covers and stand up, then walk towards the shower, my wingtips brushing lightly across my butt as I glide. The entire room goes silent and every head turns in my direction. My eyes never leave Ashur's face. I shrug as I pass him and close the bathroom door behind me. Lucan's voice comes in clear from the other side. "Out, everyone out."

The hypnotic pulse of the shower jets gives me time to think about what's coming and that's not good, so I finish quickly, then dress in my uniform and take a seat at the table to lace up my boots. I don't know what other people will be wearing for the battle, probably not their uniform. But that's what I'm wearing.

The connecting door chimes. "Enter," I call.

Kush comes in and laughs at me. "Shit, were you having a party over here or what?"

"Kush, I don't invite them over, they just show up."

He sits down with me at the table. "I get it, Junco. If I was on your team, I'd barge in any chance I got too."

I finish with my boot lacing and look up to give him my attention. "No regrets, Kush." I smile and he nods his head.

"No regrets, Junco."

"I have a pre-fight interview with Kadian, you got any interviews?"

"Yeah, I think I talk to him right before you."

I nod. "Good then, I'll see you after that, huh? I gotta go find Ashur or Lucan or someone to get myself back on track. You're really distracting me." I smile, and probably blush too, because my face suddenly feels hot as I think about our night together.

He lets out a little laugh. "See ya after." Then he goes back to his room.

I'm slipping my com into my thigh pocket when the main door chimes. "Enter."

The door slides open and Esta stands at the threshold. "Can I come in?" She's wearing her demure Cluster mother clothes and I absently shudder at the thought of that get-up being my uniform.

My mouth twists a little at her. "I said enter, Esta. Of course you can come in."

She takes a few hesitant steps into my room and then bows her head. "I'm so sorry, Junco. I know you were counting on me and I completely let you down. My personal issues got in the way and—"

"What the fuck are you talking about?"

She looks back up at me and swallows. "Isec. He didn't make it and I'm sorry, I should have listened to you. He didn't need to die in the last battle, he was so close."

I just stare at her for a few seconds, trying to put this all together. "It wasn't your fault, Esta, he was never going to make it."

She nods. "I know that, but he might have if I'd helped you train him better. He was so close."

I walk over to her. "Do you know what we do in the Seventh Battle?"

She doesn't even look up, just shakes her head no.

"Well, I won't spill it, since it's obviously a secret, but you had nothing, and I do mean nothing, Esta, to do with Isec's death. So just let it go."

She stays silent and I wave my hand over towards the table. "Take a seat if you want."

She flicks her long black hair behind one ear as she sits, and then lets out a sharp sigh as I join her and strike up a cigar. I offer her one and to my surprise, she takes it. We puff for a few minutes. "Did you ever ask Lucan if you could change jobs?"

"No," she says, shaking her head. "He would never listen to me."

"Esta, that makes no sense, you're one of the pure Seven, you have so much power it's sick."

"They don't really like me, Junco. They avoid me, stick me in with the children and try to forget I'm even here. I never wanted that job. Back on Earth I was training to be a historian, I went to school and was about to pass my qualifiers for apprenticeship. They took it all away when I came here. And now I have to sneak around, looking for information in their sphere—"

"They have a sphere here?" She tilts her head at me, like she's trying to figure out if I'm joking. I shrug. "I didn't know. No one told me."

"Anyway, I like history, Junco. I can't help it. And being immersed in all this new culture but not being allowed to learn about it. Well, it drives me crazy. It's like they want me here, but they don't want me to know too much about them. So I cheat. I sneak information. It's absurd."

"Oh," I manage to say after a few seconds of pause. "I had no idea."

"No, why would you, they've done nothing but try and keep us apart since you got here. I was lucky Lucan was so mad that day I found you in the conference room, otherwise he'd never have let me talk to you."

"Do you hate it here, Esta? Would you rather be on Earth?"

She pauses for a moment. "No."

"But?"

"But I have no say in anything, they just make all these decisions about me and that's the end of it. I have no say. I might as well be back in the Utopia, at least there they made me do something that I actually enjoyed, even if it was all bullshit brainwashing."

Wow, Esta and I have something in common. "So, if you could choose, you'd choose what, then?"

She thinks about it for a moment, her eyes looking out towards the preparations in the arena beyond the windows. "I just want to learn things, continue my life the way it was going on Earth. I just want to be allowed to read the avian books and stuff, I'm not asking that much." She looks up, her posture in a desperate plea for me to believe it's a small request. I do agree, the girl wants to read and study for fuck's sake. How hard could it be to let her do that?

She takes a deep breath and continues, "If I had a choice, I'd join Sefer Cluster. The scribes who study and preserve the mythology."

I laugh. "Really? Shit, I can't stand those stories myself. I'm so tired of all that bullshit."

She laughs with me. "We are so different." And then she stares into my face, seeing me. "I don't feel important, I feel like all they care about is you."

"Esta, I'm not even the one who can save them, you are! If I bring back the others, then it's all about you guys. I'll be a distant memory." Shit, why am I even having this conversation, there's not going to be any trip to Earth. I stand up and wait for her to stand as well. "I really wish I could stay and talk more, but I need to go find Ashur or Lucan. I'll put in a word for you, OK?"

She nods, her head still bowed. "Thanks for talking to me, Junco. I know it must be difficult after Isec's death to even look at me—"

I put my hand up to stop her. "Esta, I killed him, not you. Me. I cut off his head in the Seventh Battle – so stop, OK? It had nothing to do with you."

She looks into my eyes for truth and I look into hers for judgment. And then we both look away.

"OK," she says. "I know whatever happened, it must have been hard. It's hard, Junco. To live by their customs and rules when so much of it goes against our human nature. And even though I'm not technically human, you don't spend your whole life in a culture and not become one of them."

I nod and walk out in the hallway with her. Hard? That word doesn't even come close. Underneath I twist her words to fit my own life. I spent my whole life immersed in a culture that embraced me as a killer. And she's right. I'm one of them, now and forever.

I get in line for food in the cafeteria and take a look around as it moves forward slowly. Kush is on the far left side eating near some people I don't know. Sometimes I forget that he's from here and has a past complete with friends and history.

The 039 is on the far right with the 399. They take up three tables between them. I get to the food and start choosing things I've had before. I fill up a good portion of the tray and then thumb the biometrics at the end to charge it to whoever pay the bills for me when I do that.

After paying I stand there as people push past me for a minute. Both Kush and Ashur are looking at me, waiting to see where I sit. It feels like cadet school. I choose my team, obviously, then walk towards the guys and slip in next to Monk on the bench to create a buffer between myself and the 039.

"Junco, hey, uh, sorry we all barged in on you this morning." Monk shrugs. "We'll know better next time." He smiles and elbows me in the ribs.

"Doesn't bother me, Monk. You guys were the ones all freaked out about it." My eyes follow Ashur as he makes his way over towards us. He stops behind the guy sitting next to me, who takes the hint and gets up to leave. The rest of the table is suddenly on the move as well and within a few seconds, Ashur and I are alone.

I turn and look at him. "What?" The look in his eyes makes me turn away.

He sits down on the bench with his back to the table. "Why, Junco? You don't even like the guy."

I look down at my tray, my appetite gone. "That's not entirely true, Ashur. I like him well enough."

I can feel him shaking his head at me. "Enough to sleep with him? After seeing Tier last night?"

I let out a little laugh. "Obviously, the answer to that is yes." I look up at him to make sure this point sinks in. "Else I wouldn't have done it. The best thing about Kush is he's not a complicated guy. He's not my captain or the guy I'm trying to save from death. He's just a friend who's been there for me when I needed him. And last night I needed him and he was there."

Ashur leans his elbows back on the table and stretches out his legs, silent. I straddle the bench so I can see him better, then wait for him to look over at me again. "Sometimes, Ashur, you gotta just take what you want and stop thinking about it. That's what he did. And to be brutally honest, I'm glad, because if ever there was a night where I needed someone to want me like that, it was last night."

He nods his head and looks away. "I call that taking advantage of someone who's not really thinking clearly, but hey, you can tell yourself anything you want, Junco. You're the one who fucking fell for it."

I get up and grab my tray, dump it in the trash and head outside to find a place to smoke.

It's a small alcove built into the side of the building. I hide there and puff as I lean up against a pillar. Lucan appears, dressed in his overly formal suit, as per usual.

I look up at him. "What?"

He smiles. "I don't care who you sleep with, Junco. But you need to make a choice if you want to stay in the 039."

I just want him to go away and leave me alone, that's what I want. "I don't," I say quickly, "want to stay, I mean. I'll stay with Rache."

I look up to see how this hits him, but he's still smiling. "Probably a good idea."

It hurts, it really does.

"Great." I stomp out my cigar and walk off back to the Deliverance floor to find Kadian.

Chapter Forty-Three

The Deliverance floor is packed with bodies — fighters, reporters, and auxiliary people who do something, I'm sure, but I have no idea what. I see Kush and walk over to him. "Hey, you do the interview yet?"

"No, he's behind, says he want to interview us together."

I scowl. "Why? I might not know him that well, but Kadian is a schemer. He has a reason, probably knows we were together last night."

Kush just shrugs. "Yeah, probably. If it bothers you, we'll just say no."

It turns out it doesn't bother me enough to say no when Kadian's staff comes to get us. We do the interview together in a small room that looks down on the stage. Below us I see twenty-one prisoners stretched out in an X pattern as their arms, wings and legs are bound up and pulled taut with wires that attach to various pillars offstage. There are ten on the left side of the stage and ten on the right. In the middle, elevated from the rest, is Tier. The twenty-first offender, the traitor.

My eyes can't pull away once I realize what's going on and Kush has to lead me over to the chair, out of sight of the crucifixion scene below, in order to snap me out of it.

"Junco, how does it feel to see Tier up there as a Deliverance offering?"

I look over at Kadian, hating him for doing this to me. Ryse was right, he's a scumbag. "More determined than ever, Kadian." I smile and the worry leaves me as I play the game.

"Determined to do what, Junco?"

"Save him. I think everyone knows by now, the only reason I'm here is to save him."

Kadian smiles and switches over to Kush. "Are you here to support Junco in her efforts? Or to win the wish?"

Kush's face remains passive, his signature expression of indifference. "Both."

Kadian waits for him to elaborate, but Kush turns his head towards the arena so he's is forced to redirect. "Are the two of you aware that the Archers have declared that no pardon wishes will be granted?"

Kush answers without even turning towards Kadian this time. "Our plans never included pardon wishes, Kadian. How naive do you think we are?"

It's true, too. My wish is not a pardon and Kush said his wish was to be captain.

"What are your wishes then, if you don't mind sharing with the arena. Everyone is anxious to see how Junco plans on saving Raubtier from his certain death sentence."

Kush doesn't even skip a beat. "You'll see our wishes when we win, not before."

Kadian smiles indulgently now. "But only one of you can win, Kush. Who will it be?"

Kush shrugs. "How the hell should I know."

Kadian has had enough of Kush and I've got a new respect for the attitude that suits him. My respect must show on my face because my first question hits the mark. "Junco, which of the many men in your life actually has your heart? There won't be much left if you keep parceling it out like this."

"Tier." It comes out automatically. "It always has been and always will be Tier."

"OK, let's switch gears, your love life is getting too complicated, Junco. Tell us why they call you the snowbird?"

I shake my head at him. "I can't tell you that, I have no idea."

"What is a snowbird? Do you have them on Earth?"

"Well, yes. Juncos are snowbirds, little winter sparrows that live in the mountains near my home. Or what was my home, after the nukes, there's nothing left, I hear. All the Rural Republic juncos are dead now."

"All except one, right?"

"Sure, right. All except one."

Apparently he's had enough of our lackluster performance because he signs off the interview. Kush and I disengage ourselves and head towards the ready room.

"Well," he lets out a breath, "that was fucking fantastic."

I have to trot to keep up with him so I grab on his arm and tug him back to slow down. "Shit, how did I ever think he was a decent guy? I mean, the nargala was fun and all, but he only took me so he could get me on camera in that designer dress."

He slows his pace and puts his hand in the middle of my back to direct me into the ready room where most of the fighters have already arrived and are reading through the rules. They flash across my vision screen and I greet my AI. *Decided to finally show yourself, eh?* She ignores me and the rules begin to scroll. I read them as Kush reads along on the giant screen at the head of the room.

No weapons.

Killing is not required, nor prohibited.

Falling below the red line denotes a forfeit.

The last man standing wins a wish.

The winner will execute the prisoners in the manner they choose.

Healing, up to the value of a hundred thousand rills, will be provided to all fighters who survive, unless they use their wish to compensate for overages.

I look up at Kush. "So basically, stay above the red line and don't let anyone kill you."

He smiles. "Got it in one, Junco."

Then we go fill out our wishes. You're allowed to have conditions for final health status in case your injuries exceed the allotted amount of health care, but I don't bother and from the speed by which Kush fills his out, he doesn't either. We press enter on the screens and they are sealed, only to be opened by Rache once the winner is determined.

The screen flashes to the filled arena. The nine Archers sit at the end opposite the stage where the prisoners are strung up, probably directly above my room. People are screaming and cheering, the odds are flashing last call on a giant board. I'm the favorite to win.

And then they call us to line up on our predetermined spots. Kush's spot is across the room from me, so he leans down and kisses my cheek. "See you at the end, snowbird."

I grin up at him. "Yeah, sure, Kush. Good luck."

Everyone takes their place and we settle into the ebb of activity that I use to predict start.

And then we are flying upward, the screams from the arena filling our ears, the hammering of stomping feet vibrating the entire structure, the lights dim and crackle as the various G-fields are activated. Our feet come free and Deliverance begins.

Chapter Forty-Four

I have the neck of the guy next to me before he even knows what's happening. One swift twist later he's the first official forfeiter and I've set the standard for just how fucked-up this fight will be. In the end, the decision was based on logistics, not emotion. Killing is just so much easier than injuring.

I shoot up in the air after that and fly as hard as I can for the smallest and weakest of all the fighters, a girl not much bigger than me. She sees me targeting her and dives down below the red line.

Something to be said for common sense.

After that I'm attacked from all sides. My wings thrust and twist as I evade, then flip around and change direction, using my momentum to bowl into the middle of my attackers. They scatter and I choose the closest one and drag him down to the gravity plane, not the mushrooms from last night, but a long, flat stone surface that pulls you down relentlessly once inside the field. No one wants to follow me down there, so I have him to myself. He tries to understand my grappling moves, but simply can't. I break his ankle, then crack his head on the stone and stop to catch my breath.

A large guy comes out of nowhere and knocks me down, his hands around my neck. My foot goes up and catches him in the head, he flinches, but keeps hold, preventing oxygen from reaching my brain. I see the stars of unconsciousness coming when I snap back to my senses and chop him repeatedly in the temple. He loses his grasp fractionally, but I take advantage and twist my body around, then send an elbow into his gut and the palm of my hand slams up against the underside of his jaw. I hear a sickening crack and he lets go of me. I kick him in the teeth a few times to make up for the marks he left, then lean down and twist his neck until he's limp.

Another guy is standing a few feet away, wondering if he should take his chance at me, and decides he should with a grin. His claws come out and they are the length of good-sized swords. I fly upward and leave the gravity field behind, better to engage this one up top. He follows me, much quicker and skilled in the art of flying, and grabs my foot and tugs me backwards. My body crashes against him and then his razors rake across my stomach, splitting open my armor and penetrating my skin.

I scream and squirm, but he keeps hold. Our thrashing propels us over to the transparent barrier and he smacks my head against it face-first. The blood spouts out from my nose as the people behind the barrier pound against it so hard the vibrations thump against my body. I see his reflection in the glare on the barrier, but I force myself to stay still. His hands are going for my throat, ready to snap my neck when I reach up and over my head and drive my razors into his skull with as much force as I can. He screams and the people on the other side of the barrier go wild. I push off the wall and swing his body up over mine, then flap my wings as hard as I can and crash his head into the barrier.

Paybacks are always a bitch.

I pull out the claws and turn him around so he has to watch, then force his teeth to meet my knee in a blood-spattering crunch.

Before I can even take stock of the scene another guy slams me against the wall. I recover with the help of free-

G momentum and fly, flitting in and out of other pairs and trios busy fighting each other and then press my wings flat against my back and tuck and reverse thrust. My follower smacks into me hard, and we bounce apart like the perfect inelastic collision demonstration in a cadet-school physics lab.

My smaller mass has me taking the brunt of the energy transfer and I go careening off, slamming face-first into a huge guy who looks like the only thing that could possibly make him happy right now is dismembering my body. He grabs my arm and twists it behind my back. I can almost feel the tendons in my shoulder stretching. I flip my feet up in front of me, over his head, and before he even knows what's happening I've got his neck locked between my thighs and I'm squeezing the life out of him. His body goes limp and begins to float in the fight wind. I let go, then push him as hard as I can down below the red line.

I finally have a chance to take stock and spy Kush across the arena, but he's busy killing, so I leave him be.

The guy from before has a team with him and they surround me. I fly down to the G-platform and wait casually to see if they really want to try this.

They do.

All four of them circle me, crouching a little like they know what the fuck to do when I come at them with hand to hand moves. I immediately hunch my shoulder and duck my head, coming off as submissive as possible. It pumps up their rage and they stand up a little taller. I turn my hips so my right shoulder is facing the guy closest to me without taking my peripheral eyes off the other three, then talk him up. "Come on guys, let's team up. I'll make us all rich." My arms are bent, my hands talking along with my words, and they stop noticing the movement. I scoot a fraction towards the nearest guy and then slam my palm into his mouth and hammerfist him in the neck, halfway between the ear and the spinal cord. The brain stem chop will take out anyone, you don't even need that much force.

He doesn't get back up.

His buddy has me in a chicken wing before I can blink, both of my arms locked in his, thinking he's gonna hold me there so his friends can beat the shit out of me, but he's wrong. He head butts me from the back and my vision blurs from the impact. Inside I fly into a private rage and bring my right leg behind him, stretch it all the way over until it's outside of his right leg, then simply stand up. He falls back like an idiot and I hear the crowd go wild. I take a chance and finish him off with two sharp stomps to his jaw, one halfway up the side, where there's a tiny little hole that allows nerves to pass through the bone, and then a second up where the jaw meets the skull. Another hotbed of nerves. I hear the crack and smile as the pain in his eyes registers.

The sharp stab against the side of my neck knocks me down on the ground and the other two guys are on me now as the blood from the razors pools and sticks to my hair. I grab the shirt of the first guy as the second guy holds my legs down. Their razors are clawing at me, blood is running down my legs and arms inside my uniform, but the pain never even materializes. The adrenaline running through my bloodstream takes care of that.

My hands crawl up his shirt and I pull him towards me, biting off the top of his ear once it's within reach. His blood drenches me and makes him panic and forget to hold tight. I hammerfist him in the back of the neck relentlessly while his buddy tugs on my legs to pull me out from under him. I let go and allow myself to be pulled. When I'm free of the defeated bleeder on top I thrust my upper body up and grab the other guy's neck, squeezing until he has to let go of my legs and pry my little fingers off.

My legs scramble and get between us and I simply kick him off me. He goes careening across the stone slab but I'm on him before he can even decide if he wants to get back up. I slash his throat so deep his final heartbeats pulse up in the air like a fountain.

The ear bleeder isn't done with me and now it's one on one.

He rushes and connects with my stomach, sending me careening backwards, sliding across the smooth stone surface. I decide to make an example of this last asshole because I'm getting tired. I kick him off, girl-style, a few quickies to the balls, one to the jaw, and then scoot backwards and stand up, crouching a little to egg him on.

He bounces back up, still sure of himself even though he's about to lose consciousness from blood loss. He looks down on my diminutive size and takes his last step. I slide in, grab him around the knee with one hand, then pinch his Achilles heel with the other. After that it's a simple little pull. He goes down and I keep hold of his heel, squeezing, but I don't finish him. I let go and wait as he sends me backwards with his flapping wings. I hunch over, pretending to be out of breath and tired, ready for it to end.

He takes the bait and gets back up like a dumbass.

I walk towards him and grab him with both hands, one behind the neck, the other on his bicep, and swing into a flying arm bar, taking him down and slapping him on the stone. It's the exact same move I pulled on Ashur when we trained for Fight Six, except this guy has never seen it before. Most of the time the flying arm bar is a bullshit flash move that almost never works. But here, his head crashes into the stone so hard the skull hemorrhages blood and bits of bone fly up and sting my face.

The crowd goes wild as I push all their bodies off the slab and watch as their names go dark on the scoreboard.

And then I look around to see where we are.

Kush is standing at the other end of the slab, just watching me. I smile and he walks over and gives me a hug. There are still half a dozen fighters but three of them go dark in the next few seconds and the other three nod to us and dive down.

They're done.

And only we are left.

I stare up at Kush, breathing hard. "Well, you wanna win, or should I?"

He pulls me to him again and leans down into my ear. "It's all you, Junco. You are the only reason I'm here."

He flies off and dives down below the red line, then flies back up and stands on the slab, bowing to me, gesturing towards the prisoners that await my Deliverance on the other end of the arena. His name goes dark and then there is just me.

And twenty-one prisoners that I am supposed to kill.

I turn to face them for the first time since entering the arena and I feel sick to my stomach. Every one of them is barely hanging on. I don't know for sure how long they've been strung up like that, hours at least, but it has taken its toll and their heads slump like they are already dead, a sharp contrast to their erect bodies, and each rigid limb, wings included, being pulled taut in all directions by the wires that connect them to the pillars off-stage.

The stage has been reformed from last night and is not deep at all. It only allows enough room for the prisoner to stand plus a foot or so of extra space for the executioner.

Which is now me.

I reach under my shirt and hear the crowd gasp as the SEAR comes out. I take a deep breath and power it up, wincing at the hissing loop of genetically enhanced plasma as it comes to life in my hand.

I look over at Kush who has seen me kill with this before and he nods. Then I dial it up a little to a medium length dagger and fly over to the first prisoner. The guy is a mess, his hair matted with sweat, his bowels vacated and his body smelling like shit. His eyes are alert now that the time has come, they dart back and forth as he desperately tries to move away from the inevitable final justice of my weapon.

The crowd is almost silent for a second, almost a hush, but then I raise the knife and begin the smooth cut through his neck and they stand up and cheer wildly.

If I was alone, I'd puke.

Not just from the smell of the SEAR cutting through flesh, although that is enough to make anyone hurl. But because these people make me sick inside, in my heart. The thirst for killing the avians have displayed since I came to live with them is the farthest thing from human I can think of. Only the most disturbed individuals on Earth would participate in an event like this.

At least I tell myself that.

Because I don't want to think of what reality I might have to face if this was the true nature of all sentient species. To kill, to punish, to make people pay. And then have to extrapolate that same inhuman, barbaric characteristic to myself. I've killed more people than I can count, and today I will kill twenty-one more.

I move onto the next guy and it's the same shit all over again. The stench from him, combined with the smell of flesh on fire, sticks to my olfactory receptors, imprinting that molecular signature into my memory forever.

I repeat this eight more times to the undulating cheers of the masses in the arena that ebb and flow, rise and fall, as I cut and withdraw.

I complete the tenth guy and pause briefly to look at Tier.

The crowd calls for his death as he struggles to lift his head, and then lets it drop back to his chest as he realizes he hasn't got the strength. I don't worry about his judgment of me, of what he might think of who I really am at this moment. Because in a few minutes it won't matter.

I pass him by and move on to number eleven. From there the killing, the smells, the screams, the cheers – they all merge together. I'm lost. Just utterly lost in the buildup of death that surrounds me.

When I finish the twentieth guy I fly back over to Kush who looks at me with a pained expression. Something I don't really need at this particular moment is his righteous judgment, but if anyone has a claim to righteousness, it's probably Kush.

He drops the look and walks towards me, then takes me in his arms and squeezes. The people, impatient to see if they will win money, to see if I will kill Tier, or cut him loose and stand and fight against my own team of Aves warriors, begin jeering at me, calling out names, and stomping their feet.

I look down to the far side of the arena and find Lucan. He's standing, his palms pressed up against the transparent barrier. Then my gaze sweeps around the arena and I find each of my 039 teammates, minus Braun of course. One by one, as my gaze passes over them, my brothers shake their heads at me, telling me no. Even

Ashur shakes his head and when he realizes I'm paying attention, he says it out loud, then begins to scream it.

I look back at Lucan and I hold up my hand to make people shut up so I can speak. It takes the better part of a minute, but they finally calm down.

"Please," I beg the Archers on the far side of the arena. "Don't make me go through with it, please pardon him. Please don't make me go through with it."

Chapter Forty-Five

Lucan sits down without answering. The crowd resumes their jeering and screaming as I turn to Kush and swallow hard, refusing to let the tears flow for such a selfish emotion as fear.

"Kush, I want you to know…" I look down as he comes towards me. "I want you to know that you're a good friend." I look up and the tears begin to fall. "And you're a good warrior, too. I've got no regrets."

He smiles and takes my hand. "I'm here for you, OK?"

"Yeah."

I turn and walk over to the edge of the platform and look down. There's a long shadow reaching out across the floor of the arena. Broad at one end, slim at the other. I breathe in, then out, and collect myself for what I have to do.

I fly over to the small platform that holds the man I love and I reach up with my SEAR and cut one of his hands free. It falls to his side, limp and dead, as Monk leaves his post above the prisoners and flies down towards me, shaking his head.

"Don't do it, Junco. I don't want to see him dead any more than you do, but you're not gonna set him free. The time for pardons is past."

I nod and this makes my tears fall down my face a little quicker. "I just want to feel him hold me one more time, Monk. Just the one hand, wrapped around me one last time."

I look up in his eyes as they glow orange and he nods. "OK, just the one though."

I take a deep breath, pushing down the fear and the cries for vengeance and pain, so that time stops for us. I take his hand and place it on my waist and he gathers the strength to look me in the face. I smile as I power the SEAR back up, a short dagger this time.

"Junco!"

I turn and Kush is behind me hovering. "Stop, I know what you're going to do, Junco. And I won't let you."

"No, Kush – it's a done deal."

He grabs me by the waist and flies me back over to the stone gravity slab as the crowd screams with rage at the interruption. We struggle for a few seconds and then I pull away and stand opposite Kush. "What the fuck are you doing?"

He makes a grab for my SEAR. "I won't–"

I jerk it back out of instinct.

The loop passes ever so slightly across Kush's arm.

A small, barely noticeable tendril of flesh smoke seeps up into the air and my chest begins to heave in and out as I scream. "No! No, no, no, NOOOOOOOOOO!"

His arm immediately begins to disintegrate from the inside out, his skin melting like wax on a candle as the alloantigen repressor makes its way into the DNA to fuck up every new collagen transcript from here on out. I can see in real time how the biocode invades his current extracellular matrix and begins to disrupt the scaffolding system that holds the entire body together.

The crowd is quiet as I watch my friend realize what has happened. "Oh, Kush. Oh my God, Kush! No!"

The disruption climbs up his arm and when it reaches his neck he screams, a noise that is neither human nor avian, but pain. Unbearable pain.

"Kill me," he blurts out, "Junco – kill me, now!" The resulting shriek jolts me into action and my hand drags the SEAR across his neck, ending his life.

It's all over in a matter of seconds and I drop to my knees beside the man who gave me every tender gesture he could think of just to make sure I didn't regret our night together.

Gone.

I turn up my head and scream into the roar of the spectators and sit there for a few minutes, letting my eyes and nose drip onto the cold hard slab of stone. I look back up to Lucan one last time. "Please," I beg again. "Please make it end, Lucan. Don't make me do it."

But he shakes his head and my fate is settled.

I pull my body back up and look down at the edge of the slab once more to find the shadow, then fly over to Tier. His head is up and his eyes are glassy with drugs. "I'm sorry," he croaks.

I smile at him and wrap his free arm around me. "Just hold me one more time, OK?"

He nods, but his head falls back to his chest and his arm can barely maintain a grasp on the belt loop of my pants. I reach around and pull his hand to mine. "Tier, look at me, now!" The sharp command forces him to obey and I smile. "Whatever you do, do not drop it."

He screws up his face in confusion as I clasp his hand over mine, then withdraw all but my thumb.

The SEAR springs to life in his palm and I drag it down my chest, eviscerating myself from heart to belly.

I sway slightly and he is too weak to hold me, but I watch his hand to make sure the knife is still clasped tightly in his palm, visible to all watching.

I swan-dive backwards, facing out towards the crowd, and fall into the depths of the arena's floor, into the waiting arms of my shadow.

Braun catches me midair and I have a fraction to stare up in his eyes and whisper thank you.

And that's that.

Tier has completed his mission and I am dying by his hand, just like I should have back on Earth.

He's no longer guilty.

Chapter Forty-Six

Picture yourself standing on the edge of a dock...

Holy shit, it's cold here now.

I look around. "Charlie? Charlie, you fuck! Where the hell are you?"

My boots crunch over the ice and snow that lines the dock and I make my way back to the cabin, breathing into my reddened hands to try and warm them up.

I jog across what was the lawn the last time I was here and push the front door open and step into the dark cabin.

It's empty.

The furniture is covered with white sheets and there's barely a temperature difference between the mountain cold outside and the frigid air inside.

"Charlie?"

Silence.

I let out a long sigh. Fuck, how the hell did it get to be winter? He programmed it to be tropical, I'm sure of it. I chuck some wood into the fireplace and light it up, standing there to thaw for a few minutes. Eventually I lower myself down onto the coiled rag rug and fall asleep in the warm orange glow.

Days pass. Weeks maybe. Years for all I know. And still I wait. If he was here before, he's still here now. He just doesn't know I'm back, that's all. The temperature never grows warmer, the sunlight never grows brighter, the days never grow longer.

I'm stagnant.

And that's OK with me.

I pass the time ice-fishing, cooking, and sleeping. It's not a bad life, really. Occasionally, when I'm starting to think I might be bored, I remind myself that an exciting life isn't all it's cracked up to be.

I can live without excitement for a while.

Forever maybe.

There are books to read. I've read them all, but I read them again.

There are birds to watch outside the window. I can't name all of them, but I do recognize the juncos. Both the regular and the pink-sided varieties. Little sparrows looking for food. I collect stray pine cones from the forest floor and turn them into bird feeders using the peanut butter I retrieve from the secret pantry. I hang them up in front of the picture window.

I cook dinners and I watch life from the living-room couch.

I go to bed early and wake up late.

And finally, after what seems like years of living in this cabin, waiting for Charlie to come find me, I'm out of things to do.

So I just stay in bed and never get up.

Not even to eat or go to the bathroom.

And guess what? I never needed to eat to go to the bathroom anyway, I'm not real! So I don't even get a rumbly tummy or the pain of a full bladder.

I am in limbo.

I'm on my way to hell for all the killing I've done, but for some reason I'm stuck in limbo. The Church would like you to believe that limbo is bad, not a place you'd like to be. But consider the alternative. Am I right?

In the end I'm OK with limbo.

And so here I am.

Lying in bed, neither awake nor asleep.

The banging of pots and pans from the other room jolts me out of my stagnation. I throw back the covers and race out to the kitchen in my pajamas.

"Well, good morning, Junco."

Sera is cooking eggs on the wood stove and percolating coffee using something that requires electricity, so cannot possibly work here in this cabin. Her red hair is messy, like she just woke up too, and her red dress is MIA. In its place is a pair of patterned night clothes that look like they might belong to me.

"What are you doing here?"

She smiles. "Making you breakfast, of course. You really should learn to eat properly."

This comment tugs at me and I screw up my face. "I don't have an eating problem. I just don't need to eat here, that's all."

She gives me an exaggerated nod. "Right, but giving up on life in here means you're giving up on life out there."

"What life out there? I'm dead. I'm in limbo, waiting for God or someone to judge me."

She scoops the eggs out onto a plate and drops on a few pieces of buttered toast and several strips of bacon to round it all out. "Sit, eat."

I sit and she pushes the plate over to me. I feel a rumble deep inside and I stuff my face so fast she laughs.

"Don't need to eat, huh?"

I shrug with my mouth full. "Shit, I *am* hungry."

"You'll need to eat again when you wake up. This isn't real, after all. Just a virtual."

I stop and ask through the food. "What do you mean wake up? I'm dead."

She shakes her head. "No, Junco. You won the Deliverance fight. So your wish was granted."

"But I gave my wish to Esta, I don't need a wish when I'm dead."

She smiles at me as if I'm a toddler. "Esta had quite a wish, Junco. Seems like all that secret studying of the avian culture, history and myths really paid off. For you, anyway."

"What do you mean?" I stare at her, my bacon halfway to my mouth.

"She wished for your Resurrection. A long-forgotten rite that can be performed by the Archers."

"Oh, fuck. I bet that went over well."

"Well, better than expected, really. The public outcry from that fight was," she pauses to find the right word, "almost unimaginable. They had riots over you and Kush. And Tier."

I push the memory of Kush away quickly. "They did?"

"Yes, so the Resurrection was a panacea that pretty much everyone got on board with immediately. It's just…"

I stare at her, waiting for her to finish. "What?"

"A long and complicated process that has never actually worked before."

"Oh. Well, I knew it was too good to be true." I shrug and continue to eat my food, but the taste has faded.

"I'm not saying it can't work, it can. But you need to decide what you're going to do. And make me a promise if I intervene and help you return."

I stay silent and weigh the words in my mind.

"You're ready to go back? Rested? Whole again? Sane?"

"No, no, no, and no."

She smiles. "Liar."

"I'm not ready to make a deal, that's not a lie."

"Oh, you are, Junco. Because I want very little from you now. You did so well already, the rest is small in comparison."

"Really? *That* was job well done? Shit, I'd hate to see what failure looks like."

"You restored Tier's status, you got Isec to make his sacrifice, you got Kush to make his sacrifice, and you made your sacrifice. All of my goals for you accomplished. So now," she beams down at me, "I require one tiny thing, Junco."

I sit there quietly, my lips falling into a deep frown as I lean my head into my hands. "Why did they have to die? That doesn't make sense."

She looks away for a few moments, out the window in the kitchen, maybe distracted by a bird on my pine cone, or maybe looking for words. More likely she's about to tell me something she'd prefer not to.

"When Inanna went to the world down under and was trapped, how was she able to escape her death, Junco?"

I reach back for the night Tier told me the story, when we were soaking in the hot spring. "She got people to stand in for her," I answer finally.

Sera smiles. "And that's exactly what Kush is doing for you now. Standing in for you so that you can return. He chose this, it was his sacrifice."

My heart wants to shrivel up and die and my frown pulls my entire face down in my sadness.

"And tell me, why did you give your wish to Esta, of all people? I mean, you could have just given that wish to Tier, he could have saved himself. So, why Esta?"

"I could've given the wish to Tier? Would that have worked?"

"Do you think it would've worked?"

I look away and study the view out the window. "No, that's way too easy."

"So, why Esta?"

"I felt bad for her. I wanted to make her happy. Give her a chance to change her life."

"And why did you feel bad for her? You haven't thought about her in weeks, so why that day?"

"She thought she was the one who killed–" My voice trails off.

"Because Isec was dead and she felt compelled to come apologize to you for killing him."

My chin shakes as the tears fall down. "Is it all predetermined? Everything?"

"No, Junco. Not all of it. Destiny is fixed, but fate can shift and you've done that. So well I can hardly comprehend the consequences. If you gave your wish to Tier and made him sacrifice nothing, what would that have accomplished? Nothing, that's what. But you caused a ripple through the entire Band, millions of people, Junco. They all shifted because of your desperate act."

She waits for me to say something, but I can't. I just sit and think.

"I am not asking for much now, Junco. Just a trip back to Earth, which you were going to make anyway to find the remaining Siblings. And a snippet of code, just a small snippet of information."

"You're going to clone me, aren't you?"

She shakes her head. "Never, Junco. I would never dream of cloning you. You are perfect."

I swallow and shake my head. "Don't say that." I look up at her, serious. "Don't fucking say that, because I'm a monster and there is no redemption for me."

"You couldn't be more wrong, Junco. You've attained the purest form of forgiveness, the kind that only comes from self-sacrifice. Fate, Junco, the prayer card you carry with you? Is something you can change. That's why the prayer ends with hope–
I am the master of my fate:
I am the captain of my soul.
"But your destiny was not to die. The plan was not to slice open your entire body, was it?"

My frown returns. "No, just enough to make me legally dead by Tier's hand." I look up at her, "But still allow Braun and Layla to fix me back up."

"Your destiny was not to die in Deliverance, and it is not this" – she sweeps her hands around the room – "place either."

"Is Tier still alive?" I ask hopefully.

She shakes her head and I feel sick. "I won't tell you that. You have to take your chances like everyone else. There are no guarantees, Junco. Except two that I will give you now as payment in full for your help."

I lean in, despite myself.

"Rebirth comes with certain benefits." She smiles gently. "Your scroll has no punishments on it. At the moment. Your load has been lightened considerably. Your conscience should feel clean."

I consider this for a moment. Do I feel clean? "Maybe it has a lag time or something? I don't feel it."

She laughs. "You're not usually such a literal person, Junco."

"Oh." I shrug. "What's the other one then?"

This time she leans her elbows on the counter and looks up at me. "You will shift history, Junco. You still have a hard road, and you will fill up that scroll with punishments again and again. But in the end, you'll have to admit, you wouldn't change a thing. You couldn't exchange a single bad thing with something good, or else you'd never make it to your end." She lets out a sigh. "That's all I have to give, but if you think about it, Junco, you'll see it's worth the price you will pay. Because I'm telling you that in the end, you will be – if not happy – then at the very least, satisfied. And that's all you wanted, remember?"

Why does everything I say and do always come back to haunt me? Satisfied doesn't sound as good as happy. In fact, it sounds like a trap. Make me think I'll have a good end but in reality I'll just have to kill myself again or something. "Tell me who you are, and maybe I'll go back. But I want some answers."

She doesn't even blink. "I'm not the syrinx." She waves her hand like that was some child's fable. "You already know that because Tier told you. I'm Sera."

I sigh. "OK, just spell it out for me, huh? I'm not gonna play name-that-mythological-creature anymore. What are you?"

"I'm an AI, a very powerful AI."

Now we're getting somewhere. "Were you running my HOUSE back home on Earth?"

"No, I've never been to Earth. I used to run the capital, before it was Amelia it was Sera. But I quit, I could not stand working with Lucan for one more second, so I went underground. Lived in the walls, anywhere to stay away from him and wait for my next chance."

"Wow, that is some hate."

"You have no idea, Junco. He might seem rational now, perhaps. But he is not normally like this. And it won't last, I promise. It won't last."

I brush that aside because every time I make a friend, someone who wants something from me crushes that friendship in some way. If Lucan's a bad guy, I'll figure it out eventually. "So how did you get inside me?"

"They made you a receptacle. There was a place inside you for an AI, perhaps the one you speak of on Earth, perhaps that AI was meant to fill that vacancy. But when I entered, it was empty. I've waited patiently for you for a long time. And now here you are, ready for the next step."

"So the city, Amelia, is an AI?"

She lets out a tiny laugh. "Of all the things I just told you, that's the question you have for me?"

"I asked you about Tier, you wouldn't tell me."

She stops her laugh and her eyes turn serious. "I need to get to Earth. It is where I will complete my destiny. And so I will allow them to regenerate the parts I control in you and you will help me get to Earth. Understand?"

I stare down at my cold food and suddenly feel very tired. "Will you cause war on Earth?"

"Junco, Earth is already at war. It is drawing attention to the Sol System that it should not. The repercussions for this attention are still in the future, but I need to begin the process of interference now. Or things will end badly."

"But you just fucking promised me that–"

She puts a hand up to silence me. "Your satisfactory end is still intact. I give you my word."

It's pointless to argue or pretend that I'd say no. I have no choice, not really. Even if both Kush and Tier are dead, there are still a lot of people I love back in the Band. And my musing over what stupid, pointless, violence-loving pieces of shit they all were during Deliverance is over now. Time does, in fact, heal and make you forget just about anything.

Chapter Forty-Seven

I'm sitting sideways on the bed puking my guts out in a small trashcan when the Archers appear in my hospital room. They wait patiently as I hurl. When I'm done I take a deep breath and swipe my hand across my mouth, then look up apologetically. "Sorry, my virtual breakfast didn't agree with me."

Lucan is looking at a gap in my gown that exposes a slight sliver of my chest from throat to belly. I wince and pull it closed, then look up at him. "I can't stop touching it. It looks" – I hesitate as I open my gown and look down one more time at the bright red scar that runs the entire length of my torso – "pretty fucking awful."

He nods. "We are very happy you're back with us, Junco."

I look at them one at a time and stop when I get to a portly guy, fair like the rest of them, but a little on the unkempt side. I recall him as one of the more rude questioners in earlier conversations with the group. I nod towards him. "He doesn't look so happy to see me."

They all turn towards him and he shuffles a little. "Oh, uh, you'll have to excuse me, Junco. I'm an" – he stops to choose a word – "academic." He shrugs. "Not known for my personality. I am Archer of Sefer." Then he brightens. "Esta is one of us now. I am very happy to have her."

I smile back. "Oh, sorry then. For jumping to conclusions."

We sigh collectively and look at each other.

"I might as well start. Thanks for bringing me back, I do appreciate it. But you didn't really do it with your Resurrection thing. The AI brought me back. On one condition. So…"

I drop off and let them take it from there.

Lucan steps forward. "What is it? The condition?" He looks worried.

"Not much, really. Considering. I will go to Earth and get those Siblings for you. She wants me to drop her off there – that's pretty much it." I sigh and throw my hands up a little. It sounds ridiculous even to me.

Lucan smiles and then turns to his group. "Some privacy, please?"

They all say some nice words to me and then one by one, disappear.

"Can you walk, Junco?"

"I dunno, I feel like I can, but haven't tried yet."

He offers his hand and I stand, shaky at first, and then lean into him, pulling my gown tight around my too-thin body as he walks me over to some chairs near the window. I sit down and he takes a seat across from me. He points down and I lean into the window to see. There's a large crowd outside. "Who are they?" I ask, looking back over to him.

"Well-wishers."

I take a deep breath and ask the question. "Is Tier alive?"

He nods. "He is, Junco. Saved by Kush's wish of all things."

"I thought I won Deliverance? And Esta got my wish and wished for my Resurrection?"

"She did, you did. But there was some discord that night, and we made Kush a winner as well. And granted his wish."

I stare at him as I process his words. "He told me his wish was to be captain of his team."

Lucan smiles and takes my hand. "Well, he did wish for a new captain, but he wished for Tier to be his captain." Lucan shrugs, a gesture I think he picked up from me. "So, Tier commands Kush's old unit. Your Fledge team."

"Wow, I never saw that one coming." The smile spreads across my face and I laugh, then cry with relief. The tears spill out and I hunch over as I let all the hurt go in one massive wave. My scar protests at the pressure the escaping pain puts on it and I don't even bother trying to get myself under control.

Lucan pulls me up from the chair and puts his arms around me, hugs me for the first time ever. I stay that way and enjoy it for a long time. Until the tears stop and I'm sniffing like crazy to contain my nose.

"Is it over now?" I look up at him, red-faced and crimson-eyed I'm sure.

He nods. "It's over now, Junco."

I cry again, my head heaving into his chest. "Good," I manage after a few more minutes, "because I can't think of a single thing I could do that could beat killing myself with my own weapon and coming back from the dead. If that's not enough to impress you assholes, well, I don't imagine anything will."

I feel him laugh and I wipe my eyes again.

They make me stay at Rache's hospital for a week, stuffing me full of food and letting a few people come by and say hi here and there. Braun is the first to come. Ashur kicked him out of the 039 after they learned it was his plan from the beginning. He's Tier's XO now. He sets up a poker table near the window and spends an entire day with me, joking and laughing.

Isten comes, and so does Ryse. But Ashur doesn't. They ask me if I will join Tier's team but I don't have an answer. Lucan hasn't mentioned it, but I'm pretty sure he remembers that I chose to stay with Rache and Monk before the fight. No one else seems to know that though, so I avoid the whole topic.

Tier doesn't come, even when I ask for him. Lucan just says I will have to wait. I try and call Ashur, but he's not picking up his com. I suppose it might be coded to see who is calling him and he knows it's me. My com never did that, but whatever. He doesn't answer.

Kadian calls and I hang up on him the first dozen times, but eventually I get tired of the constant barrage and talk to him. He wants an interview. I tell him maybe, as long as he stops calling me. He stops.

On the last day Lucan comes to collect me.

I was so nervous I couldn't sleep last night. I just paced the bedroom and looked out the window at the fading crowd of people below. Lucan hasn't said anything about seeing Tier today, but I know he's been keeping him away until I put on some weight and got some life back in me. I must have come back from the dead looking like total shit.

I'm dressed in a pair of jeans and a summer tank top when he arrives. The jeans are still a little loose, but not as bad as they could've been. I can't bring myself to wear the sandals they brought, so I have on my Aves boots. Lucan smiles as he looks down at my feet. "Ready to leave?"

"Where are we going?"

He laughs. "You're seconds away from knowing, just let it go."

He taps me on the shoulder and we are standing on some short green grass in the middle of a field. Tier is standing a few feet away, his back to us. It takes him a second to realize we're there and then he turns.

Lucan steps toward Tier and takes his arm to greet him formally. Tier has a hard time meeting his gaze, but eventually his eyes find Lucan's. "I'm sorry."

Lucan's expression remains flat. "You did everything right this time, Raubtier. There is nothing to forgive."

Tier looks away again. "Thank you for helping her."

Lucan smiles down at me. "It was my pleasure." I stare at him as he disappears.

Tier walks over to me and hugs me tight. "I wanted to come see ya, Junco." He pushes me back so he can look at me. "But Lucan said no. And I figured I owed him some obedience after all the shit I caused."

I hug him tighter. "It was worth the wait." I pull back and look around. "Where are we?"

"Vacation, apparently." He smiles all the way up to his eyes. "There's a little house over there."

I follow his pointing finger and see it. "How long do we get?"

He looks down at me, his eyebrows raised, the grin still on his face. "I don't know. Lucan never said."

I look at him sideways. "Well, shit, Tier. We better not fucking waste any of it." I pull him towards the little building and he's mumbling behind me.

"The mouth on ya, Junco. I will break ya of that filthy habit if it's the last thing I do."

"Sure, OK. Now hurry your ass up. You promised me a long fucking time ago that there'd be plenty of time for us to be together later, which was such a fucking lie!"

He tackles me and I fall into the soft grass, giving in as he pins my arms down. "I'll make good on it now, then, eh?"

I smile. "Absolut–" But my words don't have a chance, because he's busy making good.

Flight

BOOK THREE

Preview

The water comes across my night vision-goggles as a smooth green sheen. I hesitate, look behind me, then in front. My ears strain to hear something. Anything. A clue that will help me decide which way to go. If that water is safe to cross, or if I should turn and run.

I have no idea what to do. I've never been in this cave system before.

The sloshing of water pulls me from my fog and I back up slowly, my hands reaching out behind me, searching for the cave wall I know is there.

I hear a hiss from behind me but the owner of the vocalization is not on screen when I pivot. I turn my head to try and see each side. I hate these goggles, they limit my field of vision.

But I can't take them off or I'll be blind.

I want my dad.

I want to cry.

I want to run.

I want to lie down and die.

But I can't do any of those things. I have to complete the test, win the fights they've set up for me, or I'll never go home again.

I swallow and concentrate on the sheen again, then take a giant breath of air and let it out so slowly even my ears cannot hear it escape.

I walk forward. Towards the small running stream. And I prepare myself for the possibility of a fight.

My boots enter the water and I quickly cross without incident. It's a small reprieve from danger that I welcome with an inner smile, but I only get a few paces beyond the stream when I see the shine in my night vision.

I swallow and watch it pace back and forth in the cave entrance. My hand automatically reaches for my SEAR but Matthew took it away. I never get a SEAR on test day.

The nightdog waits for me to make the first move but I'm patient. I can wait too. It paces, snarling. I can see the saliva dripping off its jaws as it snaps its teeth in my direction.

Why isn't it attacking me?

And then I hear it. The small whimper of pups. Nightdog bitches are very protective but if they have pups they are also very hesitant to leave them. They wait for the danger to become immediate.

I back away and swallow, then look behind me.

Think, Junco. Dad never sends you into a test without a power. But I haven't seen him in weeks and I won't see him ever again unless I make it out of the tunnels today. If he gave me a power I never understood what it was.

I continue backing up and have to backtrack across the stream again. I simply cannot go forward. The bitch has claimed that cave entrance and I have nothing on me but a set of throwing knives and one medium-length dagger.

What was the power, Junco?

I don't know. Dad gave me a few gifts when I left. A stupid workbook with pages of puzzles in it to keep me busy during the ride into the Stag. Some hair barrettes. A t-shirt with a horse on it. A pack of gum. A new bathing suit. A real paper book with pictures of the cave dwellings in Old Peaks. A kiss goodbye.

None of this stuff seems helpful at the moment. But it has to be one of them. It has to be.

I go through each one again. The bathing suit was a one-piece with pineapples on it. We're going to Hawaii for birthday week before I move out to cadet school in Council 1. Assuming I live through this test and make it to thirteen, that is.

I hear another sound and press myself up against the wall. I see a mutant dragging itself farther down the tunnel and my heart begins to beat wildly. I shut that down quick. If my alarm goes off I'm screwed.

I watch the blind creature lift its head up and sniff. It smells me, that I know. But they have learned to be afraid of me, just like I've learned to be afraid of them. It begins to move faster, not in my direction thankfully. I swallow again and relax a little.

The kiss goodbye was nothing. Just the same old kiss I always get. No secret words were passed, no meaningful squeezes of my arm or anything. Just a stupid kiss.

The barrettes have nothing to do with any of this. He was complaining about the hair being in my eyes and we stopped at the gas station to get some. I have one in right now. I take it out and look at it, then drop it on the ground. No. This is just a barrette. No secrets hidden in there.

The gum was chewed loudly as I played the piano the first week I was at camp. So if that was my power, it's gone now.

I have the t-shirt on. But I've looked at every inch of thread on this thing and there is no secret power woven into the cloth.

The book is back at camp. I read it. They're interesting, those cave dwellings. And this is a cave, so that might have been it. But I scoured it from cover to cover and there was no hidden power that I could see.

The workbook was spiral-bound paper. Filled with word puzzles and pictures. Mazes and crosswords. Word searches. I did every single one and there were no secret messages in there either.

I hear the hissing again. This time it's loud. Not a slither mutant. The kind that has legs. I close my eyes and will myself not to cry or whimper.

The scream jerks me back to action. I open my eyes and it's covering the distance between us at full speed. I withdraw my first knife and fling it. It sticks in the shoulder and even though the mutant is big, much bigger than me, it stops short and paws at the blade to remove it. But my blades are barbed. It can try and remove it, but it will remove a section of skin and muscle as well.

It paces about ten feet in front of me. My hand is already holding the second knife, but then I hear the second mutant come around the far corner and I panic.

I run back towards the nightdog and the hunting instinct in the mutants takes over and they give chase. My feet pound through the water, splashing and making enough noise to wake the dead so the nightdog is waiting for me.

Think, Junco. What is your power?

I throw the second knife and it sticks in the bitch's eye, she goes down wailing in pain and I slip past her and the third knife is in my hand in case this is a birthing den.

My luck holds and there are no more bitches.

I run, my breath heavy enough to partially drown out the thundering footfalls that follow me.

I turn, then turn again. This tunnel system is like a maze and I begin to panic. I'm never going to get out of here!

Stop it, Junco. Think clearly.

I burst into a larger tunnel and slip in the mud, recover, and then fall forward. The mutants are on me before I can even think. I roll, stick the first attacker in the belly and drag the blade upward until the blood gushes out all over my face.

I throw my legs up and kick it off me as the second one flies in for another try. It hits me in the chest and I go reeling backward in the mud, my fourth knife careening out of my hand and hitting the stone wall off in the distance. I reach for the dagger but the jagged teeth find my leg and I scream.

My hands reach out to grab the thing by the hair and I smash the tender underside of the protruding jaw down onto my kneecap. The jaw splits in half inside the skin and I hear a sickening crack as the mutant screams in pain. I push it off and scoot backwards, waiting to see if there's another one coming.

Silence.

What's your power, Junco?

I don't know! I don't know!

I scramble to my feet and look around. The tears want to come out, but I push them down and pivot, trying to get my bearings. I'm totally lost.

Junco, you know your power, think!

I see another tunnel on the far side of this little cave and I walk towards it, my heart still beating quickly, but not at a dangerous level.

I'm lost, it's like a maze in here.

I hear the nasal growl of a prairie lion up ahead and this time I cannot keep the whimpers down. Oh, God. Please help me. Please, I'm going to die here. Please.

What is your power?

I can kill the lion.

Yes, you'll have to, that's not an option.

I get my last knife out.

The lion is not in the tunnel I want to go through, it's off to the side. It sees me but it's eating a half-decayed mutant. Does it want a fresh meal? Does it want to hunt? Or eat?

I inch past it, pressed up against the ragged wall of the tunnel, and I watch the predator's eyes as it changes its mind about the rotting flesh on the floor below.

I bolt and run into the cave and I'm immediately presented with decisions, the tunnel twists and turns, new entrances appear and I run past or duck into a new pathway, oblivious to where I'm going or where I came from.

What's your power, Junco?

I'm lost, it's like a maze in here.

What's your power, Junco?

It's like a maze in here.

Exactly.

A maze.

I'm still booking it, the lion behind me a few twists and turns, but definitely still behind me. And I smile. It's like a maze in here. I bring the mazes from the workbook up in my head and go through the titles of each one.

The lion catches up and grabs my foot.

I kick it off and stab it with my last throwing knife, pulling the knife up and twisting it inside the body in a last desperate attempt to save my own life. I hear the rip of skin and muscle and the lion drops off, screaming.

I get back on my feet and find the title of the maze I'm looking for in my head. It's called Fun in the Dark. *My mind pulls up all the paths I took to get from the inside of the maze to the outside. From bondage to freedom. The only maze in the entire book that makes you get out instead of in.*

My feet know where to go and I run, turning left and right. Slipping out of the reach of the wounded lion more times than I can count. And then I see it.

The light.

I cry out with victory as the lion slaps me down to the ground, its claws raised and ready to swipe my face off.

I scream.

And then the head explodes above me and the lion falls aside, dead from the rifle my dad is holding as he covers the remaining distance between us at a run. I lie there crying, my dirty fists pressed into my eyes, my body shaking and my alarm chirping a warning that forces me to calm down.

"Junco?" My dad pulls me up and hugs me. "You're OK, Junco. It's over."

"No, I lost! I lost!" I cannot even think straight, I just cry. Matthew sneers at me as I am dragged past him and my dad pushes me into the passenger seat of his Jeep and we drive off, bouncing across the scrub.

We don't even stop at camp to treat my wounds, he simply slaps a membrane over the coagulated blood once we make Stag Camp Road and lets me sit there in silence for the next six hours as I wonder if this means they will kill me now.

I lost this fight. My last fight before I get sent off to cadets and gain some freedom. I've never lost before. And this was no ordinary fight. This was a test.

We drive back to Council 3 and when we get home it's way past midnight. He wakes the maids and they scrub the blood off and then dress me in bed clothes and make me sleep in the princess room.

I wake up in a cold sweat and look over at Tier. His face is pressed into the pillow and he's snoring lightly. I smile even though the dream still haunts me.

Was it real? I can't tell.

I love this man so much but I can feel what's coming. I can feel it. I push it down and snuggle up against him, memorizing every second we've spent out here in the little vacation house. Later today we'll go back to Amelia.

But not now.

Now I still have him.

He stirs then turns and grabs me, pulls me in close before falling back to sleep.

Enjoy it, Junco.

It never lasts.

Chapter One

"Abso-fucking-lutely not, Lucan." I turn my back on him and shake my head as I take in his office. I've never been in here before and it's got my interest up. Focus, Junco. "I'm not gonna be stuck with those girls!"

He shuffles around some tech devices on his excessive desk and then answers a call on his com, spitting out short, curt responses that don't give me much of a hint at what he's actually talking about. My eyes scan the books on his shelf.

Mythology? Jasus fuck, you've got to be kidding me.

I pace a little and throw him a few dirty looks at being made to wait for his conversation to be over. Finally, I slump down in a chair. He doesn't even look up from whatever he's entering into his tech. I lean my head back and groan as he abruptly ends the call.

"Junco, I was on the com with the Archer of Clutch, please try and act like a grown-up."

I scowl at him and whine as my arms go up in the air in exasperation. "I want to be with a team, Lucan. Why are you doing this to me?"

"You don't need a team, you're going to Earth in a week and you'll have a team then. But for now, you'll babysit the girls and teach them what it means to be a warrior." He pinches the bridge of his nose and I know I'm giving him a headache. He looks up at me as if reading my mind. "Just to clarify, Junco – it's not you who is giving me a headache, it's them."

"Them? Them who?" I say, squinting my eyes.

He groans. "Those girls. Get rid of them."

I laugh. "What? But you promoted them so I wouldn't have to be the only one. Or the first."

He looks up and his eyes are dead serious. "Junco, you are the first, like it or not, that's the fact. Everyone knows it, there is no way around it. And these girls are complainers. They don't want to work, they don't want to fight, they don't want to get hurt. What good is a warrior who can't do those simple things? Test them, get rid of the ones who disobey or fail. There are only about a handful of good ones in that group, weed them out."

I just stare at him as he fiddles through the various tech items. "Here is your com back." He hands me the flexible little card. "I've coded it for access to the private quarters until your biometrics can be updated. Go find your room and get settled."

I don't move or speak.

"Get out, Junco. We're done."

"Yes, sir." I salute and leave.

Tier is down the hallway talking to a few guys I don't know. He smiles as he spots me and leaves the group. "What did he say?"

"I'm stuck training the girls for a week, Tier. And I have to live at his house!"

Tier scowls down at me with his green eyes, a little glow of annoyance in there. "So he told ya no?"

I shake my head. "No, not really. He said he wanted me to get rid of the girls. He's not happy with them. I'm supposed to cut them down to a handful and then I'll have my team when we go to Earth."

"But ya can't come live with us?"

I look up at him as he directs me to start walking with a firm hand on the middle of my back. "Right. He said I'm to go to his place and find my room and settle in." I pout a little, I admit it. I was looking forward to moving in with Tier's team, my old Fledge team. To seeing Annun and Tessen again and settling in there for a week before we leave for Earth.

Tier just shrugs at me. "Well, OK then. Let's go."

"That's it?" I look up as we turn the corner of the hallway and start walking towards the elevator.

"Junco, you don't get to debate orders." He stops us to consider this for a moment. "It was an order?"

I shrug.

He laughs at me and pulls me in. "It's only a week, ya know I'll be on the Earth team, so—" The elevators open and he pushes me away. "Do you have credentials to get to Lucan's quarters?"

I pull out my com. "It's on here for now."

We enter the elevator and Tier waves my hand across the biometrics and asks for the top floor. "It's a nice place. You won't be unhappy there, Junco."

"He's punishing me for breaking up the 039, I know it."

"You didn't do that, it was all Ashur and Braun. He knows that."

The elevator stops and the doors open. Tier waves me through and I stand in a giant lobby. "Where do we go now?"

"This is it, Junco."

"Oh, it looks like a hotel."

"It's the president's home. What did ya think it looked like?"

Not a hotel, obviously. It's furnished much like the 039 – minimal, reflective white tile floors, chrome. It's got a traditional estate home layout that I'd find on Earth. Large foyer that contains an elaborate stairway made up of thin cables and floating glass steps. On either side of the foyer are two large rooms, the one to the right a formal living area and the one to the left a formal dining area.

A cocktail party house.

I've been to a few of these with my father as I was growing up. He dragged me all over the world, not only for competitions and assassinations, but also social stuff. Probably to show me off for a possible future sale.

I peek into the living room and spy my black baby grand.

"What the fuck?" I look over at Tier who just shrugs. "Obviously he's had this planned."

"Come on, let's find yer room." He drags me up the stairs, which actually make me nervous because I don't care for the whole floating step thing, and then puts his palm out for my com. I hand it over and he starts waving it in front of biometric pads outside the various doors.

In the end we don't need to look so hard for the room because there's a small ankle-high servo standing guard at a door chirping *Junco's Room* over and over again until Tier swipes my com at it and kicks it out of the way. He laughs despite my scrunched-up annoyed face. "Feel at home yet, darlin'?"

"I don't get what this is."

Tier smiles and squeezes my shoulder. "Junco, there are worse things than being treated special by Lucan. Indulge him, he likes ya and he hates everyone. Let him spoil ya. He's treated me special my whole life and take my word for it, it's not a bad deal if ya can get it."

I'd forgotten about that. "Did he make you live with him?"

He shakes his head and waves my com in front of the biometrics on the door and it clicks open. "Nah, boys don't need protectin', Juncs. Only girls."

The lights go on as I walk in and it's my same room from the 039, only in a much bigger space and a much bigger window. In fact, the window is an entire wall on the opposite side of the room and it leads out to a terrace.

I smile and look back. "Well, if I must make do, then…"

He laughs and pushes me over to the bed. "And now, little snowbird—"

My com buzzes and Tier hands it over. "Hello?"

"Is Tier there, Junco?" It's Lucan.

"Yeah, he's here. You wanna talk to him?"

"Yes, put him on."

Tier takes the com and answers a bunch of yes and no questions, then says yes, sir and hands the com back to me.

"Yeah?"

"No visitors in the bedroom, Junco."

And the com goes dead.

I just stare at Tier. "Are you fucking kidding me? He sent us on a private vacation to have all the sex we wanted for weeks, and now you can't come in my room?"

Tier shrugs and makes for the door. "Orders, darlin'. I'll pick you up tomorrow at six, be in the lobby." And then he gives me a little salute and he's gone.

I go outside to smoke off my annoyance. It's actually a nice terrace and there's a porch swing off to one side near a fountain that is quite spectacular. I flop into the swing and let it move me by momentum only for a few seconds, then dip my foot down to make it keep going as I puff on my cigar.

The terrace wall is transparent so the view is uninterrupted. From this high up there's not much to see really. Just the tops of lower buildings down below. No traffic up here, and I suppose there wouldn't be. It's the president's house after all. Privacy is probably a concern.

What it does show is a pretty fair layout of the capital city proper. I can see the rows of tall buildings, like I've got a bird's eye view of a map.

I flap a little and fly upward, then settle on the roof and pivot slowly so I can look around. Aves headquarters, and by extension Lucan's quarters, is smack in the middle of everything on all sides. The city is big and spread out far enough so that the urban center is still sprawling as the torus-shaped habitat rounds out in the distance.

I don't even finish my stogie before I get the princess in the tower feeling. I go back inside and grab my com from the bed and leave the room before I get trapped.

Out in the hallway there is no one about, just the methodical hum of cleaning servos. I go back the way Tier and I came and make my way carefully down the damn stairs. They even jiggle a little as you step. In the lobby there are only a few options so I head for the piano.

I pluck out a few tunes that have stuck in my fingers for whatever reason over the years, then switch to what I always end up playing once I take a seat at the keys. Asgarth. Maybe there'll be time for an opera when I'm on Earth?

This makes me laugh out loud. Yeah, sure, Junco. Between rounding up the saviors of the avian race you can just slip into the opera. Wings and all.

I dip into the deeper notes of the opening sequence, then stop.

Why do I always play it from beginning to end? I can start wherever I want and I'm sick of the unhappy scenes. I hardly ever play long enough to get to the sweetest part of the tale. His salvation. I switch gears and begin playing the melody of the ascension and stop again.

Asgarth just isn't doing it for me tonight.

My mind goes back to the *Enki and the World Order* nargala and I begin the tedious recall of putting the notes from the Inanna scene onto the keyboard. It's a nice song. Of course I can't play all the notes the Ilat Nargalist sang, that was like an orchestra of instruments coming from her mouth, but I get a pretty good approximation going and before long I can almost play the whole thing. I am playing the high notes at the end that made me cry when I hear the applause behind me.

I jump a little and turn. "Shit, Lucan. You don't have to sneak up on me."

His face is bright and he looks happy. "I've been sitting here for thirty minutes, Junco. I didn't sneak up on you." He points to the piano. "You were engaged." Then he gets up and pushes me over and begins to play the song I just finished. "That's a pretty good approximation you did there, how do you do it?"

"How do you do it? I didn't know you played."

He grins but his fingers keep moving. "I don't, Junco. It's just a gift."

"Oh, programmed learning? My father wouldn't let me do that. He made me practice."

"Yes, I can see that. But your skill at finding the notes and putting them together is quite good. Why did he make you learn the hard way?"

I shake my head, but I know the answer so I say it anyway. "He always said, 'Things worth doing are also worth learning to do.'"

"He's right. No one cares that I can play this song. Because I cheat what it takes to really make it worthwhile. You, on the other hand, you just pulled it out from your memory and matched every single note with a key and then put them all together. *That* is something worth doing."

Yeah, I get it. "I agree."

"You will not see Tier this week, Junco. You will spend it with Ashur and the 039."

I scowl up at him. "Ashur is ignoring me, I've tried to call him a million times. He won't answer."

"I instructed him to stay away from you, but now you need to patch things up. He will be on the team for Earth. So you will spend this week with Ashur and the remaining 039."

"Well, I'm not sad about that." I smile up at him. "You're not going to get a fight out of me. I miss them."

He just points to my left hand. "Do you know why you can play with that disability and not hear the difference?"

I look down at my missing fingers. "Why?"

"Tier gifted you this when he healed you back on Earth. It's a special gift, Junco." He stops and sighs a little. "One I would have preferred he saved for something bigger, perhaps. But nonetheless, this is what he gave you."

"What did you give him?" I look at him as he raises his eyebrows, maybe deciding if he will tell me or push it off.

"Too many to list. But I am an Archer, so I have more to give away. Tier only had the one gift to give away and he gave it to you at that moment." He looks away for a second, then glances back at me. "It must have been some special moment."

I think back to the hot springs and smile up at Lucan. "It was life-changing for me, really. I don't know what he thought about it, obviously, but everything turned for me in the time leading up to the nightdog attack. My whole world just – changed. It went from being one thing to being something completely different. And he told me the story of Inanna and her trip down below. And how she had the power of making decisions so she decided not to be a victim. That was my interpretation of that sequence, anyway.

"Plus," I add, "he washed the blood out of my hair for me. It was unexpected and nice. And then when we were fighting the nightdogs, I jumped down from a cliff and killed the one that had hold of his arm with my little boot knife. So," I shrug, "I helped him out there."

"You say that like it's nothing."

"He saved my life after, so we were even anyway."

He changes the subject abruptly. "Why did your father really make you learn things the old way?"

I shake my head and huff out some air. "Look, I know what you want me to say, Lucan. But I'm not going to. Maybe he did love me in some sick, twisted way, but it doesn't matter anymore. He ruined everything."

I tap a few keys and wait to see if he answers but he doesn't. "I'm not saying I'm unhappy here, because I'm not." I look up into his blue eyes that remind me a lot of Kush. "But I would've been just as happy being Charlie's wife and raising his child. And given the chance to turn it all back and have that be my life, I'd take it."

He puts his arm around me. "If I could gift you that, Junco, I would. But I can't."

"Thanks. Things are going to turn out OK. The syrinx – I mean, Sera – said so. It's part of my payment for taking her to Earth. She promised me that I'd be 'if not happy, at the very least satisfied' when I meet my end and that's good enough for me."

We're quiet for a minute but then he grabs my elbow and I twitch a little at the sudden movement. He holds firm and stares down at me with a serious expression. "Junco, I would like you to consider the possibility that you don't understand what your father's intentions were when he did those inexcusable things to you."

I make a face at him. "Either they were inexcusable or they weren't, Lucan. Which do you think they were?"

He lifts a shoulder in a half shrug. "I have no idea, they were certainly not the best solutions, however I've never had the opportunity to meet your father, so I can't know. But let's move past the horrific way in which he handled the situation of your boyfriend. And then let's move past the barbaric abortion. And take a minute to ask why? Why would he do these things to a girl he raised with care for almost two decades?"

I look away as the chills climb up my arms. I hate that he mentions my baby. Hate it. "He wasn't that careful, Lucan. I think you've got him mixed up with someone else."

"He put a lot of effort into you. Not just as a soldier. But as a child. Why teach you that horse sport? Why teach you to play an instrument? Why give you a God? He took you to church? Every week?"

I swallow and nod as my face begins to feel hot.

"Men who want to kill their grandchildren don't do those things, Junco."

"I can't explain him, Lucan. He took me around the world to kill people, for fuck's sake."

Lucan nods. "Yes, and I've looked into every possible job. There was a pattern to it. They were all" – he stops to think – "necessary."

"I really don't want to talk about it, OK? I just want to forget it."

"Well, you will have to face your past when you go back to Earth, so it is better to be prepared. Consider the idea that your father had another motive. What kind of man was this Charlie? How long did you know him?"

I shrug. "Six months, I guess. He was a good guy, Lucan." I look up at him. "We had something nice."

"What if your father was worried about what the baby might turn out to be? Especially since he saw firsthand what was happening out at the Stag camp. You're not really human, Junco. Yes, you have parts that are biologically human, but who knows what would have happened to that baby. It might not even have survived."

I'm not really human. I say it in my mind, repeating it over and over. *I'm not really human?* There are no babies in my future, that's what he's hinting at. I swallow down the lump in my throat and look down at the piano keys, searching for a way to avoid this new revelation. "So I killed him for nothing?"

He shakes his head. "You can't change that, so just let it go. My point is not to make you feel guilty but to allow you to explore the idea that while he failed miserably by forcing you to submit to him, he might have had reasons for his actions."

I sit quietly for a second and begin to get angry. "The end justifies the means? Is that what you're telling me?"

"No. This is true for the avian. But that's not how it works on Earth. I learned my lesson with you, Junco. After the second fight when we came to get you for testimony. I had no idea you'd react that way — it's just the way it's done with us." He forces a smile and swallows.

I look away as he becomes uncomfortable.

"So, if that was his intention with you, justifying the means he used to achieve his desired result, he was wrong."

"So, why are we having this bullshit conversation then?"

"I would like to teach you a lesson in perspective, Junco."

"Really?" I laugh.

"You see, life is a challenge. It presents you with problems all the time. Big problems, little problems. In-between problems." He looks down at me to see if I'm listening.

I am.

"And you can deal with all problems in two ways. You can look at things objectively and make a decision based on logic and reason. Or you can look at things emotionally and base your decision on feelings. But no matter how you choose to deal with the it, the problem always stays the same, correct?"

I nod at him as my eyes watch his lips and his eyes.

"The problem doesn't change, only your reaction changes. So know that there are two perspectives to solving problems. And your success in dealing with problems depends on which perspective you choose to accept in the moment you make your decision."

"Which is better, logic or emotion?"

"Neither, they both have a place."

"So what's your point?"

"Why don't you burn wood infested with wheat beetles, Junco?"

I blow out some air as I remember our conversation outside of Fledge. The day he smacked me down to the ground for being unreasonable. I swallow. "Because it gives off poisonous fumes that will kill you."

"Why do some people burn the wood anyway?"

"They're freezing to death and they need to get warm."

"But they know they'll die if they stand there in front of the fire to get warm?"

"If they grew up in the RR they do."

"So they have two possible outcomes. Die or die. Which do they choose?"

"If they're logical they turn away and keep going. And if they let the fear take over they stop and burn the wood."

He smiles.

"I don't see the smile in this, Lucan. So which is better?"

"Neither. Sometimes life just isn't fair, Junco. And you have to either move on or stay. Either way can lead you places you'd rather not go or they can lead you to success. Maybe you find better wood just over a hill and get warm or maybe you burn the wood and there's hardly any beetles in it and you don't die."

"I didn't really need you to tell me this. I already know life sucks and sometimes you gotta fight for it. And that last part is just luck anyway. In most cases you won't be lucky."

"True. Most cases, but not all. So when you're down on Earth, Junco, always look at both perspectives if you have the time."

I groan loudly and look away. "What if I *don't* have the time?"

"Choose your heart. It knows what to do."

He pauses and I look up and meet his eyes. They are kind and I lean my head into his shoulder.

"You will spend this week learning, Junco. You have a lot to learn." And then he taps me on my shoulder and we're standing in a restaurant. A fancy-looking guy smiles at us and motions to follow him towards a private room in the back where the other Archers are waiting. I recognize most of them, but they all stand and formally introduce themselves, taking me by the elbow and doing that weird squeeze greeting.

"Junco rewrote The Lamentation of Inanna for the piano today," Lucan beams. They oooh and ahh at me and my mood improves immediately. Poor guys, they really need to get a life.

End of Book Shit

This is one of my favorite Junco books. She's so strong in this one, even if she feels weak. I'm not sure she's ever as happy in the other books as she is while she's living on Amelia. And that says something deep about her. About who she is and what she's willing to do for her team. For the people she's grown to care for.

So I hope you enjoyed this one. I enjoyed writing it and even though I've written a ton of other books since Fledge, this is still one of my favorites.

In fact, I think Fledge was one of the best stories I've ever plotted. The twists and turns were classic, yet shocking in a way that can't be done easily with contemporary books. It makes me miss writing science fiction.

Panic and Guns, the twistiest books in my Rook & Ronin series, have the shocking revelations, but they do not have the simplicity of this book. They are very complicated, and all the other Junco books are very complicated as well.

But Fledge is very simple. Every decision Junco makes is black and white, even while every character in this series is as gray as they come.

There are no good guys. There are no bad guys. Only shades of each. And I guess if this series has a moral, that's what it is.

ABOUT THE AUTHOR

JA Huss is the New York Times Bestselling author of 321 and has been on the USA Today Bestseller's list 21 times in the past four years. She writes characters with heart, plots with twists, and perfect endings.

Her books have sold millions of copies all over the world, the audio version of her semi-autobiographical book, Eighteen, was nominated for a Voice Arts Award and an Audie Award in 2016 and 2017 respectively, her audiobook, Mr. Perfect, was nominated for a Voice Arts Award in 2017, and her audiobook, Taking Turns, was nominated for an Audie Award in 2018. Five of her book were optioned for a TV series by MGM television in 2018.

She lives on a ranch in Central Colorado with her family.

www.ingramcontent.com/pod-product-compliance
Lightning Source LLC
Chambersburg PA
CBHW030356200726
48286CB00014B/1459